Dark Horse

ALSO BY BILL SHOEMAKER

Stalking Horse
Fire Horse

Dark Horse

A Coley Killebrew Novel

Bill Shoemaker

Fawcett Columbine

New York

A Fawcett Columbine Book
Published by Ballantine Books

Copyright © 1996 by Willie Shoemaker

LIBRARY OF CONGRESS CATALOGING-IN-PUBLICATION DATA
Shoemaker, Willie.
Dark horse : a Coley Killebrew novel / by Bill Shoemaker.
p.   cm.
ISBN 0-449-90597-7
1. Horse racing—Fiction. I. Title.
PS3569.H5716D3   1996
813'.54—dc20   95-38456CIP

Manufactured in the United States of America
First Edition: April 1996
10 9 8 7 6 5 4 3 2 1

Dark Horse

1

SOUTHERN CALIFORNIA probably has more psychics, chan-
nelers, soothsayers, and fortune-tellers per capita than any other
section of the country. But not one of them had the foresight to warn
me about letting Jake Lunden use my restaurant for his pre–Kentucky
Derby party. When the young owner of Lunden Stables inquired if
The Horse's Neck would be available for a little fete the last Saturday
night in April, the only portent that I recall was the electronic beep
of a distant cash register.

Jake's a tall, boyish-looking guy, a Tim Robbins without the de-
monic glint in his eyes, whose late father made enough money direct-
ing westerns in the forties and fifties for his son to spend the rest of his
life dabbling. At the time, thanks to his wife Colleen, a former UCLA
homecoming beauty who fancied herself an equestrienne, he was
dabbling in thoroughbreds. And one of them, a beautiful warm-blood
with the awful name of Hotfoot, was the odds-on favorite to win the
Derby.

So Jake wanted to toss himself a party, and I was happy to oblige.
I led him up the stairs to view the private dining room. It was a new
addition to the restaurant, a conversion of my former bachelor's quarters, that had just been completed by a movie set designer and his
merry band of moonlighting carpenters. I suspected that the materials
had been paid for twice—by me and by Global Films. But the job was
done quickly and efficiently. And I liked the way it turned out.

The ceiling had been fitted with prefinished, slotted insulation
board that formed a subtle geometric pattern. It, like the wood trim,
was left natural, coated with a clear varnish that darkened it only
slightly. The walls were a rich deep green, decorated with small draw-
ings of thoroughbreds in frames that matched the trim. The carpet, a
pattern of muted, matching hues, was soft and thick enough to keep
the heaviest footfall from disturbing the diners below. At the far end,

a small antique bar stood proudly in front of a mirrored wall designed to make the space look twice as big.

The effect didn't quite work for Jake. "You sure this room will hold a hundred people?" he asked.

"That and more," I told him.

He paced around a little, sniffed at the green wallpaper, walked behind the bar and studied the bottles of booze and then turned to me with a grin. "Okay, let's do it," he said.

And so we did it. And so some people died and some were hurt and careers were destroyed and the fates of several humans and animals were forever altered. But, for all of that, it was a pretty good party.

It was scheduled to start at six-thirty, but only the string quartet showed up on time. The host and hostess arrived at 6:45 and the guests began to drift in at seven. The big crush took place at eight. Slightly more than sixty invitations for two had gone out, and it seemed as if everyone had shown up with friends. My maitre d', Jack Hayward, and I stood at the entrance to the busy room, watching the backslapping and handshaking and, to use a term I've grown to despise, networking, while the booze and hors d'oeuvres raised the temperature and lowered inhibitions. As the new solo owner of The Horse's Neck, I was wearing a silly smile on my face, because, with the Lunden party and the capacity crowd downstairs, we were having a record night.

"No one is listening to the music," Jack said, using the same arch British tone that he'd employed as butlers and con men, not to mention members of the nobility, in hundreds of movies. "I do believe they're playing a madrigal."

If he could hear a madrigal over the hubbub, his ears were better than mine. "The folks seem to be enjoying themselves," I said.

"Indeed. Private parties with string quartets. We are getting more like Chasen's every day," he said airily. Chasen's, a legendary Hollywood restaurant for more than a few decades, had just that week served its last meal; it was being replaced by a shopping mall.

I raised an eyebrow at Jack and asked, "Meaning I shouldn't count the receipts until they hatch?"

"For five decades, man and boy, the thespian art kept me gainfully employed," Jack said. "Alas, nothing lasts forever."

"All the more reason to appreciate these highly profitable private parties," I told him.

He sighed. "I rather liked it when the Neck was just a spot where track folk met. The crowd was raffish but goodhearted. I understand that on Wednesday night this room has been reserved by—" He gave a mock shudder. "—a porno film producer for his cast and crew."

"It's a complicated old world, Jack," I told him. "But we have a simple task—to feed the hungry, give drink to the thirsty. Provided they keep their pants on and carry the gold card."

"Troubling times, these," he said.

"Look on the bright side. The producer just might be hunting for a portly British type for his next film."

Jack rolled his eyes. As he moved toward the stairs, a brace of waiters arrived bearing a large tray with an ice sculpture in the form of a horse. Jack looked at it and shook his head. "The new Chasen's," he muttered.

I followed the sculpture into the room.

At the bar, my day mixologist, Al Grady, was filling drink orders, pausing only to send a hostile glare or two in the direction of his assistant, a college kid who was amusing the crowd by juggling booze bottles before he poured. At the opposite end of the room, prompting the proper traffic flow, was a groaning board filled with hors d'oeuvres—black bean cakes, bourbon baked shrimp, crab cakes, eggplant caviar, oysters pesto, and a few other little surprises that Chef Antony concocted for the event.

"There's the man," a cigarette-hoarsened voice said to my right. It belonged to Jeb Horvath, Hotfoot's trainer, a stocky recent widower who was trying to impress a very bored brunette young enough to be his granddaughter. Looking vaguely uncomfortable in a tweedy suit and tie, Jeb had one weathered mitt wrapped around a dark drink and the other gesturing in my direction. "Coley, come on over here and say hello, for God's sake.

"This here's Coley Killebrew," he said to the bored girl, whose name I never caught. "Used to be one of the best jocks around. Then he got into a business with a future. He owns this establishment."

It hadn't been a voluntary career move, and Jeb knew it. But he was being diplomatic. So I returned the favor. "From what I've been reading in the paper," I told him, "racing's treating you pretty well. Hotfoot's looking like a Derby winner."

"Oh, hell, the horse is a beauty all right, but the game's changed, Coley. The goddamn off-track betting. And they're legalizing all kinds of gambling now. Too damn much competition."

I'd heard it all before. From just about everybody in racing. "They'll always need good trainers," I told him, and I meant it.

"Can we go now, Jeb?" the girl whined. I would have bet on the whine.

"Hell, honey, the party's just started," he replied.

I took my leave and moved on.

I shook a few more hands, settled a bet about the last horse to win the Triple Crown—Affirmed in 1978, not Seattle Slew, who'd won the year before—and paused to watch a dignified elderly woman at the buffet table carefully placing crab cakes into her Gucci purse. She saw me gawking and, without batting an eye, deposited the final cake from the tray and said, cheerfully, "For the dog."

I wasn't the only one observing her as she strolled off to join the party. Two other women were also standing at the table. The tall, elegant one of middle years gave me a wry smile. Her name was Clara McGuinn and she had presided over Santa Rosita Raceway since the seventies, when her husband died and left her in charge. "She doesn't have a dog, Coley," Clara said. "She doesn't even have goldfish."

"You know her?"

"Corky Lunden, our host's mother."

"Well, if I'd known that, I'd have suggested she throw in some of those little goose liver pizzas, too."

"They *are* very tasty," Clara's companion said, "but pizzas get so sticky in one's handbag." She was a striking brunette dressed for success in a tailored outfit that, try as it might, did little to hide the full-figured contours of her body.

"I could get you a Baggie," I said.

"It would take more than that to win my heart," she informed me.

"Loretta," Clara McGuinn said to her, "meet Coley Killebrew, the owner of The Horse's Neck.

"Coley, Loretta Simmons. She works with Barry at SportsNet."

The reference was to Barry Gallen, an unpleasant, beefy blowhard with whom, for reasons no one could quite understand, Clara had elected to share her life. For as long as I'd known him, he'd been in charge of SportsNet cable's West Coast operation.

"Work *for* Barry, actually," Loretta Simmons said, giving my hand a hearty shake. "I'm his assistant."

"Isn't he here tonight?" I asked.

"Over by the bar with the dashing Geoffrey Paragon," Clara said.

I glimpsed Gallen through the crowd—a large, florid man in a tan suit. He was chatting with a guy who looked to be in his thirties, dark wavy hair, strong profile, easy smile. No handsomer than Errol Flynn in his prime.

"Geoffrey just flew in from London," Clara said.

"In racing over there?" I asked.

"Geoffrey's one of the owners of SportsNet," Loretta answered. "Spends most of his time in London and New York, darn it."

"What brings him to L.A.?" I asked Loretta. "You?"

Loretta sighed. "Don't I wish. No, it's something about our coverage of the Derby." She stared at him longingly.

"A bachelor, too," Clara added.

"Who's the blonde?" Loretta asked, cooling a bit.

A very tall, stunning woman had joined Gallen and Paragon, both of whom were beginning to resemble the wolf with bulging eyes in those Tex Avery cartoons. I didn't blame them. Not only was she the most beautiful woman at the party, she was the most intelligent, the most—

"That's Lea Starbuck," Clara answered Loretta's question. "Coley's fiancée."

Loretta stared at me in frank reappraisal. "Well, well," she said.

"It's all astrology," I explained.

She smiled and turned to look at Paragon again. "I wonder what Geoffrey's sign is."

"Let's go find out," I said.

"Don't mind me," Clara McGuinn said. "I've found my perfect party place, right here beside all these calories."

Lea spotted us as we crossed the room. I saw her intelligent brown eyes shift from me to Loretta and back to me again, one eyebrow going up questioningly. "And who's this?" she asked.

Paragon turned and saw Loretta. "Ah, Lea, this is Loretta Simmons. She works with us at SportsNet. I don't think I know the gentleman."

The two ladies exchanged polite nods. Barry Gallen, who did know me, watched with an amused smile as Lea introduced me to Paragon, neglecting to mention our relationship.

"Oh, of course, the jockey," Paragon said. He had an accent that was as British as Jack Hayward's.

"No more horseplay," I said. "Now I sling hash."

He rewarded the comment with a dazzling smile. "Well, Coley, what do you think? Should I fly immediately to Las Vegas? Finding oneself in the company of two such extraordinarily beautiful women must mean this is my lucky night."

"Luck can be pretty fickle," I told him.

"But unless one plays the game," he said, "one cannot hope to win." He turned to Lea. "We're having dinner later at the St. James Club, Barry and his lady, Loretta and I. I'd be honored if you would join us."

"Wouldn't I be rather like a fifth wheel?" Lea asked, amused.

"Not at all. Mr. Killebrew could come, too, as an escort for Loretta."

Without batting an eye, Lea asked me, "How does Mr. Killebrew feel about that?"

"It sounds like ten kinds of fun," I said. "But tonight is a work night."

"I could just go home alone," Loretta said sharply.

"I wouldn't dream of it," Paragon said, reaching out with his left hand to touch the side of her face tenderly. That removed the pout and replaced it with an emotion I couldn't quite read. "You and Lea can both be my dates." His fingers rested against the young woman's cheek for a few seconds. They were thin and graceful, the nails manicured and polished to a sheen. An almost too delicate gold ring encircled his little finger.

"Thanks for the offer," Lea said, "but I have other plans."

"Break them, please," Paragon implored. "I'm only going to be here for the night."

"Sorry," Lea said. "And if you'll excuse me, there's someone I have to talk with."

The "someone" was a bearlike man in a thousand-dollar tweed suit. His face was a color somewhere between pink and tan, topped by recently barbered white hair that was a bit too short near the ears. He surveyed the room with ice-blue eyes and a sour face that was transformed by a proud grin when he spotted Lea heading his way. Raymond Edgar Starbuck may have been wrong about a lot of things, but he knew quality when he saw it. And he saw it in his only daughter.

Paragon called out to her, "Wait. At least give me your phone number."

"I can do that," I told him. "It's the same as mine."

"You and she . . . ?"

"Absolutely," I told him.

"Congratulations," he said with a tight little smile.

"Looks like you'll have to make do with just one beautiful date for dinner," I said. I excused myself and followed Lea.

Behind me I heard Paragon ask Barry Gallen, "You knew they were together?"

"Sure," Gallen answered. "But you seemed to be doing all right until her daddy arrived."

Her daddy, I discovered, had not arrived alone. For about a month Starbuck had been keeping company with a woman named Vickie Salazaar. In her early forties, I guessed, with olive skin, prominent cheekbones, and a mouth that might be described as either sensuous or cruel or both, she seemed not only beautiful, but exotic, intense, and probably difficult. What she was doing with a self-centered hardhead like Starbuck was anybody's guess.

My prospective father-in-law and I were not very close. In fact, were it not for Lea's sake, we would probably not even have bothered to be civil to one another. Our enmity went back eight years to when I was still a jockey and he was chief steward of the Jockey Club. I was involved in an accident during a Breeders' Cup race at Santa Anita. Two horses hit the turf. Mine had to be put down. A jockey named Dewey Lane broke his hip, while I wound up in the hospital with a dislocated shoulder and a concussion. And an invitation to appear before Starbuck.

It seemed that my lady friend of the moment had bet heavily against my mount, the odds-on favorite. This led Starbuck to jump to the conclusion that I'd purposely engineered the accident. It was not until after he'd banned me from racing that he began to suspect he may have rushed to judgment. By then it was a little late.

Not that he's ever actually apologized for taking away the one thing I felt I was born to do well. By his way of thinking, what happened was all my fault. I should have been more convincing in pleading my case.

My innocence notwithstanding, he's never been happy about the prospect of welcoming me into the family. He's no longer with the Jockey Club. Now he's a sort of freelance troubleshooter hired by members of the racing industry. Lea works for him, and there have been times when I've suspected he was assigning her tasks primarily to keep us apart.

At the time of the party, however, her workload had fallen off drastically. Her days were spent puttering around the cottage we shared in Santa Monica, overseeing the installation of a new tile roof and wondering exactly what her father was up to. Specifically, what he was up to with Vickie Salazaar. Was the woman client, coworker, main squeeze? Thus far, Starbuck had remained characteristically mum on the subject. It was driving Lea nuts.

She was asking him some question about business when I joined them. Vickie smiled politely, and Starbuck said, by way of greeting, "What the hell is this bash costing Lunden, anyway?"

"You know how it is, Ray," I told him. "Business secrets."

I left him with that and went to the bar. Al Grady's assistant had ceased juggling and was moving the drinks faster. Al paused in his pouring to give me a quick wink. Our hostess, Colleen Lunden, looking like she'd just stepped from a Laura Ashley showroom, paused in her conversation with a prominent judge to tell me how lovely the room was and to say that I'd been right when I'd suggested they might not need a string quartet.

Two middle-age women I didn't know linked arms and began to do what looked like an Irish jig. A track official who shall remain nameless almost got sick on the carpet. The noise level rose a few decibels.

"What's the Morning Line on Ray's new companion?" Clara McGuinn asked, joining me.

"I honestly don't know."

"She's a lovely woman. But she seems a bit cold, indifferent. Not at all Ray's type."

"They say still waters run deep," I quoted, and she frowned.

According to Lea, her father had had quite a fancy for Clara. But he'd been slow out of the gate and Gallen had led him all the way. I knew how devious the old boy was and wondered if he was flaunting a young, attractive woman to tweak Clara's jealousy. If so, it seemed to be working.

A face suddenly appeared in the crowd that I didn't expect to see. Dewey Lane. I knew that he'd been tapped to ride Hotfoot in the Derby, but I didn't imagine he'd enter my restaurant for any reason. He'd always been as arrogant as a tennis champ and had felt a strong professional antagonism toward me. The accident, and his broken hip, had turned that antagonism into a personal hatred. We hadn't spoken in eight years.

He obviously wasn't there to enjoy himself. He strutted into the room scowling, paused, looked around and seemed relieved to discover the Starbucks. He joined them, and Starbuck said something to Lea that made her frown and walk away. Then he, Vickie, and Dewey Lane left the room.

I waved Lea over. "What's with your dad and Dewey?" I asked.

"You're asking the wrong person. I was dismissed. Dad can be such a . . ."

"Jerk," I supplied. "Jackass. Weasel. Ingrate. Cheapskate. Stop me if I'm getting warm."

"Men," she exclaimed, and strode off.

A few minutes later, when I left the party to check the downstairs activity, Starbuck, Vickie, and Dewey Lane were huddled at the end of the hall. Dewey was reading some sort of document.

I descended the stairs and ambled through the main dining room, shook some hands and paused to compliment a few ladies. Eventually I made my way to Jack Hayward's patch beside the entrance and asked if the evening was progressing as smoothly as it looked.

"The exception is one of your 'new' customers in the bar, who is using language he should reserve for his recorded ditties," Jack informed me.

The small lounge used to be inhabited primarily by horse players and other sportsmen who'd watch the races on a large TV screen hanging from the ceiling behind the bar. The increase in business had placed an added burden on the room. That night, the regulars were outnumbered by diners waiting for their tables.

I spotted the one Jack had mentioned right away. Or rather he spotted me. "Hey, Killebrew," the leather-clad rock star known as Halcyon called out. "Who do you have to fuck to get something to eat around here?"

He was sitting in a booth, having drinks with two barely clad women and a preppy-looking young man named Martin Grosso, the younger brother of West Coast crime family CEO Huey Grosso. Nearly a year before, Starbuck and I had been influential in closing down one of Huey's more profitable ventures—an insurance scam involving the slaughter of thoroughbreds. Several of Huey's associates went to Terminal Island, but he, of course, was still happily at large. Martin, who requested that people not address him as "Marty," had not been a part of that scam. He had gone to great lengths to distance himself from his brother's activities. He managed a select group of rock and rap music clients whose arrogance would have driven Huey to murder in less than a minute.

Like Halcyon. Pale as death on a cracker. Unshaven. Long dank dirty-blond hair. Skinny as a Slim Jim, which he vaguely resembled in his tight dark maroon leathers. Boorishly self-indulgent. Arrogant. Nasal.

"It's not bad enough, we got to sit here for a goddamn half hour, waiting for our table," he wailed, "you make us look at that shit."

He pointed to the TV over the bar, where a local newsman, at the same Terminal Island facility housing Huey Grosso's associates, was interviewing the former president of Colombia, Paolo Rodriguez, on the second anniversary of his incarceration. The interviewer looked smug and sanctimonious. Rodriguez seemed comfortable and relaxed and evil, like a poisonous toad who'd had his fill of horseflies.

"I mean," Halcyon whined mockingly, "if we gotta watch the friggin' box, at least give us our MTV."

"You're showing your age with that old slogan, Hal," Martin Grosso told him.

"You ever wonder what it would be like to get your jaw busted, Martin?" Halcyon asked.

"At least I'd be alive, Hal," Grosso replied softly.

The rocker froze and turned a shade whiter than usual. Then he gifted Grosso with a tentative smile to show no harm was meant.

I gave the room a quick scan. No one seemed to be interested in Paolo Rodriguez's video image. "I'll take care of the TV," I said, ever the genial host. Then I walked over to the bartender, Joe Dinsmore, and asked him to turn off the box.

"They're rerunning the Hollywood Park—" Joe began.

"I know the schedule, Joe. Turn it off, now, and you can commune with Hollywood Park after Mr. Music has been seated inside."

I returned to Halcyon's table. "Your drinks here are on the house," I said. "I'll see what's happening with your table."

"Fine. But hold on. I understand there's some kind of Derby party going on here, right?"

I nodded.

"Well, my horse is entered, you know. Headbanger?"

"I read something about that," I said.

"Why the fuck wasn't I invited to the party?"

"I think they decided on a string quartet instead," I said.

I quickly reentered the dining room and found Jack. I instructed him to set up a table for Halcyon's party immediately in the Backside, The Horse's Neck's version of Siberia, usually reserved for lawyers, TV reporters, daytime talk-show hosts . . . and loud and boorish rock performers.

As I headed back upstairs to the Lunden party, Dewey Lane was descending. "Leaving so soon?" I asked.

He didn't bother to reply, just breezed past me without acknowledging my presence. He seemed to be running from something, and I didn't think it was me.

The party was starting to break up.

At least a third of the crowd had departed, Clara McGuinn and her gang among them. Starbuck and Vickie had just bid their host and hostess adieu and were on their way when Lea stopped them.

"Coley thought it'd be nice if the four of us had dinner downstairs," she lied. I stood there with a blank look, wondering who I might throw out of the restaurant to make room. I needn't have bothered.

"Sorry, honey," Starbuck said to his daughter, "but tonight Vickie and I have a lot to talk about."

"So nice seeing you again, darling," Vickie said to the crestfallen Lea. To me, she said, "Your restaurant is lovely, Coley, but I'm afraid you have bugs."

"Bugs?"

"See. Something's bitten me." She displayed a tiny red welt on her upper right arm.

"I'll have the exterminators in tomorrow," I told her. "I'm sorry."

My fiancée was clearly annoyed. Glaring at their departing backs, she said, "Mosquito, huh? She probably keeps a pet snake in her purse. What the hell does Daddy think he's doing?"

"Maybe this is a reaction to your moving in with me," I opined.

"God, if that's true, I hope he doesn't marry her just to spite me."

"She'd make a rather attractive stepmother," I said.

"Right," she replied. "Just like Snow White's."

2

THE LUNDEN Stables party ended at nine o'clock, as planned. I thought it had gone well. Lea waited at my side till the bitter end, when she kissed me on the cheek and said she'd see me at home.

As kisses go, it was more a peck than a full-press. Still, it carried enough promise to get me through the next couple of hours of being the jolly host, schmoozing with the diners and keeping a benign eye on the waiters and busboys. As I made my rounds, I decided to stay clear of the Backside unless Halcyon caused some problem the staff couldn't handle. He didn't.

When he and Grosso and their ladies made their exit, a few minutes shy of closing time, the rocker paused to give me a wink and tell me he thought his steak was "butt-kickin'."

The last diners straggled out shortly after Halcyon. Even though I no longer lived just a flight of stairs away, I remained pretty compulsive about closing the place myself. The dining room, anyway. When I left a little after midnight, the bar was still open and getting a play from the folks who never seemed to have a home to go to.

It was nearly twelve-thirty when I finally arrived at our place in Santa Monica Canyon.

The cottage wasn't very large, though quite a bit bigger than either my suite over the Neck or Lea's former apartment at the beach in Venice. In the Starbuck mansion where she grew up, you could have hidden our little Spanish abode in an upstairs guest room. But I thought the place was a perfect size for two people. If we decided to become more than two, we'd have to rethink the setup.

I let myself in and walked through the house to the bedroom quietly, figuring Lea might be asleep already but hoping otherwise. When I saw her sitting up in bed, viewing the last scenes of an old movie, I made an assumption that any man might have drawn: she'd stayed awake for me.

"Hi," she said, pressing the mute button on the TV remote, shutting up William Holden no less. Both her slightly weary smile and the subdued way she returned the kiss I planted on her when I leaned over the bed were signals any disinterested observer would have recognized as purposefully nonerotic. But there were no disinterested observers present. When I did my best stripper imitation in the course of removing my jacket, I mistook her poker-faced reaction for mounting passion.

After getting the rest of my clothes off with all the urgency, and some of the clumsiness, of Inspector Clouseau, I insinuated myself between the sheets. But with foreplay barely settling in at the starting gate, she canceled the race.

"If she had something to do with the track, I'd know her," Lea said.

"Huh? Know who?"

"This Salazaar woman. Where did she come from? What does she want?"

"What we all want," I said, stroking her thigh with a hopeful palm. "Companionship. Affection. Possibly even—"

"But what does she want with my father?"

"I'll admit he's not somebody *I'd* go to looking for companionship. But I know him too well, and anyway I'm a guy myself, so you can't expect me to understand what women like."

"Coley, what are you talking about?"

"What Vickie Salazaar sees in your father. Wasn't that the topic?"

"I don't have any problem with what she sees in *him*. I'm not sure what he sees in *her*. Of course, if Dad were to find happiness with someone after all these years, nobody would be more delighted than I."

"Right."

"I *would*," she said, glaring at me. That look closed the future book on any hope of a romantic evening, but I refused to give up. I'd giggle her out of it.

"We could have a double wedding," I said. "He could give you away, and you could give him away."

She didn't crack a smile. "Vickie Salazaar isn't looking for wedding bells," she said. "She has ulterior motives."

"So does he, so they're even."

"We don't know that. We don't know anything."

In the middle of this pointless conversation, the phone rang. Though the call wasn't interrupting anything, as it would have been if I'd had my way, telephone calls at that time of night rarely spelled good news. My first thought was that something had gone wrong at The Horse's Neck. The hello I threw at the mouthpiece carried a mixture of concern and annoyance.

"Hello, Mr. Coley," said an Asian-accented voice. It was Choo-Choo, Starbuck's houseman, sounding uncharacteristically unnerved. "I must speak to Miss Lea."

"She's right here, Choo."

As I passed her the phone, my eyes locked onto the TV screen. A brief news report was on, and I recognized a shot of Temescal Canyon. Paramedics were hustling two bodies on stretchers up to an ambulance parked at the edge of the road. A wrecked car could be seen down below. It was a sadly familiar scene, but some vague notion compelled me to hit the mute button to bring back the audio. Lea threw me an appropriately annoyed look, and I immediately lowered the volume.

Still, the late news anchor's voice registered clear as a bell. ". . . in critical condition, identified as former horse-racing official Raymond Edgar Starbuck. The identity of the woman with him is, as of yet, unknown."

3

A FEW minutes and one wild drive later, I pulled my Cherokee into the parking lot at St. Thomas Hospital.

"Crowded for this time of night," I said, easing into a narrow "Compact Cars Only" slot.

Lea was out of the Cherokee even before I turned off the engine. I had to run to catch the Emergency Room door before it swung shut behind her.

A thin guy with reddish blond hair pushed away from a wall and intercepted her. With his Army-issue glasses and a bullet-sized gap between his front teeth, he could have passed for David Letterman's even more sour older brother.

"Ms. Starbuck?" Lea nodded. "And you're Killebrew, right?" he said, turning to me. "I thought you matched the description Mr. Starbuck's man gave me."

We weren't the hardest couple in the world to describe: wiry five-foot guy with drop-dead gorgeous six-foot blonde.

"Police?" I asked, trying to match his perceptiveness.

"You got it," he said, flashing his badge at us as quick as a subliminal message in a rock video. "Lieutenant Olaf Burns, LAPD."

"Can you tell us what's happened?" I asked.

"It seems a green 'ninety-three Prelude, registered to a lady named Victoria Salazaar and apparently driven by her, went off the road at about ten-thirty and rolled down into Temescal Canyon. Lady's dead. Doc says she had a myocardial infarction. Fancy way of saying her pump gave out."

"What about my father?" Lea asked.

"Got himself a concussion and various broken bones. One of his ribs stabbed a lung and he was doing a lot of huffing and puffing earlier." Burns gestured toward the entrance. "If you go right through that door, ma'am, and check in at Reception, they can give you a visitor's pass to go up to Intensive Care."

With a murmured "Thank you," Lea rushed to the entrance and I followed her.

"All part of the service, ma'am," Burns called after us. "Like to talk with you, after."

Choo-Choo was in the reception area. He leaped out of his seat when he saw us and did a quick half-step over, wringing his hands nervously.

"How is he, Choo-Choo?" Lea asked him.

He wagged his head. "Don't know. Cannot see him. No visitors allowed. They call me at midnight and I come quick. I see you not here, so I call you soon as I can."

We walked over to the reception desk and identified ourselves, Choo-Choo hovering in the background. The receptionist verified that Starbuck was not allowed visitors, but suggested we check with the Intensive Care Unit nurses' station on the second floor so they could summon the doctor who had been treating him.

The three of us went up the elevator and followed the arrows to the ICU waiting room. There we found a phone with instructions to call a four-digit extension for permission to enter the ICU. Granted that, we proceeded through another set of swinging doors and approached a counter that was both covered and surrounded by plants and floral displays. A quick glance at the cards showed they were all for Starbuck.

"I'll page Dr. Fordyce," a sympathetic nurse said. "I know he'll want to talk with you. Mr. Starbuck is obviously a widely loved person," she added, gesturing to the flowers and plants.

Not a phrase I would have chosen to describe him, I thought. "How did all these people find out so soon?" I asked.

"It was on all the eleven o'clock news shows," the nurse said.

Lea gave me a guilty look, as if she should have been subjecting herself to local news drama instead of old movie romance.

"We'll take good care of the flowers until Mr. Starbuck is allowed to have them," the nurse promised. "Living things aren't allowed in Intensive Care. That sounds funny, doesn't it? What I meant to say is—"

"We understand," Lea said. "Plants consume oxygen."

The nurse smiled, then picked up a pile of message slips and held them out. "These are calls that've come in for Mr. Starbuck," she said to Lea. "Perhaps you'd like to handle them yourself."

While we waited for the doctor to appear, Lea examined the message slips and I snooped around the gifts. Most had come from members of the racing profession. A particularly large arrangement carried Clara McGuinn's name. When I pointed this out to Lea, she nodded and showed me several message slips with Mrs. Mac's name.

In what was probably a shorter time than it seemed, Dr. Fordyce joined us. He certainly looked the part—tall, graying, whiskey-ad distinguished—and he'd mastered that gravely encouraging smile they must practice for hours in front of a mirror. He did his best to comfort Lea.

"Your father has a number of somewhat serious injuries," he said, "but I would not describe any of them as life-threatening at this juncture. I expect him to make a complete recovery, though that will take time. The puncture of his lung was the most troublesome problem, but the operation was completely successful."

Never in known history—not even when removing the wrong leg of a patient—has a surgeon said an operation was anything but successful. But I kept that little observation to myself.

"May I see him?" Lea asked Dr. Fordyce.

"He's still unconscious."

"I'd like to see him anyway."

The doctor hesitated for a moment, but apparently decided no harm would be done. He led us down a corridor to a room that was being guarded by a uniformed policeman. Fordyce nodded to the guard and opened the door.

"Just for a moment," he told us softly. Lea led Choo-Choo and me into the room.

The big man was lying there with his eyes closed, his square face so blank and untroubled it crossed my mind that he might be dead. But there was the hiss of air escaping his lips and monitors were ticking away digital readouts of his vital signs. I didn't know if they were good, but at least he had some. That he looked somewhat reduced in size should not have surprised me. Not even Raymond Edgar Starbuck could look big and imposing lying in a hospital bed, with an IV bottle hanging above him, feeding him through a vein in his arm.

Lea stared down at him without any outward show of emotion. She must have been at least somewhat relieved. Her father was clearly still among the living and resting comfortably, as they say, but just as clearly he was out and likely to stay that way for a while.

"Better let him rest," Dr. Fordyce whispered. But before we could move, Starbuck stirred, and to the astonishment of everyone, including the doctor, his eyes fluttered open. They were bloodshot and, for a second, appeared confused, but then the old intelligence lit them up, and his face approximated its normal look, one I associated with simmering resentment, withering humor, and unlimited guile.

For Lea the face undoubtedly had happier associations. But he had no kind words for his daughter. Nor did he toss any insightful medical questions at his doctor or household instructions at his butler. Instead he focused his gaze right on me, an attention I didn't particularly welcome, especially when he tried to push himself up in bed.

"Dad," Lea said, a mixture of elation and alarm in her voice.

Dr. Fordyce moved in and put his hands on Starbuck's shoulders, attempting to calm him. The patient had no apparent awareness of the doctor or Lea or anyone in the room but me. He raised his free arm to me, attempting to draw me closer.

I glanced at the doctor, who reluctantly stepped back.

Starbuck was mumbling something I couldn't make out. I leaned in closer to try to decipher his grunts. He exhaled a few words in a voice too faint for anyone but me to hear. Then he slumped back against the pillow, all energy spent, and returned to Dreamland.

The doctor pushed past me to examine Starbuck. The look he gave me implied regret he'd let me anywhere near his patient, but after a bit of probing and a consultation of the electronic readout, he seemed satisfied that we hadn't negated too much of the work he'd done on Starbuck.

"What'd he say?" Lea asked me.

I tried out what I hoped was a helpless-looking shrug. "I couldn't understand a word."

Lea anxiously turned to her unconscious father.

In a manner both patient and insistent, the doctor kicked us out of there.

4

LIEUTENANT BURNS was on the phone at the nurses' station as we walked past. He hung up quickly and rushed over.

"Is Mr. Starbuck awake in there? I've got a few questions for him, but the doc's being a hard-ass."

"He's still out," I said.

"Then maybe you folks can help me with a little problem."

We stared at him, promising nothing until he provided a bit more information.

"What can you tell me about the late Victoria Salazaar?"

"Nothing much," I said. "I suppose I've said hello once or twice."

"She and my father saw one another a few times," Lea offered.

"*Anything* you could think of might help." Burns spread his hands and lowered his voice, imitating a friend sharing a confidence. "Here's the situation. We've been having a little trouble getting any kind of a fix on Miss Salazaar. Maybe it's 'Missus.' Maybe it ain't even Salazaar. The address on her car license is a P.O. box that I won't be able to check out until the goddamn U.S. mail service gets out of bed. As of now, Miz Salazaar's got no known home address." Burns started counting off the negatives on his fingers. "No known friends except Mr. Starbuck. No known family. The computer finds no matches for her prints. She's not registered with Social Security. No history whatsoever. Did she speak with an accent, maybe?"

I shook my head.

"None that I noticed," Lea said. "I'm sorry, Lieutenant. I simply didn't know the woman that well."

"So be it," Burns said, throwing us a gap-toothed smile. "You think of anything, you be sure to let me know." He handed us each a small white card with his name and phone number, then walked back over to the nurses' station, again commandeering one of their telephones.

Lea, Choo-Choo, and I sat down in the waiting room. I assumed

Lea would probably want to hang around until her father's mentis was again compos. But I should have known better than to try to second-guess her.

"Choo-Choo, would you mind staying here and calling me as soon as Dad wakes up?" she said.

"Of course, Miss Lea. But your father will be asking for you."

Lea gave me a sharp glance. "He'll probably be asking for one of us. We'll be at the beach house for a while. If you can't get us there, try our home. At the very least leave a message on the house machine."

Choo-Choo agreed, but he seemed as puzzled as I was that Lea was taking off.

In the Cherokee, circling up the ramp onto a freeway that would take us in the direction of the Marina Del Rey peninsula, I asked, "Why are we going to your dad's house?"

"Our choices seem pretty cut and dried," she said. "We can wait around until Dad wakes up on his hospital bed. Or we can try to find out what put him there."

5

"WHAT DID Dad tell you?" she asked as we sped along the Santa Monica Freeway.

"What makes you think he told me anything?"

"I know him and I know you," she replied. "Whatever he said made your eyes nearly pop out of your skull."

"My eyes never pop out."

"What'd he say?"

"He said, and I quote, 'They killed her.' "

"Damn," she said. "Can't you drive any faster?"

To my mind, I was already in training for Le Mans. "Any faster and we'll need oxygen helmets."

"We have to find out who 'they' are, before 'they' go after Dad again."

"His head was still full of drugs, Lea. Burns said Vickie died of a heart attack. I'm assuming that was a medical opinion and not just a guess."

"Don't you think she was a little young and healthy-looking for her heart to give out?" Lea objected.

"You can't tell about those things."

"If she and Dad worked adjoining desks at the corner savings and loan, I might buy it. But you know the sort of things he gets into, and she's this mystery woman. At least let me have my doubts."

So I pushed the Cherokee a little harder and we reached Starbuck's bleached wood beachfront house in record time. I followed Lea through the front door and down a hall, past an art gallery of great jocks of yore, into her father's spacious but cluttered office. The computer on the black oak desk should have brought some neatness and order to his data, but there wasn't a flat surface in the room that wasn't covered with notes, books, or memo pads.

Significantly, Lea ignored the computer and started in on the papers strewn on top of the desk. I turned the full force of my disinterest on the filing cabinets.

Most of the stuff that had been properly identified with neat typed tabs was too old to have current significance, so I uncovered nothing that might shed any light on Vickie Salazaar's death. But I came across one file of more than passing interest. It was labeled Coley Killebrew.

It dated back to the original eight-year-old investigation that had resulted in my leaving racing forever. I'd assumed I had put all that behind me, but feelings of frustration and bitterness welled up in me anew as I read for the first time some of the negative statements made by people I'd always supposed were friends. One jock I played poker with every other Monday night said I was always taking dangerous chances in races and it was only a matter of time until I got somebody killed. A former valet claimed I had been more interested in the odds and betting action than any rider he'd ever known. That was a crock; jockeys can't place bets, of course, and the whole time I rode horses for a living, the only bets I'd ever had an interest in were the ones owners and trainers made for me. I don't know why the valet lied.

I flipped to the end of the file and got my biggest surprise: the Killebrew investigation was apparently ongoing. The last report concerned my recent outright purchase of The Horse's Neck from my former partner Johnny Rousseau. According to the file, an investigator named Andrew H. Gunderman prepared the original report and the most recent.

"Lea . . ."

"Hm?" Standing at her father's desk, she looked up from a document she had been scanning.

"What the hell is this all about?"

With surprising quickness she strode over and snatched the file out of my hand. "Those are private," she said.

"He's having me investigated," I said.

"That's what he does. It's his business."

Fighting a rush of anger, I tried to keep my tone level and moderate. "So you approve of this? Of your father hiring some asshole to stick his nose into my bankbooks?"

She thought about that and softened just a bit. "I can understand your being upset, but you shouldn't have gone into his files." With that, she replaced the file in the drawer, slammed it shut and pushed in the locking device, preventing any more unauthorized snooping by me.

"I was only trying to—" I heard my voice rising with my anger and broke off. I counted to ten and started again more calmly. "I understand the strain you're under. But I'm not the one who sent that car down into the canyon. Why don't we both go home and—"

"I'd better stay here tonight," she interrupted. "I want to go through all of this before that dim bulb Burns gets his hands on them."

"Okay, so how do I help—"

"You'll help," she interrupted, "by going home and getting some rest. I'll get through all this faster alone."

No compelling counterargument came to me. All I could do was nod helplessly and start for the door.

"Coley?" she said.

I turned around, hoping for a smile, a wink. Maybe even a goodnight kiss.

"It annoyed me that Dad chose to speak with you and not me."

"He's got a concussion. He didn't see you. Hell, he might have even thought I *was* you."

"No," she stated flatly. "It's just the way men are. When the chips are down, women don't count."

As little respect as I had for Starbuck, I thought she was way off the mark. Male, female, or anything in between, Lea was the only human he ever counted on. She was being . . . I paused. She was being a loving daughter who, probably for the first time in her life, was beginning to realize that her father was not a stand-in for Superman.

"You're all he cares about," I said. "That first night you and I met, he told me you were the best *man* he'd ever worked with. He used that word, remember?"

She remembered. I could tell because she started to smile. She didn't finish. "That was before he met Vickie Salazaar and decided to keep me out of the loop. And now, he regains consciousness and doesn't know if he's alive or dead and he just . . . ignores me."

She teetered on the verge of tears, fought the feeling and won. As she turned back to her stacks of paper, I moved to her and, more awkwardly than I'd planned, put my arms around her. She resisted for a minute, then dropped the paper she was holding and hugged me back. We kissed and I felt some of the tension leave her.

Then she stopped the kiss, but not the hug. "Oh, Coley," she said. "He looked so helpless."

"He'll be back on his feet before you know it."

"But what's happening? Why is he hiding things from me?"

"I don't know. If Vickie really was murdered, maybe he's been trying to keep you away from that kind of danger."

It was the wrong thing to say. I realized it as the words left my lips.

She pulled away from me. "I hope you understand why I have to do this," she said.

I understood. She was going to prove to Starbuck just how wrong he was to keep her out of the loop. I nodded and told her I'd leave the porch light on.

6

IT WAS five A.M. when Lea came home. I was in bed, but I hadn't slept more than a fitful twenty minutes or so and was wide-awake when she began bumping around the darkened bedroom. I watched for a minute as she struggled to drag something from the closet before I decided to have mercy on her and turn on my reading light.

She jumped, startled. "Oh! I woke you. I'm sorry." She was holding a suitcase.

"Going somewhere?" I asked.

"Yes," she said. "Louisville."

"Derby fever?"

"Dad booked two seats on a flight to Louisville—for himself and Victoria Salazaar. He also made hotel reservations."

"Single room?" I asked.

"Two, thank God. The flight leaves in just a couple hours. I'm catching it."

"Your dad will probably be up and screaming in a few hours."

She considered that. "And what he'll be screaming is for me to go to Louisville." She continued throwing objects into her suitcase. She packed like I do, with more speed than order. I got out of bed and started dressing with a comparable frenzy.

"Aren't you tired?" she asked.

"Sure," I said. "But I can sleep on the plane. I'm going with you."

I half expected her to put up an argument, but instead she gave me a sweet smile and said, "Gee, I guess you do love me."

I was trying to fashion an appropriately romantic reply when the phone startled us with a shrill chirp. It was still too odd an hour to expect any good news.

"This is St. Thomas Hospital. May Ah speak to Miz Starbuck

please?" asked a woman with a Dixie accent so thick she might have worked for Atlanta General. I handed the phone over and tried to read the news on Lea's face as she listened. No luck.

When she put down the phone, she turned away from the packed suitcase and stared at the door, frowning with what I suspected was worry and indecision.

"Dad's had a relapse of some sort. He's asking for me. I have to get over there."

"I'll drive you."

She shook her head and said decisively, "No. I'll drive myself. You'll have to catch that flight."

"Without you? Why?"

"Because of this." She took a sheet of paper from her pocket and handed it over.

It was a torn page from an appointment pad, with that day's date. In the space for nine P.M. was the scrawl, *AHG at B12.*

I looked at her quizzically. "You'll have to translate. What's it mean?"

"Daddy apparently made an appointment with someone at nine to-night, at B12, wherever or whatever that is."

"The only B12 I know is a vitamin."

"I think we can rule that out," she said.

"Wouldn't it make more sense to hand this over to the police? They're usually better at this sort of thing than ex-jockeys."

"Oh, Coley," she said, "can't you understand? If I simply turned it over to the police, my father would never forgive me. As it is . . ."

"As it is, he'll probably never forgive you for turning it over to me. Is that what you were going to say?"

"No. I was going to say he'll never forgive me for choosing to stay here with him rather than going to Louisville."

"It's the choice any human would make. Don't worry about Louisville. I'll give it my best."

She smiled and blessed me with a quick kiss good-bye. "I'll try to join you," she promised.

I put a finger to her lips, quieting her. "Get going. If your dad is awake, ask him about B12."

She nodded and said, "Also the meaning of AHG."

"That I already know."

She gave me a puzzled look. "How—"

"When we have more time," I said, leading her to the door.

"As soon as I've seen Dad, I'll phone your hotel and leave a message with the details."

I watched from the front door as she got into her Saab convertible and headed off down the tree-lined street. For just a second I had the chilling feeling she was driving away forever.

7

IN SPITE of the late hours Jack Hayward labored in my employ, he was an early riser. It was probably a holdover from palmier days when five A.M. casting calls were the rule rather than the exception. I have a mental image of him rising with the rooster's call, performing his morning ablutions, getting togged out in his Adolph Menjou model three-piece worsted, and sipping drip roast by the telephone, waiting for some desperate assistant director to summon him to a soundstage where they needed a touch of elegance and class. But he was in the wrong decade for that. What he got that morning was me, telling him he would be in charge of the Neck for a while.

He'd been reading about Starbuck's "tragic accident" in the paper and wanted to talk about it, but I hadn't the time.

It was typical of "Diamond Jim" Starbuck to have bought coach seats for himself and the late Vickie Salazaar—another bit of circumstantial evidence that theirs was a business trip. Using the bogus rationale most executives do, I decided Starbuck would want me to be as bright and alert as possible when I arrived. So, for his sake, I tried to trade the two tickets in on one First Class.

Alas, that section of the plane was already filled with other weary execs. I had the opportunity of glaring at their smug faces as I passed through on my way to the no-frills coach area.

One of the smuggest faces was familiar.

Barry Gallen, the SportsNet cable executive, was comfortably ensconced in a soft leather seat next to a small, wiry man in his forties who sported one of the few crew-cut toupees this side of the late fifties. Gallen didn't look happy to see me, for some reason, but he nodded and said, "Hello, Killebrew."

I nodded and would have continued on, but his companion stopped me with, "Coley Killebrew? Hey, this is a real honor."

Stopping too long in the aisle when a planeload of passengers are trying to get to their seats can get you pretty well mauled by luggage and pointy shoes, so I stepped into the empty row in front of the two men. "I'm Lew Totter," the crew cut said, extending a hand with a sports watch tied to it.

"Lew's a producer at our shop," Gallen informed me.

"You were a hell of a jockey, Killebrew," Totter said.

I thanked him and started on my way again.

Again Totter stopped me. "Weren't you and Ray Starbuck involved in that Dresner murder?"

"A little," I said.

"I was just reading about Starbuck's accident in the *Times*," he said, waving the paper at me as proof. "Anything new on how he's doing?"

"Nothing new," I said, deciding not to stir up the rumor pot by mentioning the early morning call from the hospital.

"Clara kept me up half the night, checking on his condition," Gallen said. He seemed mildly outraged at the idea she should care.

"Well, they've known each other a long time."

"I suppose so," he said, and abruptly changed the subject. "On your way to the Derby?"

"Good guess," I said. Actually, I didn't expect to be in Louisville that long, but it seemed simpler to shade the truth. "You, too?" I asked.

"We'll be there."

"Is Clara joining you?"

He flushed and said sharply, "This is a business trip."

"We'll be going over the details of SportsNet's coverage of Derby Day," Totter explained.

"What exactly will you be doing, Barry?" I asked, amusing myself by adding to his discomfort.

Gallen's eyes narrowed in annoyance. "I'm exec-producing the taping."

Totter commented on that by issuing a mildly derisive snort.

"Well, actually, Lew does most of the production work," Gallen said. "I'm just mixing a little business with . . ."

He was looking directly behind me. I turned and saw his assistant, Loretta Simmons, enter the plane.

Even if she hadn't been wearing a suit of some soft, curve-hugging fabric, she would have been enough to make the steward's morning. He stood there like a hat rack, holding her hanging bag until a female flight assistant broke the spell with an elbow to his side.

"Coley, what a pleasure," Loretta said, giving me full benefit of those big brown eyes. She proffered a smooth, pink cheek as if we'd been pals from way back, and I pecked it. Then she cocked her head and lost the smile. "How's Lea's father doing?" she asked.

"Still in Intensive Care," I said.

"It's an awful thing, just awful."

"Yes, it is," Gallen said with complete insincerity. "But at least he's better off than the poor woman he was working with." Perfunctory regrets duly conveyed, he turned to Totter. "Lew, you're not going to let Loretta stand in the aisle all day, are you?"

Totter rose awkwardly and with a sigh vacated the seat.

"Thanks for keeping it warm and cozy for me," she said.

Lew gave her a mirthless smile. "I even ordered you a Bloody Mary," he said.

He and I sauntered to the coach section. It was only half filled. When we found our respective seats, it turned out there was a human hippopotamus spilling over onto part of Totter's. "It's gonna be one of those days," the producer said.

"I think everybody's on board who's coming," I said. "Sit here." I pointed to the vacant seat next to me.

He didn't need a second invitation. He dug out a pillow and a blanket from the overhead compartment and flopped onto the seat. Fixing the pillow just right behind his head, he said, "Now, if only this pilot isn't on drugs or about to have a heart attack . . ." He dug under his rump for the safety belt and clicked it over his thin waist.

"You nervous about flying?" I asked.

"No," he said. "Just an incurable pessimist."

The flight didn't give him much food for pessimism. It was without event. The meal was breakfast, the hardest one for the airlines to screw up. Totter was a congenial seatmate.

The movie I didn't need, but I watched it for want of something even remotely entertaining. It was the kind of action-adventure pot-boiler that had at least one explosion every five minutes and a ratio of three stunt doubles to every speaking part. The plot concerned a team of ex-cons hired by a millionaire to follow a hard-nosed ex-CIA agent into a South American country to execute the dictator/drug lord responsible for the death of the millionaire's grandson.

"They shoulda called this one 'The Jim Carmody Story,'" Totter said, chuckling.

It was close enough to what the media told us about billionaire entrepreneur James Deth Carmody's little project of two years ago. But there had been at least a half-dozen movies selling that same brand of vigilante romance before Carmody tried it for real. What he did was send a group of mercenaries into the Magdalena mountain range to find and capture Paolo Rodriguez, the powerful civilian president of Colombia.

The basic difference between Carmody's caper and the one we'd been force-fed by the airline was that Rodriguez had aided the CIA in some unspecified manner that had prompted them to overlook his little peccadilloes, like murder and drug-trafficking and racketeering.

Instead of merely killing Rodriguez, which would have been the simpler way to go, Carmody's paid patriots dragged him to this country and turned him over to the Drug Enforcement Administration, which performed the official arrest. Though his defense attorney tried to prove that Rodriguez's illegal activities had been ordered by the CIA, the former Colombian president was found guilty in a U.S. federal court of conspiring to market in drugs, racketeering, graft, and money-laundering. He now resided in a maximum security prison in California.

"Why do you think Carmody did it?" I asked. "The reports were a little soft on his motive. He didn't have a murdered grandson, as far as I know."

"He told us why, Coley," Totter replied sarcastically. "He did it to help this great country of ours 'throw off the yoke of illegal drugs.' "

"What a guy," I said.

"Of course, he's also been positioning himself for a run at the presidency," Totter said. "And that might have played some little part in it all."

"Well, the guy's got enough loot to become President," I said. But, knowing Carmody, the idea made me wince.

"He's got a horse in the Derby," Totter said.

"He's quite a man among horses," I said.

"You know him?"

"Rode for him a couple of times," I said.

"What was he like?"

"An owner." I could have said a lot more, but what was the point?

My mind flashed back to a scene at Saratoga nine years before, when Carmody had "disagreed" with the way a jockey named Laborde rode one of his horses. We losers were all trudging back to the jockey room comparing alibis when Carmody appeared out of nowhere and blindsided Laborde. I think he might have killed him if a couple of us hadn't stepped in.

We'd all figured the incident was over, a heat-of-the-moment kind of thing, but that night two unknown assailants attacked Laborde and beat the hell out of him. The thugs were never caught. And there was absolutely no evidence linking Carmody to the beating. But I decided that day it was time for me to be going home to Southern California.

Totter's voice brought me back to the present. "Well, the odds-makers don't have much faith in his horse, For Cupid's Sake. Panamanian. A beautiful filly, color of midnight. What do you think?"

"She can run a little," I said. "She started slow, but you can't argue with her record over her last few starts."

"Still, she's a filly," Totter mused, "and it's hard to compare the animals she's been facing with colts like Hotfoot and Headbanger."

"Tough horses," I said.

"Where the hell are they getting these names this year?" Totter asked. "*Hotfoot.* How can you expect a horse to win a classic race with a name like that?"

"You'll have to ask Lil E. Tee and Seattle Slew," I told him.

Totter shrugged. "Well, anyway, For Cupid's Sake figures to be lumped in with the field horses. Might turn out to be a real dark horse. A very tempting long shot."

"You like long shots?" I asked.

He sighed with mock regret. "Actually, I prefer the conservative approach, as a rule. I suppose that'd put me in the Hotfoot camp. *Sports Illustrated* thinks he'll win the roses. Maybe even pick up the Triple Crown."

"The Triple Crown isn't that easy."

"You do it?"

"Nope. I've had my fair share of Derby and Preakness and Belmont winners, but never with one horse in the same year. It doesn't make me feel lonely, though. In over a century, only ten riders have pulled it off."

For a second Totter looked puzzled. "Wait a minute. I thought there were eleven Triple Crown winners."

"Eleven *horses*, but Eddie Arcaro managed it twice as a jock. With Whirlaway in 'forty-one and Citation in 'forty-eight. After that it was twenty-five years before Secretariat did it, and we've had another pretty long dry spell since Affirmed in 'seventy-eight."

"I guess you're telling me I shouldn't bet the farm that Hotfoot'll make it an even twelve," Totter said.

"There's bound to be another Triple Crown winner one of these days, and he may be it. But my suggestion is to take it one race at a time."

We briefly returned our attention to the plane's video screen, where the movie mercenaries had just mowed down about half-a-hundred wild-eyed jungle warriors working for the drug lord. Totter removed his earphones. "You want a drink?"

"Seven A.M. is a little early for me."

"Yeah. Me, too," Totter said, waving to a stewardess.

He was into his second Bloody Mary and scribbling on a legal-size notepad when I asked him, "Have you been working for SportsNet long?"

"Seems like forever." He paused. "Actually, it's a pretty good gig. Except for . . . some people you have to deal with."

"Gallen?" I ventured.

"Mr. Horn Dog, you mean?"

"He likes the ladies?"

"The guy probably celebrated the Big Five-O by throwing a birthday party for his schlong."

"Why does Clara McGuinn put up with it?"

"Who's gonna tell her?" Totter asked.

"Maybe me."

He gulped. "Hey, look, you didn't hear anything from me. . . ."

"Don't worry. I don't mix in other people's affairs. But there are more than enough who do."

"Barry plays it straight in L.A.," Totter said. "That's why we wind up doin' these dumb docs in faraway places. Just this year, he and I have hit jai alai in Florida, soccer in South America, bike races in Italy. You name it, we been there. Me producing the documentary and Barry in some four-star hotel screwing anything with big knockers and the breath to keep 'em flying high."

I smiled. "Sounds like he might be the subject of a good documentary himself."

"It's an idea."

"Seriously, though, don't your viewers want to see soccer and bicycle races?"

"Sure. But we don't exactly have deep pockets over at SportsNet. ESPN and the commercial nets have the loot to make the proper deals for live telecasts. Their crews get cooperation, setups with an undisturbed line of sight. Our guys have to hang from palm trees. Take the Derby, for example. We'll be lucky if they let us shoot from the grandstand after we've bought our tickets."

"You can get a pretty good picture from anywhere at Churchill Downs," I said.

"Yeah. Too bad we need words to go with those pictures."

"That a script you working on?" I asked, looking at the notepad.

"In our operation, the producer does everything but load the cameras. Right now, I'm trying to think of some angle—" He broke off and stared at me. "You ever do any TV?"

"I rarely even watch it."

"Yeah?" he said as if he didn't believe me. "Well, you're a good-looking guy, seem to be in pretty good shape. Got a nice well-modulated speech. How'd you like to be in our documentary?"

Considering my opinion of over-the-hill jocks who wind up wearing makeup and blue blazers with television logos on the pocket, I automatically started to turn him down. Then I realized that Totter might be offering me just the excuse I needed to hang around the track and keep my eyes and ears open for whatever Starbuck had been working on.

"I'm not in the union," I said.

Lew Totter grinned. "That's perfect. We don't pay union wages."

"What would I have to do?"

"You're here to hang around and watch the Derby. That's about all you have to do. Only there'll be a cameraman to capture each magic moment on tape."

"Exactly how much is my privacy worth, in nonunion wages?"

"I . . . I'll have to ask Barry." Totter's enthusiasm was slightly dampened by the thought. "The problem is, he doesn't want to spend a penny more than he has to on these things."

"What have you got left in the budget?" I asked.

"Budget? Man, when you're talking SportsNet budgets, you're talking 1950 ZIV-TV budgets."

"But if you can't do a decent job—"

"You still don't get the big picture, amigo," Totter said. "Barry doesn't give a damn about a decent job. All he cares about is getting his ashes hauled."

"He's off to a good start."

"You mean Loretta? No way. He may be cooze happy, but he sure as hell isn't gonna risk one of those sexual harassment suits."

I yawned. "Well, if I'm going to be on camera, I'd better get some beauty sleep."

"Sweet dreams," Totter said. "Me, I think I'll just have another Bloody for the road."

8

BACK WHEN I was racing, I took so many cross-country flights at odd hours that I could nod off just by lowering my lids. But I was out of practice. Instead of sleeping, I just slumped in my seat with my eyes closed, listening to the scratch of Totter's pencil on paper and the clink of ice cubes in his Bloody Marys. And I thought about going to the Derby.

For the first time I wouldn't be enjoying the laughs and the insults in the jockey room, all overlaid with that special Derby Day tension. Nor would I be riding out on a perfectly trained thousand-pound thoroughbred before a crowd of a hundred thousand plus. I'd be *in the* bloody crowd. I wouldn't be getting that special view of the twin spires of the grandstand, hearing the sentimental music, drinking in the sweet anticipation of the post parade. There'd be no pounding around the track, looking for ways to save ground, to string through a wall of horses, to get my mount there first.

Instead, if I followed through with Totter's plan, I'd be there as a representative of the media, and a minor one at that. The prospect of being at Churchill Downs as a mere observer was not a pleasant one. One more thing keeping me awake.

Finally, the plane landed and my depressing stroll down memory lane segued into a walk to the luggage area, where Totter suggested to Gallen that I share their limo into town.

"We'd be happy to have you, of course," Gallen said with all the sincerity of an infomercial pitchman. "But we're a little shy on room. Wouldn't want Loretta's lovely baggage to get all bent out of shape, would we?"

"I've just the one flight bag," Loretta pointed out.

"I didn't mean that baggage," Gallen said, wiggling his eyebrows and staring at her rounded rear end.

It was the worst Groucho Marx imitation I'd ever seen, and Loretta, who rolled her eyes, didn't seem terribly amused, either.

"Anyway," Gallen continued, "I'm sure Killebrew will be more comfortable driving in on his own."

As Gallen and Loretta moved on, Totter hung back for a moment and said confidentially, "Maybe this is better, Coley. I can sound out Barry about your being in the documentary a little easier if you're not there."

I nodded. I wasn't disappointed at all about missing the limo drive. In Gallen's company, even the five-mile trip from Standiford Field to Louisville would seem an eternity. I headed for the car rental desk and fifteen minutes later was floating through morning traffic that may have been heavy by local standards, but to anyone from Southern California seemed like clear sailing.

At the hotel I asked the reception clerk for any messages before I even registered and was both annoyed and concerned when he came up empty. Lea had promised to phone me as soon as she could about the meeting that night at nine P.M. "at B12." That might mean that Starbuck had not regained consciousness.

Upstairs in the room I cut my bellhop short in his spiel about the hotel's restaurants and facilities and, as soon as he was gone, clutching an overgenerous tip, placed a long-distance call to St. Thomas Hospital.

At Intensive Care I was informed by a cheery female voice that Starbuck had been moved to a regular patient floor. The not-quite-so-happy voice at that floor's nursing station told me that Lea Starbuck was not with her father. "Mr. Starbuck has been asking about her all morning."

"She didn't arrive there at five or six this morning?" I asked.

The nurse allowed as she hadn't been on duty then, but it was her understanding that Mr. Starbuck had been waiting for his daughter to arrive even since he awoke at seven. "Who is this calling, please?" she asked.

"Could I speak with Mr. Starbuck?"

"He has a private phone in his room. Could you give me your name, please?"

I gave her my name and asked for the number where I could reach Starbuck.

"I'm sorry, Mr. Killebrew," the nurse said. "We're not allowed to give out that information. If you'd care to contact Lieutenant Olaf Burns of the Los Angeles Police Department . . ."

I thanked her and replaced the phone. I wasn't about to call Lt. Olaf

Burns, who'd no doubt want to know what the hell I was doing in Louisville. I myself didn't know what I was doing there. I was perplexed and more than slightly worried. Instead of suffering a relapse, Starbuck seemed to have improved enough to leave Intensive Care. And if Lea had not arrived at the hospital, where was she?

I dialed my home number, and the results didn't improve my frame of mind. After a couple of rings, the message kicked in—Lea notifying callers that we were not at home. As much as I liked hearing her voice, I interrupted it and retrieved the solitary sound bite that had been left.

"This is Lieutenant Burns speaking. This is for Miss Starbuck and Mr. Killebrew. Please call me at once at police headquarters." He recited the number with insistent precision.

The hell with calling Burns. I tried Starbuck's home number and got Choo-Choo, who was all atwitter. "No, Miss Lea not here," he said.

There was a crashing noise from somewhere in the background. "What's going on there, Choo?"

"Policemen. They just come in here with this paper says they can mess this place up. They even dig into Mr. Starbuck's files. Mr. Starbuck is crazy mad, but there is nothing I can do. They are police."

"You spoke to him today?"

"Yes. He sounds weak. But very angry."

"Do you have his direct line at the hospital?"

Choo-Choo hesitated. "He say not to give it out to anyone. Except Miss Lea."

"Sure, but couldn't you—"

"I'm sorry, but it's what he say."

"Okay, I understand. Any idea where Lea might be?"

"Hospital, maybe."

"Not there."

"She probably working. She just like her father when it comes to work."

"Ain't that the truth," I agreed. "Well, ask her to call me if she happens to drop by. She knows where I am."

I stayed at the hotel through the afternoon, but there was no word from Lea or anyone else on that coast. When the phone finally rang at six o'clock, I grabbed it eagerly.

"Coley, it's Lew Totter. I talked to Barry about our idea."

"Right," I said. "Our idea."

"Barry ate it up."

"I'll just bet he did."

"He did, really. I've been authorized to offer you a flat nine thousand long ones to appear in the documentary. I tried for more, but . . ."

I paused as if mulling it over. I knew I was going to take it, mainly because of the protective coloration doing their documentary would offer me. And nine thousand dollars was not exactly a pittance to anyone not in television. But I didn't want to seem too eager.

"Your budget really that small?" I asked.

"Okay, we bump it up to ten thou, but that's tops. Look at it as an hourly rate, Coley, and it's not all that bad. And you're here in town for the Derby, anyway."

"I suppose. It'd be nice if SportsNet picked up my hotel bill, too."

"Okay, can do. But you take care of your airfare, tourist or not."

After waiting a beat, I said, "Deal."

"Terrific. This could be the start of a whole new career for you. We need to get going on it right away. Can you meet me at the Bridle and Bit?"

"Don't know it."

"It's a pub near the track." He gave me directions.

Before I left, I stopped at the hotel desk to leave word where I could be reached. "In case anyone calls," I said.

9

THE BRIDLE and Bit was on Central Avenue, a few blocks from Churchill Downs. Since in all the times I'd ridden in the Derby I'd never heard of the place, it couldn't have been in business long. But the owners had done their best to make it look as much a Louisville institution as the mint julep. Horse pictures lined the walls, including a shot of Aristides, who won the first Derby back in 1875. The age of most of the other shots suggested they'd bought some old horseman's collection—or maybe acquired the decorations of another bar now out of business.

Totter was seated at a rough-hewn table with a slightly plump woman wearing khaki pants and a bright green T-shirt complete with shamrock and the slogan "Kiss Me, I'm Irish." I could believe it. She had closely cropped brown hair, a pug nose, and cheekbones prominent enough to make her face look considerably less round than it was.

"Coley," Totter said, "meet Kate Donlevy. She's my cameraman."

"Could have fooled me," I said.

She grinned. "It's a step up from camerabroad or shutterbabe. Lew's got a quaint notion of what political correctness is all about."

"That's why she loves me," he said, shoving out a chair for me with his foot.

I took a seat, caught a waitress's eye and ordered a glass of tap beer.

Totter said, "I've arranged press credentials for us all to gain entry to the backside at Churchill Downs. Before the sun goes down, I want to tape Coley strolling around the stables, visiting the various Derby horses."

"How about audio?" Kate asked.

"We'll just wild-sound it," Totter said. "I'm thinking we go with an overall narration. Later, when we line up interviews, we'll have to be a little more careful about sound quality."

"Right," I said as if I knew or cared what he was talking about.

Before we headed for Churchill Downs, I let my fingers do the walking over the Touch-Tone buttons of a modern pay phone disguised as an 1890s artifact.

"Still no message, Mr. Killebrew," my hotel clerk's regretful voice said. "We'd have called you if there had been."

I apologized for letting my anxiety imply inefficiency on his part and told him I'd be out of reach for a while but would check in from time to time.

"Very good, sir," he replied crisply.

But it wasn't very good. I was playing the poor man's Jim McKay in Louisville when I should have been back home finding out what had happened to Lea.

10

MOST RACETRACKS are more or less out in the country. Churchill Downs is right smack in downtown Louisville. When we got there, Totter led us past the security phalanx surrounding the entrance to the backside.

Racetrack grandstands differ. So do racing surfaces. But stable areas are all pretty much the same in their sights and smells. Wooden buildings with pervasive fire extinguishers. Grooms and hotwalkers cooing at their big nervous charges. The fact that this was Churchill Downs, even more the American racing Mecca since it added the occasional Breeders' Cup to its annual Derby festival, changed the atmosphere very little. Nor did it need changing. To someone involved in racing, it was automatically both comforting and exciting, as full of memories as a school reunion.

Our first stop was a barn where a number of the out-of-town Derby candidates were concentrated. Though the media representatives might have found it more convenient, the track management didn't gather all of the big race runners in one barn. Those already stabled locally would naturally stay put with the rest of their trainers' strings, and often an out-of-town trainer would borrow stall space from an in-town friend to get his charge out of the limelight and into a calmer and more homelike atmosphere.

If I'd been the trainer of a Derby contender like Hotfoot, I'd have wanted him as far away from the media hordes as I could manage. But as Kate followed with her camera and I began my rounds of the contenders, Hotfoot was the first one we approached. Conveniently, his owners were paying a visit. Colleen Lunden was stroking her charge's nose, while Jake, less comfortable around horses than his wife despite his family's western movie heritage, stood a few respectable paces back.

"Coley! What a surprise!" he said. He walked over from Hotfoot's stall to shake hands, and his wife followed.

"You didn't say a word about coming to the Derby," Colleen chided me in a friendly way.

"SportsNet asked me to work on their documentary," I said. I introduced Totter and Kate.

The presence of Kate's camera seemed to formalize the occasion. Suddenly, no one was talking. "When did you guys get in?" I asked.

"Just this afternoon," Colleen said, enunciating carefully. "We came here straight from the plane. Oh, there's Jeb."

Jeb Horvath was walking toward us with a worried expression on his face. He nodded to me, distractedly, then addressed Colleen. "I been tryin' his hotel, Miz Lunden. But he still isn't—"

He frowned as Kate Donlevy moved in on us with her handheld camera. "I'm sorry," he said, "but what the heck . . . ?"

Totter stepped forward and made the explanation. Jeb seemed mildly surprised that I was part of the SportsNet team, but instead of any comment pro or con, he said, "We've got a little problem that isn't for the public."

"We're just filming a documentary," Totter assured him. "We're not 'Hard Copy.' " He gave Kate a wink and she lowered her camera.

"What's up?" I asked.

Jeb looked at Kate's idle camera and said, "That's turned off, right?"

Kate told him it was.

"Dewey Lane didn't show up at the track this morning to work Hotfoot, and I been trying to get hold of him all day. Hotel says he never checked in."

That was bad news for them, and not much better for me. I'd been hoping to ask Dewey about his meeting with Starbuck and Vickie Salazaar the night of the Lundens' party.

Jake apologized and said they'd better all go man the phones, trying to get a line on Dewey. He and Jeb agreed to sit still for interviews the following day, assuming that their jockey's whereabouts would no longer be a mystery.

Kate, Totter, and I moved on to other stalls and barns. We didn't run into any more owners as we surveyed the West Coast entries, but we did manage cordial but unenlightening exchanges with some of their trainers and handlers.

We spent a few minutes with The Loan Arranger, owned by the president of the still solvent South Coast Mortgages. The animal looked like a mean one, the kind who'd foreclose on your fingers if he got a chance. Next up was Sabisa, an apparently kindlier, gentler animal owned by a Mexican-American manufacturer of salsa products.

Our wandering eventually led us to Headbanger, the rock star Halcyon's bay thoroughbred. Kate hoped we might run into the great man himself, but instead we were treated to Martin Grosso, looking a little like Ragtime Cowboy Joe in his brand new Levis, plaid silk shirt, and polished, elaborately stitched boots. The mob king's little brother greeted me like an old pal.

"Excellent dinner in your restaurant, Killebrew," he said. "Somebody in your kitchen must have grown up in Parma, the pasta's that good."

"You minding the horse, Martin?" I asked.

"Hal's off in town somewhere," he said. "I hope to hell he's not buying another thoroughbred. What brings you to the barns?"

I gestured to Kate and her whirring camera. "Getting a little footage for a TV special."

"You're a real Renaissance man, aren't you?" he said. "Well, if you're unhappy with your personal management—"

"I thought you stuck to music performers."

"Even the Pope cuts a record now and then."

Grosso went on to describe the benefits of his management company, but he'd lost my attention. I was staring at the side of Headbanger's barn, where the letters B7 were painted in red. I waited for Grosso to take a breath and closed our conversation.

"Hal'll be around tomorrow," Grosso called to my back. "If you want to tape him and the horse."

I nodded and waved and joined Totter. "Who's in Barn Twelve?" I asked him casually.

The producer consulted the photocopy sheets he'd been given to locate the Derby starters.

"Jaydee Farms, James Carmody's outfit. That's where his filly, For Cupid's Sake, is stabled."

"Let's pay her a visit," I said.

I picked up the pace as we moved along the shed row, probably passing a bunch of Derby hopefuls. Totter and Kate stayed with me as if I knew something they didn't.

Barn 12 was busy. It had the usual stable crew with a few extras. Five thugs who didn't seem to have a role in taking care of the horses were stationed at regular intervals around the barn. They didn't make a move to stop me from knocking on the door to the office, but they watched me, Totter, and our camerawoman very carefully.

Carmody was not in attendance, nor did I expect him to be. The person who answered our knock was a clean-cut man in his forties. He looked kind of like Ward Cleaver from the old "Leave It to Beaver" TV show, but his eyes spoiled the effect. There was something odd about them, a kind of dullness. He introduced himself as Richard Sandford, For Cupid's Sake's trainer.

"What happened to Gandy Dawes?" I asked.

Sandford stared at me. "What do you mean, what happened?" he asked, as if I'd just suggested that Dawes had met some horrible fate.

"Last I heard, he was Carmody's trainer," I said innocently.

"You a jockey?" Sandford asked.

"Not lately."

"Well, Dawes hasn't been doing any training *lately*, either. He retired a couple years ago, when I took over. Is that all?" The guy was unusually testy.

Totter explained that we were from SportsNet. The name of the cable network didn't get much of a reaction from Sandford, but I had the feeling ESPN or ABC wouldn't have fared any better.

"Sorry, but we don't want any unauthorized cameras around here," the trainer said flatly.

"How might we get authorization?" Totter asked.

A very slight smile appeared on Sandford's lips. "That would have to come from Mr. Carmody himself."

As the two of them continued talking and getting nowhere, I concentrated on something more diverting. A gorgeous filly who was being groomed in the stall nearest to Sandford's office had me enraptured.

I strolled closer, away from the conversation. She was a splendid animal with a dramatic ebony color. Her conformation was perfect, her bearing somehow regal. There was a feeling of superiority about her I couldn't quite define, the kind of aura for which racetrack poets thought up inadequate expressions like "the look of eagles." This had to be Carmody's Derby entry, For Cupid's Sake.

The groom finished his work, patted the great black neck, and disappeared into a room off the stall. An African-American stable hand shuffled close to For Cupid's Sake, carrying a rake. He was spreading straw. The filly whickered, and the black man looked at her without apparent comprehension. She tucked her ears back and her eyes seemed to change color, going from brown to black. The hand shrugged and continued to rake.

I called out, "Hey, you with the rake. Come here a minute."

The black man looked at me, confused. Then he shuffled over. "Yes, suh?"

"How long have you been working here?"

Sandford called out from the door to the office, "You got enough to do, Andrew?"

"Yes, suh, surely do."

"Then go do it." Sandford turned to me and said with forced amiability, "This is a working stable, Jack. You know how it is. Not a lot of time for chitchat with strangers."

I nodded. In my experience, stables have always allowed a little time for polite conversation, but the dull-eyed Sandford apparently ran his operation his own way. Or Carmody's. I turned as the groom led For Cupid's Sake back to her stall. Andrew continued raking his straw.

"Coming Coley?" Totter sang out, walking away with Kate.

I smiled at Sandford. "Thanks for your time," I said.

11

WE MANAGED to get a little more footage of the backside activity before the gathering darkness put us out of business. We trudged back the way we came and found the Lundens still talking to their trainer at Hotfoot's barn.

"Coley, wait a minute," Jake called.

He took several fast strides away from his wife and Jeb Horvath. "Colleen and I don't know much about the restaurants around here," he said. "Any suggestions?"

"Eight years ago, the Hot Box was the place to go," I said as Colleen joined us.

"Sounds like a good omen for Hotfoot," she said.

The restaurant's owner, Stoney Hilton, was another former rider and an old pal. He'd named the place after an instrument of torture we jocks used to keep our weight down. Once I'd asked him why he picked the name; he told me it was mostly to celebrate the fact that he'd never have to enter one again. In overcompensation for all the years of starving and sweating, the food in his place was almost as notable for its large portions as for its quality.

"We'd love to have you folks join us," Jake said.

Kate begged off. "Got something else lined up," she told us. "But I thank you all the same."

Lew was happy to accept, and I, after checking my watch, said I'd be glad to have cocktails, but I had an errand to run at eight-thirty.

An hour later Totter and I rejoined the Lundens in the bar of their hotel. Barry Gallen had joined the party. He'd been in the bar also, alone and not enjoying it. He seemed so starved for company, not to mention food, that he forgot to be arrogant.

When the five of us arrived at the Hot Box, Stoney Hilton came out of his office to welcome us warmly. He was almost as wide as he was tall. Last time I'd seen him he was merely a little chubby.

"The food here must be even better than I remember," I said.

Stoney looked at his girth, grinned and patted it. "The food here's at least as filling as it is at your place, Coley. But actually, I eat like this for my health."

That was a setup if I ever heard one, but I played along. "How do you figure that?" I asked.

Clasping me around the shoulder as he led us to our table, he said with a straight face, "You remember that New Year's Day when the jockeys threatened a work stoppage over disability insurance?"

I nodded.

"All those old ex-riders were gonna come out of retirement and offer themselves as substitute jocks. Don Pierce, Ray York, guys like that."

"Uh-huh," I said.

"Well, it's damn tempting to try to prove to yourself and everybody else you can still cut it. But a guy who hasn't ridden in years can get himself killed out there. If I kept in shape like you, you dog, I might just take a shot at a comeback and have to be scraped off the track."

"So you won't be a substitute jock," I said, "but gee whiz, Stoney, if you get any healthier, they may ask you to be a substitute horse."

He thought that was just hilarious and wandered back to his office laughing as if elves were tickling his feet with feathers.

I had one cocktail with the diners, then, as promised, at eight-thirty I excused myself. I told Jake I'd try to make it back in time for dessert.

On the way out, Stoney intercepted me. "You ain't eating?" he needled.

"Just shilling for you."

"And I appreciate the business, but won't you have just a little filet mignon? I mean, you're not still trying to make the weight, are you?"

"My riding days are over," I told him. "But I've got something to take care of. Where's your pay phone, Stoney?"

"Pay phone? You tryin' to make me feel bad?" He led me to his office near the maitre d' station and pointed to the phone on his desk. "Make it long distance," he said. "London, Paris, Tokyo. On me."

I settled for my hotel. Still no word from Lea.

It was just this side of nine o'clock when my rental entered the nearly empty racetrack parking lot. I knew there wasn't any legitimate way of

returning to the backstretch and Barn 12 that night. And given the security of Churchill Downs in Derby week, I wasn't about to try it il-
legitimately. Besides, I knew who I was waiting for, and he was bound
to turn up eventually.

I'd been sitting there awhile when Andrew the stable hand came
shuffling away from the backside, carrying his lunch box. As he approached an ancient, rusted Mustang, he lost some of the shuffle and
stood a little taller.

I started up my car. Andrew had unlocked the Mustang's door and
was about to get in when I drove alongside and said, "Hi, Andrew.
Quitting time?"

The black man immediately bowed his back obsequiously. "Oh,
you gave me a start, suh."

"You talk like that back in L.A., Andrew? Or is it just something
you put on for the Kentucky folk?"

"I doan unnerstan' . . ."

"If you can take a little constructive criticism, you tend to lay it on
too thick. You sound like you've been taking lessons from Willie
Best."

"Mistuh, ah . . ."

"Come off it, Andrew. You're no stable hand. You don't even know
that when a horse puts his ears back he's getting ready to do some
damage. I'm surprised you haven't got your butt kicked already—if not
by the horse, then by that horse's ass of a trainer."

Andrew said nothing, but his slack jaw tightened and he gave up the
slouch.

"Starbuck was supposed to meet you tonight at nine. I imagine you
know he isn't going to make it. I'm here in his place."

He still had nothing to say.

"C'mon, Andrew." I took out the crumpled memo slip that
Starbuck had written and held it out. "AHG. Andrew H. Gunderman—the same private detective Starbuck hired to look into my
background."

Gunderman sighed in resignation. "I guess you're the ex-jockey,
Killebrew, huh?"

"Who else?"

"Well, you got it slightly wrong. Starbuck wasn't going to meet me
here. The plan was for him to phone the barn at nine to tell me where
we would meet. See, this isn't a good place for me to be spotted talking to him or anybody else."

"Then where is a good place?"

"Back where I'm staying, I guess."

"Lead the way."

I followed the Mustang for about seven miles to a run-down motel in an even more run-down section of the city. I pulled my car alongside his and was by his side as he got out his key.

"Won't you come in?" he said sarcastically.

He flicked on the lights as I followed him into one of the most depressing motel rooms I'd ever seen.

"Nice, huh," Gunderman said, indicating the cracks in the walls and the dust devils under the cotlike bed.

"The price of going undercover," I replied.

He sat down on the bed and gestured at the only chair in the room. I stayed standing.

"What do you want, Killebrew?"

"What are you working on?"

"Next question."

"Look, I'm just trying to find out what happened to Starbuck."

"Paper says he was in a car accident."

"Starbuck thinks the driver of the car may have been murdered."

"Yeah?" Gunderman didn't seem terribly surprised.

"What's James Carmody got to do with it?" I asked.

"Far as I know, nothing."

"What's your assignment?"

"You're gonna have to get that from Ray Starbuck."

"I'm representing him."

Gunderman smiled. "I don't think so. Else he would have mentioned it when I talked with him this afternoon."

"He called you? How is he?"

"For a guy fresh from the operating table, he sounded lively and pissed off. As usual."

"Did he mention his daughter?"

"Daughter? Hey, man, Starbuck isn't the kind of dude who spends time chattin' about the family. He only wants to know if he's getting his money's worth out of me. I dig that kind of arrangement, because I earn my pay."

"Considering what happened to him and the Salazaar woman, you must be a little nervous," I suggested.

"My insurance company says I'm a good risk," Gunderman replied. "Not a single accident in twenty-five years of driving."

"Starbuck told you it was an accident?"

"He didn't say dit about dat. All Starbuck and I discussed was my progress. Period."

I could believe it. I had experienced the hard way Starbuck's method of never letting his left hand know what the right is doing. Gunderman was not going to be of any help.

At the door to the dismal room I said, "Starbuck's fondness for secrecy almost got me killed once. You better take care."

"Ever see me play football when I was at USC, Killebrew?"

I shook my head. I had no idea he was a football player.

"That's okay. I never saw you race, neither. But here's my point: reason I never made pro is because I felt I had to do everything myself. I never could trust my teammates to do the right thing. That makes for a lousy quarterback. But the attitude that's no good for a team player is right on for a private detective. I always watch my own back."

"Well, in case that back winds up against the wall . . ." I gave him the name of my hotel and my room number. He didn't seem to make any special note of either.

12

I ARRIVED back at the Hot Box to find the party had grown. The diners had been joined by Hud Barrow, the aging racing columnist for *Sports Week* magazine. At his side was a voluptuous redhead he referred to as his "niece."

Running into Barrow was not the highlight of my day. For reasons that I've never understood, he has always refused to give me a break in print. Back when I was on top of the game and picking up winners in bunches, he would always find something negative to say about my performance. And long after the news value of my fall from grace had ended, he continued to mention it, usually in the form of some snide allusion.

Barrow pretended to ignore me when I joined the table. He was too busy quizzing the owners of the Derby favorite about their missing jockey.

". . . and if Dewey Lane doesn't turn up, what happens then?"

"I'm sure he'll turn up," Jake Lunden said with a thin smile.

"But if he doesn't? You got a replacement in mind?"

"Look, Hub," Jake said, "I don't know where you heard about Dewey, but it's no big deal. He'll probably be here tomorrow, in plenty of time."

"If not, you could always use Killebrew," Barrow said nastily. "Most of the dirt seems to have rubbed off him by now."

"You'd know if anyone would," I said. "You're the dirt expert."

"Would you consider getting back in the game, Killebrew?" Barry Gallen asked. He seemed surprisingly interested in my reply.

"If I did," I said, thinking of Stoney's excuse for gluttony, "I wouldn't pick the Derby for my comeback. I'd find a nice small-town track on a quiet afternoon when a guy like Barrow here is at home pretending to be a family man with the wife and grandchildren."

"Grandchildren?" Barrow's redheaded "niece" said, drawing back from him.

The reporter gave me a venomous glance, then turned to Jake. "If you're so sure Dewey Lane's gonna be here tomorrow, why'd you put in a call to Eddie Delahoussaye?" he asked.

"What makes you think I did?" Jake asked.

"Tell him, Killebrew. Tell him what a persistent son of a bitch I can be."

"The son of a bitch part is right," I said.

Barrow gave me another of his glares. "I hear you're shacked up with Ray Starbuck's daughter."

I didn't reply.

"Musta left her sittin' vigil by his side in the hospital, huh?"

I still said nothing.

"They say the L.A. cops are coming up empty on the dame. What's her name? Sanchez? Something like that. Anyway, they can't find out anything about her. A real mystery woman. What about that, Killebrew?"

"You know more about it than I do."

The old newsman cocked his head and gave me a crooked grin. "You helped solve the Dresner murder, right? So what's the deal now, you think you're some kinda private dick, working with Ray?"

"I'm an ex-jockey with a little free time and I'm here to see a horse race," I said. "And I guess I'm edging into your territory, Hud, narrating a documentary for SportsNet."

"Hell, Barry, you must not give a damn who you employ," Barrow said, shifting his gaze to Gallen. "Who's your ice-skating commentator, Tonya Harding?"

"Think she's available?" Gallen asked genially, treating the writer's venom as if it were light table conversation.

Hud Barrow turned back to me. "I think you're snooping around. You break bread with these good people and you're probably hoping to catch 'em pulling some little stunt like the one you tried eight years ago. Misery looking for company."

"There's only one snoop at this table that I know of," I said, getting up to go. "And in this case, it's one too many. It was nice seeing the rest of you folks."

"Still not eating?" Stoney Hilton said as I passed by.

"If you ever decide to drop a few pounds, here's a diet tip," I said. "Hang out with Hud Barrow. You'll lose your appetite every time."

13

THERE WERE still no messages for me at the hotel, so I figured the most productive thing I could do was get a good night's sleep. But as my head hit the pillow, the phone rang. The voice on the other end was not the one I'd been praying to hear.

"Just what the hell do you think you're doing in Louisville?" Starbuck's voice sounded a little weak, but his hostility was in mid-season form.

"Why shouldn't I be in Louisville? It's Derby week."

"You're interfering with my business, Killebrew, and you're endangering lives."

"Whose life besides my own?"

Starbuck hesitated, then said, "Andy Gunderman's, for one."

"He looks like he can take care of himself."

"I still don't get what the hell you're doing there."

"I'm here because you're not. Didn't Lea tell you?"

There was silence at the other end of the line. I tried waiting him out, but he was better at it than me.

"Didn't she tell you about it?" I asked again.

"Lea's on a job," Starbuck barked. "But you're not. I don't need your help."

"Right. You're doing just fine. So's Vickie Salazaar. Who killed her, by the way?"

"What are you talking about?"

"At the hospital. You said she'd been murdered."

More silence. Finally, he said, "I must've been high as a kite."

"Then it's not true?"

"They say she had a heart attack. It sure as hell seemed like a heart attack. She couldn't catch her breath and then she just folded. I tried to grab the wheel, but by then we were flying down through the trees."

"Who was she, anyway? The police can't get a handle on her."

"I know. I've had a meeting with a Lieutenant Burns. A total idiot masquerading as some sort of supercop. I'll tell you what I told him. 'Vickie and I were casual acquaintances.' I don't have any idea why they can't find any trace of her past. She didn't talk much about herself."

I knew he was lying. Vickie and he had to have been working on something involving the Derby. But here I was, an agent in place in Louisville, and Starbuck didn't seem inclined to make use of me. It was a blow to the ego, but I decided to rise above it and provide him a little intelligence information even if he didn't want it.

"Dewey Lane didn't make it to Louisville," I said.

"So Andy told me. Look, Coley, you're not doing anybody any good in Louisville. Come on back to L.A. and we can talk."

"It was your daughter who asked me to fly here," I said. "If she wants me to close up shop and come home, she can tell me herself. Mention that to her when she reports in."

Starbuck started to reply, but I didn't give him the chance. I put the phone back on its cradle and made a renewed effort at a night's sleep. This time it worked.

14

LOUISVILLE FOLLOWS a predictable pattern during Derby Week. The closer the big day comes, the larger the purses and the fiercer the competition. The town was crawling with print and broadcast reporters, many of whom never covered a horse race any other time of the year and had no concept of an intelligent question. As more and more horse people, media people, and celebrities arrived on the scene, the cost of living adjusted itself upward: a $3.95 breakfast was hiked to $12.95; a $90 hotel room went for $300.

On Derby Day minus one I was again at the track, with Totter and camerawoman Kate, checking out the horses and their human connections. I had no idea what kind of documentary we'd wind up with, but there would be no shortage of footage to choose from.

Up to then I'd been so professional I impressed even myself. But that morning I ruined one of Kate's setups, letting my eyes and my brain drift during a close-up as a black limo with smoked glasses glided through the backside area. Kate groaned and said, "Where are you, Coley!"

"Sorry, I guess I need a break," I said, walking after the limo. Though I didn't tell Kate not to follow me with the camera, I was glad she didn't.

I kept the vehicle in sight. Not many owners would make that kind of dramatic entrance, so my hunch that the limo's destination was Barn 12 seemed an odds-on bet.

Anxious not to be spotted, I found a cranny beside Barn 10 where I was able to spy, partially hidden, as the limo pulled up in front of For Cupid's Sake's barn.

The chauffeur jumped out with the speed and solemnity, if not the firepower, of a SWAT team member. As he beat it to the rear door, a heavyweight lumbered out of the front passenger seat and four security guards who had been stationed at the barn rushed the limo. By the time the chauffeur had the back door open, the guards and the heavyweight had formed a protective human shield around the vehicle's wiry passenger as he hopped out and headed for the barn. Not quite obscured by the phalanx of guards was gray hair, a simian face tanned the color of birch, a rumpled seersucker suit, and a thin black four-in-hand tie. Put them all together, they spelled my one-time employer: James Deth Carmody.

Shifting my eyes back to the now unguarded limo door, I spied the other two passengers: a beautiful brunette in a white Chanel suit, and a slightly younger but equally attractive blond woman. Seemingly oblivious to the backstretch activities, they were watching a small television. Judging by the sound, it was a talk show, Oprah or Sally Jessy. The pair were so intent on the screen, I wondered if the topic was "Bimbos Who Love Billionaires."

The chauffeur closed the rear door on the women, then got back behind the wheel. I edged past the vehicle, convinced I was inconspicuous if not invisible, and moved closer to Barn 12.

Finding a vantage point I hoped was far enough away it would not prompt the curiosity of the guards even if they spotted me, I watched For Cupid's Sake being given the once-over by her owner. Trainer Richard Sandford stood by Carmody as he ran his hand over the filly's back, muttering something to the animal. Judging by the way Carmody treated people, he should have been saying something like, "Win tomorrow or you're dog food." But I could tell by his expression the animal meant more to him than any mere human being. I'd seen that look on owners' faces before. It was as if Carmody were in the presence of a deity.

Andrew circled the barn, bent and shuffling, pretending to collect refuse. He startled Carmody out of his reverie. "Jesus, Richard," the old man said, his nasal voice rising in pitch as he ducked behind the horse. "Get him."

Suddenly, the guards turned on Andrew, guns drawn and pointed. Willie Best couldn't have done a better job of eye-rolling fright and perplexed terror than Starbuck's private eye, but under the circumstances, at least some of the fear must have been real. I took advantage of the distraction to move a little closer.

"Guns up!" Sandford ordered, and the men raised their pistols before returning them to their holsters.

A shaken Carmody rose from behind his horse. "Gaw-damnit," he bellowed. "This Nigra coulda blasted me, the horse, and you before your boys got their peashooters out of their pants."

"He look dangerous to you, boss?" Sandford said. His tone sounded surprisingly sarcastic, considering his employer's lack of geniality. But Carmody was apparently too wrought up to notice a little thing like sarcasm.

"Real sorry, gentlemens," Andrew drawled. "Just cleanin' up." I still thought he was laying it on too thick, but they seemed to buy it. Never underestimate the power of a stereotype.

Carmody stared at Andrew for a few seconds, then relaxed.

Sandford said harshly to the black man, "You muck out those stalls yet?"

"Gettin' right on that, suh," Andrew replied.

Sandford gave him a look that could have cracked a diamond. Andrew turned and scuffled away.

Shaking his head, Carmody started to say something else to Sandford, but his eyes fell upon his jet-black filly and his mood softened. He smiled. "You gonna win for me, Cupe?"

The filly shifted her weight and took a backward step.

"We didn't come here to lose," Sandford said.

"Keep that thought," Carmody said and nodded to the guards. They surrounded him on the way back to the limo, moving so quickly I barely had time to slip from their line of vision.

I watched the billionaire hop back into the limo. Just before the chauffeur closed the door, the blonde looked up and stared past her companion, through the guards and straight at me. The Killebrew luck. It probably should have been flattering that the private army of bodyguards hadn't noticed me, but a beautiful blonde had.

The door closed and the chauffeur got back behind the wheel. I turned to go, but there was no escape.

The limo pulled up beside me and down came one of the rear windows. From inside the car I heard Carmody asking, "What're you up to, honey?"

The blonde called out to me, "Hello, there."

I paused, staring at her radiant smile. From the corner of my eye I could see Carmody's security team closing in on me from the barn.

The girl asked, "Don't I know you?"

"Do you?"

Carmody moved to the window, too. "Killebrew?" he asked.

"Of course," the blonde said. "Coley Killebrew. Don't you remember me, Coley?"

There *was* something familiar about her. The clear blue eyes. The dimples.

"The little girl on the white horse," she prompted, and I suddenly remembered.

"Angela," I said. Until that moment I'd forgotten Carmody had a daughter.

Sandford approached the limo through a hole in Carmody's defensive line. "You know this guy, Angie?"

"I used to steal brownies from the kitchen for him and that other jockey. Ricky."

"Ricky Fox," I said. "They were the best brownies I ever tasted, too. You've certainly grown up, Angela."

"It's been a long time, Killebrew," came Carmody's grating voice from the limo.

I nodded.

"I hate to be brusque," Carmody said, "but we're on a real tight schedule this morning. Good to see you, though. Drop by some time."

"Please do," Angela said as the limo pulled away.

Drop by where? I wondered.

Sandford glared at me. "You didn't tell me you knew the Carmodys," he said.

"I rode for him for a while."

"Yeah, that's right. You said you knew Gandy Dawes. Well, see you around."

He turned and headed back to the barn, followed by the security guards. Beyond them, Andrew Gunderman stood beside the barn, staring at me with a puzzled frown.

15

I WAS waiting that evening at seven when Gunderman's Mustang clunker returned to his grim motel. I watched from a discreet distance as the private detective took out his room key and started to put it in the lock. He drew back a little when he discovered the door was open.

He entered warily. A few seconds later, apparently having satisfied himself no one was waiting to ambush him, he shut the door.

I got out of the renter and moved quietly to the window of the room. I knew the intruder wasn't inside waiting for Gunderman, because the intruder had been me. When I'd been in the room earlier, I had adjusted the curtain so that there was about an inch of space to give a clear view into the room. Through it, I watched Gunderman rush to the closet and take down a battered suitcase, tossing it on the bed.

He unscrewed two studs on the bottom of the suitcase and loosened the marred leather section. From behind it he withdrew a notebook. When he saw it, the tension seemed to go out of his body. He was relieved, and so was I.

I retreated to my rental car and drove away. Early tomorrow, when Gunderman was busy at Churchill Downs with his stable-hand impersonation, I planned a return visit to have a look at that notebook.

The clerk at my hotel had a smile on his face when he spotted me coming across the lobby. It seemed he finally had messages for me. Two of them. Neither was from Lea.

The first was from her father, ordering me to return to L.A. I stuck it into the cigarette sandbox beside the elevator. The second was another dinner invitation from the Lundens. Apparently, they'd made it a personal goal to get me to devour food in their presence. I decided to give them the opportunity.

I had slightly less than an hour to take a shower, dress, and drive across town. Before I left, I made one more unsuccessful try to reach Lea by phone. Of course, I was worried and concerned, but not as much as I would have been if Starbuck hadn't told me she was working, and if I hadn't already experienced the way her cases tied her up for days on end.

Ironically, if Starbuck had only told me the truth about her whereabouts, he wouldn't have had to ask me twice to leave Louisville. I'd have flown home on the first plane out.

The Lundens were dining at a restaurant in the Kentucky Center for the Arts, which overlooked the Ohio River. As befitted owners of a top Derby prospect, they had scored a window table for just the three of us. But they weren't too concerned with the view. Jake looked a bit haggard. And, instead of being her usual calm and collected self, Colleen was definitely distracted.

A waiter rushed the table and left with my request for a dry martini and another for Colleen. As nervous as the Lundens were, they seemed reluctant to talk. We sat there watching the river as one of those floating casinos came drifting by from Indiana. Its glitter was pretty, but to a lot of racing people, it couldn't have been an uglier sight.

"Is casino gambling really going to kill racing?" Jake asked suddenly.

I shook my head. "Nope. Disinterest is the problem. Something has to be done to get the attention of younger fans. And that won't be accomplished by a philosophy of if-you-can't-beat-'em-join-'em."

I was referring to the efforts of those involved in racetracks, including Churchill Downs, to combat their competitors for the gambling dollar by petitioning state legislatures to give the tracks exclusive permission to operate games of chance. So far, that form of gaming had not gotten the nod. And because of the fairly recent Boptrot stings, in which the FBI clocked a number of local politicians taking bribes to influence racing legislation, it seemed highly unlikely that the legislature would be eager to grant that sort of exclusivity, whether it was a good idea or not.

Though we kicked that subject around for all it was worth through my first cocktail, it soon became clear the Lundens' main concern was not legalized casinos in Kentucky.

Jake stared at me and said, "It looks like we're going to have to pull Hotfoot from the Derby."

"Why?"

"No rider."

I told them that I'd heard that Dewey had been suspended by the Churchill stewards for not showing up for his mounts.

"The damned little ingrate doesn't even have the courtesy to call us," Colleen said as new martinis arrived. "And that frumpy wife of his says she doesn't know where he is. Like hell."

Jake patted her hand. "His agent hasn't heard anything, either," he said.

I frowned, thinking not only of Dewey's disappearance, but Lea's, and wondering if there might not be a connection.

Jake watched with some concern as Colleen downed half her martini in one gulp. She dabbed at her lips with a napkin and said, "Even if he could ride, I'm not sure we'd want him."

"Oh, I'd want him all right," Jake said. "I wouldn't have much choice. I can't find another jockey."

"The country's full of 'em," I said.

"I can find *a* jockey all right, but not one of Derby caliber."

I couldn't believe it. "There are lots of excellent riders out there."

"Don't you think we've tried?" Colleen asked impatiently.

"And now it's too late," Jake said.

"Call Cal Ramirez," I said.

"I did that two days ago," Jake said. "He was available. But then, two hours later, he called back to decline. The same with Val Cullum."

"These guys agreed to ride Hotfoot, then said no?"

"Not only them," Colleen added. "Johnny Luther. Wes Snyder."

"Tell us we're not being paranoid, Coley," Jake begged. "Tell us that nobody is out there, trying to keep our horse from running in the Derby."

"Did you hear that from one of the guys you tried to hire?"

"No. They gave me no reasons at all," Jake replied, "and I pressed them plenty, believe me."

I raised my eyebrows. "Well, I suppose somebody might think of buying a Derby. But it's a goofy idea. They'd be risking a whole lot of loot and the probability of criminal action. And they still couldn't be a hundred percent certain their horse would win."

"I know it sounds crazy," Jake said. "But how else can you explain it?"

I shrugged. "It's a tough one. I hope you're not going to ask me to ride for you. After eight years, I'm a little rusty and about fifteen pounds overweight."

"We don't want you to ride Hotfoot," Jake assured me, a little too decisively to suit my ego. Then he looked at his wife sheepishly.

Colleen blurted out the question that had been behind their dinner invitation. "Was Ray Starbuck investigating that rock and roll person, Halcyon?" she asked. "Is that why you're here?"

Their connecting me with Starbuck's investigations made me uncomfortable. "Don't tell me you believe that nonsense Hud Barrow was spouting about me being some sort of sleuth?"

All hope went out of Colleen's face. She looked wretched enough to make me hate myself. "If we thought that somebody was trying to get the goods on that bastard," she said, "it would have made this whole mess a little more bearable."

"I'm sorry, but I don't have any idea what Starbuck was up to," I said. "I'm just here to see what the Derby looks like from the stands and pick up a few bucks from SportsNet."

Our waiter reappeared to notify Jake he was wanted on the phone. My host excused himself and strode out, leaving Colleen and me staring at the river.

Our silence was uncomfortable, but I couldn't think of a thing to say to her. Finally, she said, "Ray told us he and his lady friend were coming to the Derby. But I've known him long enough to realize it wasn't just a pleasure trip. Couldn't he have been investigating Halcyon?"

"Why pick Halcyon? There are sixteen other owners in the race."

"Because he has the most likely winner if Hotfoot is pulled. Headbanger almost beat Hotfoot at the Breeders' Cup Juvenile at Santa Anita last November. Halcyon took the defeat very personally. Since then, whenever our paths cross—and they do, since the racing world is relatively small—he's . . . confrontational. Insulting. He . . . gets fresh. But you know how Jake is, peace-in-the-valley at all costs."

I nodded. "Like those strong, silent types in his dad's westerns," I suggested, trying to put a positive spin on it.

She smiled ruefully. "Even they eventually put on their guns," she said. "I don't know what it will take to make Jake fight back. Maybe I should start carrying a gun myself. Then we could get Mr. Drugs-Sex-and-Rock-and-Roll to crawl back into his primordial ooze and stop trying to keep our beautiful Hotfoot out of the goddamn Derby."

This last was said with such emotional heat that diners from the surrounding tables fell suddenly silent. Colleen took a deep breath, then gave me a little half-embarrassed smile. "Whew," she said. "Sorry about that. It's just that we worked so hard, and now this disgusting, foul-mouthed thug thinks he can just buy the Derby."

"The guy's a jerk," I agreed. "But I've known Headbanger's trainer, Eddie Krayle, for a long, long time, and I can't see him being a party to anything crooked."

"Maybe Krayle isn't a party to it." Colleen put her hand on my arm and looked at me imploringly. "Please be honest with me, Coley. You swear you don't know what Ray was up to?"

"I really don't."

"But you and Lea . . ."

I was about to tell her with absolute truthfulness that my relationship with Lea definitely did not make me privy to Starbuck's business. But before I could, Jake returned to the table, looking even more unnerved than before. He didn't sit down.

"I'm terribly sorry, Coley, and I certainly want you to stay and enjoy your dinner. But we have to leave."

"Leave? Our food hasn't even arrived," Colleen said, staring at her husband as if he'd just sprouted another head.

"What's up?" I asked as Jake was dropping money for the waiter.

"We have to . . . make arrangements. We're going back home tonight."

"What?" Colleen's anger was creeping up on her again.

"It's best," he told her in a manner so definite she quieted down.

"That must have been some phone call," I said.

"A— It's a personal matter," Jake said. "And it won't wait. We'd already resolved ourselves to withdrawing Hotfoot. Please stay and dine."

Jake obviously wasn't going to satisfy my curiosity, so I just said, "I hope everything works out for you. See you back in L.A."

Colleen gave me a quick peck on the cheek, squeezed my hand, and they were gone.

The waiter arrived with our orders a moment after they'd left. I looked them over and told him, "I'll keep my trout. You can take the others back."

"But—"

"Okay, maybe you'd better leave the steak, too. Just in case."

"But . . ." he repeated. He was only in his twenties, but I pegged him for a career waiter. He hadn't asked us to call him by his first name. He didn't provide gossip about the chef. He actually seemed to be more interested in customer satisfaction than in bonding with us. I told myself I'd been in L.A. too long.

The waiter seemed genuinely distressed at the idea of his patrons missing out on a great dinner.

"They had to leave," I told him. "I think that should cover it." I indicated the wad of money Jake left.

The waiter picked up the bills. "Yes, sir."

"Tip okay?"

"Yes, sir. Thank you, sir."

"It's Mr. Lunden's treat," I said. "By the way, I don't suppose you know who phoned him just now?"

"The lady did not mention her name," the waiter said, "just that she wished to speak with Mr. Lunden."

"Did she sound upset or anxious?"

"Not at all, sir. She seemed pleasant enough." The waiter seemed puzzled at the question but not reluctant to answer. "Didn't mind repeating her request."

"Why'd she repeat it?"

"She was kind of difficult to understand," the waiter replied. "Her Kentucky accent was thicker than the stuff we put on pancakes."

16

WEARY BUT extremely well fed, I drove back to the hotel. A sudden wind whipped the car and there was the smell of rain in the air. It was beginning to appear that the sun might not be shining on the Derby that year.

I was yawning as I strolled past two maids resting by the linen closets on my floor. I heard one of them say, ". . . then, next time I look, it's right there on the hook where it's supposed to be."

"You musta been dreamin'," the other maid replied.

Idly wondering what they were talking about, I got out my key card, shoved it into its slot and heard the door to my room click open. I entered, still yawning mightily. No sooner had the door closed behind me than I saw a flickering light in the bedroom.

The TV was on, the sound muted. I wasn't alarmed. I might have left it on, and if I hadn't, I didn't put it past the maid to provide herself some entertainment while changing the sheets.

I was reaching for the remote to click the set off when I saw the figure slumped in the overstuffed chair just to the right of the bed.

It was Andrew Gunderman. He had traded in his track costume for dark slacks and a sport coat. His face was bloated and purple. His tongue, looking the size of a horse's, protruded from his mouth. Someone had twisted a silk tie around his neck and choked him with it.

It was my tie, one of the three I owned. My favorite, too—the Countess Mara stripe.

Without any foolish optimism, I felt for a pulse. None existed, but the flesh was still warm.

I swiftly checked the bedroom, the bath, and the two closets. Satisfied that Andrew and I were alone in the suite, I bent over the body and carefully drew back the flap of the dead man's jacket. A gun was nestled in a holster clipped to his belt.

What had happened exactly? There were heel marks plainly visible in the carpet, leading from a spot not far from the hall door into the bedroom and over to the chair. So Gunderman must have been attacked and downed near the door, then dragged across the floor. There was no sign of any struggle, and his gun was still on his hip, so he must have been taken by surprise. That meant the killer was waiting in the suite.

Waiting for whom? Certainly not for Gunderman in my hotel room. Waiting for me, then. If Gunderman hadn't gotten there first, it would have been me in that chair wearing my favorite tie and sticking my tongue out at the world. If the killer could overpower a big guy like Andrew, what chance would I have had?

Of course, the unfortunate Gunderman came to see me, too. And found what? The door half open? No. He was a pro. He would have been on his guard, just as he'd been when he found his motel room unlocked. I paused a beat and came up with the logical answer.

When Gunderman discovered someone had broken into his motel room, he must have guessed it was me. He came to my hotel to complain, or make sure. But when he knocked on the door to the room, he got no answer. I'd heard the hotel maid talking about losing something. It didn't seem unlikely Gunderman had borrowed her pass card from the hook on her linen cart. Maybe the murderer did, too. If it vanished and reappeared twice, it would really drive her nuts.

In any case, the killer had been waiting, choosing a weapon from my closet that could not be connected to him. When Gunderman took a step inside the suite, the killer either knocked him out and strangled him while he was unconscious or was strong enough to kill him with the silk garrote before he could fight back. The fact that the killer was able to drag Gunderman to the bedroom suggested a certain amount of strength.

But why drag him there instead of leaving him where he lay? Maybe to reduce the chance of someone out in the hallway seeing the body when the killer slipped out of the room. Or maybe he got Gunderman out of the way because he still intended to wait for me, turn it into a two-killing evening.

The ringing phone made me jump. I didn't answer, just stared at the phone. Whoever was calling would have to try again later, when I was slightly saner.

The absolutely correct move for the ordinary citizen would be to contact either the hotel detective or the police immediately. But I was no ordinary citizen. The consequences of reporting the detective's death were just too daunting. Here I was with a corpse in my hotel room, a dead man who had once been involved with Raymond Edgar Starbuck in getting me thrown out of racing. I'd be behind bars faster than Secretariat won the Belmont. They couldn't make it stick, of course—the waiter at the restaurant could probably give me an alibi, and a guy my size wasn't a likely candidate to overpower Gunderman, even with the element of surprise on my side.

But even if they couldn't hold me for long, I didn't want to spend the next several months in and out of Louisville jails.

There was only one way to go.

Gunderman's chair was on rollers. It took some effort on my part, but I got it to move. I took out my key chain, which held a silver knife, a birthday gift from Lea. I used it to cut through the tie and peel it from Gunderman's neck. It didn't much improve his appearance.

I found a blanket in the closet and covered up the body, tucking the edges under the dead man. Then I opened the door a crack and peered up and down the hall to make sure that the maids were gone and nobody else was in sight. Then I began the tricky process of pushing the chair and its contents into the hall. The door was a little too narrow. I had to reposition Gunderman's body to squeeze through.

Once out into the hall, we were past the point of no return. Mildly panicked, I pushed the blanket-covered load down the hall to the stairwell door. I opened it, stepped through, and dragged the chair and body after me.

That was the easy part.

Now I started the long, torturous trip down seven flights of stairs to the basement level where my car was parked. The chair was now useless. I dumped poor Gunderman's heavy corpse onto the metal deck. Then, abandoning the chair, I grabbed an edge of blanket and began the downward trek.

As with any new activity, you have to get into the rhythm. Right away I learned it was possible when dragging a corpse downstairs to be too successful in building up momentum. The thudding body, setting its own speed of descent, threatened to bowl me over.

After I made it down the first two levels, I began to feel more confident. Sure, I'd get it done. Absent a fire, earthquake, or power failure, who ever used a hotel stairway anyway? If I took my time and didn't make too much noise, there was little danger of being discovered.

Thinking you're safe tempts the gods. As I passed the fourth level, I heard a door open, followed by drunken laughter.

"The hell I will," a man's voice slurred. "The hell I will."

I had no idea what the man would or wouldn't do, but I prayed he wouldn't do it in the stairwell. I reached out a hand and flipped off the light.

"Jesus, now I know I ain't gonna run down four flights of stairs, not in the goddamn dark, no matter how much we bet."

The door closed. I breathed a sigh of relief, switched the light back on, and continued dragging the body downstairs.

At the door to the B level parking, I left the body in the corner, covered with the blanket. If anyone passed while I was getting my car, I hoped they would be drunk enough or self-absorbed enough not to notice it or speculate on what its shape suggested.

At that time of night, there wasn't much traffic in the parking lot. Still, a few cars were trickling in as I walked to mine.

I started up the rental and drove it to within a few feet of the stair exit door. It was another moment of high jeopardy, since the odds of somebody happening by were much shorter than they'd been on the stairs.

I dragged the blanketed mound through the exit into the garage and opened the passenger door of the rental car. "Now for the slapstick part," I said to myself.

I could have been pumping pure adrenaline through my arteries, and I still wouldn't have been able to hoist up Gunderman's body and plop it onto a car seat. Even alive the guy outweighed me more than two to one. Dead, he wasn't any lighter. So my game plan was to lift the lifeless but still pliable legs and drape them into the car. Then I'd lift the bulk of Gunderman's body as high off the concrete floor as I could, move my own body underneath it, and shoulder the corpse onto the passenger seat.

The first try wound up with both me and the corpse splayed out on the garage floor. But on the second try, with Herculean effort, I managed to shoehorn the body into the rental.

I slammed the door and, gasping for breath, circled the vehicle, slipping into the driver's seat. When my hands touched the steering wheel, I was surprised at how sweaty they were. I looked in the mirror and saw that my hair was matted and my face wet with perspiration and white as chalk. If I'd seen me on a TV screen, I'd have assumed I was watching an upset-stomach commercial.

Enough self-admiration. I took a deep breath, turned on the ignition, and drove out of the garage and back onto the stormy streets. I had no trouble returning to Gunderman's motel. I drove past it and parked a block away, under a shade tree that seemed to intensify the darkness.

Earlier, when I'd broken into the motel room, I'd used a credit card. This time, though, I decided to search the dead man's pockets for his key. I found it, and another set as well: his car keys. The battered Mustang must have been parked somewhere near my hotel. Hopefully, not too near.

I removed Gunderman's wallet. In the light from the dash, I saw that it contained very little: sixty-four dollars in cash, one hundred-dollar traveler's check, a temporary Kentucky driver's license, a picture of Gunderman and a thin black woman with orange hair and a nice smile. There was nothing to indicate the dead man's residency or true occupation. I put back the wallet.

Then I got out and walked to the motel, which seemed remarkably quiet. Evidently, it was too run-down for even the hot-sheet trade. The only sound was the wind. Clouds bumped and rolled through the night sky, collecting directly overhead. In the distance was the rumble of thunder. I managed to reach the motel before the skies opened up.

I entered Gunderman's room cautiously. I hadn't ruled out the possibility that a murderer might be skulking nearby. But as far as I could tell, the room had not been searched. I found the worn leather suitcase in the closet, unscrewed the studs in the bottom and removed the notebook.

A crack of thunder brought me to my feet. I took a few deep breaths and carried the notebook to a bedside lamp.

It turned out Gunderman had been a very scrupulous recorder of events, including a detailed account of the goings-on at Barn 12. Even a cursory look told me that he was a considerably better detective than he was a stable hand.

A few heavy raindrops splatted against the window. Deciding I'd better get out of there before the heavens really opened up, I tucked the notebook into my coat pocket, repositioned the leather panel on the suitcase, twisted the studs back into place, and rubbed them and the case with my handkerchief. I returned the case to the closet where Gunderman had left it.

Backing toward the door, I continued to use the handkerchief, rubbing every surface I'd touched during either of my visits. I walked out of the motel room and headed quickly toward the car, getting just enough rain down my collar to make it uncomfortable.

The street where the rental was parked was still dark and quiet, except for the more frequent flashes of lightning and claps of thunder. I opened the passenger door and struggled to pull Gunderman's body from the car. It fell heavily to the wet sidewalk.

With difficulty, I dragged the corpse a few feet to the tree and propped it against the base. That's where I left Gunderman, sitting up, legs stretched out, swollen head lolling on one shoulder. The rain was starting to really come down, forming tears on the dead man's face.

Another flash of lightning lit up the sky. Lit up Gunderman's open dead eyes, too. I ran back to the car and drove away.

17

I SPENT a few minutes patrolling the rain-slicked streets around my hotel, but I couldn't find any sign of Gunderman's old car. Then I drove slowly through the hotel's two parking levels. No grunge Mustang there, either.

Using a pay phone a block away, I called the Louisville police. Raising my voice a few frantic octaves, I reported the sighting of a dead body, giving the location with careful accuracy but hanging up before they could ask any questions. That was the most I could do by way of giving the detective a proper send-off.

Back at the hotel, I rode the elevator up to my floor. Before returning to my room, I checked the emergency stairwell. The chair was still resting where I'd left it. If any hotel staff had passed, they presumably would have removed it. Any guests would probably have ignored it. I wheeled it all the way to my room without meeting anybody.

I was about to apply my key card to the lock when the door was swung open from the inside and a man I'd never seen before stepped through it.

He didn't look very threatening. He was in his sixties, a bit paunchy, with no more seams on his face than the average bloodhound, wearing a rumpled suit and a wary expression. He stared at the chair, then at me. "You Mistah Killebrew?" he asked, making a song of it.

"That's me. And that's my room you just walked out of."

"The name is Mawks, Mistah Killebrew. Awtimus Mawks. Hotel security." He flashed a license that read Artemus J. Marx. "You takin' a stroll with that chair?"

I looked down at the chair and grinned sheepishly. "Aerobic exercise," I said.

"Well, we got a real fine gymnasium in the hotel, third floah."

"I'll have to try it sometime." I pushed the chair past Marx and into the room. "Do you visit all the guests' rooms while they're out, Mr. Marx?"

"Ackshully, suh, I came up heah in response to a guest complainin' a noise comin' from yo' room."

"Sounds pretty quiet to me," I said.

"Yessuh. Anyways, I knocked, an' when you didn't respond, I just sorta let my—"

He was interrupted by the sudden strum of a guitar and loud laughter down the hall. We turned to see a mob of people heading to a room a few doors away.

"Neighborhood's going to hell," I remarked.

At the center of the group and carrying the guitar was the rock star, Halcyon, and among his entourage was Martin Grosso. They were all obviously high as Goodyear blimps, but I wasn't sure on what: booze maybe, or drugs. For some, just the anticipation of the Derby could do it, but I doubted that was enough stimulant for this bunch.

"Maybe the noise wasn't coming from my room at all," I suggested to Marx.

"I see yo' point, suh," the hotel detective replied, turning toward Halcyon and his party.

The rocker noticed me. "Hey, the food jock. Maybe he can get 'em to open the fuckin' kitchen."

"Kitchen's closed for the night, gents," Artemus Marx said, his tone gentle but firm. "It's real late and the othah guests'd like to get some sleep. So what say we keep it down, huh?"

"Keep it down?' Halcyon said, with a grating laugh. "Man, this is the time to keep it up." He grabbed one of the women in the party and kissed her. Martin Grosso, more in control than most of his companions, was studying the hotel cop, as if gauging the man's potential for posing a problem.

Marx threw me a sheepish look as he waited for Halcyon to finish his kiss. He turned to the rock star. "Suh, if you'd just take all this into yo' room and keep it quiet—"

"Sure, we'll keep it quiet," Halcyon said, raising his voice even louder. "You heard him, dudes. Quiet!"

Martin put his arm around Halcyon's shoulders. "Cool it, Hal. Tomorrow's the big race, remember. Let's save the celebration for after the win, huh?"

Halcyon nodded. "Yeah, yeah, sure, you're right. I wouldn't want old McGruff the Crime Fighting Dog here to think we don't know how to behave." He turned to me. "Hey, Killebrew, c'mon over and join us. We'll have a quiet little party."

"Thanks anyway, but I've had a long, hard day."

"Your call," Halcyon said. He handed the key card to Marx as if he were the duty doorman. The hotel detective scowled but opened the door, putting on a fake smile as he handed the key back to Halcyon.

Just before I closed my door I heard Marx say, "I'm askin' you folks to keep the noise to a dull roar, okay?"

I shoved the chair back to its original position and sagged down onto the bed. Then I noticed the phone light blinking angrily.

According to the desk, a Mr. Starbuck had phoned three times. No, Mr. Starbuck had not left a number where he could be reached.

Exhausted, I stripped off my jacket. I opened the door of the No Host Bar, viewing the selection and deciding on an imported beer. Then I settled down to read the late Andrew Gunderman's notebook.

It began, neatly penned, with his showing up for a job Starbuck had prearranged for him at Churchill Downs. A week later he'd been assigned to the task of preparing the barn on Derby Row for Jaydee Farms.

"Operation of Barn 12B seems normal, except for excessive security," said an early entry in the notebook. "Richard Sandford is, as V predicted, a hard-nosed asshole."

Who the hell was V? Vickie Salazaar seemed to be a safe guess. If so, what was her connection to Sandford, the man running Jaydee for Carmody?

The series of entries that followed were filled with the details of everyday track activity. Gunderman scrupulously listed all visitors, by name if he knew them, otherwise by description. He indicated no suspicion of any kind, except for Carmody's girlfriend, whose name, it seemed, was Lula Dorian. The sophisticated-looking brunette was, according to Gunderman, a former waitress who caught the billionaire's eye while toiling in a Chunky Chicken fast food emporium in Lexington.

"She's supposed to be your typical Southern fried bimbo who grabbed the brass ring," the detective had scribbled in one of his last entries, penned just that evening, "but I caught her chatting it up in Spanglish with some scarface Chicano never seen before. When Sandford showed, the conversation ended fast. Scarface booked. Check Dorian out."

His final entry had been, "Break-in at my motel room. Maybe Killebrew. Maybe somebody else. Check out tonight."

As I flipped back through the earlier pages, my name caught my eye. Gunderman had logged in my meeting with Angela Carmody at the barn. His comment was a large question mark. Then, almost as an afterthought, he'd added, "Check out missing Lane re Killebrew race."

It wasn't paranoia on my part to conclude what "Killebrew race" had to mean. Had Gunderman been so annoyed with me he was going to reopen that ancient can of worms?

I leaned back in the chair, took a swallow of the beer, shut my eyes and tried to shift my mind to more appealing subjects. The image of Angela Carmody appeared, then melded into a vision of Lea, opening her arms to me. It wasn't until three hours later that I woke up to realize I'd fallen asleep in the chair.

18

THAT WAS about all the sleep I got. I knew we documentarians would be starting early on Derby Day, but they hadn't told me just how early. I've always wondered what time that complimentary paper appears outside your hotel door. That a.m. I found out. Happily, it was the Louisville *Courier-Journal* and not the generic *USA Today* that plopped on the hallway carpet at a quarter to five.

I only had to scan a few pages before I found a brief item titled MYSTERY DEATH BY STRANGULATION. The name of the victim was being withheld pending notification of family. I wondered what family of Gunderman's would be found. Was that pleasant-looking, orange-haired lady in his wallet photo a wife or a girlfriend?

It was no surprise that the murder, a minor news item to begin with, would get less attention on Derby Day. The major coverage was given to the rain-soaked condition of the Churchill Downs racing surface and the fact that Jake Lunden had withdrawn the favorite, Hotfoot, at the last minute, causing the odds on the race to shift.

As Colleen Lunden had suspected, the new favorite was Halcyon's Headbanger. But the absence of Hotfoot definitely made it more of a wide-open race. Where Hotfoot had been listed at 8-to-5, with a possibility of being odds-on by post time, Headbanger was being listed at a generous 5-to-2, and several other contenders, including The Loan Arranger and Sabisa from my part of the country, were drawing increased support.

I'd put down the paper and picked up my razor by the time Lew Totter called to invite me to an early breakfast.

Totter's hotel was an easy walk from mine, and since the heavy rains of the night before had lessened to a mist, and I'd seen enough of that parking garage for a while, I decided to go by foot. Maybe I'd work up an appetite.

I found the producer and Kate Donlevy, the camerawoman, already seated and digging into heaping plates of eggs, grits, and chicken liver from the breakfast buffet. Loretta Simmons, Barry Gallen's assistant, was there, too, bright and alert and nibbling on a croissant.

I filled a plate of my own and joined them. We were discussing how the wet track would affect the race when Gallen joined us briefly, looking a bit weary and frazzled. He barely had time for a few sips of coffee before someone caught his eye.

At first I didn't recognize the handsome young man in the white raincoat. When he waved, I realized it was Geoffrey Paragon, the transatlantic SportsNet bigwig who'd taken such a fancy to Lea at the Lundens' party.

Gallen leaped to his feet and followed Paragon out without another word for the rest of us at the table. That was apparently Loretta's cue to take her last sip of coffee, bid us good day, and move quickly to catch up with the departing men.

"Mis-tah Geoffrey Padagon beckons," Totter said, laying on an ultraphony British accent, "and men and women rush to do his bidding."

"Guy seems young to own a piece of a network," I remarked.

"No doubt born of privilege and wealth."

"His being here probably explains why Gallen's so shaky," I said. "The big boss is in town."

Totter waved off the suggestion. "Barry doesn't sweat the brass. My guess is he probably screwed the pooch last night. Literally."

"Now, boys," Kate said. "Remember, there's a lady present."

"My profuse apologies, hot stuff," Totter said, winking at her lasciviously. He reached for her hand and planted a kiss on it.

She withdrew the hand with a chuckle. "Idiot!"

"Anyway," Totter continued to me, "I've been making the rounds with Barry for a while now, and the only time I ever saw him shaky like this was down in Panama when he got caught in the kip with a teenager. The catcher was her big brother. Who happened to be a local cop. I still don't know what black magic he used to get out of that one, but it sure scared the bejesus out of him. Hell, it musta been another whole month before he started screwing around again."

"Sounds like quite a guy," Kate said. "But there are other things besides sex that put big business types on edge."

"It's a woman," Totter said with conviction. "Trust me, I know the signs. And he's keeping her as low profile as he can."

"What makes you so sure?" I asked.

"I went by his room last night to drop off the Derby tickets. He took about fifteen minutes to unlock the door. And when he did, he only opened it a crack, like there was somebody else in there he didn't want me to see. He had that dopey kicked-in-the-head-by-a-mule look he gets when his testosterone level gets higher than his IQ."

In point of fact, I couldn't have cared less about Gallen and his girlfriends, except that I was fond of Clara McGuinn and sorry to learn she'd backed such a loser. With a sigh, I asked, "What's on our card for today?"

"We've got at least *some* footage on all the real contenders," Totter said judiciously. "I thought we'd spend our time this morning on mood stuff."

"Meaning?"

"Oh, hooves digging into the turf. Hotwalkers and horses in the mist. All in slo-mo. Maybe we'll use time-lapse on the stands filling up." He looked over at Kate, asking her if that was possible.

She seemed unenthusiastic. "I've got an extra camera in the car, if we can con some track guy to stand guard on it. But this is pretty hokey stuff, Lew."

"You're forgetting our motto, sweetheart," Lew replied. "Nothing is too hokey for SportsNet."

19

THE MIST-SHROUDED morning moved by so quickly, I barely noticed the dampness. Wandering around the stables would have been a pleasantly nostalgic experience at any time. Being there at that moment, picking up the pre-Derby excitement, pushed me past nostalgia. Did I wish I was going to ride out on the track that afternoon? Did I want one more shot at bringing home a classic winner? What do you think?

Just before the first race I visited the jocks' room, where the riders were sparring with one another, pretending the tension wasn't building inside them. Some of the guys here I'd ridden against countless times. Others had no idea who I was. I kibitzed with a couple of old friends while Kate's camera rolled. But the nostalgia was so powerful I couldn't hang around for long.

"What's the matter?" Kate asked me. "You look like you've seen a ghost."

"Something like that," I replied.

As the big moment itself drew closer, we got plenty of footage of the horses being saddled and the freshly pressed and groomed owners and trainers in the walking ring. When they headed out for the track, Kate followed me to my seat, taping the crowd all the while. Then she was off to catch the horses and riders as they readied to move into the chute. The tape of the race itself we could pick up from the network that had bought the rights, but everything else in our documentary would come from Kate's camera.

Glancing around during the ceremonial playing of "My Old Kentucky Home," I was impressed by the location of my seat—four off the aisle, with a clear view of the finish line. Looking around, I saw I was surrounded by owners and trainers, several of whom nodded in recognition. Four rows above me was the James Carmody party—Carmody and his trainer, Richard Sandford, along with two very serious men in dark suits, were looking out over the crowd toward the chute. Neither his daughter nor Lula Dorian was present.

Totter appeared, slipping into the seat next to mine. "Sorry we couldn't get you on the back of a horse, but is this close enough?" he asked with a grin.

"How'd you score these seats?" I asked him. "We're closer than Carmody."

"Power of the press, my good man. What my sire demands, my sire gets. Even if I have to grovel like a worm in heat."

I looked at the two empty seats beside ours, counting the probable members of our party. I assumed Barry Gallen and Geoffrey Paragon would be along before the race started, but that seemed to leave us one seat short.

"Isn't Loretta joining us?" I asked.

"Loretta is, ostensibly, back at the hotel, taking care of business odds and ends," Totter said. "I get the feeling she's not much for spectator sports."

Gallen and Paragon turned up as the horses for the Derby were shaking out the kinks on the backstretch. If Gallen was impressed by our seats, he didn't mention it. He was jumpy and distracted. By contrast, Paragon exhibited grace and charm, congratulating Totter on "this quite remarkable proximity to the track."

I couldn't quite peg his accent. It was British-influenced certainly, but there was something else there. Australian maybe.

"Mr. Killebrew, I didn't have much chance to speak with you at your restaurant," Paragon said. "I was a bit distracted by your lady."

I replied with a bland, amiable smile.

"Actually, I was privileged to see you race. Twice. And both times you rode a winner."

"Where was that?" I asked.

"The first time was at Longchamps, on Arc de Triomphe day. The second was at Santa Anita, perhaps eight years ago. It was on one of my first visits to America."

"I believe someone told me you lived in London?" I asked.

"Sometimes I do," he said. "I am, what shall we say, a citizen of the world."

"The world is a pretty big place."

"Yes," Paragon said, smiling. "We have offices in London, Paris, Rome, and, of course, New York. I do spend most of my time in Europe."

"Selling SportsNet to the masses?" I asked.

Paragon seemed amused by the question. "How would you describe it, Barry?"

Gallen jumped as if surprised to suddenly become part of the conversation. "What?"

"How would you describe what I do?"

"Uh, international telecommunications."

"Yes. I rather like that. International telecommunications."

He winked at Gallen and made a Gallic gesture indicating perfection: right thumb and forefinger forming a circle. The delicate ring on his hand had some sort of crest on it, too small to make out even if I knew one crest from another.

Having completed their warm-ups, the sixteen horses gathered in the mile-and-a-quarter chute to our left, preparing to load into the starting gate. I checked the odds board. Whether because of For Cupid's Sake or not, the five horses blanketed in the mutuel field had been bet down to 4-to-1, not much of a potential windfall for those who liked the looks of Carmody's filly.

Headbanger was a 2-to-1 favorite, with a tough New York campaigner named Glory Regained at 3-to-1. The Floridian Warm Regards, a consistent runner with only a maiden race win and a frustrating series of second-place finishes on her scorecard, was going off at 7-to-2. Of the Californians, I thought Sabisa, at 8-to-1, was a pretty good value. I thought less of The Loan Arranger's chances: the odds of 10-to-1 seemed about right. Longest shot on the board at 80-to-1 was Waterskier, least well regarded of the horses not lumped with the field. I figured if For Cupid's Sake were running uncoupled, she would be no more than 5-to-1, given the buzz she had created in the past week.

This being the Kentucky Derby, a race that commonly led owners and trainers to follow their hearts rather than their heads, not many hopefuls had been discouraged by the early entry of the now-absent Hotfoot. Sixteen horses comprise a large, unwieldy field, though not as bad as the maximum of twenty the Derby rules now allow. Since the regular starting gate held only fourteen, two horses had to break from the auxiliary gate attached on the outside. With such a long run to the first turn, though, they didn't figure to have a serious problem getting position. The muddy track would be more of a factor in individual horses' chances than post position would.

The big field was loaded into the gate by the starter's crew with brisk efficiency. The Loan Arranger, as hard to handle as he'd looked in the barn, did a little jumping around in his stall, causing his jock to get off his back and hang onto the superstructure of the gate for a few seconds. A European entrant named Apostle, who'd been trained over a dirt track specifically created for potential invaders of North America, took some convincing to enter the metal monster at all. Still, for such a big group, the fifteen colts and a filly were mostly well behaved.

The hundred thousand present in the stands were hushed as the sixteen thoroughbreds stood in line. Then the gates flew open and they were off.

It appeared to be an even break and looked clean and uneventful from the grandstand view, but I knew from experience the horses were not all running in a straight line. A lightly regarded colt named Vaquero surged immediately into the lead. Since he was widely thought a sprinter with no chance, none of the other riders tried to go with him. Five contenders, including both Headbanger and For Cupid's Sake, were content to follow three lengths behind the leader in a tight little group. Sabisa, The Loan Arranger, Apostle, and Warm Regards were farther back, while Glory Regained, a notorious stretch-runner, dropped all the way to the rear of the pack, though not far enough back to avoid getting ample mud kicked in his face.

Entering the first turn, For Cupid's Sake was parked three wide, but not far enough out to hurt her chances. In fact, the footing might have been better out there than down on the rail.

Into the backstretch, Vaquero was still in the running. Headbanger had made a stout move, though, looming up beside the pacemaker. The jock on Headbanger was still sitting chilly, hadn't even started to ride Halcyon's colt for real yet. The rest of them, I thought, had better not let him get away. Vaquero was bound to crack, and if he left Headbanger with the track all to himself, the race would be over.

They must have read my mind. As the field turned for home, Vaquero started his vanishing act, stopping on the rail and making the whole field come around him, but Mulligan Stew was head and head with Headbanger, and Warm Regards, the perpetual runner-up, had made an impressive move on the outside to join them. For Cupid's Sake, in fourth place by herself now, still seemed to be going easily, and I wasn't about to count her out. The Californian Sabisa was having seven kinds of hard luck, taking up slightly to avoid the slowing Vaquero and then getting trapped behind a wall of horses.

They turned into the Derby stretch. There's no longer homestretch in American racing, and it seems even longer when you're trying to hold a young runner together at the end of a mile-and-a-quarter race. Headbanger and Warm Regards were a couple of lengths in front of everybody else. But For Cupid's Sake was really motoring in third place, edging up on them from the outside. I could hear Carmody four rows behind me shouting, "Go, For Cupe! Go!"

Now there were three leaders across the track, but it was far from a three-horse race. The colts in the second group were coming fastest of all, closing yards of ground with every stride. In mid-stretch at least six different runners looked like possibles.

Then the distance got to Warm Regards, who started slipping back between horses. But For Cupid's Sake kept going, challenging Head-banger. At a sixteenth of a mile out the filly got her handsome ebony head in front of the favorite's. For a few strides it looked like the Derby was going to have its fourth female winner. Behind me, Carmody was cackling and yelling like Walter Brennan on speed.

Then the filly's luck turned bad. Just a few yards from the finish she lost her footing in the mud. For a terrifying second it looked like she might go down, which, with the big field right on her heels, would have spelled tragedy for somebody. But she stayed on her feet and her jock managed to hang on. So all the slip cost her was the race.

Headbanger, a colt who wouldn't quit, surged past her to win by a half length.

The Loan Arranger came flying up on the outside to almost nose Carmody's filly out of second place. Glory Regained, the New Yorker, was less than a length back. Warm Regards finished fifth, ahead of the troubled Sabisa and the European hopeful, Apostle.

Paragon stood up and turned to face the crowd. Barry Gallen watched him nervously. The main TV cameras moved in on Halcyon, above us and to the right, draped in a pale blue cutaway and top hat that made him look like a parody of the actors in the Ascot scene in *My Fair Lady*. All around us, owners and trainers were either shouting their congratulations to the rock star or mumbling disgruntled oaths at his success.

Carmody looked too stunned to be angry. But that would change before long. I wondered who was going to take the heat for his filly's loss. Fluky as the misstep in the stretch had been, I was sure the billionaire wouldn't just write it off to racing luck. If Carmody didn't get what he wanted, somebody had to pay the bill.

Paragon seemed to have his fill of the scene. He sat down again, and the worried look suddenly left Gallen's face. Paragon looked bored. "Ah well," he told Gallen, "so much for the Derby. We'll have to do this all over again in Baltimore in two weeks."

Gallen nodded without expression.

Paragon turned to me. "Shall we have the pleasure of your company, too, Mr. Killebrew? At the Preakness?"

"I'm not sure."

"Aren't you the star of our Triple Crown film?"

"I thought it was a *Derby* film," I said truthfully.

Paragon turned to Gallen. "Don't tell me you're letting Mr. Killebrew get away from us?"

Gallen replied distractedly. "No. Of course not, Geoffrey. I'm sure Killebrew and I can work something out."

Totter mumbled, "My my," under his breath.

"That's settled, then," Paragon said, rising to his feet. "You'll excuse me, gentlemen?" He nodded to us and trotted down the steps.

Gallen tracked his departure so intently, it was as if he wanted to convince himself that the man was really gone.

Halcyon, the most bizarre owner of a Derby winner I could recall, was making his triumphant descent to the winner's circle, shaking every hand offered him from either side of the stairway, followed by a cool and controlled Martin Grosso and a bruiser with shifting eyes. It was evidently a very big year for bodyguards.

In the winner's circle, Halcyon and his much more conventionally dressed trainer, Ed Krayle, stood by while their jockey was awarded the blanket of roses. I could identify with the rider, having felt the weight of those flowers a couple of times. But I could also identify with For Cupid's Sake's rider. He'd saved a piece of the purse and maybe even a few lives by staying on the filly's back in the stretch. But his reward from Carmody wouldn't be roses. He was a good bet to wind up designated scapegoat.

"Well," Totter said, "now that you're the new shining light of SportsNet, Coley, maybe you'd better hop down there so we can get a shot of you congratulating the rock-'n'-rollmeister."

That seemed to remind Gallen he had to follow his boss's dicta. Putting his arrogance on temporary hold, he said, "Killebrew, I'd appreciate it if you'd stick with the documentary through the remaining two races. I think you know we don't have tremendous budgets for these things, so I hope we can extend our original deal."

"Plus transportation, hotels, and expenses," I said.

"Of course."

"First-class transportation," I added.

Gallen glared at me but managed to keep a smile on his face. "Naturally," he said between clenched teeth.

I considered adding a few totally unreasonable demands just for the fun of it, but Totter was urging me to follow him. As we headed through the mob toward the winner's circle, the producer told me, "Kate's set up. What we'd like is for you to sort of hug the guy like you're an old, old friend."

"No problem. Eddie Krayle *is* an old, old friend."

"Not Krayle. He's just a trainer. I'm talking about star material. Halcyon."

"Me hug Halcyon without proper inoculation? Not even if you flew me to Baltimore in a private jet. A quick handshake is almost asking too much."

20

AT THE airport a few hours later, waiting for my departure to LAX, I looked up from my newspaper and saw Hud Barrow scuttling toward me.

"Well, Killebrew, how goes it?" he asked, taking the seat next to me.

"It goes," I replied, returning to the paper. The way my luck was going, I should have assumed the so-called journalist would be booked on my flight. My only hope was to make him know how little I wanted to be in his company.

"You're looking fresh and relaxed this evening," he said in a not unfriendly way. I got the feeling he wanted something and would wait till he had it before he got insulting. "How'd you like the Derby?" he asked.

"I'd love to give you a quote for your column, Barrow, but my every thought on the subject belongs to SportsNet."

Barrow made a snort of contempt for the broadcast media. But he didn't, as I had hoped, go away.

"So how's that niece of yours, Hud?" I asked. "Nice girl, but I can't say I noticed much family resemblance. Unless your hair was red three toupees ago."

"Funny man," he said. He still didn't go away.

"Look, Hud, I'm every bit as fond of you as you are of me. Why risk ruining a perfectly good animosity with polite conversation?"

"You telling me to get lost?"

"I'd like to tell you to go play on the runway, but the other side of the room will do."

"You misjudge me, Killebrew," the writer said slyly. "Fact is, I got some info might interest you."

"Not likely," I said, picking up my paper again.

"See anything in that sheet about a guy from L.A. got himself murdered in Louisville?"

"Must've missed it."

"P.I. named Gunderman," he said with relish. "Black guy. Ever hear of him?"

I shook my head no and did my best to appear disinterested.

"Cops're calling it a 'senseless' crime on account of Gunderman's wallet was still on his body with money in it. 'Senseless' is cop talk for 'we don't have a friggin' idea why the guy was killed.' "

Hud grinned wolfishly. "They got an eyewitness, however, who claims to have seen some gent coming out of Gunderman's motel room last night. Some jockey-size guy. What do you think of that?"

"At this time, in this part of the world, Louisville is definitely the place for jockey-sized guys."

"Yourself included," Hud pointed out.

"Come to think of it, Hud, you're only a few inches taller than me. A witness wouldn't have to jump center for the University of Kentucky to describe *you* as jockey-sized."

"Yeah, maybe," he said. As I hoped, my reference to his height was the last straw. "Keep it out of the mud, smart guy."

I watched the elderly sportswriter storm away. I knew it was only a matter of time before the Louisville police would turn up Gunderman's car. I wondered if there was anything in the car, or hidden somewhere in the hotel room, that might lead the police directly to me. I shivered, looked at my watch, and hoped the plane wouldn't be too late in departing.

21

NOT ONLY did Barrow keep away from me on the plane, but he went out of his way to avoid me as we collected our luggage on the ground at LAX. All in all, a successful flight.

The sun had just about dived into the Pacific as I drove home through the evening traffic. There is always traffic in L.A., but the evening variety is special. It's slower, wearier, and its nerves are more frayed. If you're in your car looking for trouble, evening is when you'll find it.

I spent the time trying to convince myself that Lea would be waiting at our cottage. Or if not actually there, at least she would have left me some kind of message telling me not to worry. Of if not an actual message, there would be some clue I could follow to locate her.

At dusk, the darkened cottage and five plastic-wrapped copies of the L.A. *Times* littering the driveway were my first indication the answer was going to be none of the above. Then I saw the junk flyers and bills jamming the mailbox. Well, maybe she'd been too busy to get the papers and the mail in.

When I'd let myself in, I could no longer deny the obvious. The house had been unoccupied since I'd left. Nothing had been moved, nothing disturbed. The only activity was the blinking red light on the phone answering machine.

I turned on a living room lamp and with a last burst of hope— maybe she had left a phone message for me—I played back the tape. Most of the calls were from either Lt. Olaf Burns or Starbuck, each seemingly trying to outdo the other in anger and frustration.

I obviously had no intention of responding to Burns's demands for an immediate reply. I did want to talk with Starbuck, but Mr. Secrecy had left no hint of a callback number. I phoned St. Thomas Hospital.

The evening receptionist asked me to repeat the name of the patient I was trying to reach. I wound up spelling it and was all the way to "buck" when a male voice came on the line. "Who's this calling?" he asked.

"I'm trying to reach Raymond Starbuck."

"And your name, sir?"

Maybe Starbuck was having his calls screened. But the voice on the other end of the line didn't sound like it belonged to a social secretary. I disconnected. If the hospital had one of those gizmos we recently attached to the Neck's reservations line, a little computer readout that tells you the number of the person who's phoning in, there'd be a knock at the door shortly.

I tried to ignore that possibility as I phoned Starbuck's home. After six rings Choo-Choo's recorded voice announced, "No one is here to answer call. Please leave message and phone number at beep."

After leaving my number, I made my final call. Jack Hayward answered on the second ring. In the background were the sounds of the restaurant getting ready for its first sitting. The flap of tablecloths, the clink of glassware.

"Everything is progressing on well-oiled wheels, sirrah," he chirped as soon as he heard my voice. "I was even able to sneak in an audition this morning for Steven Spielberg at Universal."

"How'd it go?" I asked.

"It was for an elaborate contemporary version of 'Rip Van Winkle.' "

"Sounds perfect for you, Jack."

"Alas, it appears that Robin Williams has been cast as Rip, and Mr. Spielberg felt I was not quite elfin enough for the other parts."

"That's show business," I said. "Has Lea been in the restaurant, by any chance?"

"No. But a glowering member of the constabulary has paid frequent visits, looking for you and/or the beauteous Miss Lea."

"A Letterman look-alike?" I asked.

"I suppose, though I'd say more of a Buddy Ebsen without the charm. Will we be seeing your smiling face anon?"

"With any luck," I said.

The doorbell rang. Actually, it bonged. The choice of sound had been Lea's—I preferred an old-fashioned ring or buzz.

"I'll talk to you later, Jack." I hung up and went to check out my visitor through the front door peephole.

The porch light was not on, but there was enough dusk left for me to make out a man I'd never seen before. Rugged-looking, late twenties, dark. Wearing a bright Hawaiian shirt. Either he saw my shadow against the peephole or I hadn't been as quiet as I'd hoped, because he asked, "Mr. Killebrew?"

"What can I do for you?" I said through the door while I flipped on the porch light.

"We're here to take you to Raymond Starbuck." The brighter view of him added a couple days' growth of beard to his face.

"We?" I asked.

"My partner and I." He pointed to a nondescript sedan parked behind my Cherokee at the curb. At that distance through the peephole, it was impossible to identify the shadowy figure at the wheel.

"You guys work for Starbuck?"

"We work for everybody."

"Oh?"

"The government," he explained.

"The U.S. government?"

The man smiled. "Most of the time. We're with the Drug Enforcement Administration."

"ID?"

"No, DEA."

"I don't want you to think I don't have a sense of humor or anything, but I'd like to see some ID."

"Sorry. We don't carry 'em when we work the streets. But here." He lifted his shirt and pulled a gun from behind his belt. "Know how to use this?"

"More or less."

He cocked it and bent down to rest it on the porch in front of the door. "Hang onto it if it'll make you feel more comfortable."

Feeling more foolish than comfortable, I opened the door and stepped onto the porch. I picked up the gun, a Beretta Centurion. I uncocked it and tossed it back to my caller. "Be with you in a minute."

I went to the den, grabbed a coat, and paused before a wooden table. From its single drawer I plucked a gun that Lea keeps there—a Smith & Wesson Bodyguard that she assures me can be fired right through one's coat into an assailant's midsection. I slipped it into my jacket, certain that it was fully loaded. The Beretta, who knew?

As we drove toward the Santa Monica Freeway, me all alone on the rear seat, the men introduced themselves. Hawaiian shirt said his name was Marquez. The driver, dressed in a gray pullover and khaki pants, was Dougherty. Other than that and the name of their agency, they imparted no information whatsoever.

"Is Lea Starbuck at the hospital?" I asked.

"We'll see," Marquez said.

"Just tell me if she's with her father."

"In good time," Dougherty said.

"Why's the DEA running errands for Starbuck?"

"You're a basketball fan, Mr. Killebrew?" Marquez asked.

We were on the Santa Monica Freeway, passing the Robertson off ramp. The Robertson off ramp leads to St. Thomas Hospital.

"Where exactly are we headed, boys?"

"Downtown," Dougherty said amiably.

"I don't suppose you could narrow that a little."

Marquez looked at Dougherty and said, "The Lakers did better than I thought they would this season."

Dougherty replied, "The Clippers were another matter."

I quit asking questions.

Our destination turned out to be the Brompton, an ancient luxury hotel in the heart of downtown Los Angeles. It was so steeped in history and tradition and snob appeal that it had retained its class while the neighborhood around it went to hell. It rested like a bright jewel-box relic in the midst of the aimless and the homeless, fast food emporiums, porno movie houses, and flea market operations that offered real fleas.

The sedan dropped down into the narrow recess leading to the Brompton's underground parking. It was the most immaculate garage area I'd ever seen. They must have put on an extra shift of security just to keep the street people from sleeping in it.

With my two guides leading the way, I strolled past Rolls-Royces and Bentleys and Aston Martins to an ancient open-air elevator with grillwork polished to a sheen. It was probably the last remaining elevator in the free world to have an operator, a pale young man in a gray and black uniform. He nodded to Marquez and Dougherty and pressed the top button on his brass panel.

The elevator took its time making it to the twenty-fourth floor. We exited onto a short hallway with dark purple walls and cream-colored wood accents. There was only one cream door, marked 2400. I guessed it was what you called the penthouse.

The men didn't knock. Dougherty placed a key in the lock and opened the door. Another man, similar in every respect to my two pals except for his dress—warm-up shorts and shirt and Air Nikes—

greeted us. Marquez called him La Nasa. He used his head to gesture toward French doors that opened onto a rooftop garden.

There, in the midst of an assortment of colorful flowers, Raymond Starbuck sat in a wheelchair, observing the night skyline with headphones clamped over his ears.

"Here's Killebrew," Marquez said. And when that got no reaction, he shouted it. Starbuck tore off the headset and spun around in his chair to offer the fond and courtly greeting I'd come to expect from him.

"You stupid son of a bitch!" he shouted.

"Has he been checked for distemper?" I asked Marquez, who shrugged.

"What the Christ did you think you were doing in Louisville?" Starbuck asked angrily.

"As I told you, I was following Lea's request. She asked me to go."

"When was this?"

"The morning after you went down the canyon. She was going to go herself, but when they called from the hospital and said you'd had a relapse—"

"Who called?" Starbuck asked, glancing at the other men.

"A nurse, I guess. Heavy southern accent." I paused, remembering the words of the waiter in Louisville. An accent thick enough to spread on pancakes, he'd said. I stared at Starbuck, getting the picture pretty clearly by now. "You didn't have a relapse, right?"

"And Lea never made it to the hospital," he said, his voice flat. He turned to the two men. "Shouldn't you boys go check with the people at the hospital about the southern accent?"

Marquez and Dougherty both left the garden without question or hesitation. Starbuck had everybody else intimidated, why not the DEA? After they had disappeared into the suite, he said to me, "Not a lot of brainpower there, but we make do with what we have. Which brings me to you."

"What's happened to Lea?" I demanded. "And why didn't you tell me—"

"Grab a chair."

As I pulled up a deck chair, Choo-Choo appeared with a glass of iced tea for me, a clear fluid and pills for Starbuck, and a plate of bagels, Starbuck's comfort food of choice.

Realizing he apparently was going to provide me with at least a morsel of information about Lea, I controlled my impatience, sipping tea and waiting for him to take his medication. The night was as humid as a sauna. The natterings of drunks and panhandlers drifted up to us from the sidewalk. Starbuck didn't seem to mind. He was taking his time selecting just the right bagel.

"Have one," he said. "Choo picks up a fresh batch every night at midnight from the House of Bagels. That way, they're perfect for breakfast."

"It's a little past breakfast time," I pointed out, wishing he'd get to the point.

"Even now, they're pretty springy," Starbuck said, munching away.

Choo-Choo waited until he was certain nothing else was required of him and returned into the penthouse.

"Where's Lea?" I asked again, not really expecting a straight answer.

He surprised me. "The people who killed Vickie Salazaar have her," he said without emotion.

Something cold and sickening took control of my stomach. I put the barely touched glass of tea down on the tile and leaned forward, wanting to hear more and dreading it at the same time.

"She was alive and well as of this morning," Starbuck said. "Calls to my hospital room are transferred here. I get two a day from the bastards who grabbed her, at eight in the morning and eight at night. They let us have a brief conversation."

"And you're sure she's okay? Maybe they're forcing—"

"Lea and I set up a series of signals a long time ago," Starbuck interrupted. "She's all right. And they say she'll stay all right as long as I keep my mouth shut."

"Who're 'they'?"

"I don't know for sure. All I know is what Vickie told me."

"Which is?" I was sitting on the edge of my chair, tensed, like a sprinter waiting to be given the direction.

Starbuck gives out information about as easily as a mother lion gives her cubs up for adoption. Finally he said, "I suppose I have to tell you. I'm not doing Lea any good sitting here in this goddamn chair. And I don't have much confidence in the Frat Pack out there. I don't see as I have any other choice."

22

"YOU KNOW, of course," Starbuck said, "that the DEA confiscates all sorts of property from drug dealers—cars, boats, houses, and so forth—then sells it off to finance its antidrug operations."

"Sure," I said.

"They occasionally seize horses, too. I was asked to look into certain allegations concerning the auctioning of several confiscated thoroughbreds."

"Is this leading to Lea?"

"Yes. And we will arrive there sooner if you just sit quietly and try to look intelligent. Where was—yes, the seized racehorses. Apparently, they were sold off in the standard manner the DEA handles most of its confiscated property."

"So what was the problem?"

"The Racing Commission got an anonymous letter claiming the agent in charge of the sales had purposely undervalued certain horses."

"You mean," I said, "he lowered the sale price to friends?"

"Precisely," Starbuck said. "The problem is that the letter didn't provide many details. And, by itself, it is merely an accusation, not actual proof. The Racing Commission asked me to supply that proof, or to discredit the accusation."

"And where did Vickie Salazaar come into it?"

"She was with the DEA. As much as I hated having to deal with a government agency, I didn't think I could proceed without seeking their cooperation. Naturally, I was very cautious. If an agent was playing fast and loose with confiscated goods, I needed to find out whether he was doing it on his own or with others. For all I knew, it could have been a standard operating procedure at the DEA."

"Our government at work."

"Well, they put on a pretty good show of being outraged at the suggestion. But they didn't give me any guff about it being the impossible dream. If they had a bad apple, they were perfectly willing to let me weed him out. They assigned Vickie to be my contact."

"And you didn't let Lea know about any of this?"

He scowled at me. "Of course not. It had nothing to do with her."

Fathers and daughters, I thought. Out loud I said, "The cops are having quite a time trying to get a line on Vickie."

"It wasn't her real name. I have no idea what her real name was. She'd been working undercover, moving in and out of the drug cartels for so long, she may have forgotten it. If the drug lords weren't able to check her past, it's a cinch that Burns idiot won't stand a chance."

"Sounds like she was a good agent."

"Damn good. And a step ahead of her own agency. Though they did cooperate with me, as I said, the DEA brass took a dim view of that anonymous note. They tried to convince me it was the work of some crank, or maybe a disgruntled drug dealer trying to blacken the agency's reputation. But Vickie took a more pragmatic view. Even though the agent in question wasn't named in the letter, she knew who he was."

"How?"

"The guy had participated in the arrest of Paolo Rodriguez, and was also involved in selling off Rodriguez's U.S. possessions. One of his holdings was a small horse farm near Sarasota. Shortly after the sale, this same agent quit the DEA to work for the man who purchased several of the horses. We were going to Louisville to brace the ex-agent and see which way he jumped."

"I assume we're talking about James Carmody and Richard Sandford," I ventured.

Starbuck cocked his head. "What makes you think so?"

"Well, for one thing," I said, "Carmody was involved in Rodriguez's capture. For another, your man Gunderman was snooping around the Jaydee barn. And For Cupid's Sake, who just missed taking the Kentucky Derby for Carmody, was a Panamanian import. One of Rodriguez's, right?"

"Sandford was our suspect, all right," Starbuck replied, "and For Cupid's Sake was the horse whose sale we thought we could nail him on. But we went over the paperwork with a fine-tooth comb, and everything seemed in order. The animal doesn't have the kind of bloodlines that would boost her price. She was a beauty, sure enough, but nothing special otherwise. And that's the kind of money Carmody paid for her. Nothing special."

"You should have seen her run at the Derby. On dry ground, she'd have wound up wearing the roses."

"Even if the horse wins the Preakness and the Belmont, all Carmody had to say is she's a freak," Starbuck said bitterly. "God knows there are enough examples of those."

A "freak" is a horse that outperforms its pedigree. They do turn up now and then—Holy Bull being a notable example—but not as frequently as royally bred equines who can't run a lick.

"You think that Sandford and Carmody pulled a switch?" I asked.

"What I think is, they created a new horse by giving a well-bred animal a new name and printing a new set of papers to go with it."

The frustration that had been building in me finally rose to the surface. "I frankly don't give a damn about Carmody or his horse or the DEA. Why don't we cut this little chat short and move on to something really important? Like finding Lea."

"The agents are working on it from this end," Starbuck said. "Aren't you a little bit curious what I'm doing here in this glorified old folks' home?"

"What I'm curious about is why you aren't doing more to find your daughter."

Starbuck shook his head angrily. "For Christ's sake, I'm doing everything I can, and I feel like crap because I can't do more. And I don't need some stupid little twerp mouthing off and making things worse." He took a few deep breaths to bring himself down and went on in a calmer voice, "I was still doped up when the bastards called to tell me they'd taken her. They said she'd stay alive and unharmed as long as I kept quiet about anything that Vickie Salazaar might have told me."

"About For Cupid's Sake?" I ventured.

"They weren't specific, but I assume that's what this is all about."

"The voice tell you anything about who they are?"

"Listen for yourself," he said. "The guys have been taping the calls since I got here."

Starbuck wheeled himself across the tiles and into the suite. By the time I followed him inside, he had the young agent, La Nasa, rushing to set up the tape recorder.

Each call began with a male voice with no discernable accent— low-pitched, a little muffled, with no background noises to offer any clue as to the location of the caller. First he would warn Starbuck to say nothing to the police or any law enforcement agency about anything "your companion of last Saturday night may have told you. Miss Starbuck is with us, still in good health."

Then it would be Lea's turn.

On the original call she said, "Daddy, I'm fine. Just do as they say and everything'll be okay."

On the second call, later that night, she repeated the same phrase, adding, "I hope to see you soon."

The following day Lea said the same basic thing. "Everything is okay." Likewise that night.

"The key word being . . . ?" I asked Starbuck.

His eyes moved to the agent who was operating the machine. He didn't reply. Instead he said, "Keep listening."

On the next set, Lea began to sound a bit different, clipping off the words. Slightly breathless.

"What's the matter with her?" I asked.

"We'll discuss it in a minute."

More recorded calls. More of the same, except that Starbuck was by then asking what was wrong with Lea. The male voice assured him that his daughter was fine. "Just a bit unnerved by the situation."

Lea herself assured Starbuck that she was all right. "Don't worry, Dad." But her comments grew shorter and her speech more ragged. I could feel my heart pounding in my chest.

Finally, in that morning's conversation, she spoke haltingly. "Dad . . . please listen to them . . . Do as little . . . as possible . . . In fact . . . do nothing . . . I'm fine . . . Trust me."

Starbuck performed a wheelie and rolled back out onto the terrace. I followed.

"Haven't they tried tracing the goddamned—"

"Of course they've tried. But it's impossible with all the electronic garbage on the market today."

"She could be anywhere," I said hopelessly. "And she's not well, no matter what she says."

"She's still in the city, but she's not well," Starbuck said softly, glancing toward the suite and making sure that the DEA agent remained inside. He obviously didn't trust anybody. Except me. Perhaps.

"Your private code?" I asked.

" 'Okay' means 'L.A.' 'Daddy' means she's in good shape. 'Dad' is marginal. 'Father' would be really worrisome."

"So she's here and what? Wounded?" I asked.

He shook his head helplessly. "Not seriously hurt, but hurting."

"Now what?" I asked him.

"You heard the tapes. You tell me."

"We look for a doctor," I said.

Starbuck nodded. "Maybe you aren't dead between the ears after all."

" 'Do as little . . .' " I repeated. "As in Dr. Doolittle."

"Lea's usually more resourceful than that, but under the circumstances—"

"Do they," I asked, indicating the agents in the suite, "have any leads on a doctor?"

"I haven't brought the Doolittle business to their attention," Starbuck said. "I trust them only to a point. Richard Sandford was with the DEA for nearly ten years. I have no idea who his friends are within the agency. That's why I've been trying to get hold of you. You'll have to find our Dr. Doolittle."

"How do I do that?"

"I'll narrow the search a bit. As I tried to tell you a while ago, I'm in this so-called safe house because somebody was able to get past hospital security, enter my room, and switch the intravenous they'd prepared for me with a lethal dose of levorphanol."

"Bad medicine," I said.

"That, and the fact that Carmody's people—if that's who they are— knew exactly when I came out of my coma, suggest someone at the hospital is in on this. I leave it up to your own ingenuity to find the right one and get him to lead you to Lea."

"Him? It was a woman who called to lure Lea to the hospital."

"I wouldn't ignore the women on staff," Starbuck said. "But I doubt our doctor would be foolish enough to let you hear his or her voice. That would be an accomplice."

"I'll get on it," I said, and started for the door.

"Coley?"

I stopped and turned back toward him.

"Do you know anything about . . . Andrew Gunderman's murder?"

Starbuck only told me as much as he figured I needed to know, and there was no reason I had to be any more forthcoming with him. What was to be gained by my telling him the truth about Gunderman?

"Just what I read in the newspapers."

"I guess I can put him on my dance card, too," Starbuck said flatly. "Damn it, but guilt is a miserable thing to live with."

I nodded with some degree of sympathy. As far as Gunderman's death was concerned, I'd been feeling a sizable guilt of my own. After all, the detective had almost certainly been killed in my place.

23

SPINOZA & CO. was a small bookstore on Melrose Avenue. It had a dandy location, sandwiched between Dracula's Drive-In, a fast food place specializing in raw hamburgers and Bloody Milk Shakes, and Weirdmobile, a store selling, well, weird mobiles. I hadn't been in the bookstore since its opening several months before, partly because its stock didn't conform to my notion of bedside reading. Instead of my favorites—Dick Francis and Bill Murray—its shelves were filled with paperback editions of the works of Aquinas and Machiavelli and Descartes and Locke and, of course, Baruch Spinoza.

The rest of Melrose was pulsing and jiving in the warm night, but Spinoza & Co. was properly quiet and contemplative. The ringing of the vesper bell over the door brought a pretty little curly-haired woman in from the rear of the store. She took one look and rushed over to embrace me. It didn't seem to disturb the five or six very solemn types studying the philosophic tomes.

"Hi, Gigi," I said, returning the hug. "The big guy around?"

"John's in back," she said, taking a step away from me and looking me over with suspicious appraisal. "You're not here on business, are you?"

All I could give her was a helpless look.

She pressed her lips together as if she wanted to tell me to buy a book or get the hell out of the store, but of course she didn't. She just said, "Come on along," still friendly but a few degrees cooler in her manner.

As we walked to the rear of the store, I paused at a counter I didn't remember noticing at the store's opening. On it rested an assortment of tarot cards, dowsers, books of palmistry, gizmos to test ESP, crystals, and various oils and unguents. "What's all this?"

"My contribution to the store," Gigi said proudly. "John thinks it's nonsense, but I think his obsession with philosophy is pretty much bullshit, myself."

"Sounds like you two are made for each other."

"Actually, we are," she said with a smile, leading me past the black curtain at the rear of the shop.

The space we entered was a comfortable office, with two desks, matching computers, a refrigerator, more books, and a large mint-green sofa on which rested a huge man, reading a tiny paperback that was almost lost in one of his massive hands.

John "Walrus" Walnicki looked up and his relatively small face broke into a grin. With unexpected grace he leaped from the sofa and crossed the room to shake my hand.

"What're you reading these days, Walrus?" I asked.

"Hume. 'The science of man' and all that stuff." When I'd first met Walrus, he'd been assiduously studying the great religions, but his intellectual turf covered the whole range of philosophical thought. "Want a brewski?" he asked.

"No brewski. I need a little help."

Walrus's eyes went to Gigi's. She turned and started to walk away. "I need your help, too, Gigi," I said.

I understood that her feelings toward me were mixed. If it had not been for me, she and Walrus would never have met. But the reason they did meet was that she'd been the nurse assigned to the big man when he was brought into the hospital with a bullet in his side, a bullet he'd received in the line of duty working as my bodyguard.

It had taken very little convincing on her part for the convalescing Walrus to decide to give up his dangerous profession in favor of becoming a purveyor of the works of the great philosophers that he loved to read. The tidy nest eggs they both had amassed would get them through a few years on Melrose, even if sales remained thin. They had turned the second floor of the building into pleasant living quarters.

"Me?" she asked. "How can I help you?"

I explained that I needed information fast about the doctors at St. Thomas Hospital.

"But I never worked there," she pointed out.

"I know. I was hoping you might know somebody who does."

She hesitated. The lady really was cautious. All I was asking for was a name. She was probably visualizing a nursing school classmate caught in a gang cross fire because she had referred her to "Jonah" Killebrew.

"Look," I said, "Lea's been kidnapped. I have to find her. A contact at the hospital might help."

Gigi quit vacillating. "I know somebody," she said. She sat at her desk, punched a few keys at her computer, then another key, and picked up the phone.

She worked her way through St. Thomas's switchboard with remarkable speed, Walrus watching her with a mixture of pride and utter devotion.

In less than three minutes of phone chitchat, Gigi turned to me and asked, "Can you meet her in half an hour?"

24

WALRUS WENT with me, to a coffee shop across the street from the hospital. Jilly Margolis was precisely where she told Gigi she would be, at the booth farthest from the door, having a melted cheese sandwich before going home.

She was a thin, moderately attractive woman with frizzy blond hair and large breasts that were well displayed under her nurse's blouse. She was an outgoing, self-confident lady who almost immediately began flirting with Walrus. Not knowing her relationship with Gigi, I couldn't tell if the heavy vamp number was a gag or not, but it looked real enough. She was selling, but there was little chance of Walrus buying. He was more in danger of being struck by lightning on his green sofa.

When I finally managed to get Jilly's attention, I said, "I need to know the names of any doctors at the hospital who've turned weird lately."

"Honey, they're all weird. They're doctors."

"I mean, really weird. An easygoing guy who became uptight and angry overnight. A hard worker who suddenly isn't around much. That kind of weird."

She shook her head. "Nope. They're all business as usual."

"What about drugs?" I asked.

"Whoa, now," Jilly said. "Look, I told Gigi I'd talk to you guys, but . . ."

"What's the matter?" Walrus asked.

"I'm not getting involved in any of that, that's all."

"Any of what?"

"You know what. I heard about those goons."

"Goons?" I asked.

"Oh, those ETAs or whatever they call themselves."

"DEA?"

"Whatever. They scared the pee-pee out of a friend of mine. And never mind her name, okay?"

Walrus and I exchanged looks.

"I mean she just happened to be seeing Carl at the time and she got this call at the hospital. The DEAs, they . . . threatened her. It coulda been me or any one of a dozen of us. Carl isn't exactly a monk. He must've dated every woman in the whole building."

"Carl who?" Walrus asked.

"Dr. Carl Forrester."

"What did he have to do with DEA guys threatening your friend?" I asked.

"Well, according to my friend," Jilly said, filled with intrigue now, "they wanted to know if she'd ever done drugs with him. Did he provide the drugs? Did he ever talk about prescribing drugs for famous people? Like that."

"What'd she tell them?"

"She hung up on them. They called right back and said they'd have her in a jail cell in less than an hour unless she answered their questions."

"This was all done by phone?" I asked.

Jilly nodded. "And so she told 'em all she knew about Carl."

"And that is . . . ?"

She shrugged. "Whatever she knew. She didn't tell me." I couldn't decide if she was being cute or if she thought we were both simpletons.

"You say you've dated him," I pointed out. "Did he do any of those things?"

"Look, I was only having good times with the guy. I wasn't making his appointments for him. And no, we didn't do drugs. At least, nothing serious. No heroin or crack or anything like that."

"How long ago did the DEA agents talk to your friend?"

"Just a few nights ago. Maybe a week."

"Has anything else come of it?"

"Like what?"

"Is Carl in any kind of trouble at the hospital?"

"Not that I've noticed."

"What's his home address, Jilly?"

"I don't know." She took a bite of her sandwich.

"You said you dated him. Maybe did a little coke?"

"I didn't say that." She was closing down.

"You didn't do it at your place, did you?" I asked.

"Absolutely not."

"His place, then," Walrus said.

"Oooh. I don't want to get into any trouble, and I don't want to get him into any."

"We only want to talk with him."

"You're just saving us a little time, Jilly," Walrus said, turning on the charm. "There are other ways to find out. He'll never know you told us."

He broke down her resistance. She gave us an address in Westwood, and Walrus got on the phone to tell Gigi he'd be a little later than he thought.

Dr. Carl Forrester lived near the top of a posh high rise on Wilshire Boulevard. As we approached the door, I asked Walrus, "You've seen *Pulp Fiction?*"

"Seen it? I've lived it."

"Good. That's our model." I pressed the door buzzer.

Judging by his outfit, the great heeler was expecting somebody else entirely. His black silk shirt was open to the navel, tucked neatly into white silk slacks. No socks. No shoes. Probably no underwear. Judging from her fascination for Walrus and her indifference toward me, I had figured Jilly liked them big, but the doctor was a relatively short, thin fellow with a goofy brown comb-over and a tiny nose that almost got lost on his puffy, decadent face.

Walrus and I entered the apartment fast, pushing Forrester out of the way. Walrus shut the door and put the chain on the hook.

"What the hell is this?" Forrester demanded.

I strolled into a spacious living room with a wide modern bay window looking down on the sparkling lights along the Wilshire corridor. The air was filled with the smell of cooking spices.

"You alone, Doc?" I inquired, peeking into a kitchen going at full tilt. Something was in the oven. Pots were bubbling on the stove. There were recently chopped vegetables on a wooden sideboard beside a half-filled wineglass. Sensual Latin music emanated from a built-in speaker.

"I'm expecting a guest any minute. And I still have to do the salad dressing. What the hell is this?"

"We're a little disappointed on the Starbuck thing," I said casually, leading the doctor back into the living room, away from the butcher knives.

Dr. Forrester took a step back and stared at us. "Who are you guys? I've never seen you before."

I relaxed a little. Until that moment, I hadn't known for sure if Forrester was our man. Walrus nodded his head.

"The boss wants to talk to you," the big man said.

"You guys get out of here. Now." Forrester's face was flushed with anger.

"Look, Doc, we're just the messengers. You got a problem, you take it up with the boss."

"Tell him I'm busy tonight. I'll see him tomorrow."

"Then you know how to reach him?" I asked.

"Of cour—" Forrester froze, realizing we'd been conning him. He tried to make a dash for the kitchen. Walrus grabbed the back of his shirt and lifted him off the ground.

The one button holding the shirt popped off and Forrester fell to the carpeted floor. He tried to push off the rug, but I kicked his arm out from under him. Then I leaned close to the doctor, who was panting for breath.

"Where's Lea Starbuck?" I asked calmly.

"I . . . I don't know."

"Then where's your bathroom?"

Forrester's frightened eyes flickered in the direction of a hallway.

"Watch him," I said, and went off to locate the bath.

I smiled at the sight of a marble tub as well as a shower. I flipped the metal stopper closed and turned on the water in the tub. On my way back to the living room, I paused to stroll through the kitchen.

Back in the living room, I saw that Forrester was still on the floor. Walrus's foot, the size of a wooden duck, was planted on the small of his back.

"Wh-Who are you?" the doctor asked.

"There's a bathtub," I told Walrus, ignoring the question. "But the burners in the kitchen are already heated up, and there's a garbage disposal in there. So the kitchen gets my vote. It'll be faster."

"I don't know," Walrus said, wincing. "It gets so messy using the garbage disposal, puts me off my food."

Forrester looked back and forth from Walrus to me, wild-eyed.

"So let's use the stove top."

"I hate that burning flesh smell," Walrus said. "And it's too hard to muffle the screams. We'll do the tub."

"Have it your way," I said, sounding like a long-suffering spouse.

Walrus grabbed the doctor's ankles and hoisted him upside down, carrying him into the bath. The water was now about a foot deep in the tub.

"This'll take forever," I said.

Hanging upside down, staring at the water, Forrester said, "What do you want to know?"

"Who are you working for?"

"The DEA, for Christ's sake. Please put me down. I have high blood pressure."

Walrus looked at me, a bit perplexed.

"The DEA?" I asked. "The DEA told you to kidnap Lea Starbuck and then try to kill her father?"

"Kidnap? Kill? Look, that wasn't how it was put to me at all. This guy, Dover, said nobody would get hurt." His upside-down face looked at me pleadingly. "I'll be glad to talk to you in a civilized manner. Can't you get him to let me down?"

I nodded and Walrus lowered the doctor to the floor of the bathroom.

"Who's Dover?" I asked.

"The head man," the doctor said, the purple starting to leave his face. "There are a couple others, but Dover is calling the shots."

"Description."

"Not a bad-looking guy, I guess," Forrester said, staring at the water rising in the tub. "Maybe a little dusky."

"An African American?"

"No. Chicano. I don't know. Maybe not."

"Anything else about him? Beard? Mustache?"

"Uh, no. The guy's neat. Slicked-back hair in a tight ponytail. Armani suits. Anyway, somehow he knows I've been assisting Dr. Fordyce with Starbuck. So he pushed me to do some things."

My jaws began to hurt and I realized I'd been clamping them too tightly. The water was nearly two feet deep. I closed off the faucets. "How'd he push you?" I asked.

"He said he'd stop me from practicing medicine if I didn't cooperate with them. Maybe even put me in jail."

It wasn't the worst idea I'd ever heard. "So they blackmailed you into doing what? Helping 'em kidnap Lea?"

"No, no, no. I wasn't involved in that. I didn't find out about it until later."

"What were you involved in?"

"All I was supposed to do," Forrester said, "was make sure the duty nurse on Raymond Starbuck's floor was away from her station for ten minutes. No big deal. She's a friend."

"Friend enough to desert her station?"

Forrester nodded. "Well, we, uh, find an empty room and do a little blow together every now and then. To clear the head."

"You're a real poster boy for the AMA, aren't you?" I said. "Why'd you think they wanted the nurse away from her station? So they could get Starbuck's autograph?"

"No. I . . . It wasn't like Starbuck was in the room. He'd been wheeled off for X rays and his police guard had gone with him. Dover told me that Starbuck was refusing to assist the DEA, and he wanted to leave something in the room that would convince him to change his mind."

"Like what? A horse's head in the bed?"

"I don't know what. It never occurred to me he was going to switch the intravenous solution."

"And when he did, weren't you a little skeptical about him being with the DEA?"

"I . . . I don't know. Everything I've heard about him, like that '60 Minutes' story, makes you think they play pretty fast and loose."

"Including murder?"

"But if they're not DEA, then who . . . ?"

I shrugged. "We'll know when you tell us where they are."

"I can't . . ."

I looked at Walrus, who lifted the doctor by his ankles and dunked him head first into the tub.

Forrester flailed and tried to get his head clear of the water, but Walrus wouldn't let him. Finally, the big man lifted him free.

Sputtering, Forrester gave us an address in the Hollywood Hills.

"Is that where they're keeping Lea Starbuck?"

He nodded.

"You've seen her there?"

He hesitated, then nodded again.

"When?" I asked him, feeling my heart begin to pound again.

"Three evenings ago. I . . ."

"You what?"

"Nothing."

"How was she?"

"In good spirits. Fine," he said.

"Tell me what's wrong with her or, so help me, I'll drown you myself."

"I helped her. She'll tell you. That's why I went there. To help her."

"Helped her how?"

"She was—" Forrester, sensing he might be getting into deeper waters than the bathtub, let the sentence trail off. "—hurt a little."

I grabbed the doctor by his wet hair and yanked back. "Hurt how?"

"She broke her leg. I don't know how it happened. I swear. All I know is Dover called me and I went out there and set the leg for her that evening. I had to do it by portable lights. There's no electricity. But I did a damn good job."

"How bad off is she?" I asked.

"It was a simple break, but it makes it a little tough for her to, ah, take care of herself, if you know what I mean." He stared at my face and seemed alarmed by what he saw there. "Please. She was okay when I left."

I glared at him as if I were trying to make up my mind whether to kill him or not.

"If this weasel is telling the truth," Walrus said, "it's a good sign. They wouldn't bother setting her leg if they were gonna . . . you know."

I nodded. It made sense.

"What about the doc, here?" Walrus said. "How long?"

"About an hour."

Forrester looked at us, puzzled. Then, realizing what was happening, he lifted a hand to his head. But he was too late to ward off the leather sap Walrus was bringing down.

The doctor slipped to the floor. "I'll put him in his bed," Walrus said. "That way, when he wakes up he won't feel quite so bad as on a cold floor."

"Frankly, I'd just as soon he wake up with his head in the toilet," I said.

As we were exiting the building's elevator, a pretty young woman was approaching, carrying a bottle of wine wrapped with a ribbon. "Going to Dr. Forrester's apartment?" I asked.

"As a matter of fact, I am."

"Then you must be . . . ?"

"Dorothy."

"Dorothy, right," I said. "I'm sorry, Dorothy, but the doctor is out."

"Out?"

"Called away on an emergency. Somebody in Bel Air needed Percodan, pronto. Try him again in about an hour."

"An hour? Percodan?"

"Percodan, B-12, heroin, crack cocaine, crank. Something like that." I gave her a wink. "It all comes out of the good doctor's gladstone, doesn't it?"

She backed away from me as if I'd just started to drool on her pumps. Then she turned and began walking quickly to her car.

"We're not exactly making the doctor's night, are we?" Walrus asked.

"I hope not," I said.

25

THE ADDRESS Forrester had given us proved to be an earthquake-cracked, cantilevered two-story Spanish home near the top of Topanga Canyon. It looked abandoned. It was isolated from its nearest neighbors by a forest of bramble and bush on one side and a muddy wash caused by floods on the other. Even with the flickering diamond lights of Hollywood below, the place had a cheerless, dangerous atmosphere.

The moonlight was bright enough for us to see that vines wound around and through broken mullioned windows. A cherub stood on tiptoe in a parched fountain just beyond the broken gate, playing host to scattered flyers and brochures. Hanging on a wobbly four-foot-high iron fence was a For Sale sign.

Walrus took one look at the place and suggested we call in some sort of law enforcement.

I frowned at him. "Becoming a small businessman has made a profound change in you," I said.

"By certain standards of measure, I was always a solid citizen," he protested. "And you do have friends in the police—"

I shook my head. "No police. Not until we're sure Lea is safe."

He sighed, stepped over the fence, and then reached back and lifted me over. We walked silently to the front of the house. Walrus put his ear to the door, listening, then turned to me and shrugged. He removed a small flashlight from his pocket and handed it to me. Then he took a gun from under his shirt and daintily tried the door handle. It turned and the door opened with a creak.

Walrus entered and I followed him through the door into the darkened house, shining the flash ahead of us.

The main floor of the house consisted primarily of a large unfurnished room with floor-to-ceiling windows that looked down into the canyon where the red taillights of cars were like little ladybugs crawling up a thin vine.

We stepped into the kitchen, past a small area that apparently served as a breakfast nook. Ants, beetles, and other night crawlers swarmed over pizza rinds and grease-soaked hamburger cartons tossed casually on the floor, along with empty beer cans and plastic soda bottles. It didn't take long to establish there was nobody on the ground floor, so we started up the stairs.

There were four rooms upstairs. Three of them were unlocked and obviously empty of anything but accumulated dust and cobwebs. The fourth didn't open when I turned the knob. I suggested Walrus apply a heavy shoulder to the door, and he broke through it as easily as I open a cereal box. That's where we found Lea.

When my flashlight caught her, I was half elated and half horrified. She was lying on a pallet of foam rubber, hand raised to keep the light from her eyes. Her leg, in a plaster cast, rested on several filthy, uncased pillows. She'd been living in squalor. They had provided her with a bedpan, but she hadn't bathed in days.

"I can do it," she said, slurring a bit. "I can make the call."

"No more calls, honey," I said, and turned off the flash.

"Coley, oh God."

"Here's one of those battery lamps," Walrus said.

"Don't turn it on," she pleaded.

"We've got to get you out of here," I said.

Walrus moved into the hall before turning on the lamp. Only a little light came through the doorway, but it was enough. The helpless, totally demoralized creature looking back at me wasn't the Lea I knew. She shrank back as I moved toward her. I realized she didn't want me or anybody to see her in that condition.

Whether it was a good idea or not, I couldn't stop myself from bending down and embracing her. At first I thought she was going to recoil from my touch, but slowly she accepted my arms.

And she began to cry.

"We have to get her to a hospital immediately," I told Walrus.

"No," she protested in a painful croak. "I want . . . to see my father."

Walrus added his own suggestion. "The kidnappers will be coming back one of these hours. We'd better make up our minds."

"Four of them," Lea said. "No. Five."

"Four would be enough," Walrus said.

"Take me to Daddy," Lea whispered in my ear.

"Okay," I said soothingly. "Okay. Daddy it is."

She allowed Walrus to carry her to the car.

It crossed my mind that either he or I should stay behind to keep a watch on the house. But as much as I wanted to see the people who'd done this to Lea rot in hell, it was more important that we take care of her first.

26

WHEN WALRUS carried Lea into the Brompton penthouse, Starbuck stared at his daughter's shattered appearance and his eyes filled with tears. He suddenly turned away from her to glare at me. "Get a bloody doctor—"

"All taken care of," I assured him. "On the way, courtesy of your caretakers."

Walrus carried Lea into a bedroom and placed her gently on the bed. She reached out a hand to me, while Starbuck wheeled beside her. Walrus, obviously uncomfortable, left the room.

"Coley," Starbuck said, "would you give me a few minutes with my daughter?"

I looked at Lea, who somehow managed a wan smile. She squeezed my hand. "I knew you'd find me," she said, and took my hand and kissed it. "I knew it would be you."

"Anytime," I said softly, and left the room.

Walrus and I were telling the DEA agents about the house in the hills when La Nasa arrived with Lea's doctor. She was dressed and carried her instrument bag, but she was still wearing her house slippers. Without a word to us, she strode into Lea's room and closed the door.

Marquez dispatched La Nasa, obviously the junior agent in the group, to the kidnap house. His instructions were to do nothing except report back if the kidnappers returned.

Marquez wasn't amused by Forrester's claim that his blackmailers were DEA agents. "The name Dover doesn't ring any bells, and these guys sure as hell aren't DEA."

"You know your organization better than I do," I said. "Maybe they're former agents . . ."

"Or maybe this asshole doctor made that part of it up."

"I don't think so," Walrus said. "The guy was scared. And he wasn't very bright to begin with. Maybe they weren't DEA, but he *thought* they were."

"Walrus has a good instinct for that kind of thing," I said.

Marquez stared at me appraisingly. "If you believe that, why the fuck do you still trust us?"

"I trust you and whoever else in your agency knows where Starbuck is. Because if you were untrustworthy, he'd be dead."

"Unless we were even more devious than you think," Marquez said nastily.

"That's too complicated for a simple country boy like myself."

"Simple, maybe. Lucky, definitely. We've been working on this kidnapping for five days, and you come in here and find the lady in about an hour and a half." He grabbed the phone, dialed a number, waited a few beats, then repeated the name Dr. Carl Forrester twice into the receiver, spelling it once. He followed that with Forrester's address and the request that the subject be picked up and detained for questioning.

He replaced the receiver and, without another word, left the suite.

"Guy's got a little public relations problem," Walrus said. "He's easy to hate."

"Just got his nose out of joint because we did his job for him."

I stared at the closed door to Lea's bedroom.

"We kinda missed dinner, Coley," Walrus said. "Suppose they have room service in this place?"

"Starbuck brings his own room service," I told him.

27

WALRUS AND I were sampling some of Choo-Choo's sweet and sour soup in the kitchen when the great man came wheeling through.

"She's sleeping," he said. "The doctor wants to get an X ray of her leg first thing tomorrow. But she thinks it was set well enough. It isn't the break that's got Lea in this condition. It's the goddamned drugs those idiots were feeding her, ostensibly to help with the pain." He wheeled away from us.

I stood to follow him. Walrus started to get up, too, but gave me a grateful smile when I suggested he relax and continue his late dinner.

Starbuck was in the center of the vacant living room. "Where are Marquez and the others?"

"One of them's just outside the door," I said. "The others are running errands."

"Don't you have any?" he asked me pointedly.

"I was hoping to see Lea."

"The doc said she'll be out until morning."

"Then what?" I asked him. "How long do you figure on keeping holed up here?"

"Until we're both on our feet. Then I'm going to James Carmody's farm in Lexington to give him a real lesson in intimidation. And I suspect Lea may want to put in her ten cents."

"You're that positive Carmody's the one behind all this?"

"Any other suggestions? I keep an open mind."

The hell he did. "What does Lea say?"

"There were five men. They grabbed her in the hospital parking lot. Used a taser. Some spoke Spanish. She'd recognize at least three of them, especially the one called Dover. A pretty boy with a ponytail."

"They let her see their faces?"

Starbuck nodded gravely. "It was good timing on your part. She'd be of use to them only as long as she could ensure my silence."

"Which brings us to the big question: What do they want you to be silent about?"

"I wish I knew. Evidently something that Vickie kept to herself, possibly due to some former misguided friendship with Sandford."

I mulled that over. "Well, the up side of it all is that, with Lea safe, when Carmody or whoever's secret still doesn't surface, they'll probably realize you're no longer a threat."

Starbuck glared at me. "They kill two of my associates, kidnap my daughter, and try to kill me, and you say I'm no threat? Hell, man, as far as they're concerned, I'm the bloody wrath of God."

"I mean, they'll figure their secret is safe, that Vickie didn't pass it on to you."

"Eventually, they may arrive at that conclusion," he said. "But for the while, I'm afraid Lea and I are stuck with our junior G-men protectors. Especially since she can identify her kidnappers."

I stared at him, wondering if he really thought they were in danger, or if this was yet another of his schemes to keep Lea and me apart.

"What I don't understand," I said, "is if Carmody is holding the reins on all this murder and mayhem, he surely didn't seem terribly interested in me."

"Why would he be?" Starbuck asked.

"If he's that focused on you and Lea, he must certainly be aware of my connection to the family."

"Perhaps he doesn't feel you're significant."

"You mean he realizes that kidnapping me wouldn't stop you from putting on your wrath-of-God suit?"

Starbuck smiled. "What a thought. A sociopath like Carmody setting his sights on you. It makes my mouth water."

"Nice talk to your future son-in-law."

Starbuck's eyes narrowed. "If you're really worried, I imagine the boys could let you bunk on the sofa, all safe and secure, until Lea and I are strong enough to take care of Carmody ourselves."

Machiavelli couldn't have expressed it better. "I appreciate the thought," I told him. "But I'll just keep risking fate on the outside."

"Good man," he said dismissively, turning his chair to go.

"I'm puzzled by something," I said.

He turned back, eyebrows raised.

"You and Vickie Salazaar were in her car, driving, and what happened exactly? How did she die?"

The self-amused expression left his face. "I'm not completely sure. We were driving, as you say. She was acting a little odd. Sort of angry, on edge. I was asking her if somebody said or did something to offend her at the party. I heard her sharp intake of breath and turned to see her gasping. Her body jerked convulsively and fell forward on the steering wheel. I tried to grab the wheel, but I was a little late."

"The coroner initially said she died from a heart attack."

"He still does, according to Marquez," Starbuck said, his mouth twisted as if he were tasting something sour. "But it's been obvious to me all along that she was murdered. With everything that's happened since, it's an inescapable fact."

"But how? The coroner evidently found no signs of foul play. It was just the two of you in her car."

"Hell, I don't know how they killed her. But Marquez's people aren't satisfied with the coroner's report, either. They're looking into it."

"Maybe Lieutenant Burns would help out if you were to talk to him about the attempt on your life and Lea's kidnapping."

He lifted a lip in disgust. "That guy couldn't find his own big flat foot without patting down his leg. Besides, Marquez wants to keep the police from messing things up for as long as possible."

Marquez this, Marquez that. As if picking up my thought, Starbuck said, "Ordinarily, I wouldn't give a damn what some scruffy bureaucrat wanted, but I happen to agree with him about the police."

"What do you think changed Vickie's mood at the party?" I asked. "Something Dewey Lane said?"

"I doubt it."

"What *were* you and Dewey chatting about, by the way?"

"Business," he said.

"Not about me?"

Starbuck's eyes opened wide in surprise. "Why the hell would we be talking about you?"

I was stuck. I couldn't tell Starbuck about the entry in Gunderman's book without telling what I knew about the private detective's death. "No reason, I guess."

"Lane and I met because of something a little more pressing," Starbuck said.

"Like what?"

"Lane called earlier that day to say he wanted to meet with me to discuss a problem. I suggested the party. What he told us was that he'd been offered twenty-five grand to make sure that Hotfoot did not win the Derby."

"Offered by whom?"

"To use his own words, 'some broad.' She phoned his home. At that point Carmody's filly was still considered a rank outsider. Dewey figured the threat had come from that rock singer, whatsisname."

"Halcyon."

"Whatever."

"What did the Lundens say about the threat?" I asked.

"Dewey didn't tell them. The mysterious woman warned that if he told anybody, the only thing he'd be riding would be a coffin."

"Gaudy talk," I said. "But he did tell *you*. Why you?"

Starbuck reacted defensively. "I've got a reputation for helping racing people in trouble."

Naturally, he was holding something back. I said, "And now, nobody's seen Dewey in days."

"I know," Starbuck said, frowning, possibly toting up a body count in his head. "I don't suppose you'd care to . . . check with his wife Milly, see if she's heard from him?"

"That's a phone over there," I pointed out. "Call her yourself."

"Damnit, the guy may be dead. And if he is, I sure as hell don't want to hear about it from his wife."

First fatherly affection, now increasing guilt pangs. Starbuck's injuries seemed to have left him a changed man. I was curious enough to take pity on him. "I'll go talk to her."

Starbuck's attitude did a total 180. "Be sure to pump her for anything she might know about Carmody," he said eagerly, giving me a wink.

"Will do," I said. I hadn't felt so manipulated since my last visit to the chiropractor.

28

THE LANES lived on a quiet, tree-lined street in Glendale. Their small wooden house was dark, which was not surprising at a little after ten-thirty at night. But their garage door was wide-open and carless. Walrus pointed out three mornings' worth of print journalism resting against the front door.

"Ran off in a hurry," he observed. "Forgot to notify the newspaper. Left the garage door open for people to help themselves to the garden tools."

Given the Lanes' level of security consciousness, I wasn't surprised to find an unlocked window at the rear of the house. Mumbling something about breaking and entering, Walrus boosted me through the window.

"Give me your flashlight," I told him.

Reluctantly, he obeyed. The flash helped me wend my way through living and dining rooms so pristine they looked unused. In the kitchen a plate of putrid stew rested beside a glass containing a pale brown liquid that was probably tea and melted ice. I moved on past a telephone sharing a waist-high shelf with a pencil.

In the bedroom a closet door hung open, showing a gap in the hanging clothes. Two drawers appeared to be spilling out of a chest, their wooden bottoms showing in areas where blouses and undergarments had been removed.

It looked like Dewey's wife had left the place in haste three days before. She'd probably taken off around the dinner hour, unless she ate heavy meals at lunch. She'd packed only a few clothes, which meant either that she intended to return fairly soon or that she had to get out of there fast. In the case of the latter, she might never return.

I was on my way out when I noticed a paperback book lying open on the bed, front and back covers visible. It was a romance novel, its bright cover showing a muscled man in tights and a busty woman in a low-cut ball gown locked in passionate embrace in a moonlit grove. She hadn't taken her book with her, one more indication of a hasty getaway.

I picked up the broken-spined book and turned it over to the page she had been reading. In the top margin an 800 phone number had been scrawled in pencil.

So Dewey's wife is eating dinner alone, reading her book. The phone rings. Her caller (Dewey?) tells her something that compels her to rush to the bedroom, throw some clothes into a suitcase or two, run to the garage and drive away.

I looked at the book again. While Mrs. Lane—what did Starbuck call her? Milly—while Milly Lane is talking on the phone, the caller gives her a number. But if it was Dewey, why an 800 number?

I looked at the phone number again and repeated it to myself a few times until I had it memorized. Then I rubbed the surface of the book with a handkerchief and put it back on the bed. I returned to the open window.

Walrus was waiting nervously. He lifted me up and deposited me on the ground. "Can we go now?" he asked hopefully.

"Sure."

"Was this B and E really necessary?" Walrus asked as we drove away.

"Let's see."

I pulled into the nearest gas station, jogged to the pay phone and dialed the 800 number. A male voice answered, repeating the number but saying nothing else.

"Hello," I said.

"Who's this speaking?" the voice on the other end demanded.

My mind whirred. "Dewey Lane," I blurted.

The silence seemed like an eternity, but was probably no longer than twenty seconds or so. Then the line was disconnected. Guess I hadn't picked the right magic words.

It was eleven-fifteen when I dropped Walrus at Spinoza & Co. One dim light showed in an upstairs window.

"Gigi's still awake," Walrus said. "Freud thought the big question was 'What does a woman want?' I'm beginning to believe it's, 'What will a woman do when she doesn't get what she wants?' "

"Let me know if you find the answer," I told him.

29

IT WAS a good thing Starbuck's suite at the Brompton was so big, with all the people in residence. He himself was asleep in one room, Lea in another. La Nasa was sacked out on a sofa. Choo-Choo had his own room elsewhere in the hotel. I found Marquez in the kitchen, seated at a table, nibbling a bagel. Maybe he was planning on sleeping in the corner, near the fridge.

"They picked up the sawbones, Forrester," he said.

"Get anything out of him?"

"Oh, yeah. A lot."

"Do I have to ask? Okay, what did you get out of him?"

"Intestines, blood, guts," Marquez replied. "Like I said, he got picked up. Off the sidewalk alongside his apartment building. It looked like he jumped." Marquez took another bite of bagel. He might have been giving me an update on the weather.

"When?"

"Maybe five minutes before my guys got there. They spotted the crowd and stuck around and played lookie-loo while the cops did their thing."

"Forrester didn't strike me as the suicidal type," I said.

Marquez shrugged. "Dead is dead. He's no use to us, so how he got to the pavement isn't too important." He smiled. "But I did check the time, just to make sure you and your big buddy didn't do the pushing. You were still here with Starbuck when it went down. When *he* went down."

"What about the house in the hills?" I asked him.

"If the kidnappers tossed the doc out of the window, I doubt they'll be returning to the vacant house. The place had been used to sell narcotics, by the way."

"How do you know?"

"There was paraphernalia in the basement. We pulled some prints and they're trying to match 'em as we speak. Maybe we'll get lucky."

"Assuming they killed Forrester, why?" I asked.

"Maybe you and the giant were spotted leaving the house with Lea Starbuck," Marquez said. "They would have figured the doc sold 'em out. Or maybe he called 'em to warn 'em a little too late and that riled 'em. Whatever. He could identify 'em."

"Well, here's something a little odd." I gave him the phone number I'd found at the Lane home and asked him if he could trace it down.

With a bored shrug he crossed the room to a telephone on the wall. He punched a few buttons, waited less than a minute, and read the phone number once into the speaker.

He yawned.

I opened the fridge and found a bottle of acidophilus milk. I got a glass from the cabinet and half filled it. It tasted sweeter than regular homogenized.

Marquez replaced the receiver and said, "Number doesn't exist."

"Somebody answered when I dialed it less than an hour ago."

"Nobody's answering now. Listen." He dialed, then held out the receiver. An annoying recording was suggesting that the caller consult his or her phone book because the number dialed was not in service.

"It got disconnected in a hurry. There must be some record of it."

"There's no listing for it anywhere. Not even in FBI files."

"I don't care if there's no listing for it. If you call it and somebody answers, it exists."

"Look, man, I checked—"

I raised a conciliatory hand. There was no point in getting heated about it. "Okay, okay, the question has to be, what kind of numbers wouldn't be on your computer?"

"Hardly any."

"But some, right? What are they?"

"Some government numbers. The FBI doesn't list all its own numbers. Could be CIA."

"How about DEA?"

"Sure," Marquez said. "We've got numbers that are D.B."

"What's D.B.?"

"Deep-buried. But they're in service. This one ain't."

"It was in service earlier tonight," I said, getting weary of this conversational treadmill.

Marquez was weary, too. He got to his feet with a stretch and a yawn. "Good night, Killebrew. If I don't get my five hour's sleep, it makes me real cranky."

"You sleeping on the floor?" I asked.

"Naw. I'm throwing La Nasa on the floor. Rank has its privileges."

Before I departed the suite, I paused at Lea's closed door. I opened it quietly. Moonlight fell across the bed where she slept, her propped leg making an odd tent of the thin coverlet.

I walked over to her bedside. She seemed to be barely breathing, but there was a faint rise and fall of the cover over her chest. It must mean she was having an untroubled sleep, and the thought of that would help me do the same. So would the memory of her usually suntanned face pale in the moonlight and breathtakingly beautiful.

Suddenly she smiled. Although her eyes were still closed, I couldn't help returning the smile. Was I in her dreams? I knew she'd be in mine. I backed from the room as quietly as I'd entered.

30

DESPITE ALL the good thoughts, I had a lousy night's sleep. The bed was too big for me. Or maybe I was not destined to sleep well alone, ever again. I tossed and turned and just when it seemed I'd dozed off, the doorbell rang. Gonged.

The bedside clock read six-thirty A.M. Too early for any ordinary visitor. I eased out of bed and moved to a window. By pressing my face against the windowpane, I could barely see someone standing on the front porch. The someone backed up suddenly, revealing himself as Lt. Olaf Burns of the LAPD.

I got away from the window just in time to prevent his seeing me. Sooner or later I'd have to deal with him, but not just yet.

Burns rang three more times before he gave up. I waited until he had retreated down the path before I even made the noise required to walk to the bathroom.

After a shower and a shave, I called Starbuck's suite. Four rings. Five. I started to get impatient. With all the people in residence there, you'd think one of them could pick up the phone promptly. After ten rings I began to realize no one was going to answer, but I gave it another five anyway. Nothing.

I jumped in the Cherokee and drove to the Brompton as fast as the morning rush-hour traffic would let me. A little faster, truthfully. I did a bit of the shoulder driving and lane darting that usually makes me curse other drivers.

When I got to the hotel, things weren't quite the same. The elevator with its gleaming grillwork arrived empty. There was no pale-uniformed operator to ask for my floor, just the ordinary self-service. I pressed the penthouse button myself with a growing feeling of foreboding.

The door to Suite 2400 was ajar, increasing my alarm. What kind of a scene of carnage was I going to walk in on? I imagined murdered agents draped over furniture soaked in blood. And in the bedrooms . . .

I rushed in, startling two Asian cleaning ladies dressed in gray-and-white-striped uniforms and white aprons. The rest of the suite was empty. Vacant. No DEA agents. No Choo-Choo. No Starbuck. No Lea.

One of the ladies said, "No one here."

"Where'd they go?"

She gave me a puzzled look and rattled off some unfamiliar patois to her associate.

They followed me from room to room as I made a quick search. Nothing. I was looking at the spotless garbage pail when the talkative housekeeper said, "All clean."

"Where's the garbage? Where's what you cleaned up?"

"No clean up," she said. "All clean before we get here. All clean. All gone."

The hotel lobby was on the first floor, one flight up from the street. I approached the desk clerk, a woman in her forties, brisk and efficient.

"What happened to the party in Suite 2400," I asked, trying but failing to sound casual.

She gave me a puzzled look. "Suite 2400 has been vacant for several weeks."

"And the elevator operator?"

"The what?"

"When I was here yesterday, there was an elevator operator," I said, hearing a slight shake in my voice.

"Sir, our elevator has been self-service for as long as I've worked here. Ten years. Perhaps you're thinking of some other hotel. The Biltmore."

"Where's a public telephone?" I demanded.

She directed me using the wary, patient tones reserved for mental patients. But halfway to the bank of phones I made a sharp right face and went back to the parking garage. At the moment, I didn't trust the dignified old Hotel Brompton enough even to make a phone call from its lobby.

I drove about a mile before I pulled over and stopped at a phone booth. I flipped through the government agency pages in the front of the book and found the number I wanted. With impatient fingers I attacked the buttons.

"This is the Drug Enforcement Administration," a no-nonsense female voice informed me.

"I'd like to speak to Agent Marquez."

"What was that name again?"

"Marquez."

"Would that be spelled M-A-R-Q-U-E-Z?"

"I imagine so."

"I'm sorry. We show no one by that name in this office."

It should have surprised me, but I'd felt it coming.

"How about Dougherty or La Nasa?" I asked, and dutifully spelled them, but by now my voice had the toneless drone of a guy who knew he was wasting his time.

"No La Nasa. Have you a first name for the Dougherty?"

"Afraid not."

"Just a minute."

The phone was silent for a few beats before a male voice said, "This is Agent Dougherty. How can I help you?"

The voice was wrong. It was more seasoned, huskier than the young guy who'd been with Marquez. I replaced the receiver.

31

MY HEAD spinning, I drove the Cherokee to The Horse's Neck, and tried to go through the motions of business as usual. The effort failed. My main chef, Antony, was listing a series of kitchen problems real and imaginary when I snapped.

"How long have you been working here?" I demanded.

"Five and one-half years. Since you dismissed that . . . that sous-chef you'd been using."

"Then by now you ought to be able to handle these goddamn petty problems yourself without bothering me with them."

The whipped-dog look on Antony's face told me I'd overreacted. I had my mouth open to apologize, but the damage was done.

Antony drew himself up to his full height and said, "So sorry to be a *problem.*" Then he turned on his heel and retreated to another section of the kitchen.

With a sigh, I fixed myself a cup of coffee and took it and the morning paper into my office before I could alienate any more staff. I sat there turning pages until I found the small two-inch article about the apparent suicide of the hapless Dr. Carl Forrester. I'd rarely come across a more worthless human being, but I still didn't like the idea that I'd probably precipitated his death. First Gunderson and now Forrester. I was a walking disaster area. Stop me before I kill more.

I gave my head a good shake. Enough of that crap. It was time to take positive action. Time to start thinking like a guy who had a chance of winning the race.

Okay, Coley, how do we ride this one? Let's look at Marquez and his cronies. Fake or the real stuff? If they had the clout to take over the penthouse, install their own elevator operator, and seal the lips of the hotel staff as they left, they surely must have some kind of official status. But maybe I was underestimating the power of liberally applied palm grease. I could go back to the Brompton and try rattling a few cages, but I doubted the results would be worth it.

If the bunch were not DEA, they still seemed to be trying to keep Starbuck and Lea from harm. Who could they be, and what were they after? Were they just keeping their captives alive while they got whatever information they needed from them? And then what?

My imagination got too vivid again. I had to keep this on an analytical level, not let my emotional involvement take over. I began to make little notes on a pad of the facts I knew and the probabilities they suggested. I suppose it was therapeutic, in a way, but I wasn't coming up with anything very useful. I was still at it when Jack Hayward applied a knuckle to the open door with a flourish.

"Excuse me, squire, but the time arrives for us to lower the drawbridge for the ravening hoards. And one of our doughty crew is exhibiting a petulance that threatens our very existence."

"Antony?" I ventured.

"I asked him for the luncheon special and he replied, 'Steak tartare.' Now, we just might be able to convince some of our clientele to sample a hamburger deluxe, a Salisbury steak perhaps. But raw and bloody—"

"I'll talk to him," I said wearily.

Jack withdrew a pink slip of paper from his coat pocket and placed it on my desk. "Our moody master of the culinary arts asked me to bring this to you."

The note, in Antony's oddly delicate handwriting read, "Miss Lea called. Says she's all right."

I leaped out of my chair. "When did she call?" I may have screamed it.

"I am merely the messenger," Jack said, taken aback. "It was our sullen chef—"

I didn't wait for Jack to complete the sentence. In the kitchen, I found Antony studying a mound of ground beef. "When did Lea call?"

Antony didn't answer. He merely raised one eyebrow.

"Look, Antony, this is not the morning for temperament. Lea's in trouble and I want to know exactly when she called and exactly what she said."

Antony's face showed sudden concern. "Your woman is in jeopardy? Ah, that explains it. I accept your apology. She phoned shortly after I arrived. Nine-thirty or thereabouts. She said to tell you not to worry, that she and her father were fine."

"How did she sound?"

"Sound? Like she always sounds. Feminine. Beautiful. Desirable."
Antony is almost as enamored of Lea as I am.

"And those were her exact words?"

"Let me see. Oh, yes, I forgot. She said they'd moved to another location and she would call you later. It made very little sense to me, but
I suppose to you . . ."

I felt my body and soul relax a bit for the first time since I walked
into that empty hotel suite. I started back to my office, then returned
to the chopping block, pausing by the mound of red meat. "What do
you plan on doing with that ground beef?"

"Ground sirloin."

"Same question."

The chef approached the meat, studying it like a sculptor studies a
chunk of quarry-fresh rock. "Perhaps I will prepare Antony's pesto
meat loaf."

"You're cooking it, then?"

"But of course. What else would I do? I am familiar with the ple-
beian palates of our diners."

Shaking my head, but with spirits raised by Lea's call, I left the
kitchen and ran straight into a downer: Lt. Olaf Burns, in full fury.

"All right, Killebrew. Why the hell have you been dodging me?"

"What do you mean, dodging you?" I said innocently. "You come
to my place of business, and here I am."

"Why didn't you return any of my calls?"

"I've been away."

"With Lea Starbuck?"

"No."

"Where is she?"

"I honestly don't know where she is," I said.

"C'mon. You're engaged to her, you live with her, and you don't
know where she is?"

"We both lead very busy lives, Lieutenant. These are the nineties.
Even married couples aren't joined at the hip."

"So that's your story," Burns said. His Letterman grin was turned
upside down. I was a big disappointment to him.

It occurred to me that there was nothing to lose by throwing him
a bone. Especially if it might just shake the complacency of that
forked-tongue clerk at the Brompton.

"Look," I said, "I honestly don't know where Lea or her father are
at this moment, but I do know where they were until this morning."

"You want me to ask where," he said. "Okay. Where?"

I hesitated only long enough to make my answer seem less voluntary and therefore more credible. "The Brompton Hotel in downtown L.A.," I said finally.

"What were they doing there?"

"I asked them the same question and got no answer. Then, when I found out they'd moved, I couldn't get the clerk to tell me. In fact, she insisted they'd never been there."

Burns stared at me. "I hope you're not screwin' with me, Killebrew," he said wearily. "I get the feeling everybody I talk to is screwing with me on this one."

"Why are you still on this, Lieutenant? Isn't Vickie Salazaar's death still listed as accidental?"

"Sort of. But she's still a mystery woman. And the only guy who knows anything about her barely escaped another 'accident' while he's in the hospital. And now he and his daughter seem to be, ah, unavailable for questioning. So I can't exactly close the book on this thing, now can I?"

"You've got a tough job," I said sympathetically.

He looked at his watch. "Hope I haven't been keepin' you from your lunch," he said.

"Our special's meat loaf," I said. "Care to join me?"

"That's damn decent of you," he said. "Be some good body fuel for that trip downtown to the Brompton."

I phoned the kitchen and put in our order.

"My mother used to make meat loaf," Burns said.

"This is not your mother's meat loaf."

"I sure as heck hope not."

Since it was the luncheon special, our orders couldn't have come faster if we'd gone to a McDonald's. Accompanying the main meal was a slice of apple pie à la mode. Though food had been the farthest thing from my mind, we both ate like we'd spent the morning climbing a mountain.

The food seemed to have a mellowing effect on the detective. He relaxed and our conversation drifted off to other things: the weather, earthquakes, riots—the stuff of L.A. life. And, of course, racing.

"Man, wasn't that Derby something?" Burns said.

"It was a good one."

"You said you were away. I don't suppose you were there. In Louisville, I mean."

"As a matter of fact, I was," I replied, sensing a hint of trouble.

"While you were there, you didn't happen to bump into a black guy named Andrew Gunderman?"

I did my best to look blank. "No."

"But you know Gunderman?"

I frowned, like a guy searching his memory. "Gunderman? I don't think so."

"A sometime employee of Raymond Starbuck's," Burns said, finishing his pie. "Does that help?"

"I haven't met everybody who works for Starbuck."

"Matter of fact, he's the guy who investigated your little problem at the track way back when."

"Oh?" I said, hoping that I looked convincingly confused now. Apparently both Starbuck and I had been wrong about Burns being a bumbling cop.

"Seems kinda curious," Burns went on, "that the guy who gathered evidence against you is murdered. The guy who got you kicked out of racing is damn near murdered. And the guy who gave testimony against you, a jockey named Dewey Lane, turns up missing. What's a homicide detective to think?"

"You're saying I had something to do with these things?" I asked.

"I'm not accusing you, but these little coincidences are sorta piling up, aren't they?" And he hadn't even tied in the Forrester "suicide."

"Should I call my lawyer?" I asked, hoping my face showed nothing except befuddlement.

"I don't think that's necessary," Burns said, standing, dabbing at his lips with his napkin, then folding it neatly and resting it carefully on the desk beside his empty dessert dish. "But you might want to keep his number handy. Thanks for the lunch. Next time it'll be on me."

32

"**H**ELLO, HONEY."

My eyes went to my watch. It was two-twenty in the afternoon of what was turning out to be a good day after all.

"Hello, Lea," I answered. "I love you."

"I love you, too. And, boy, do I need the reassurance. Oh, Coley, it's been so awful. Letting myself get caught that way at the hospital. And then trying to climb out of a window and falling and breaking my leg and getting captured again. So stupid. If it hadn't been for you and Walrus—"

"How's the leg?"

"Healing. The X rays indicate a clean break. And that unfortunate Dr. Forrester apparently did a good job of setting it. I . . . I can't talk long. We promised Agent Marquez we wouldn't use the phone at all, but I had to call you."

"Are you sure Marquez is DEA?"

"I . . . don't know. Why?"

"The DEA has no Marquez listed in Southern California. Or La Nasa. And their Dougherty isn't your Dougherty."

There was a brief silence, followed by, "I'll tell Dad."

"I want to see you."

"That's . . . not possible right now," she said. "The reason we moved so quickly is because the other place was compromised. Sonny Marquez says this time no visitors at all."

We had evidently progressed from Agent Marquez to Sonny Marquez. "How long is this going to go on anyway?" I asked.

"According to—"

"Sonny," I said, interrupting her.

"Yes, according to Sonny . . . oh, Coley, thank you for being jealous. It does wonders for my self-esteem. Anyway, according to Sonny,

Dad and I will be here until something happens to change the situation."

"In that case—"

This time, Lea interrupted me. "Got to go," she said, "and I really can't wait to be with you again."

Abruptly, the connection was broken.

I replaced the receiver and finished the sentence for myself. "In that case, let's see about changing the situation."

My first step was to visit the offices of SportsNet. The cable network's address was more hip than fashionable. They did their business out of a refurbished warehouse on the Venice boardwalk, about a hundred sandy yards from the Pacific Ocean.

The information desk was empty, but in a room just off the reception area, I found Loretta Simmons chatting on the phone, using her version of a proper British accent. She saw me and held up a hand with one finger, indicating that she'd be just a minute.

She finished her conversation, replaced the phone and, smiling, explained, "That was my transcontinental voice. I use it when I have to get tough. For some reason, people aren't as put out when they're being put down by an Englishwoman."

"You would've fooled Prince Charles," I said. "Did you study voice?"

"Like ninety-nine percent of the people who move to Southern California," Loretta confided, "I wanted to act. And if you come from a little town about ten miles outside of Winnipeg—that's in Manitoba, eh—and you want to act, voice lessons come right after you get your composite taken."

"How long ago did you make the trip?"

"Six years and eight months. Three years ago, when the five hundredth film executive promised me a part if I'd just get him off in between his phone calls, I decided to sample the below-the-line jobs."

"You preferred below the line to below the belt."

"Exactly. And here I am. You looking for Lew?" I nodded. "Follow me."

She led me up a concrete stairwell with high-tech red pipe handrails to Lew Totter's office on the second level. The producer was standing behind his desk, looking out through barred windows at the sand and ocean and sunbathers.

"Getting inspiration, Lew?" Loretta asked kiddingly.

"More than I need," Totter said, turning around and walking toward us. "I love to work in stimulating surroundings. Coley, grab a chair."

"Work hard, gentlemen," Loretta said ironically.

As I settled into a modern contraption pretending to be a chair, Totter walked back to his desk and parked. Gesturing at the bars on the windows, he said, "You probably think that's to keep crooks out, right? Wrong. It's to keep the employees in. Especially on days like this. It looks like the tryouts for the *Sports Illustrated* swimsuit issue out there."

On another day I'd have enjoyed the view with him. Today I wanted to get right to the point.

"Lew, I've got an idea."

"This is Idea Central. Shoot."

"We saw how well For Cupid's Sake did in the Derby. Without that one false step, she's a winner, right?"

"Absolutely."

"A filly Derby winner would have been a rarity. Only Regret, Genuine Risk, and Winning Colors have done it, so she would have been the fourth. But here's what people usually overlook: a filly winner of one of the other two Triple Crown races would be as unusual as a Derby winner."

Lew Totter looked surprised. "Yeah? I thought fillies won the Preakness all the time."

"Wrong. Four fillies won the Preakness in the early years, but the last one was Nellie Morse back in 1924. We've had two fillies win the Derby since then. Just two have won the Belmont. One of those, Ruthless, won the very first running in 1867; the only other one was Tanya in 1905, and since then it's been zip for the ladies."

Totter looked impressed. "I think I picked us the right expert commentator. You're like a racing encyclopedia."

Actually, I'm no track historian, but I'd done some preparation for this conversation. I threw him a few more filly facts and he said, "This is fascinating stuff, Coley, but where are you going with it?"

"Stand to reason that a great filly will attract a big female audience, something that a lot of SportsNet's programs don't."

"Maybe."

"Why don't we narrow the scope of our documentary to just the one horse?"

"One horse. For Cupid's Sake?"

"Right. We could go to Lexington to Jaydee Farms and tape them getting the animal ready. Maybe interview the trainer and Carmody himself."

"Whoa, kemosabe," Totter said. "Aren't these the same folks who were telling us to take get-lost pills. It seems like only yesterday."

"That was before I discovered I had a friend in court."

He looked at me questioningly. "Oh?"

"Carmody's daughter."

"Aha," Totter said with a leer.

"Nothing like that. She's way too young for me, barely out of her teens. She was just about *into* her teens when I was working for her father. A sweet little kid who loved horses. And she liked me. We were friends, nothing more, but we're still friends. I think she might prevail on the old man to let us take some pictures of him and the horse."

By Totter's expression, he obviously still wasn't convinced, so I plodded on. "If we just grind out another Triple Crown documentary, who's going to care, really? Who's going to watch? But if we come up with an hour or more with the horse, make that the filly that wins the Preakness and/or the Belmont Stakes, we'll have a special that's really special."

Lew Totter considered for a moment. Then he said, "I like the idea of a fresh approach. Pushing the envelope a little. But I see a risk here."

"Where?"

"Consider this analogy. Covering the three races in general is like investing your money in a balanced portfolio. Whatever happens, you end up with something at the end and you don't lose too much. Betting all our resources on a filly that might turn out to be a loser is like plunging our whole life savings into municipal bonds."

"Lousy analogy. SportsNet's whole future isn't riding on this documentary. There's not a whole lot of downside if the horse runs out of the money. But if she wins, the network's reputation gets a sharp spur upward."

Totter nodded. "Okay. Let's say we use a solo subject. Why not focus on the animal with the best chance to win, Headbanger? He's already picked up the Derby. He has a chance at the Triple Crown. And we get all that rock-star carryover, too."

"Good point," I admitted. "But think about it. You'd have to deal with Halcyon's recording company and manager and publicity manager and Huey Grosso's little brother, Martin. Besides which, every media outlet is going to be concentrating on the potential Triple Crown winner, so you'd have less chance of getting something really unique. And, frankly, if it's a matter of handicapping, I don't think Headbanger can take For Cupid's Sake on a dry track."

"Hell, I don't know . . ."

"For Cupid's Sake is the perfect choice. It's politically correct from a gender point of view. Even if she loses, you can still have a good documentary, just not one with a storybook ending. Lew, if I were a vaguely ambitious producer, I'd see this as a way to make that jump up to ESPN."

Now I had him.

"ESPN, hell," he said. "How about ABC?"

"Exactly."

"Let's give it a shot," he said, and reached across the desk to shake my hand.

After a moment his expression, a gleaming amalgam of creative ambition and greed, came back to normal. He was revved up, but not to the point of throwing all practicality out the window.

"Uh, you realize, Coley, I have to run this past Barry first."

"Sure, Lew, I understand."

Running it past Barry took the better part of an hour and a half. First Lew had to locate him. Then we both had to make our case to him on the speaker phone in Lew's office. Barry listened, asked questions, got answers, asked the same questions in a different way, got the same answers in a different way, and finally declared himself agreeable.

"But you guys realize, I have to run this past Geoffrey Paragon first."

"Sure, Barry," Lew Totter said.

"This may take a while. Geoffrey's not in the States at the moment."

The run was becoming a marathon, but that's television. Lew obviously wanted to make our case to Paragon directly, but Gallen said he'd take care of it.

"And maybe take credit for it," Lew muttered under his breath, too softly for the phone to pick up. After Gallen had hung up, Lew said, "Come on down to the beach with me, Coley. I know a place where we can wait this out."

As we exited the building, we were followed by a young guy who seemed to have stepped from a daytime soap opera. Handsome, dashing, and athletic, he wore a white tennis outfit that made his deeply tanned skin look even darker. He swung a racket from side to side and bestowed on Lew a dazzling smile, a wink, and a mock salute just before he jogged off down the boardwalk.

"The SportsNet tennis pro?" I asked.

"Roddy?" he said. "I don't think he's a pro at anything except playing with the ladies. Guy reminds me of that old actor, what's his name, Gilbert Roland, except for the dumb horsetail he's got dangling over the back of his collar."

"He work for SportsNet?"

"Yeah. But I couldn't tell you exactly what he does, except maybe cash his check. He usually doesn't even bother to come into the office. Paragon forced him on Barry."

"I wonder why."

"He's a legacy. Somebody's cousin or nephew."

"Paragon's?"

"Who knows?"

We strolled to an empty table in front of a nearby dive, where we drank beer and talked and observed the human scenery jogging, walking, vamping, and skating by. Lew was optimistic about our proposal's chances. "I'm pretty sure Paragon'll go for it," he said.

"What makes you think so?"

"He's a big fan of Carmody's. Our seats at the Derby? Paragon made the special request that they be on the aisle in front of Carmody's. He told Barry he'd like to see the guy elected president. With a businessman in the White House, maybe the FCC would keep its big nose out of cable entirely."

Less than an hour after we settled in, Loretta arrived with the news that Paragon liked the idea.

"What'd I tell you?" Lew said, and ordered another beer.

33

WHEN I got home that evening, I found Sonny Marquez sitting in the living room, smoking a cigar, feet up on the couch like he owned the place. My first impulse was to ask him what the hell he was doing in my house, but of course I realized it was Lea's house, too, and she presumably had given him her key. The sight of one of her suitcases by his chair seemed to confirm that.

"Finally," he said.

"I'm glad you're here," I told him. "We have a few things to talk about."

He raised his hand, showing a pair of fingers. "Just two," he said.

"Okay."

"First, I came to pick up some things for Lea to wear. They're in the suitcase. That's okay with you, isn't it?"

"Sure, but why don't I deliver them personally?"

"That's the second thing. Don't be a smart guy and try to find her. All you'll do is put her in further danger."

"I'm the guy who rescued her, remember?"

"That was then. This is now. No interference."

I stared at him. "The DEA says there are no agents here named Marquez."

Marquez grinned. "You checked on me? I like that."

"So who the hell are you?" I asked.

"Jee-sus, what do you expect?" he asked, no longer smiling. "I'm not some fucking office agent who pushes paper downtown and goes home to Orange County every night. I work undercover, down and dirty. Marquez is my street name."

"And La Nasa and Dougherty?"

"Same deal. It's the names we use when we're working. You sure as hell don't want some fucking Colombian hit man wiping out your whole family tree. He'd have his work cut out for him trying to go after all the Marquezes in L.A."

It made some sense, I suppose.

"Look, Killebrew, we've got this thing controlled. Just stay cool and let us do our job."

"Maybe I'll take a trip," I said.

"Great idea. Get your mind off all this. Your lady's in good hands."

"I might visit Lexington," I said.

"Pretty country around there, or so I've been told," Marquez said.

Apparently satisfied I'd agreed to stay out of his hair—the idea of my going to Lexington didn't seem to faze him any—Marquez picked up the suitcase and made his exit.

I closed the door and locked it behind him, wondering how he could have anything under control if Lexington meant nothing to him. Obviously, Starbuck still hadn't mentioned anything about James Carmody to him, which suggested that he didn't place much trust in him, either.

34

"GOOD MORNING, Santa Rosita Raceway, track of the fakes and glowers," said the rumbling voice.

"God, Roger," I said, "I hope they told you it was me. If that's your usual telephone greeting, you must be closer to retirement than I thought."

"Two-thirds of the racing world seems to be on the unemployment line. Why not me? Who the hell is this, anyway? Some other track dropout, probably."

Sitting in my relatively pristine office, I could picture Roger Willetts at his impossibly untidy desk at Santa Rosita, a honey bear wrapped in an off-the-rack suit that may have fit him twenty years and thirty pounds ago. He was the assistant general manager, a lowly sounding title for the guy responsible for the smooth day-to-day running of the place.

"I need some information from you, Roger."

"Why else do you ever call? Keeping this bullring from descending into bankruptcy isn't enough of a job, I have to run an information service for over-the-hill jockeys, too. What is it? More facts and figures on fillies in the Preakness or the Belmont?"

"Look, if you're too damned busy to help a friend, forget it," I said, playing along with his standard irascible act. "You probably wouldn't have what I need, anyway."

"Wanna bet?"

"If I wanted to bet, I'd go to the two-dollar window. All I want is James Carmody's home phone number."

"Oh, is *that* all. How about Bob Dole's private number, while I'm at it? And Phil Gramm's?"

"In other words, you don't have Carmody's number."

"So I'm useless. So take back the dinner you owe me for that filly info. You know that Carmody hasn't run a horse on this coast in years."

"Don't get defensive, Roger. Nobody's perfect. Babe Ruth struck out, Steve Young throws an interception every couple of years, and I caught you once when you were cheerful."

"When was that?"

"The day of some national disaster, I forget which. Here's an easier request: How about the number for Gandy Dawes?"

"Carmody's old trainer? Piece of cake. He's not running for anything." A minute later, Willetts read off a number.

"Two-one-six. What area code is that?"

"I think it's Cleveland, Coley, home of Thistledown. Maybe you and I *do* have something to be grateful for."

"Thanks again for all your help, Roger."

"You ever need anything at all, call somebody else, okay?"

A serious-voiced child answered the phone when I dialed the number Willetts had given me. I asked if I could speak to Mr. Gandy Dawes, and I heard the little voice calling for Grandpa.

"Yeah?" said a raspy voice.

"Gandy? This is Coley Killebrew."

"Well, I'll be damned." The voice brightened a bit. "How ya doin', Coley?"

"Good, and you?"

"Can complain but won't. I'm living with my son's family, some of whom seem to like me a little bit. And don't believe what you hear about Cleveland. It's not nearly that exciting. If you're hustling mounts, Coley, I can't help you. The closest I come to a horse these days is when I feed the dogs."

"I'm trying to reach your old employer, James Carmody. Have you got his number?"

"Yeah. I guess you could say I got his number." Dawes followed that with a mirthless chuckle and the phone number from memory. "I sure as hell called him enough. I put in my best twenty-two years with that Southern gentleman. And he had the brass balls to put me out to pasture at the ancient age of sixty-three. Sixty-three! That's middle-aged for trainers. Guys like Jim Fitzsimmons and Max Hirsch were just getting into their stride at sixty-three."

"And what about Charlie Whittingham?"

"Right. But Carmody had this mean-spirited son of a bitch he wanted to use as his trainer, so I was out."

"You mean Richard Sandford?"

"I mean Richard 'tell me everything you know about horses, then get the hell out of my barn' Sandford. Fella didn't know jack shit about trainin' horses. But I'll say this for him: he was a good learner."

"Carmody must be a real sweetheart," I said.

"Aw, J.D. ain't so bad. 'Least he wasn't till he got it into his noggin about that filly. Man, I never saw a man wanted an animal more."

"We're talking about For Cupid's Sake?" I asked.

"Uh-huh," Dawes replied.

"Any idea why Carmody was so anxious to own her?"

He hesitated before replying. "Nope. Not really. Guess he knew what he was doin', though. I been follerin' her progress enough to put a few bucks on her in the Derby. If that ground had of been solid, she'd of gone for the roses. I tell ya this: it's dry for the Preakness, my bookie's gonna be payin' me back big-time."

"It's not a bad bet," I said.

"What you want with Carmody, anyway? You not thinking of ridin' for him again?"

"No. I'm not riding for anybody these days. But it is a business thing. I'm doing a little work for SportsNet."

"They pay big?" Dawes asked.

"Not me they don't."

"You want to make yourself a bundle, bet on For Cupid's Sake."

"I'll give it some thought," I said. After a pause I asked, "You remember Joey Laborde, Gandy?"

The former trainer took his time answering. "Yeah. I remember little Joey."

"After he ran that ragged race, was it Carmody ordered his beating?"

"Aw, Coley, that's ancient history."

"I bet it's just like yesterday for Joey. Was it Carmody?"

"Hell, you know how J.D. is. Man can't stand to lose. You ain't plannin' to ask him about Joey on the air, are you?"

"No, we're not looking to offend him," I said. "We need his cooperation. I just wanted to get it straight in my mind the kind of man I'm dealing with."

"Just like everybody else, he wants to win all the time. Difference is, he's got the money and the clout to make it happen."

Two calls down and one more, the tough one, to go. But instead of making it right away, I stood up, walked to the kitchen, and had a Danish with a cup of coffee. Slightly fortified, I returned to the phone and punched out Carmody's number.

The voice on the other end was female and officious. My plan had been to talk with Angela, but I changed my mind on the spur of the moment and asked to speak with Carmody himself.

"I'm sorry, but Mr. Carmody will be in conference all day."

"This is Colman Killebrew," I said. "Please tell him I called and would love to speak with him regarding his ownership of the horse, For Cupid's Sake."

"Could you be more specific, Mr. Killebrew?"

"Not on the phone, ma'am," I said, and left her my number.

Carmody called back within the hour. "Hi, Killebrew," he said. "I've been wonderin' about somethin' since seeing you the other day. How long did you work for me?"

"Long enough for thirty-six races, of which we won thirty-one." That stat I had at my fingertips without getting it from Willetts.

Carmody made a harrumph noise that could mean anything, then said, "Well, what's on your mind? The girl said it was about For Cupid's Sake."

"As you may already know, when I was at your barn at Churchill Downs the other day, I was working on an assignment for SportsNet. We'd like to make a short documentary on For Cupid's Sake."

"Oh?" The one-word question was delivered with deliberate wariness.

"Because, after seeing her almost win the Derby, we're betting she's going to win either the Preakness or the Belmont and possibly both."

"Not interested, son. But if I was, I'd have gone along with ESPN and *Sports Illustrated*. They both called right after Cupid showed her stuff in the Derby. Sorry."

"A beautiful horse like that should be given the attention she deserves right now. You can see the interest she stirred up by just coming close to winning. Once she crosses that finish line, she'll be famous enough. But you won't be able to reproduce the preparation that went into her big win. Let us do our documentary, and you'll have a record of it."

After a brief silence he said, "What is it you're asking for, exactly?"

"Permission to tape at Jaydee Farms for a couple of hours. Short interviews with you, your trainer and jockey, plus anybody else you feel should be interviewed. Then some footage of Cupid going through her daily routine."

"The questions to be approved beforehand?"

"If that's what you want." I suspected I was giving up one of the prized elements of a free press, but when did I ever claim to be a journalist? It wasn't the documentary I was interested in. It was the access to Carmody.

"And all this stuff's to run only on SportsNet?"

"I . . . I'm not sure about that. It's possible they may sell off excerpts to the networks or other cable companies. We're hoping to get as wide a coverage as possible."

"When will it run?"

"As soon after the Belmont as we can put it together."

"What's your end of it, Killebrew?"

"I'll be doing the interviewing."

"You like that better than riding a horse?" Carmody asked, as if he couldn't quite believe it.

"No. There's nothing better than riding a horse. But that ended for me a few years ago."

"Yeah, I seem to recall a bit of bullshit gettin' tossed your way. Tell you what. Fly on up tomorrow and come to dinner here. Bring your questions for me to look over. If they're okay, I'll spare you an hour, no longer, for your movie."

"Sounds fair."

"Dinner's at eight. Now this is just you I'm inviting. Not the other birds involved in your little movie. We'll pick out a time when I'll be ready for them."

I hung up the phone and called for Jack Hayward to tell him he'd likely be overseeing the restaurant again for the next five or six days.

35

M Y NEXT step was to get over to the SportsNet offices again to fill Lew Totter in on my arrangements with Carmody.

"I agreed he could approve the questions in advance," I said. "I hope that doesn't compromise—"

"Hey, Coley, do we look like an organization with a lot of integrity to compromise? Seriously, getting Carmody's cooperation is a big break. If he wants to look at the questions, mazel tov."

He took out a pad of paper and between us we drafted some fairly standard, mostly innocuous questions to present to Carmody. Lew added one about his presidential aspirations. "You got to give him one he can toss out. Makes him feel in control and creative."

He said he'd get them typed up and fax them over to me at the restaurant.

"One other thing, Lew."

"What's that?"

"I'd like a buddy of mine to be the cameraman on this shoot."

"Shoot? You're picking up the lingo, Coley. But I have to tell you, I think we'd be pressing our luck asking Barry to add anybody else to the payroll."

"No added expense to SportsNet. I'll handle his expenses. I'd just prefer to use my own man."

"Sounds fine to me. I don't have to ask you if he belongs to the union, because we haven't hired a union cameraman in our glorious history. But is he any good?"

"The best."

"What's this guy's name?"

"John Walnicki."

.   .   .

Convincing Totter was a cinch compared with convincing Walrus.

"Coley, what do I know about operating a camera?" He waved a big arm around the shelves of his bookstore. "I spend most of my time with the works of guys who never heard the word 'video' in their lives. . . ."

"So what? Most of them never heard of cars either, and you can drive."

"Okay, so it's a bum analogy, but taking pictures requires skill and talent. Doesn't it?"

"Why? You just need to be able to hold the camera steady, and if anybody I know has a steady hand, Walrus, it's you." I lowered my voice, knowing Gigi was in the back room of the store. "I need somebody I can trust on this deal. I don't know just what to expect."

"Rough stuff?" he said, his interest improving. Maybe the slow life was getting to him.

"Could be."

That was when Gigi emerged from the back room, looking at the two of us as warily as usual. I know she loved Walrus, and I think she was fond enough of me as an individual, but the two of us together seemed to give her bad vibes.

"I was on the phone with Jilly Margolis for an hour," she said accusingly. "She was frantic. She gave you and John the name of some doctor, and just a few hours later the doctor committed suicide."

"Baby," Walrus said, "I told you Coley and I didn't have anything to do with—"

"I'm worried about you, John," she said sternly. "I know that Jilly is an hysteric, but the man's death obviously wasn't just a coincidence. So you had *something* to do with it."

Walrus was silent.

"You told me you were through with that life," she said.

"This is my fault," I said. "I should never have dragged—"

"No," Walrus interrupted. "Listen, baby, I am through with that life. Never again will I risk my future for money. But Coley is my friend, and if he needs my help, he'll get it."

"I don't want you hurt," she said, moving into his arms. She looked like a little girl being embraced by a bear.

"I love you, Gigi," he said, "but you have to understand I'm not the kind of guy who turns a friend down."

"Wal—John," I said. "It was a mistake to drag you into this. I can handle it from here on."

I started for the door.

"Hold on, Coley," Walrus said. "I'm in this with you."

"But—" Gigi said.

"I'm in this," he repeated, staring at her. "Nothing's going to happen to me. Or to Coley."

She shook her head. "The last time, you were shot."

"I was a bodyguard for a lot of years, honey, and I got shot a few times and stabbed a few others. All of those times I was careless. Freud says we don't really make mistakes, so maybe, subconsciously, I wanted to get hurt because I had low self-esteem. But now, I've got you, honey. No more mistakes for this boy."

She glared at him until her eyes filled with tears. She rushed into his arms. "You're the most impossible man I've ever known," she said, and stood on tiptoe for him to kiss her. He bent to that task, a grin on his face.

"I'll . . . just let myself out," I told them.

Ah, romance, I thought. And where was mine?

36

A S SOON as I set foot in The Horse's Neck that evening, I was approached by a customer who'd been sitting at the bar, a young African American in a conservative gray suit.

"Mr. Killebrew?" he asked in a well-modulated voice.

I nodded.

He removed his wallet and showed me an ID stating that Lawrence B. Singleton was a member of the Central Intelligence Agency. The card was disappointingly understated. I was hoping it might have had a little logo on it, Casper the Friendly Ghost, maybe.

"What can I do for you, Agent Singleton?"

"It's what I can do for you, Mr. Killebrew. Might we go somewhere a little less public, like your office?"

It seemed a reasonable request. We strolled through the restaurant without another word. Once we were behind closed doors, he got right to the point.

"We'd like to know exactly what your interest is in James Deth Carmody."

"Strictly business," I replied, quickly enough for it to have been the truth.

"It's a business dinner you're having with him tomorrow night at his farm in Lexington?"

"You guys really do have your ears to the ground."

"We believe in being informed," Singleton said without a hint of amusement in his face. "Which is why I ask: What exactly is your *business* with James Deth Carmody?"

Using as much shallow enthusiasm and trivial detail as I had bestowed on Totter and Gallen, I told him about the documentary. I put everything I had into depicting myself as an empty-headed ex-jock bedazzled by the prospect of a broadcasting career.

The reviews of my performance that I read on his face were at best mixed. Agent Singleton gave me a skeptical, sidelong look, as if he wasn't quite sure I was a deceitful, two-faced bastard but felt the odds were favoring that opinion.

Finally he said, in that same unaffected, unemotional monotone, "It will be in your best interest, and in the best interest of your country, to postpone or, better yet, cancel your documentary."

"Any particular reason?"

"Several. But none that I'm at liberty to discuss."

"Well, if it's in the country's best interest . . ." I said.

"Then you'll be staying clear of Carmody for the time being?"

"That sounds like the prudent thing," I admitted.

Singleton rewarded me with a polite smile and a nod of the head. Possibly the broadest gestures he allowed himself. "That's being smart," he said.

As soon as he'd marched off, I turned on my computer and wrote a brief note to Lea. It included my plan to visit Carmody to see what I could turn up. I printed the note, added a few very heartfelt personal comments by hand, placed it into an envelope that I sealed. I wrote her name on the front. Then I went back into the main dining room and caught Jack Hayward's eye.

"You rang, sirrah," Jack said as he followed me into the office.

"I'm taking off, Jack. I'm not sure when I'll be getting back in town, but I don't want anybody to know I've left. Understand?"

"Not at all."

"If anyone asks to see me, I'm downtown at the market. Or I'm having lunch or dinner away from the restaurant. Or I've got the flu. Whatever works."

"Be I so bold as to inquire where you'll be?"

"You don't want to know," I said. I handed him the note I'd printed. "Put this in the safe. If something should happen to me . . . this is for Lea."

He accepted the envelope with a worried frown. He asked, "This isn't a 'far, far better thing' you're doing, is it?"

"Me wind up with my head in a basket? I hope not."

"And it has Miss Lea's approval?" he asked.

"Not exactly," I said.

"Does she know you're leaving Lotusland?"

"Not exactly," I repeated.

"What do I tell her when she calls?"

I hesitated. Lea had enough on her mind without worrying about me. And I didn't want to raise her hopes until I was sure what I could pry out of Carmody and Sandford. And I definitely didn't want Marquez and his cronies to get wind of the fact that I was trying to do their job for them. "Tell her the same thing you're telling the others."

"As you would have it," he said. He looked confused and worried and a bit disappointed in me. I felt the same way myself.

37

WALRUS AND I were on a jet to Lexington the next day. Usually my companion was about as good-natured and cheery as anyone I'd ever known, but starting out he'd been a little testy. He wasn't very happy in airplanes to begin with, and he didn't like being separated from the little woman. I probably should have felt guilty about dragging him along, but I had my own problems.

On the way east I eased him out of his mood by recapping what we knew and didn't know about the whole mess. Walrus labeled it a Socratic dialogue, but Socrates had at least some of the answers he was trying to draw from his students, and the two of us were majoring in questions.

There were several obvious reasons for the DEA to be keeping watch over Starbuck and Lea. Vickie Salazaar had been one of their own. She and Starbuck had been investigating Richard Sandford, a former member of their team.

"Are there any ties between Marquez and his pals and Sandford and Carmody?" Walrus asked.

"Unknown," I said. "Hell, we don't really know that Sandford and Carmody were involved in Vickie's murder."

Walrus sighed. "We don't really know for sure that she *was* murdered," he said.

"It's all pretty dim. But obviously somebody is feeling hostile to Starbuck. And now the CIA is mixed in, from Carmody's end. Singleton didn't mention Vickie or Starbuck."

"What's their interest in Carmody?"

"Probably not benign," I said. "When Carmody sent his mercenaries into Bogotá to get the drug lord Paolo Rodriquez—"

"The word 'mercenaries' is a little harsh," Walrus said, reminding me of his former occupation. "Let's call them professionals."

"Okay, those *professionals* ended a bunch of operations the CIA had going through Rodriquez. So my guess is, as payback, they're probably trying to nail Carmody with something big enough to nip his political plans in the bud."

Walrus shook his big head. " 'Out of timber so crooked as that from which man is made, nothing entirely straight can be carved,' " he quoted. "Emmanuel Kant."

"Ain't it the truth," I said.

"Still, it's possible we're all working toward the same goal," Walrus suggested. "Getting Carmody."

I nodded.

"You really think he's capable of having people murdered?" Walrus asked.

I thought about the beating of the jockey, Joey Laborde. "Yeah. He's capable."

"Okay, but assuming he's a thinking man, he would need a reason. If Lea's father and the Salazaar lady were going to the Derby, maybe there was something about the race. You said his horse would have won if he hadn't slipped. . . ."

"She. The horse is a filly," I said. "Maybe Carmody is crazy enough to try to buy a race. He's used to getting what he wants by money and threats."

"But does he want to win a race, even the Kentucky Derby, more than he wants to be President of the United States?" Walrus asked, not without logic. "Because that's what he would be risking."

The result of our Socratic dialogue? By the time our plane touched down at Blue Grass Field, we knew less than we had when we started.

38

WE PICKED up a rental at the airport and drove to our hotel, where I unpacked, showered, redressed, and left Walrus to take his chances with the hotel dining room. Actually, he liked the looks of the menu and didn't at all seem to envy my foray among the rich and powerful.

Carmody's spread, Jaydee Farms, wasn't hard to find. It just went on and on and on. The nearly everlasting perimeter was marked by high tension wire. Past it, armed guards patrolled with hunting dogs. We'd wondered about Carmody's connection to the CIA—this fortified compound could have *been* the CIA. Back in the days when I had ridden for him, Carmody's ranch on the other side of Lexington had been less than half this size and one-tenth as uninviting.

At the gate my car and its contents were subjected to an elaborate electronic search. Carmody's men had sophisticated scanning devices I'd never known existed. The high-tech methods didn't extend to the traditional pat-down I received from two of the guards.

There may have been more indignities to come, but Richard Sandford arrived at the gate to speed me through the ordeal. He got in the passenger seat of my rental and directed me around the property. Jaydee Farms had all the white-fenced paddocks, cobbled roads, and statues to departed runners you'd expect to find on a bluegrass breeding farm, but the overelaborate security made it all seem a subtle front, as if other things, far more sinister and far more secretive, were going on within the fences.

Finally we arrived at the main house, which was at least two miles from the gate. It was a large two-story, plantation-style building, and it looked familiar. I mentioned this to Sandford.

"You an old movie fan?" he asked.

"I've watched my share."

"The house is called Harrow," Sandford explained. "It was built to resemble a plantation home that appeared in a forties flick called *The Foxes of Harrow*. It's one of Mr. Carmody's favorites."

We were greeted at the door by a liveried black servant whose Old South manner made Carmody's acceptance of the late Andrew Gunderman's shuffling sycophant act easier to understand. If a billionaire chose to occupy another time, from the house he lived in to the people he populated it with, he had the means to do it.

Sandford parked in front of Harrow and then took me for a stroll through the side garden toward the rear of the house. I was beginning to wonder if he were showing me the servants' entrance when we took a sharp turn, crossed a patio, and entered through open French doors.

We were in a small sitting room, decorated in cost-is-no-object antebellum style. Lula Dorian, Carmody's stunning brunette girlfriend, was sitting on a purple velvet chair, wearing a short dress that almost wasn't there and sipping what was probably not her first drink of the day.

The former Chunky Chicken waitress waved me over and suggested I try "one of Sam's absinthe frappés." Sam, I assumed, was the sad-faced African American standing next to a sideboard on which the booze rested.

"Maybe a gin and tonic," I told him, and he nodded as if it had been the wisest decision he'd heard in years.

Lula patted the couch next to her. As I perched there, waiting for my drink, Sandford poured his own. Lula launched into a long and winding tale about how she found the dress she was wearing in this "tiny little shop in Louisville."

I leaned forward attentively, which she no doubt expected from any man who came into close proximity. But she might not have been flattered to know I was more interested in her voice than her cleavage. My ears were anxiously listening for a syrupy southern accent. But I could find no trace of Dixie or the Hispanic background that Gunderman had wondered about. Just a slight Texas twang, with a touch of absinthe slur.

"Will you be going to Baltimore, Ms. Dorian?" I asked.

"Call me Lula, honey. Miz Dorian's my mama. Jamie hasn't said anything to me about Baltimore. What do you think, Dickie?"

Sandford shrugged. She turned back to me. "Tell me now, are you as vain as so many of 'em?"

"So many of whom?"

"Jockeys. So many of 'em are terribly self-conscious about their size.

I've seen some who wear heels higher than mine." I glanced at her slender feet, which may have been the point of the reference. "You ever wear elevator shoes, Coley?"

"Nope," I said honestly.

"Good for you. I find small men dreadfully attractive, you know. Lots of women do." She leaned forward confidentially, waving her nearly empty glass. Now I was finding her cleavage more interesting than her voice. "I understand that small men aren't exactly small all over. Is that right?"

"Compared with what?" I asked.

I was about to find out when Angela Carmody joined us and made a big thing about how pleased she was to hear I was coming for dinner. She took my arm and led me toward the French doors. Sandford watched us sullenly over his drink.

On the patio Angela whispered, "Isn't she the most tacky thing you've seen?"

I gestured helplessly and said nothing.

"Was she coming on to you? I swear, I can't believe Daddy puts up with all her flirting." Fathers and daughters, I thought.

Deciding to change the subject, I stepped back, looked at Angela's cocktail dress and said, "A definite improvement over Levis and those boots with the hole at the toe."

"Thank you, sir," she said, and gave me a mock curtsy. Then the smile left her face and she lowered her voice again. "There's something I really would like to talk to you about."

"Boyfriend advice?" I asked lightly.

Her eyes moved back to the French doors. Sandford was standing there, scowling at us. "No, not about that," she said. She frowned, causing unnatural lines to appear between her delicate brows. For the first time, I realized that there was an odd, shiny tautness to the right side of her face. It hadn't been very noticeable before. Or maybe I just hadn't been paying attention.

"Tell me," I said.

Sandford started toward us, pasting on a thin smile to conceal his hostility.

"Later," Angela whispered.

The butler announced that dinner was ready, and we filed into a dining room no larger than the grounds at Santa Anita. Carmody, wearing a velvet dinner jacket with a gold-embroidered crest on the pocket, stood at the head of an oak table that could have seated thirty or forty without brushing elbows. It was set for just the five of us,

Angela and I to his left, Lula and Richard to his right. The formality of the service and elaborateness of the menu reminded me of a state occasion.

The meal began with a generous allotment of oysters on the half shell, served on a bed of ice with horseradish, Tabasco sauce and lemon juice at the ready. I wondered how Walrus was faring back at the hotel.

Not surprisingly, Carmody ruled his table the same way he did his life—with autocratic power. Lula, Angela, and Sandford had very little to say, other than to nod in agreement with whatever the man at the head of the table happened to be espousing.

Carmody put away quite a few oysters, but of subsequent courses he ate lightly, as if he didn't need many calories to keep him at full speed. Still, it seemed important to him to keep us abreast of the effort he'd made on our behalf. The salmon, poached with champagne mustard sauce, had been "swimmin' in the lochs just yesterday," he told me. It was accompanied by minted red potatoes tossed in butter, and fresh asparagus. The accompanying beverage was Swedish aquavit.

In between his ruminations on how the country should be run (isolationism), what was wrong with the present administration (too liberal, too soft, too ineffective), and what was wrong with the world in general (drugs, lenient courts, overtaxation), he pressed me with questions about corruption in racing.

"You must know some pretty good stories about puttin' in the fix," he said.

"None that I can think of," I said.

"C'mon now. In all your years at the track, you never heard of an owner or a trainer telling a jock to hold a horse back?"

"You hear all kinds of things, but it's always secondhand. When I was riding for you, I don't remember you giving that kind of orders."

Carmody studied me carefully. He seemed amused. "And of course you made sure every one of your mounts moved as fast as they could."

"I never held a horse back that had a chance of winning," I said carefully.

"Sounds like weasel-words to me."

"Not at all. I just never felt like breaking a whip on an animal I knew had no chance. I didn't believe drawing blood was worth placing fifth or sixth."

"And the race that got you tossed out?"

"It was as honest as any I ever rode."

"Well, hell," Carmody said. "Either you really are that rarity, an honest man, or you're a pretty damn good liar. I'd almost prefer the latter. They're more interesting to have around."

As the evening wore on, Carmody kept returning to the subject of crooked races. By the time we reached the dessert course—cheese and biscuits, grapes and other fresh fruit, with a port that dated to the Ford administration—I was so tired of the game, I decided to change the rules and see how he'd react.

"Actually, I did hear of something that happened quite recently," I said.

"Yeah?" Carmody leaned forward expectantly.

"It's only a rumor, of course. But the story is that somebody tried to buy one of the biggest purses in racing."

"Buy?" Carmody asked. "You mean by bribing the jockeys to lose?"

"It was more threat than bribe." I looked from Carmody to Richard Sandford, who was frowning at me.

"What race might we be talking about?" Carmody asked.

"The Derby," I said quietly.

Carmody grinned. "This past Derby?" he asked.

I nodded.

Carmody unleashed a high-pitched laugh that suited his simian features. "What do you think about that, Richard? Mr. Killebrew says somebody tried to buy the Kentucky Derby."

Sandford shrugged. "Bullflop. If anybody'd given Alfie any trouble, he'd have told me." Alfie Quinn was For Cupid's Sake's jockey.

"Alfie may not have been approached," I said. "For Cupid's Sake wasn't considered to be a serious threat."

"What about the horse that won?" Angela asked. "Headbanger? Did anything happen to that jockey?"

"If Mr. Killebrew's rumor is true," Carmody said, "I suspect that would mean that that greasy little musician with the earrings is the party who was doing all the threatening." He smiled. "Now isn't that a lovely thought."

Carmody was confusing me. He was acting genuinely innocent. Even more vexing, so was Sandford, who appeared much more interested in Angela than in any stories about fixed races.

"Well, I must say you disappoint me, Mr. Killebrew," Carmody said. "Here I was hoping for some juicy racing scandals I could sink my teeth into, and you give me a rumor that is dubious at best. But

I'll look into it, all the same. Now, how about a brandy in the den?"

Before I could consider the consequences of brandy on top of port, Angela said, "I was hoping to show off Sandy to Mr. Killebrew."

Her father stared at her sweet, slightly lopsided grin for a few seconds, then said, "Fine with me, if it's okay with Mr. Killebrew."

"It'd be my pleasure. And please, can't we make it Coley?"

"Sure enough. Give me a call tomorrow. By then I'll have looked over your questions and we can proceed with your movie," Carmody said, leaving the table.

Angela and I got up a moment after Carmody, and I followed her out of the room. Sandford watched us go.

It was a coolish, pleasant evening, and it was nice to get outside for a while. Not so much as a blade of grass along the well-lit pathway was out of place. If anything on the Carmody spread was found in less than immaculate maintenance or repair, the slaves must have been in for a proper whupping.

As Angela and I walked to the stable area, I was aware that she was limping slightly. I was curious but didn't want to ask her about it directly.

"Are the stables in the same zip code as the house?" I asked.

She smiled. "It's not much farther."

"Sandy's *your* horse?"

"Yes."

"Do you have your own colors to race him in?"

"Oh, Sandy's not a racehorse. I'm not really into racing. Show horses are my thing."

At last we arrived at the stables, which smelled like stables smell, but not overpoweringly so. The horses' homes were as immaculate as everything else on Carmody's spread.

Sandy had the small head and gorgeous conformation of a high-strung Arabian. Somewhat haughty in manner, he didn't exactly come rushing to greet us. But he did deign to acknowledge our presence by rising and allowing Angela to run her delicate hand over his neck.

"I bought him myself," she said. "When I was at the Sorbonne, I did my thesis on 'The Horse As Art.' A history of paintings featuring horses."

"What painters did you write about?"

She started naming them: Géricault, Bonheur, Micas, and others I'd never head of plus one or two that I had, like Picasso and Toulouse-Lautrec.

"Books about horses often do well, so I was able to turn my thesis into a coffee-table art book that was popular both in Europe and in America. With the money I earned from it, I bought Sandy when he was just a colt."

I'd been searching my memory but couldn't recall too much about this odd, otherwordly young woman. She told me that she had spent most of her first eighteen years on horseback. "But I never ride anymore."

"Not even Sandy?" I asked.

She looked at the animal wistfully. "No. Not even Sandy." She touched the ultrasmooth section of her face. "I had a . . . little mishap six years ago. In France. I was careless. Something—a bee perhaps—caused my horse to buck. Not only did I fall, but the animal rolled onto me. The poor beast was in such a panic he kicked me." She touched her right cheek. "The bone was shattered. But surgeons can do wonders, don't you think?"

I nodded. "You're very beautiful."

"Dickie thinks so," she said.

Sandford didn't strike me as a Dickie, but I said, "Dickie is smarter than he looks. Are you and he . . . ?"

She smiled. "No way," she said. "Dickie's like my older brother. He looks out for me."

"Looks out how?"

"Well . . ." She rolled her eyes. "I suppose I'm a bit . . . impulsive at times. Nothing terrible, mind you, but I'm always afraid that if I don't do things I want right away, I may never do them at all."

"Example?"

She took a minute, wrinkling her face in thought. "Last week in town I saw this really lovely painting of a show horse in the window of a gallery. The gallery owner told me it was five thousand dollars, but I had to have it. Anyway, Dickie went to the gallery the next day and there were several other paintings by the same artist, some even larger canvases than mine. Dickie priced them and discovered they were selling at half what I paid. You see, I go to galleries all the time, and they know who I am and, of course, the price goes up. I don't mind, usually, but this was a bit much."

"Did you return the painting?" I asked.

"Of course not. I love the painting. But Dickie got the gallery owner to lower the price a little."

"How'd he do that?"

"I suppose he must have had words with the man," she said, kind of airily and unconcernedly. "Dickie doesn't mind telling people what he thinks."

She focused her attention back on the horse. "Pretty baby, pretty Sandy," she said.

I thought Sandy was a very lovely animal and told her so, adding, "Haven't you ever wondered what it would be like to ride him?"

"Not more than once a day," she said.

"You must not be as impetuous as you think."

She stared at me solemnly. "I'm afraid to ride him. But I'd still love to."

"Then it'll happen. One day your desire will overcome your fear."

"But it's been so long," she said. "Maybe that's part of my fear. I was an experienced rider when I fell."

"I went seven years without getting on a horse," I told her. "But I found myself in a situation where I had to do it. Your body remembers more than you think."

"I couldn't do it alone."

"Somebody to give you a leg up?"

"Something like that, yes."

"Well," I said, "I thank you for showing me Sandy."

I started to move back in the direction of the house, but she stopped me.

"That's not . . . why I asked you out here. There's something . . . I don't know how to begin. It's so difficult to explain to people unless their minds are open."

"Mine opens and shuts like a mailbox," I told her. "You might just be catching me in an accepting mood."

She considered that for a moment. "Okay," she said. "I saw you with my father about six weeks ago."

"No way," I replied. "Eight years ago, maybe."

"You don't understand."

"I guess I don't."

She looked at me in deadly earnest. "Since my . . . accident, I've had . . . odd sensations. Images flash in my mind. When I saw you tonight, I was reminded of an image I received six weeks ago. It was of you and Dad fighting with one another."

"Fighting? I barely know your father, Angela. And I usually stay clear of fights."

"These images are not to be taken literally. Though I saw you both fighting, the interpretation could mean that you are at opposite sides of an issue. I . . ." She shook her head in frustration. "I know this sounds so foolish. But the image was a sign."

I was staring at her, not sure how to react. "Do you have these . . . images often?"

"Thank heaven, no. They're terribly draining and upsetting. But they do signify future events. A month ago I dreamt that For Cupid's Sake fell into a swimming pool. I saw her swimming with all her might, but she simply couldn't reach the edge of the pool. And it happened."

"She fell into a pool?"

"No, no," Angela replied, frowning at my lack of understanding. "She lost the Kentucky Derby because of rain, don't you see?"

"Mmmmm," I said. It was supposed to sound noncommittal, but it just frustrated her.

"I shouldn't have even mentioned it to you. You're like Dad and the others."

"So you've told your father about the images?"

"I made a mistake of telling him my early dreams. He called them nonsense. My father is a very pragmatic man. He thinks dreams are the result of diet. But I know they're reflections of the future, the windows to our destiny."

I have to admit I was beginning to wonder about the blow Angela took to her head. I said carefully, "Dreams are always open to a variety of interpretations. The vision you had of me and your father, for example. Perhaps we were in a situation where I was actually shoving him out of danger's way."

"You were both angry, snarling at one another like savage animals. Though I could hear nothing that was being said, I could hear animal sounds. Animals in a fury."

"Lions and tigers?"

"Horses, actually," she replied, a bit miffed.

"Maybe your dad and I were both angry at a third party who was not in the dream."

She nodded as if that were a possibility. With a wan smile she said, "Maybe it was Mrs. Barker you both were shouting at."

"Mrs. Barker?" I asked.

"Vida Barker."

I knew the name, of course. Almost everybody in the country did. But I didn't see the connection. Vida Barker, whom the media had labeled "Ma Barker," was the forty-five-year-old widow of Emmett

Barker, the founder of the Evangelical Church of the Divine Savior. When her fundamentalist, slightly fascistic husband had passed away—in the bed of a woman of easy virtue, according to at least one supermarket tabloid and a television talk show—Vida Barker, white gown flapping in the purified breeze of her television studio, assumed leadership of the ever-growing flock.

"What's Vida Barker got to do with anything?" I asked.

"Daddy says he's not going to commit the same error Mr. Perot did when he made his bid for the presidency. He wants to have a proper running mate in place."

"Ma Barker for Vice President?" This was a nuttier idea than Angela's dreams.

She nodded. "I myself find her narrow-minded and rooted in the past. But she is an independent woman with a very large following."

Calling Ma Barker an independent woman was like saying Adolf Hitler was an effective politician. It left quite a lot unstated.

"Anyway," Angela continued, "the image was so very vivid. I felt I had to discuss it with you."

"Don't worry about me doing physical damage to your father," I assured her.

"Oh, that wasn't my concern at all. The final image was of you, Coley. You were lying on the ground. And you were broken and bleeding as if you'd suffered some terrible fall. A shadow passed over your mangled body while this horrible roar blocked out all other noise."

"What kind of a roar? Another animal?"

"I can't say. Just a hellish sound. Anyway, I wanted to tell you about the dream. To warn you." She moved toward me quickly. "And I wanted to do this."

She kissed me, and the little girl I'd known vanished forever.

For a moment I was too surprised to react in any way. Then I pulled away from her.

She looked hurt. "I . . . I'm sorry. I thought maybe . . ."

"Two years ago and I wouldn't have pulled away," I said.

"Two years ago, I was only twenty," she said.

"Then maybe I would have pulled away." I smiled. "Maybe not."

"What happened two years ago? Did you get married or something?"

"Or something," I said.

"And you love her?"

"Oh yes."

She smiled. "And she loves you?"

I nodded.

"But she wouldn't be upset if you and I were good friends?"

"No. She wouldn't be upset at all."

We both heard footsteps outside.

"Angie?" Richard Sandford called before entering the stable. He seemed relieved that we weren't writhing on the floor in passion. He stood beside Angela and, not too casually, placed a protective, or maybe even proprietary, arm around her shoulders.

"Well," I said heartily, "it's been a terrific evening, but I think it's time I was leaving."

Sandford and Angela walked me to my car.

As I got behind the wheel, Sandford bent down and gestured for me to open my window. He moved closer and, his face barely a foot away from mine, whispered, "You got a dab of lipstick on your mouth."

"Oh," I said, "thanks for the tip."

"Here's another. Mess with her and I'll tear your fucking head off."

I calmly turned on the engine and backed away, rubbing my lip with a finger. Sandford returned to Angela's side. She waved at me and called, "Come back soon."

The look in Sandford's eyes sent me an entirely different message.

39

BACK AT the hotel, I gave Walrus a play-by-play of the evening, omitting the kiss. When I'd finished, the big guy nodded thoughtfully, as if something was on his mind.

"What?" I asked.

"There was this guy, Peter Hurkos. Considered to be a genuine psychic. I was reading about him in one of Gigi's books. He even helped the police catch the Boston Strangler."

"Isn't there some doubt today that the guy they caught really was the Boston Strangler?"

"I don't think so," Walrus said. "But anyway, this Peter Hurkos claimed his clairvoyant abilities began after a blow to the noggin. Just like Carmody's daughter."

"Maybe Peter Hurkos has been dreaming about me, too."

"Don't scoff," Walrus warned. His tone of voice was persuasive.

"See you in the morning," I told him.

In my room, I picked up the phone and dialed The Horse's Neck. Jack Hayward gave me a real ego boost. He told me that he hadn't had to lie once about my whereabouts all evening. Nobody had asked.

The next call was to my home phone. The only message on the machine was from a real estate agent who wondered if I was interested in selling the cottage. Not just yet, thanks.

Well, they were probably keeping her from a phone, I thought.

That night, while lying in bed, I tried to send Lea a telepathic message. "I love you," I kept repeating over and over in my mind. I don't know if she ever received the signal, but at least it put me to sleep.

40

LEW TOTTER flew into Lexington the next day, and that afternoon all three of us went through the Jaydee Farms security check. But though we were closely watched by innumerable pairs of suspicious eyes, it seemed as if we were being given the full cooperation of the staff.

Carmody was the toughest subject to pin down. "Set up in my office," he suggested seconds after being introduced to Lew.

"Right now?"

"Hell, yes. I want to get this damn thing over with."

It was a showplace office, the walls covered with English sporting prints, apparently unread Morocco-bound volumes, and a huge polished oak desk devoid of clutter. It seemed highly unlikely any actual work was done in there, but it would serve as a nifty setting for Carmody to tape some folksy TV spots for his presidential campaign.

We looked at the prints and the book bindings and the maroon rug and the antique lamp on the desk for about twenty minutes before Carmody canceled the appointment without explanation. "Make it tomorrow morning instead," he snapped. "Ten sharp."

"No problem," Lew said with a wave of the hand. "We'll have plenty of other things to keep us busy."

And so we did. Walrus, full of surprises as always, did a good job with the camera. Either he knew more than he'd let on, or he was a quick study. I'd half expected Lew to start making suspicious sideways remarks about why I'd wanted my own man on the job, but Walrus's efficiency seemed to supply its own answer to the question.

The next morning we were out of our hotel before the crack of dawn to get our first shots of For Cupid's Sake's daily routine. She was being stabled at her Jaydee Farms home until it was time to ship out for Pimlico and the Preakness. The procedure was a bit unusual, but Carmody's tight security dictated that his filly not be exposed to the dangers and distractions of a racetrack any longer than was absolutely necessary.

"We're giving her a workout over at Keeneland this morning," Sandford told me.

"You mean Carmody didn't build his own mile oval here at the farm?" I inquired.

"It's an idea," the trainer said, poker-faced. "I'll suggest it to him." With that he strode off. It didn't look as if we'd ever be close friends.

I suggested to Lew we try to get some footage of the workout. We could probably be back in time for our ten o'clock appointment with Carmody.

On the drive over, the producer suggested that Walrus shoot out of the window. "And you can give us a little voice-over," he told me.

"What about? The back of Cupid's van or the foliage along the roadside?"

"Anything that rekindles some of those fabulous Killebrew memories. Remember the first rule of sportscasting: never let the pictures speak for themselves."

So, while Walrus's camera caught the passing countryside, I waxed nostalgic, mainly about riding at Keeneland. "It's a horseman's track," I found myself saying, "and the scene of some of the world's most important yearling sales. The crowds there know racing so well, they don't have to be spoon-fed. Back when I rode there, the fans could be trusted to figure out what was going on down on the track without a public address announcer. They relied on their own eyes or the comments of the guy with the binoculars standing next to them."

And so it went. We taped For Cupid's Sake unloading from the van on the Keeneland backstretch, then got some footage of a fast early-morning mile. The filly's regular rider, Alfie Quinn, was on her back for the work. We had the tape rolling when he dismounted, close enough to pick up his conversation with Richard Sandford.

"One thirty-seven and four," the trainer said, peering at the stopwatch in his hand. "A little quicker than I wanted."

"Well, boss, *she* wanted to go even faster," Quinn said. "I wore myself out just holding her."

"Can we have a word, Alfie?" I said.

Quinn grinned for Walrus's camera and reached over to shake my hand. "Well, Coley Killebrew, I'll be damned. How you doin', jock? I knew that restaurant of yours would go bust and you'd have to go to work for a living."

"Running a restaurant's harder work than this, and I'll have you know I'm still in business. What about this filly? You got a Preakness winner?"

"Hell, we had the Derby in our back pocket, and the Good Lord just said, 'Not today, Alfie.' Sure, we can take the Preakness. With just a little luck. Can't count on a thing in racing, Coley. You should know that better than anybody."

"Too true," I agreed ruefully.

While For Cupid's Sake was still cooling out, we hustled back to the farm for our ten A.M. interview with Carmody. The billionaire could keep us waiting all he wanted, but it didn't seem advisable to return the favor.

We were set up and ready on time, but Carmody came scurrying by, waving an impatient hand and saying, "Not today, gents. Sorry. Let's try again tomorrow." Then he was off without further explanation. Lew, Walrus, and I looked at each other in bemusement.

"Why's he jerking us around?" Lew asked. "He knows what we're going to ask him, and he's been interviewed on TV enough not to be camera shy."

"Power," Walrus said. "And as Friedrich Nietzsche observed, 'The love of power is the demon of men.' Still, what's the point of having it if you don't exercise it once in a while?"

Lew stared at the big man, open-mouthed, then looked at me for some explanation. "Student of philosophy," I said. But Lew's mouth remained open.

Since Carmody had given us the brush-off, we goofed around until that afternoon, when we caught up with Richard Sandford outside For Cupid's Sake's stall. Evidently, he'd had a pleasant lunch, because he was only mildly antagonistic and agreed to be interviewed without much hesitation.

"Nice work this morning," I said when Walrus had set up.

"Well, like I told Alfie Quinn," Sandford said, a bit stiltedly since he was aware of the camera, "I was hoping for a little slower. But Cupid was well within herself. I think it sets her up well for the Preakness. She won't leave her race on the training track, I'll guarantee you that."

I fed him a few more innocuous queries, then said, "You're a pretty amazing guy, Richard."

"Oh?" He stared at me, the light of suspicion dancing in his eyes.

"It's not every day that a trainer with only a few years on the job has the success you've had with For Cupid's Sake."

He relaxed, tried a smile and settled for a smirk. "I've loved horses ever since I was a little kid."

"What sort of work did you do before?"

He hesitated only a second. "I was with the government."

"Politics?"

"Law enforcement. I spent twelve years with the DEA."

"The Drug Enforcement Administration. Interesting work?"

"You could say it was interesting. But this is what I really wanted to do. So when the opportunity presented itself, I jumped at it."

"A pretty big jump, wasn't it? From DEA agent to head trainer for a major stable?"

"As I say, I've always been around horses. Maybe Mr. Carmody took a chance on me, but I don't think I've given him any reason to regret it."

"Tell us a little about the DEA. What were some of the cases you worked on?"

"Past history," Sandford said.

"C'mon. No false modesty here. Weren't you one of the agents that arrested Paolo Rodriguez?" Lew, standing out of camera range but in my line of sight, raised one eyebrow.

"Stop the tape," Sandford ordered.

Walrus looked at Lew, who nodded.

"I thought we were going to stick to the questions on your list," Sandford said.

"We are," I lied.

"The questions are supposed to be about For Cupid's Sake," Sandford said.

"Right. Actually, I was just getting around to that."

Sandford frowned. "Getting around to what?"

"I heard For Cupid's Sake was once owned by Rodriguez."

Sandford paused a beat, then said neutrally, "That's right."

"And she was part of a stable of animals confiscated because they'd been purchased with drug money?"

"That's right. So?" Sandford asked, looking vaguely uneasy now.

"Were you involved in the auctioning of the horses?"

"There were a couple of us working that, yes."

"And shortly after the sale of For Cupid's Sake to James Carmody you began working here. . . ."

"What the hell are you implying?"

"Nothing," I said, my voice cracking in innocence. "Just getting the facts straight."

"Well, here are the goddamn facts," Sandford said. "I grew up on a ranch near Rawlings, Wyoming, and I've always loved horses, like I said. I was lucky enough to meet Mr. Carmody through my work at the DEA. He offered me the job and I grabbed it with both hands."

"When you were with the DEA, did you ever work with anybody named Sonny Marquez, or Dougherty or La Nasa?"

Sandford frowned in concentration. "I don't think so, but agents change their names more often than they do their shirts. What's that got to do with anything?"

"What about Vickie Salazaar?" I asked.

Sandford blinked but stayed relatively unruffled. "She an agent, too?" I nodded. "Look, the DEA's got a hell of a lot of people working for it. I'm happy I'm no longer one of them."

"You didn't like the work?"

"I was there a long time. It's a tough job and you don't get much back. Not the kind of occupation that makes you feel glad to be alive. That's how I feel now. Glad to be alive. Glad to be training a fine stable of horses."

"Can we go back on the record?" I asked, gesturing toward Walrus.

"Sure. If we're going to discuss horses and not what I did or didn't do with the DEA. That part of my life is behind me."

Walrus started rolling again, and Sandford and I discussed the advantages and disadvantages of the tongue tie.

On the drive back to the hotel Lew asked me, "What was that DEA stuff all about?"

"Just trying to loosen him up," I replied.

"Loosen him up? He practically walked out on you."

"Hey, I'm still a bug boy in this interview business," I said. "The only way we learn is by making mistakes."

41

THE NEXT day was the last before Carmody and company would be taking off for the Baltimore area, so I figured the billionaire would finally be ready to carve us a few minutes out of his schedule. But when we arrived, he was not there to greet us. In his stead the considerably lovelier Lula Dorian informed us that he was in an emergency meeting.

Lew scowled and asked, "How long will he be tied up?"

Lula shrugged her shoulders, causing her silk blouse to expand and contract. "Could be minutes, hours, or days. But he did say he wanted you to have run of the house while you wait, so he must be feeling a little guilty. He's not usually that thoughtful."

Lew turned to me. "What do you think? Do we wait or—"

"Oh, Coley, I forgot," Lula interrupted. "J.D. did want to see *you* when you got here."

Lew rolled his eyes. Walrus sighed and said, "Do you have any Calistoga?"

"What's that?" Lula asked.

"Fizz water."

"In the bar, next room over."

"Got something ninety proof or more to put in the fizz water?" Lew asked.

"Anything your heart desires," Lula told him over her shoulder as she led me to the showplace office.

She did not enter, merely made an about-face and hip-switched away.

In the room were several men and women who seemed to be in the midst of hatching something devious. "Ah, Coley," Carmody said, greeting me with unusual cordiality. "Vida, this is Coley Killebrew."

Vida "Ma" Barker offered me her hand. The evangelist was even more startling than her video image. She towered over me, of course—many women do—and her demure business suit managed to conceal her voluptuousness about as well as her tower of blond cotton-candy-style big hair downplayed her height. Her blue-eyed gaze held a potent combination of warmth, strength, intensity, and come-hither. I think calculation was in there somewhere, too, but you had to search for it. In that instant I'd have followed her myself, even though my head knew her destination was nowhere I wanted to go.

She said, "It's a pleasure meeting you, Mr. Killebrew. J.D. has been telling us of your skill as a horseman. I'm sorry I've never seen you in action."

"I'm happy to say I have seen *you* in action, ma'am."

She smiled, taking my statement for a compliment.

Carmody briefly introduced me to the other half-dozen people in the room, mostly male and much less memorable. It turned out they were his media experts, the best known of them Burt Lincoln, a gent with a sour, slightly bloated face. The guy so reeked of cynicism that he'd have been a disaster on the tube himself, but he'd engineered the successful broadcast assaults of any number of conservative office-seekers.

"These folks want to package me like a box of dog biscuits," Carmody cackled. "Can you beat that?"

"Can't be done," I said, playing up to his ego. "You're too unique to be packaged."

"That's what I think, but I'm paying these boys a lot of green. They're supposedly the best in their business."

I stood there smiling and waited for him to get to the point. It didn't take long. "The thing of it is, Burt here tells me I shouldn't be doing this documentary of yours."

"I can't imagine why," I said, looking inquiringly at Lincoln. "It could only be good publicity." The spin doctor stared at me as if I were the main reason for his indigestion. He said nothing.

"Of course, I had to explain to him I'd given you my word," Carmody said. "And Burt understands what that means, right, Burt?"

Burt's overripe face broke into a pained smile. "It means you're the boss, J.D.," he said.

"Pre-cisely," Carmody replied.

I had no idea what the dynamics were of the relationship between Carmody and Burt, and I didn't care. Not as long as the big boss man was still going to let me hang around.

"Now, if you'll excuse us, Coley . . . ?" he said.

"Sure." I edged toward the door. "I'll be here whenever you're ready for our interview."

Carmody wagged his head. "Not today, señor. These birds are gonna have me and Vida tied up for another couple hours at least, and I got a whole list of stuff to take care of before we fly to Baltimore. But I got an idea. It'll save me time and give that oversized cameraman of yours some good shots—what Burt calls photo ops. It'll also save your network some bucks, so everybody benefits."

"Sounds good so far. What's the idea?"

"You and your cameraman join me and For Cupid's Sake on our flight tomorrow. Interview me in the air. It's an hour from here to Baltimore. That should give you enough of me, and then you can leave me alone."

"It's the kind of plan I'd expect from the next President of the U.S.," I said with a reasonably straight face. Carmody beamed. Vida chuckled. Burt glowered.

The change in travel plans required another selling job on Walrus, who was not happy about sharing a private jet with what he called "a herd of thoroughbreds."

"Think how I feel," Lew told him that night at dinner. "I wasn't even invited."

"The passenger space is limited," I explained. "Carmody's girlfriend isn't invited, either."

"You can take my place," Walrus told Lew.

"Not if we want video of the interview," I reminded him.

"It's easy to do," Walrus began. "I only—"

I kicked him under the table.

"It's easy for a pro," I said. "No offense intended, Lew, but we don't want some amateur shooting this documentary, do we?"

"I guess not," Lew said. "And, to tell the truth, I'd be a little nervous myself with all that horseflesh stomping around."

Walrus's eyes opened wide and he turned pale. I pretended not to notice.

42

THE FOLLOWING morning, Sandford and the traveling grooms were walking the horses up the ramp into the side of the jet when we arrived at the private plane hangar at Blue Grass Field. Walrus dutifully aimed his video camera at the loading process, but he looked more skittish than the animals.

"Nothing to worry about," I told him. "They've been flying racehorses for fifty years."

"What happens if they don't like being off the ground?" Walrus asked.

"The flight attendant gives them a stiff vodka."

"Don't joke with me, Coley."

"Remember what Roosevelt said about fear?"

"Remember what Alexander Pope said about fools rushing in where angels fear to tread?" he replied.

We waited to board until the more important passengers were settled in. The horses had been placed in wooden boxes bolted to the center of the plane, facing front in a single line. Their heads and necks stuck up past the top bar of the boxes. In front of the boxes were two rows of double seats, a couple of which Walrus and I occupied.

"I wish I didn't have the horses behind me," Walrus said.

"Relax," I said, "they're not packing handguns, and you'll hear them coming if they break loose." He didn't look comforted.

The other human passengers at the front of the plane were Carmody, Richard Sandford, and a guy named Franklin, who was almost as large as Walrus. A bodyguard, I guessed. While our seats were similar to what we would have had in a commercial airline's business class, Franklin's was in a jump seat attached to the right bulkhead, permitting him to see more of the plane. He wasn't a talkative fellow, but I did hear him mutter that the seat reminded him of flying in troop carriers in 'Nam.

The traveling grooms and Dr. Julio Alvarez, Carmody's personal veterinarian, took the remaining bulkhead jump seats in the rear.

At takeoff the grooms stood beside the animals, calming them. Walrus closed his eyes and began to hum to himself.

"Your man airsick?" Carmody asked me.

"No. Just meditating."

"You flown with horses before, right?"

"No. I always made separate travel arrangements."

"Smart man," Carmody said. "There's a story about Determine flying across the country to the Derby back in the fifties. Before takeoff, the pilot handed the horse's trainer a pistol and said if the animal started kicking up a fuss, he'd have to shoot him. The trainer said, 'I'd shoot myself before I'd shoot Determine.' "

"Are those the instructions you gave Richard Sandford? To shoot you before he shoots For Cupid's Sake?"

"Nope. Much as I love that filly, she'd have to take the bullet."

We'd been in the air for almost forty minutes when Carmody said, "Okay, Killebrew. Let's do this thing."

I nudged Walrus, and he pried his bulk out of the seat and rolled the video camera. I hoped the activity would take his mind off his fear.

I started slowly, sticking to the preapproved questions.

"What made you buy For Cupid's Sake?"

"She was such a sweet little yearling. I just sort of fell in love with her. I had to have her."

"You could tell she had potential?" I asked.

"Nothing about her bloodline suggested it. But I had a gut reaction. And those I always follow."

"What are your plans for the filly after the Preakness?"

"It depends on how she does and how well she comes out of the race. If she runs good, I'd sure like to try for the Belmont. Obviously, if she wins one or both of those races, I've got the Eclipse Award for best three-year-old filly in my pocket. If she doesn't win, we may point her for some of the big filly races in the summer, just to make sure she gets her due. If she does win the Preakness and the Belmont, I'd say the heck with the filly races and look for what it'd take to make her Horse of the Year."

"You mean the Breeders' Cup."

"Sure, and not the Distaff, but the Classic."

"Pretty ambitious," I said.

"Well now, Coley, I may not be everything the press says about me, but I do admit to being just a tad ambitious."

"Is that ambition what's leading you to run for public office?"

"I've heard that vague rumor about me seeking the greatest office in the land. But right now I think it'd be more appropriate if we kept our conversation on the sport of kings."

So that brought us back to horses again. I asked him about Cupid's rider, and he allowed as how Alfie Quinn, even though he let the horse down at the Derby, certainly knew his way around a track.

"What's your trainer, Richard Sandford, think about your plans for For Cupid's Sake?"

"Well," Carmody said, grinning at Sandford sitting one seat back, "Richard and I see eye-to-eye on just about everything. When it comes to our filly, I mean."

"It was a pretty bold move to turn your stable over to a guy with relatively little experience."

Carmody didn't blink. "Like I said, I go by my gut reactions. And this one paid off. Richard's a natural. Grew up around horses."

"It's sort of ironic that you've got Paolo Rodriguez to thank for both your horse and your trainer," I said.

That one stopped him. His face was blank for a second or two, then relaxed into a smile. "The Good Lord works in wondrous ways," he said. "I set out to do something for my country. And in so doing, I wound up with one of the best trainers around and *the* best thoroughbred."

"Could you fill in the blanks about the events that led to your meeting Richard Sandford?"

"Oh, I think that's been part of the record for a couple years now. I wouldn't want to bore anybody with old stories. And besides, we seem to be descending, Coley. Your cameraman ought to sit down and fasten his seat belt."

End of interview. End of flight.

The landing at Baltimore-Washington International Airport seemed smoother than average to me. The pilot probably took special care since, with a boss as capricious as his, anything less than a three-point could have gotten him fired.

The plane taxied across the tarmac toward the private hangars, and as soon as its forward thrust stopped, a dark sedan drove out to meet it. Four men got out wearing dark *Reservoir Dogs* suits, more security guards of the breed that followed James Deth Carmody wherever he went. They fanned out around the plane.

The four-legged passengers were the first to disembark, their handlers easing them down a special ramp. That accomplished, we mere humans followed, led by Franklin, who surveyed the scene, gun in hand. Carmody and Sandford stayed in his wake, leaving Walrus, Dr. Alvarez, and me to fend for ourselves.

As I was descending the portable steps, a powder-blue stretch Mercedes limousine roared up. Not an authorized vehicle. The security force responded like antibodies ready to fight off infection. They surrounded Carmody with guns drawn and pointed in the direction of the limo. Its back door swung open and a professional wild man, wearing a leather jumpsuit that perfectly matched the car in color, leaped out.

"You monkey-faced old bastard," Halcyon shouted at Carmody.

Franklin was a bit unnerved by the rock star's failure to be intimidated by all the hardware. "Hands high," he ordered in a commanding voice.

The rocker seemed not to have heard him. He continued to move toward Carmody and the armed group. Sandford stepped forward to intercept him.

"Stay where you are," the trainer warned, putting restraining hands on the jumpsuit.

Sandford's involvement didn't make Franklin any happier. He appeared unsure whether to let the trainer handle it or not. But he was pro enough to realize that firing his weapon might not aid the cause.

Halcyon's focus remained unwaveringly on Carmody, who peeked out from behind his guards.

"You can't threaten me and get away with it!" Halcyon shouted.

"Who the hell is threatening you?" Carmody yelled back, his voice even higher-pitched and screechier than normal. "Who the hell is this crazy asshole?"

"He owns Headbanger," Sandford said, his eyes steady on Halcyon. He seemed strangely calm. Maybe he'd realized that no weapon could possibly be concealed under the rocker's tight leathers. "You better get back in that zootmobile of yours, pal," he said. "Or else your nice colt's gonna be minus an owner."

Halcyon didn't seem to hear or see Sandford. For him, Carmody was the only other person sharing the tarmac. "You fuck with my horse, you limp-dick old monkeyman, and I'll fuck with you."

"What the hell is this gooney-bird shouting about?" Carmody yelled. "Goddamnit, Richard, this is the kind of shit you're supposed to take care of."

Franklin looked to Sandford for guidance. The ex-DEA agent nodded. That's what it took for Franklin and two of the other security guards to advance on Halcyon. It also served as a cue for another figure to emerge gracefully from the rear of the limo. Martin Grosso raised his arms, his hands clearly empty.

"Gentlemen, gentlemen," Grosso said, his voice pleasantly conversational. "There's no need for drastic action here."

He was so self-possessed, he riveted the attention of everyone. We could have been posing for a group photo.

"Hal, you've delivered your message," Grosso told his client softly. "Now it's time to get back in the car."

"Must be on drugs," Carmody said, just loud enough for everyone to hear. His words set Halcyon off again.

"What're you on, Carmody?" the rocker asked. "What makes you think you can pick up a phone and threaten me and my horse like I was shit or something?"

Martin Grosso slid between the guards and Halcyon and turned to face the musician. "You've made your point. Now it's time to get back in the car." His words were still soothing, but his actions became more forceful as he grasped the rocker's shoulders, spun him around, and pushed him toward the limo.

As soon as the musician was safely back in the car, Martin turned back in Carmody's direction. Raising his voice only slightly, he said, "My friend merely wanted to tell you that you've made a serious mistake. We don't respond well to intimidation."

"What're you talkin' about?" Carmody asked.

"Save the innocent act for the gullible masses," Martin said. "Whatever kind of bullshit you're trying to pull is your business. But when you drag us into it by issuing your insipid little threats, you're making a serious mistake. Headbanger will be racing this weekend. And if by some bizarre chance your threat was serious—that is, if you try to harm the horse or the jockey or Halcyon—please understand that you will be repaid in kind."

"Why you arrogant little punk—"

Martin Grosso sighed. "You're lucky I'm . . . more temperate than my brother." With a gesture toward the private plane, he added, "Otherwise, you might have developed engine trouble up there." He paused, a businessman considering his options before he said with an illustrative tap on his chest, "Or maybe heart trouble. I understand you're hypertense."

"You dare to threaten—"

"Mr. Carmody," Martin Grosso said, holding up his hands. "You started this."

"You're talking like an idiot. I started nothing."

"Then our mission has been a success. Have a good day." Martin smiled again, turned and slipped inside the limo. As it glided away you could almost hear the tension level drop.

Carmody marched toward me.

"Killebrew, what do you know about that little prick?"

"He's a rock and roll performer."

"Not the musician. The other guy."

"Martin Grosso. His big brother is Huey Grosso."

"The mobster?"

"That shoe fits," I said.

"Then what you were talking about is more than a rumor. This friggin' Halcyon cretin and his hoodlum partner are using thug tactics to get horses out of the race."

"It sounded more like they were accusing you of that," I pointed out. But I might as well have said nothing.

"Where'd your rumor come from? I want Richard to put somebody on it."

By now I was sorry I'd ever mentioned the bloody rumor. "It was going around."

"Around, huh? Gimme a name, damnit."

I've never responded well to demands, and I wasn't about to expose the Lundens to Carmody's charming ways. "I don't have a name."

"No? Well then, sonny boy, when you get one, I'll continue to co-operate with your friggin' movie. Right now, it's on hold, and you can find your own goddamn transportation into Baltimore."

Walrus and I watched Carmody and his crew walk to the hangar where two Lincoln Continentals awaited them. When the sedans departed, our flight bags remained abandoned orphans on the tarmac.

"There's a man who doesn't take I-don't-know for an answer," I said, watching the Lincolns get smaller and smaller.

"Misplaced aggression," Walrus said. "He wasn't really mad at you."

"That'll make the walk to the cab stand much more bearable."

"Maybe we'll get a ride after all," Walrus said, gesturing to a neutral-colored sedan that was bearing down on us.

"And maybe not," I replied when the car came to a stop scant inches from where we were standing.

CIA Agent Singleton rolled down the passenger window and shook his head like a disappointed schoolteacher. "I thought you were a man who knew how to get along in this life, Killebrew. Now I have to tell my supervisor I misjudged you. That's bad for me. And even worse for you."

Not waiting for any kind of reply, Singleton rolled up the window and his poker-faced partner drove them away.

"Who was that?" Walrus inquired.

I told him.

"How'd he know Carmody was landing here?"

"I'm not sure, but I think I know how Halcyon found out. Singleton told him."

"Secret agents, organized crime, rock music, and us, all in some sort of cosmic jumble. It's a weird world, isn't it?"

"But the world isn't really to blame," I said, lifting my suitcase and heading for the terminal.

43

"SO HOW did that in-flight interview go yesterday?" Lew Totter asked brightly, carefully bedecking a half slice of toast with
butter and grape jelly. He'd just arrived at our Baltimore hotel and was
joining Walrus and me for a late morning breakfast.

"Not bad up to a point," I said, "but that's the good news."

Lew picked up the toast and bit into it with exaggerated care, looking across the table at me warily. "Okay. Let me have it."

"Carmody has withdrawn his cooperation."

"Shit." Lew put down the toast. "What happened?"

I hesitated.

"The man is moody," Walrus said.

"Good answer," I said.

"Well, you better bring what you have and come up to Barry's suite
with me," Lew said glumly. "He'll be thrilled to hear this."

"Gallen's in town?"

"Sure. Having no real work to do, he naturally had to get here a
couple of days before the rest of us."

And, as we discovered an hour later, he had to have accommodations of royal, or at least presidential, standards to do his no work
in. Loretta Simmons, lovely as always in a long skirt and white silk
blouse, met us at the door and ushered us into the suite's reception
area, which was no larger than the downstairs dining room. She had
set up an office for herself in there, and, judging by the scattered papers, notebooks, and humming computer, she at least had plenty of
work to do.

She suggested we loiter in the equally spacious living room beyond.
Barry would be with us shortly, she said, gesturing to the closed bedroom door.

After watching her elegant ankles carry her back through the door,

I turned my attention to the other sights in the tastefully and expensively decorated room.

The hotel named its suites after Preakness winners, and Gallen's could only be the Secretariat. An original painting on the wall depicted the 1973 finish, Ron Turcotte's confident ride on the Meadow Stable colt contrasting with Lafitt Pincay's desperate efforts on the second-place Sham.

"The *Daily Racing Form* clocked him in track record time that day," I told Walrus and Lew as we waited for Gallen to emerge. "One fifty-three and two. But the track's clocking was one fifty-five."

"Which one went in the books?" Lew asked.

"Neither one. They finally compromised on 1:54.2. Canonero II's record still stood."

"Isn't modern technology wonderful?" Walrus remarked.

"It's what keeps us in business," Barry Gallen said from the bedroom doorway. The cable executive was finally ready to join us. Though it was gaining on noon, he still wore a bathrobe and a bleary-eyed expression. "What's so important?"

Before any of us could answer, the phone rang once. Loretta Simmons picked it up in the reception room and appeared in the doorway a moment later.

"Clara McGuinn for you on line two," she told Gallen.

Gallen grabbed the living room extension with a vengeance. "Thanks so much for returning my call," he said with heavy sarcasm, apparently oblivious to the rest of us in the room.

He waited for her reply, then asked, "Then where the hell were you?"

Lew got up from his chair, looking uncomfortable. He indicated the door with his head. As the three of us filed out into Loretta's makeshift office, we heard Gallen say sharply, "Well, I do think it's my business where you are at ten-thirty at night. You sure as hell weren't home."

Loretta raised an eyebrow at Gallen's implied accusation. "The pot calling the kettle noir," she whispered.

Lew seemed to be on the verge of giggling, but he restrained himself. He sat on a couch near French windows that led to a balcony looking out over downtown Baltimore.

From the other room came Gallen bellowing, "Well, maybe you should," and slamming the phone down hard enough to rattle the glasses on the portable bar.

"I think Barry is ready for you, gentlemen," Loretta said gaily.

When we reentered the room, he said, "Well?"

"We've got some excellent footage," Lew said with transparently phony brightness. Actually, he hadn't sampled any of it.

"Okay," Gallen said. "Then why aren't we happy as kings?"

Lew offered me the floor. I recounted once again Carmody's latest decision.

Curiously, though, Gallen didn't seem all that interested in my news. He was distracted, presumably by his conversation with Clara McGuinn. He excused himself and went back into Loretta's office. A second later she joined us and Gallen closed himself off from us in her temporary office.

A red light glowed on the phone in the living room and Lew whispered, "He's off again. Hunting the most dangerous of all games."

"Naughty, naughty," Loretta cautioned.

"He ever hit on you, Lo?" Lew asked her.

"You're the only one who ever hit on me. Barry's smarter than that. Though not much, I grant you."

"Well, he's liable to be all day trying to find happiness," Lew said. "Do we have to sit here . . . ?"

Loretta shook her head. "There's another exit, fortunately."

Lew turned to me. "I suppose I should take a peek at the stuff you got."

I handed the tapes Walrus had shot over to him and he began to screen them on a VCR that was among the Secretariat suite's amenities. About a half hour into them Gallen stormed into the room, glanced at the television screen, then continued on to his bedroom without another word to us.

Loretta returned to her area, and Lew nodded toward the screen with an approving smile on his face. Apparently Walrus's camera work made the grade; he could add cinematography to his other dubious achievements.

"I think we might just have enough for an acceptable documentary," Lew said. "But we'd better put in a little more time at the track adding to the footage. Walrus, you can use your telescopic lenses on For Cupid's Sake."

We agreed to meet in the lobby in half an hour.

44

WE SPENT the better part of the day strolling and shooting. Neither Halcyon's nor Carmody's barns were open to the press. They were at almost opposite ends of the stable area, guarded by equally alert, hard-looking types.

Walrus, Lew, and I were on hand to enjoy the spectacle of reporter Hud Barrow trying unsuccessfully to gain entry to Headbanger's stable. The ancient scribe approached a guard who could not have been more serious and determined if he'd been watching over Buckingham Palace.

"What the frak's this all about?" Barrow complained. "I've never heard of the press being kept out of a stable."

"Those are my orders, suh," the guard said stolidly.

"There's something goddamned weird here," Hud said, turning back to me. "You know what's going on?"

I shook my head.

Noticing Walrus, Hud said, "Keep that camera out of my face, muscle boy."

"We're not taping now," Walrus said.

"Yeah, well, try taking my picture without permission and I'll make you eat that camera."

Walrus smiled at him and said, " 'A man of my spiritual intensity does not eat cameras,' to almost quote George Bernard Shaw."

"Huh?" Hud turned to me. "Is this son of a bitch for real?"

"Real enough to snap your spindly bones like dried twigs," I said. With a growl the old reporter stomped off.

Lew was staring at the stable guards. "Walrus, why don't you get some tape on these guys?"

"Don't even think of it," the guard who'd dealt with Hud said, glaring at Walrus and his camera.

Walrus stared back at the big guard and told Lew, "I'll do it if you want. But there might be some damage to the camera."

Apparently offering obeisance to the bottom line, Lew told him to let it go. But as we walked away, he instructed Walrus in soft tones to use a zoom on the guard. We later got similar shots of the forces arrayed outside Carmody's barns. Then we visited some more hospitable outfits, catching up on the doings of several of the other horses who'd been at Churchill Downs—notably Sabisa, The Loan Arranger, Warm Regards, and Apostle.

We also covered the newcomers who hadn't made the Derby starting gate, the most notable being the Maryland local Ducks in a Row, who was on a five-race winning streak against lesser competition. The trainers, the grooms, and a couple of visiting owners were all glad to talk, about their horses, about the weather, about the racing game generally, which made a welcome change from the paranoid connections of Headbanger and For Cupid's Sake.

At the end of the day Lew seemed in high spirits. "This could turn out all right for us, you know? Assuming Cupid comes through and wins. What do you think her chances are?"

"Headbanger's still going to be even-money," I said noncommittally. "For Cupid's Sake figures to be a three-to-one shot in the Morning Line, maybe shorter by race time. The colt's a logical favorite over the filly."

"But the filly's got the biggest bodyguards," Walrus pointed out.

45

B Y THE time I woke up the next morning, the odds had changed.

Sometime during the previous night, the TV in my hotel room reported, Headbanger had fallen victim to a virus. Halcyon's veterinarian had worked on the animal throughout the night. According to CNN, the horse's condition was serious.

I ate breakfast alone in the hotel coffee shop, listening to the buzz from the tables around me. The withdrawal of the Preakness favorite was apparently imminent, and the ramifications of such a cataclysm were the only topic of conversation.

"Glory Regained's people are going to be kicking themselves for skipping the Preakness now," said one self-appointed expert.

"Are you kidding? He'd never have been able to get up in time at a mile and three-sixteenths. They're smart to wait for the Belmont."

"Aren't you guys worried about the poor *horse?*" an exasperated feminine voice demanded. I wondered if they knew what she was talking about.

Even my waitress got into the act. "It's like the Triple Crown is jinxed this year, huh?" she said, pouring my second cup of coffee.

"Not a good year for favorites," I agreed.

"What's goin' on, do you think?"

I wished I knew. I was almost desperate enough to ask for her opinion.

When I got back to my room, I turned on CNN again and discovered there had been new developments. Halcyon's trainer, Eddie Krayle, had gone before the cameras, looking weary but somewhat relieved. Eddie was a decent guy, and I felt for him.

"The infection seems to have been halted," the trainer said, "but Headbanger is much too sick to be running in any race just now."

"How about the Belmont, Eddie?" an offscreen reporter demanded.

"Too soon to say, but I would doubt we could have him ready in time. I'll have to talk to the horse's owner about things before we can determine any future plans."

"Will Halcyon be making a statement himself?"

Eddie looked a little annoyed. I'm sure he wanted to ask what they thought a rock singer could tell them about the horse that his trainer couldn't. But Eddie understood how publicity works and said he didn't know.

"Will Headbanger be staying on the East Coast?"

"As soon as he's well enough to fly, we'll be taking him home to L.A."

I wished I were going with the horse. I felt that I was in over my head, confused and without a plan.

46

THAT NIGHT, Walrus and I were walking back to our hotel from a dinner of Maryland crab cakes in a nearby restaurant when Halcyon's powder-blue limo pulled up at the curb. The back door opened and a smiling Martin Grosso stepped out.

"Gentlemen, we'll give you a lift," he said in his soft, even voice.

"It's just two more blocks," I said.

"We have a slightly farther destination in mind."

One of Martin's traveling companions joined him, powerfully built, wearing a dark leather jacket and dark pants. He gestured with the gun in his fist that we should get into the car.

We got in.

Halcyon patted the leather rear seat next to him. Walrus sat next to me. Martin and the muscle took the jump seats. The limo promptly pulled away, whizzing past our hotel in seconds.

The rock star stared at us without expression. It was as if he'd been recently sedated, not exactly the impossible dream.

"Gentlemen, we need your assistance," Martin told us.

"You've got a very unique way of asking for a favor," I said.

"Perhaps. But sometimes necessity takes precedence over politeness."

" 'Politeness is to human nature what warmth is to wax,' " Walrus quoted.

Martin stared at him and raised one eyebrow. "Schopenhauer?"

"Who else?" Walrus said.

I'd had enough of that. "What do you need?" I asked.

"We want you to get us into Carmody's barn."

"You picked the wrong guys," I said. "You'd have a better chance of getting in by yourselves. We're on the outs with Carmody."

"You flew in with him," Martin said. "Word is you're working with him on some television project."

"That's kaput. We're off his guest list."

"Too bad," Martin said. "I was hoping to avoid violence."

Walrus, sitting next to me, tensed.

"I'm not like my brother, Killebrew. Anybody'll tell you that. I abhor his way of life and I've done everything I can to avoid it. However, I am not a pushover, and it was unwise of Carmody to think I was."

"You think he's responsible because Headbanger got sick?"

"Not sick," Halcyon said, surfacing from his stupor. "The animal was poisoned. His food was full of . . . whatever that stuff is."

"Potassium thiocyanate," Martin said. "It's a medication humans use to lower their blood pressure."

"And guess who's got high blood pressure?" Halcyon said. "Mr. James Fucking Carmody, that's who."

I almost laughed. "Let me see if I have this right. You think Carmody used his own personal medicine to make your horse sick?"

Halcyon looked at Martin Grosso, who replied, "A more pertinent question is: Who else would profit from Headbanger's toxicity?"

"How bad off is the horse?" I asked.

"He'll recover, but not in time for this weekend's race."

"But he will recover, right?"

"He better fuckin' recover," Halcyon said.

"There's a matter of honor to be settled," Martin Grosso said. Here, his manner indicated, was a serious young man to whom all other possibilities had been closed.

Martin took a cellular phone from his pocket and dialed a number, informing the answering party, "We'll be there in ten minutes. No sense waiting for us, though. Just go ahead with what we talked about."

He closed the phone and slipped it back into his pocket.

"It's idiotic to kill somebody because he made a horse sick," I said.

Martin grinned. "No one is going to be killed."

"Then what, For Cupid's Sake?"

"Hell, no," Halcyon said. "Nobody hurtin' any horses with me around."

"Halcyon loves horses," Martin said, with just a touch of sarcasm.

"Then . . . ?"

"You'll see," Halcyon promised. "You'll have a fuckin' ringside seat."

.   .   .

When we arrived at Pimlico's security gate, our passes were checked and we were waved through, though not before Halcyon had obligingly signed his autograph for one of the younger guards. The leather-jacketed leg-breaker still had his gun, but he was carrying it in his pocket.

The limo pulled up inside the stable area, and we were invited to disembark. Martin Grosso led us in a little procession. As we passed the darkened barn where Headbanger had been stabled, we were joined by two more leg-breakers, part of the team that had been guarding Headbanger. We proceeded, as threatening-looking as a lynch mob. If the inhabitants of any of the other barns observed our progress, they probably were happy to see us pass.

"How'd the medicine get into Headbanger's chow?" Walrus asked.

Martin hesitated. "We're looking into that right now," he said, his eyes darting to Halcyon. Evidently he was keeping something from the rock star.

"Access would be limited," I said, pushing the issue to see where it would go. "Somebody close to the animal."

Martin, obviously annoyed, lowered his voice. "We've got a missing groom. Joe Ramirez. We're looking for him, but for all I know, he's back in Mexico, or wherever the hell he's from. He was a drinking buddy of Ha—"

"What are you guys sayin'?" Halcyon asked.

"Nothing important," Martin told him. "Small talk."

At the Jaydee barn, one of Grosso's leg-breakers had established himself where Carmody's guard once sat. Inside the barn, three other of Carmody's team had been gathered and tethered in an empty stall.

Halcyon looked around and his face fell. "The old fart's not here."

"Don't worry," Martin said. "He'll get the news very quickly."

"I want to see his monkey face when he does."

Martin's eyes canvassed a section of the room. He spotted a cellular phone, which he carried over to one of the captured guards.

"I want you to call Carmody," he said.

"I don't know how," the guard said, poker-faced and monotoned.

"You look old enough to know how to use a phone."

"I don't have any number for Mr. Carmody," the guard said, not rising to the bait.

"If something happens around the barn, how do you let him know?"

"I don't let him know. I call his trainer, Richard Sandford. That number I have."

"That'll do fine. Tell him Cupid's acting up. He should bring his vet with him."

"And Carmody," Halcyon added.

"He's not going to do that, Hal," Martin said. "And that sort of request would be like a danger-alert flag. We'll have to settle for Sandford and the vet."

Halcyon was clearly disappointed, but he nodded his agreement. The guard made the call, and only minutes later Sandford and Dr. Julio Alvarez were picked up by leg-breakers just before they reached the barn.

Entering with his unexpected escorts, Sandford took one look at me and asked, "What's going on here, Killebrew?"

"Ask Grosso," I said. "Walrus and I are here under duress."

"I hoped we might use him to distract your guards," Martin Grosso said. "But it wasn't necessary. Everything was accomplished with no harm to anyone. Just a bit of inconvenience." To illustrate this last, he pointed to the guards, tied and gagged now, sitting on the dirt floor of the empty stall.

Sandford stared at Halcyon. "They're gonna love you in prison, Hailstone," he said. "Shave off that hair and pull out those earrings and serve you up on a silver platter to the head con."

"You shut the fuck up," Halcyon said.

"Nobody's going to prison," Martin said confidently, slipping a black case from his pocket. In it was a hypodermic needle and a small vial of liquid.

"In the interest of protecting the horse, I'd like your veterinarian to do the honors," Martin said to Sandford.

"You lowlife bastards," Sandford said. The former DEA agent apparently had had enough. He rushed toward Martin and Halcyon, but hadn't a prayer of getting to them. He was quickly intercepted by one of the leg-breakers.

Walrus threw me a look that was too subtle for others to notice but gave me a clear message: "Maybe now's the time." I shook my head.

Sandford didn't give in easily. He kept struggling with the leg-breaker. It took two more of them to subdue him and tie him to a hitching post.

"It's a goddamn defenseless animal you're hurting," Sandford yelled.

"Headbanger was just as defenseless," Martin said.

"You're blaming us for your horse getting sick?" Sandford asked incredulously.

"Who the hell else—" Halcyon began.

Martin Grosso raised a hand to quell his client. "Not sick," he said. "We explained it all to Killebrew. You can talk to him about it later. Doctor . . . ?"

Dr. Alvarez looked at the vial and read the label. "Procaine penicillin." He looked at Sandford without expression.

"What the hell?" Sandford asked. "An antibiotic?"

Dr. Alverez nodded. "I've used it before on Cupid. For an upper respiritory problem," he said. "It shouldn't cause her any difficulty."

"What's really in the vial?" Sandford asked with some skepticism.

"Just what it says," Martin Grosso replied. "Procaine penicillin. Enough chat. Inject the animal, doctor."

Dr. Alvarez looked at the bound Sandford for guidance.

"If you don't do it, I'll have to ask one of my associates here," Martin said. "Well-meaning and careful as they are, they are not practiced in giving injections to thousand-pound animals. They could easily make a slip. They might actually do the animal some damage. Asking a trained veterinarian to do it is a humane gesture on our part and one that should demonstrate our good faith."

"Good faith," Sandford snorted, but he gave the veterinarian a helpless nod.

Dr. Alvarez performed the injection, and the filly took it in stride. "Now what?" Sandford asked.

"You're not very up on your track history, are you?" Martin said. He turned to me. "You understand what's going on here, don't you, Killebrew?"

I nodded. I'm sure Dr. Alvarez understood, too. Sandford was fairly new to the game, but he'd been around long enough to figure it out, also, as soon as he calmed down.

Employing a mock sports announcer's voice, Martin Grosso said, "The year, 1968. The horse, Dancer's Image. Winner of the Kentucky Derby. But then tragedy. It was not a clean win. The horse's blood test showed evidence of the drug phenylbutazone. No prize money. Lots of bad press. 'Bute's legal now, but procaine penicillin isn't. If Carmody tries to run this fine animal in the Preakness, it will be, in the immortal words of Yogi Berra, déjà vu all over again."

"That monkeyman tries to fuck with us, he gets fucked," Halcyon said somewhat less elegantly.

"That about sums it up," Martin said, returning his voice to its natural low-keyed menace. "Killebrew? Do you and your friend want a lift back to your hotel?"

"No thanks," I said. "We like to walk."

As Halcyon, Grosso, and the thugs started to go, Sandford growled, "The cops'll be on your ass before you go five blocks."

Martin Grosso seemed to mull that over a bit before he answered. "I believe I'd check with your employer before you bring in the police."

"We'll tell them——"

Martin raised a hand. "You'll tell them something. We'll tell them something else. No one will be sure who's telling the truth. But what they will know and *remember* is that For Cupid's Sake had been medicated. If Carmody pulls the filly from the race, there may be a little ripple of curiosity. But if it gets out that she's racing with an illegal substance in her blood, the animal, not to mention Carmody, will drown in the notoriety. Think long and hard about that, Sandford. Adios."

As soon as Martin and Halcyon had left with their thugs, Walrus and I began to untie Sandford and his guards. Dr. Alvarez was examining For Cupid's Sake to make sure no other damage had been done to her.

Sandford rushed to the phone, punched out some numbers, and reached Carmody almost immediately. He filled his boss in on what had happened, finishing with a statement that "Killebrew and the giant camera guy got dragged along."

Sandford listened grim-faced for a moment, then held out the phone to me. "Mr. Carmody wants to talk to you."

Carmody's voice, never a musical instrument at the best of times, was cold, hard, and grating. "I want to know what your involvement is with Halcyon, Killebrew, and I want to know now. No more holding out on me."

"I don't have any involvement with Halcyon. He and Grosso abducted Walrus and me because they thought we were friends of yours and could help get them into your stable."

Carmody made a grunting noise that could just as easily have indicated scorn for or acceptance of my statement. After a moment he said, "Is the situation with the horse as Richard described it?"

"Your vet is here. He can give you a better read on that than I can."

"You ever hear of anything like this?"

"I've already told you I'm no expert on fixed races. Maybe there's a way of getting the medicine out of Cupid's system in time."

Dr. Alvarez stared at me and shook his head from side to side. "This stuff stays with the animal quite a while. We'll be lucky if she's clear in time for the Belmont."

"Your vet is saying no," I relayed.

"I want to talk with him. But first, if it was your goddamn horse, what would you do?"

After a moment's thought, I told him I might take a chance and run her. "If Cupid wins, maybe she'll pass the drug muster. Even if she doesn't pass, losing the purse shouldn't put you on relief, and people will still remember who finished first in the race." The hot water Sandford would be in under the trainer's responsibility rule, I didn't mention.

"The difference between me and you, Killebrew, is that you've got no reputation left to ruin. I've got to be squeaky clean if I expect to run for public office. The bastards're right. Even if it's just medicine, the drug word is a dirty one. I can't afford to let it smear me. I hope I can trust you to keep your mouth shut about all this."

"It's your call," I said.

"That go for your confederate?"

I looked over at Walrus, who was intently studying the horse. "I can vouch for him, too," I said.

The word "thanks" didn't seem to be in Carmody's vocabulary. "Okay, then," he said. "Put Doc Alvarez on the horn."

Walrus and I left the party. The security guys at the main gate were nice enough to hustle us up a cab.

47

BY BREAKFAST time of Preakness Stakes day, television had spread the word: in less than forty-eight hours the top two contenders in the race had been withdrawn. Speaking on James Deth Carmody's behalf, Richard Sandford told the cameras that For Cupid's Sake had a bruised hoof, a minor injury but one that would not be healed soon enough for her to be in top shape for the race. He went on to mouth one of the standard clichés of racing public relations.

"If this were an ordinary horse and an ordinary event, I wouldn't hesitate to run her. But For Cupid's Sake is something special, and there's no way I would recommend to Mr. Carmody that she run in a classic race in anything but the very best of condition."

The reporters followed the standard answer with a standard question. What about the Belmont?

"Oh, yes, we definitely hope to have For Cupid's Sake ready for the Belmont Stakes. She should be back training within a few days. We believe the added distance will pose no problem at all for her."

After breakfast Lew and I approached Barry Gallen's hotel suite with some trepidation. We could hear raised voices through the door, the clipped tones of Geoffrey Paragon lambasting Gallen, and Gallen, with slightly less anger, answering back. The main topic was the removal of For Cupid's Sake from the race.

"How much time and effort did we expend on a bloody nonstarter, Barry?"

"Just tell me how we could possibly have known that, Geoff? Shit happens."

"You just tell me how you could possibly know any of the shit that happens when you're spending all your time bloody bird-watching instead of taking care of business."

Lew looked at me and whispered, "Barry said we should come up."

I shrugged and pressed the buzzer.

Conversation stopped abruptly inside the room. The door was opened by an uncharacteristically glum Loretta Simmons.

Gallen, red-faced, was standing by a window, staring down on Baltimore.

Geoffrey Paragon, as unruffled as ever despite the towering rage he'd been projecting through the closed door, welcomed us almost affably.

"Have a good day, gentlemen," the network chief said. "Enjoy whatever is left of the bloody race."

With that, he headed for the door.

"You're going?" Gallen asked stupidly.

"Is there some reason I should stay?"

Gallen didn't answer. Before exiting, Paragon winked at Loretta, but it didn't cheer her.

"I . . . I'm sorry the documentary on Cupid didn't work out," I said to Gallen.

"Yeah. Well . . . what the hell," Gallen said, somewhat listlessly. "Maybe it's for the best."

"We can still salvage our first idea, Barry," Lew said with forced brightness. "We simply do our usual coverage of all the horses. Coley and I can go out to Pimlico right now, catch the crowds coming in."

"Whatever." Gallen turned to Loretta and said, "Get me on the next flight to L.A."

She raised an eyebrow, and he explained, "I don't have much interest in the race anymore. I want to get home, see what the hell is going on there."

"Then you want us—" Lew began.

"Do whatever it is you do," Gallen said heatedly. "Just don't bother me with it."

Lew started to say something, but I thought a silent retreat was preferable to any more words. I tapped him on the shoulder and pointed to the door.

Outside, where Walrus was waiting for us, Lew admitted he'd never seen Gallen so down.

"He took a pretty good brow-beating from Paragon," I said.

"Yeah. And I gather things ain't so good at home, either. I hear Mrs. Mac's stopped sitting home all alone while he's out on these little 'business trips.' "

"Good for her," I said.

"Man, Paragon was really pissed off. I mean, it's not that big a deal. So we shot some footage on a horse that got scratched. I remember a whole reel from a bullfight got lost or stolen and we had to cancel the goddamn show and he just shrugged it off."

"Well, you never know what these big business types have on their minds," I said. "Boxes within boxes."

"I know what you mean, brother. What say we find a nice little boite where I can have one perfect martini before heading out to Pimlico?"

"I'd like lunch," Walrus said.

"Swell," Lew replied. "That'll give me time for at least *two* martinis."

48

WALRUS JOINED us at the Preakness, using Gallen's ticket. "This is the best seat I ever had for any sports event," he said. "I mean, my high school basketball seats weren't this good."

"Gallen picked 'em," Lew said. "But it took the wiles of a true dog robber to come up with them."

"These are almost the exact seats we had at the Derby," I said, considering our distance from the track and our view of the finish line.

"Technically, I'd say we're over one section," Lew said.

Turning my head, I saw a line of vacant seats in the fourth row behind us. "Do you suppose those empties belong to Carmody?"

"I do, indeed," Lew said.

Walrus began to aim his camera at the crowd. Lew suggested he go down to the rail to pick up the post parade. "Then hustle on back here, and we can get footage from the best seats in the house. We'll be able to borrow the network feed, but it'll help to be able to intercut some shots of our own."

For the Preakness post parade they play a tune I always thought was "O Tannenbaum." The locals claim it's "Maryland, My Maryland." The field that paraded to the familiar melody certainly wasn't the best ever to go postward in the race, but it was among the most contentious.

Preakness fields are traditionally smaller than Kentucky Derby fields, but the series of defections of name horses this year had served to embolden some moon shooters, and fourteen hopefuls were on their way to the post.

Always known as the "Middle Jewel," the Preakness normally has one edge over the more famous Derby and the more challenging Belmont: in almost every year, a single potential Triple Crown winner is in the Preakness field. But with the withdrawal of Headbanger, that wasn't true this time. With no clear favorite in the race, the betting action was interesting to follow.

Off his fast finish in the Derby, The Loan Arranger had been made a lukewarm Morning Line favorite at 5-to-2, but a local plunger's early bet of some thirty grand on the nose of Ducks in a Row had made that colt, an 8-to-1 Morning Line pick little regarded outside his native Maryland, a surprising tote-board favorite for a period of about twenty minutes before post time. Cooler heads had prevailed by the time Walrus scrambled back up to his seat to snap a blank cassette into his video camera, and The Loan Arranger was favored at 3-to-1. Ducks in a Row and perpetual bridesmaid Warm Regards were at 7-to-2, and my personal pick, the Californian Sabisa, was a generous 4-to-1. The salsa maker's colt had had all kinds of hard luck in the Derby, and I thought a sensible crowd would have favored him today. It was almost enough to drive a man to make a wager, but I sat on my hands.

The European Apostle, back to try his luck again on a drier dirt track, was held at six, while bettors were offered eight on the roan Appetizer, a New York runner who had skipped the Derby.

The field of fourteen broke cleanly. Unlike the Derby, there was no single speed horse expected to set the pace, Vaquero's connections having decided to confine him to sprints. For reasons of his own, the jock on Appetizer made his move early, and the roan from New York had a clear lead of two lengths by the first turn. But I was pretty sure he'd be gobbled up by the rest of the field before the mile and three-sixteenths were over.

By the time the cavalry charge got down the backstretch and entered the far turn, however, I thought I may have underestimated the animal. Appetizer was now leading by three lengths and nothing seemed to be running at him. Warm Regards and Ducks in a Row, who had been moving together like merry-go-round horses in second and third place, certainly weren't making up any ground. The Loan Arranger, a favorite by default, was well to the rear and didn't seem likely to make up enough yardage off such a slow pace, and as for Sabisa, I'd lost him in the pack.

The Pimlico stretch is much shorter and consequently more favorable to front-runners than the Churchill Downs stretch. When Appetizer swung into the lane four lengths to the good, I'd about concluded one wily jock had stolen himself a Preakness. Then a challenger appeared, charging through an opening on the rail.

"Sabisa!" I shouted. "Go get him, baby. Go get him, baby. You got him, baby. You got him."

By the time they reached the Pimlico finish line, Sabisa had prevailed by a long neck over Appetizer. It was some twelve lengths back to Warm Regards, who held Apostle off for third by a half.

Lew was looking at me in surprise. "How much did you have on that horse?" he demanded. "And more important, why didn't you tell me he was going to win?"

"Not a penny," I said honestly. "I just like a good race."

It was amazing. Murders, skulduggery, Carmody, the CIA, Halcyon, and Grosso had all been pushed into the background. Watching that Preakness finish was the purest pleasure I had had for some time. Sport of kings, king of sports, you betcha.

There was someone only a section away even more excited by the finish than I was. Sabisa's owner was a squat, florid man wearing a dark pinstripe suit, the diamonds on the frame of his eyeglasses sparkling in the sun. Apparently he was a man who never stopped eating, even when his horse was pounding down the stretch in a classic race. He had been munching on something, a croissant, that he handed to his surprised associate before he began hopping down the steps toward the winner's circle.

"Shoot him," Lew told Walrus. "Stick with him and shoot him."

He turned to me. "You ought to get down there to congratulate the winner, too."

"Sure," I said, rising to obey the request. I took one more look at the croissant and smiled. I was twice grateful to Sabisa's owner. Not only had he given me the pleasure of watching his horse's thrilling win, he had shown me the way to find my lady.

49

THE FLIGHT back to Los Angeles with Lew, Walrus, and an assortment of happy and dejected Preakness-goers was like a vague dream. There was only one thing on my mind.

Thanks to the difference in time zones, we arrived in the early evening. I made my good-byes to Walrus and Lew and headed straight for The Horse's Neck. Business before pleasure. I entered through the kitchen and immediately summoned Jack Hayward to my office.

"Ah, sirrah, you have returned from the Crusades," he said. "And you just missed her."

"Who?"

"Lea, of course. You didn't mention her infirmity. But she's handling it excellently, hobbling about with her crutches."

"Here, in the restaurant?" I asked incredulously.

Jack frowned. "You didn't know that she and her scruffy companion were here?"

"Scruffy companion? You mean Sonny Marquez?"

Jack shrugged. "Six-foot-two, leather jacket, a five o'clock shadow that was at least three days old. This is not good, sir. If you didn't know they were here, then you probably did not give them permission to consult our catering files."

"No, but it's no big problem," I said. No sense getting Jack in a dither. "I'd better take a look at the book, though."

"Right away."

He returned with a brown-suede-covered ledger. As I flipped through its pages I asked, "Did I get any messages while I was gone?"

"Several. Mainly from Lieutenant Burns. He also dropped by once or twice. He seemed even more saddened than usual to find you were elsewhere."

I stared down at the pages devoted to that fateful Lunden party. "I assume this was what they were interested in?" I said.

"I . . . I can't tell you, I'm afraid," Jack said.

I looked back at him quizzically. For once my maitre d's suave self-assurance was showing signs of strain.

"I, ah, left them alone in your office to peruse the book. They did use your Xerox machine."

"How do you know?"

"They left a Xerox page behind that I discarded." He pointed to the wastebasket.

I retrieved the rumpled sheet of Xerox paper. Evidently, the yellow ledger sheet had copied too dark the first time. But not so dark that I couldn't make out the names of the Lunden partygoers.

I sent Jack off with the ledger and phoned home. I listened impatiently to more messages from Lt. Olaf Burns, then perked up at the sound of Lea's voice.

"Coley, I was hoping to catch you. Sonny has this interesting lead that has to do with the party at The Horse's Neck. You could help us with it. I'll try back tomorrow."

I hoped that her call was for a reason more personal than Sonny Marquez's desire to see the catering list. In just a few hours I'd be able to ask her.

50

SHORTLY BEFORE midnight I was parked on Robertson, down the block from the House of Bagels. Most of the residents of Beverly Hills and Brentwood buy their sinkers there. As Starbuck had announced that evening at the Brompton, it was also the place where Choo-Choo picked up his supply each night, fresh from the oven.

At twelve on the dot, precise as always, Choo-Choo guided his spotless Camry into the parking area. At ten after twelve he emerged from the House of Bagels with a pleated brown bag which he placed very carefully on the passenger seat.

I followed the Camry west on Pico past the darkened restaurants and the blinking night lights of the Westside Pavilion, until, near the 20th Century Fox studios, it turned left into an upscale residential area known as Cheviot Hills.

The Camry bounced up onto a steep driveway beside a two-story home with a winding path that cut through a lawn with a dramatic upward slope. I parked and on foot moved closer to the lawn area. Just to the right of the path a large divot had been hastily replaced. My bet was that a For Sale sign had recently been removed.

I walked to the front door and rang the bell. There was no reply and no sound from inside. I rang the bell again. Sensing someone staring at me through the peephole, I smiled and winked.

The door was opened by the still unshaven Dougherty, who gave me a look of rueful resignation and stepped aside for me to enter. La Nasa was beside a stairwell, his hand resting on a pistol in its shoulder holster.

"The bagels, huh?" La Nasa said.

I nodded.

"What'd I tell you, Dougherty? I knew the bagels routine was a bad idea, but the old man is a real hardhead. Sonny's gonna be truly pissed."

"Isn't he here?" I asked.

"Be back any minute," La Nasa said.

"What about Lea Starbuck?" I demanded.

"Upstairs, helping her old man get ready for his date," Dougherty told me.

"Come again?"

"Try the second door from the head of the stairs," La Nasa said.

I nodded and trotted up the stairs. I found the door and knocked. Starbuck's voice replied liltingly, "Come in, sweetheart."

I opened the door. He was on his feet, using a cane to move haltingly around a nicely appointed bedroom. He was dressed in elegant silk foulard pajamas and an apparently new black flannel robe. The wheelchair was nearby. He looked at me for a moment with naked astonishment before a scowl took over his face.

The hell with his scowl. I shifted my glance and feasted on the sight of Lea, stretched out on a green and white sofa, her cast propped on its arm. She was wearing a bright yellow sweater and a tan canvas wraparound skirt. She looked like heaven on a cloud.

"Mi amore," she said, holding out her arms to me. At just under the speed of light I moved inside them.

And we kissed.

Warmth, tenderness, sex, love. All of that . . . and Starbuck, grousing, "Can't you two do that out of my sight?"

"Whoa, mama," Dougherty said from the doorway.

So much for romance.

Remaining on the sofa beside Lea, I turned to the drug agent in time to see him tucking his gun into his belt.

"Didn't mean to disturb you," he said.

"Better than shooting me," I said.

He looked down at the gun and gave me a sheepish smile. "We're supposed to be guarding these folks. You don't look like you're here to do anybody any harm, Killebrew." He snickered. "But Sonny says we don't trust anybody."

"How'd you find us?" Starbuck asked.

"He followed your guy with the bagels," Dougherty said. "Speaking of which, I might just go get me one."

"Lea," Starbuck asked with deceptive sweetness, "could you hobble off and give me a minute alone with Coley?"

"Not if you're going to shout at each other."

"Nothing like that," Starbuck assured her.

I stood and helped Lea lower her plastered leg to the ground, then walked her to the door.

"Close that, will you?" Starbuck said as soon as Lea had gone. "And come over here where we can't be heard, *even if somebody has her ear to the door.*"

Instead of the ass-chewing I'd come to expect from any "chat" with Starbuck, the big man gave me a worried look. "Marquez was driving Lea all around town today," he said.

"They were at my restaurant."

"Exactly. Marquez is only about half as smart as he thinks he is, but he's not an idiot. And parading Lea around is an idiotic way of keeping her safe."

"I'm with you so far," I said. "In fact, I'm not so sure these guys are really drug agents."

"Lea mentioned that. I think they have to be. Nothing else makes any sense. But that doesn't mean they're on our side, exactly."

"I don't understand."

"Marquez's got his back to the wall, and I suppose his superiors are demanding some action. So I think the son of a bitch has decided to use us for bait."

"Did you ask him about it?"

Starbuck shook his big head. His face twisted in frustration. "I can barely walk with a cane, damnit. And Lea's not much better off. I'm not in any position to have a face-off with the only guy standing between us and Carmody's hit men." He sighed and said, "So it looks as if it's up to you."

"I'm not overwhelmed by your confidence in me," I said.

"Don't get sensitive on me at this late date." He grunted and plopped down on the bed. He winced as he shifted his weight. "Here's the way I see it. Marquez and his crew would prefer to chase after shadows than consider the possibility that an ex-DEAer like Sandford could be involved in Vickie's death. That means it's up to you to get close enough to Carmody and Sandford to hand 'em to Marquez on a plate."

"I'm a little ahead of you on this," I said. "I've just spent a few days at the Carmody compound in Kentucky."

He was very generous with his smiles that night. "Well, God damn," he said. "What'd you find out?"

"That he's not acting like a guilty man."

The smile transformed into a scowl in jig time. "Of course he isn't. What sociopath does? Jesus, you're in the guy's house and all you bring back is an observation? For them to risk killing a government agent and kidnapping Lea they've got to be wading in some deep, dark waters. It shouldn't be that hard to find signs of rust."

"Maybe they only dipped one toe in. Maybe the worst thing they did was rig a horse sale. Maybe they're not the master criminals you think they are."

Starbuck's frustration level went up a few notches. "Why am I surrounded by idiots?"

"Some men would start doubting themselves," I said.

He glared at me.

"I didn't say they weren't the bad guys," I told him. "Just that I'm not blessed with your certainty."

"Then keep at it," he said. "Somebody has to do something or . . ."

He paused because there was the sound of a woman's voice as she ascended the stairs. A voice I recognized. Asking, "How's he doing?"

"We'll talk later," Starbuck said to me and hoisted himself to his feet.

Just outside the door Dougherty said, "He's feeling better every day. Probably because of your visits."

Starbuck struck a pose beside the bed that suggested he had been on his feet for hours and really didn't need the cane at all.

There was a knock at the door.

"Come in," Starbuck said, almost making a song of it.

Clara McGuinn entered the room.

She was at least as surprised to see me as I was to see her. Part of my surprise came from her wearing, instead of her usual tweeds, a clinging silk dress with a scoop neckline that showed off a very feminine figure I confess I had never noticed before.

The all-business owner of Santa Rosita Raceway was also wearing makeup. Lipstick. Eyeliner.

"Coley? What in the world are you doing here?" she asked.

"Visiting," I suggested.

"I mean in Los Angeles. Didn't you stay for the party after the Preakness?"

"Party?" I asked. "Nobody mentioned a party. Anyway, I wasn't in a party mood."

I might have said more, but Starbuck, who was gawking at the newcomer like a lovestruck bull moose, took command of the conversation. "My God, Clara," he said, "you make Liz Taylor look like a bag lady."

"I hope so," she said, "I'm nine months younger than she."

"More like nine years," Starbuck said gallantly.

"I'm sorry I'm so late," she said, "but the concert went on and on and then they insisted I join them at the Oliver Club."

"You're here. That's the important thing."

"Is that Clara?" Lea asked, limping to the door, taking the place of the departing Dougherty.

"I guess I just can't stay away," Clara McGuinn said.

"Do you think Clara and I might have just a little privacy?" Starbuck whined. "This room is starting to resemble the Farmer's Market."

"I wouldn't mind a little privacy myself," I said, joining Lea and leading her away. We were barely out of the room when Starbuck's cane cracked against the door, sending it shut.

Lea's room was directly across the hall. We were stepping into it when the front door to the house opened and Sonny Marquez's voice inquired, "How's it going?"

"It's like Honeymoon Hotel," La Nasa remarked dryly. "The McGuinn lady is with Starbuck, and Killebrew's upstairs with the blonde."

I made a face. Lea put a finger to her lips and reached out to shut the door.

The blinds were closed, giving the small room a claustrophobic feel. The furniture was utilitarian and basic: bed, chair, and dresser. With my help, Lea lay back on the bed, resting her cast on a sponge pillow.

I switched off the overhead light and Lea turned on a lamp beside the bed. Then I lay down beside her, just staring at her for a while until neither of us could resist touching one another.

"God, I missed you," she said.

I didn't bother saying anything.

When we finally came up for air, I asked her in a hoarse voice, "Is this okay?"

"It's okay with me."

"With your leg, I mean."

"The cast only goes to mid-thigh," she said.

"Another triumph for modern medicine," I said.

Much later I lay awake listening to her even breathing as she slept. Was there ever a more comforting sound than that of your lover totally at peace?

There were questions I wanted to ask her, of course. They'd flown from my mind the moment I saw her, and now they would have to wait. I eased myself from the bed, dressed, and went downstairs to find someone who could provide some answers.

La Nasa was alone in the living room, watching commercials interrupted by the Late, Late, Late Show.

"Marquez still around?" I asked.

La Nasa pulled himself away from a pitch for a feminine hygiene product to point to the rear of the house.

Marquez was in his favorite room, the kitchen, alternately eating a tuna sandwich and cleaning his Police Special, which was laid out in several pieces before him. He seemed to be studiously ignoring me.

"Hi," I said, sitting down across the table from him.

He didn't look up from the hunk of metal he was wiping clean. The smell of oil was almost as strong as the tuna odor.

"How much longer do you plan on keeping the Starbucks here?" I asked him.

He put down the gun hunk and stared at me. "Before I kick your ass out of here, Killebrew, I'll try to explain one final time how this all works. We've got two main objectives. One, we want to catch and remove from society the person or persons who murdered our agent, the woman you knew as Victoria Salazaar. Two, we want to keep the Starbucks alive and well until objective one has been accomplished."

He was bristling as he snapped the now-clean gun hunk together with another gun hunk. Starbuck had been right: the guy was evidently under great pressure, probably from his supervisors. Almost obsessively, he began cleaning another piece of his weapon. "Objective one is a matter of almost routine detective work, and that is progressing as we speak. The second part is turning into a goddamn joke. As witness your sitting here. As witness the lady upstairs with Raymond Starbuck. We are not keeping a tight ship here. Grab me a brew from the fridge?"

"Grab it yourself," I said.

He shrugged, placed the gun parts on the table, took his time getting to his feet. He strolled to the refrigerator, removed a can of beer and brought it back to his chair. He seemed to be ready to explode, but he said with elaborate calm, "Now, where was I?"

"Not keeping a tight ship."

His eyes narrowed. "The point is: there is only one way to stop a professional killer. You have to keep him or her away from the prospective victim. Am I getting through to you?"

"You're very good at simplifying things," I said.

"The problem is, time is against us. No matter how careful we are to keep the Starbucks hidden and guarded, eventually a window of opportunity will open up. There will be the moment that Starbuck gets too near a window or the houseboy lets somebody follow him from the goddamn bagel shop. And there the killer will be, with guns blazing." Marquez took a gulp of the beer.

"You don't mean guns literally?" I asked. "It could be knives or a bomb. Maybe arrows. Poisoned darts."

"You mocking me, you little smart-ass?"

I didn't have anything in mind when I started goading him. I was just fed up with his whole attitude. "Me mock you? Hell, you're the pro. Of course, Lea might still be sitting in a deserted house in the hills if it had been left to you pros."

He snapped his gun together angrily and began filling it with bullets. "Yeah," he said. "And maybe you found her a little *too* quick."

"Arrogance and paranoia," I said. "Good traits for a government agent."

"Fuck you, Killebrew. You're gone. Don't let me catch you here again."

"For the sake of Lea's safety," I said.

"Damn straight."

"Were you thinking of her safety when you took her to my restaurant today?"

"That was her call," Marquez said. "She wanted to go."

"And you needed her to get my maitre d' to cooperate," I said.

He glared at me. "She's a big girl. She knew the risk, but she also knew that the list might be important."

"Is it?"

"Maybe," he said. "Tomorrow I'm gonna run the names through the computer to see if anything pops out." He stood up. "That ends our conversation. You're outta here."

"Or what? Are you going to shoot me?"

He pasted a fake smile on his face and took a step toward me. Then his hand shot out and grabbed my coat. He jerked me forward. "Hardheaded asshole doesn't listen."

I was the asshole, but he was the guy getting physical while wearing tennis shoes. I stomped down hard on his toe.

He let out a scream that segued into a howl of rage.

I moved away from him and waited to see where the pain would send him.

He leaped for me.

I stepped aside and pushed him into the table. The beer bottle and the plate with the tuna sandwich went flying.

Behind us, La Nasa and Dougherty rushed through the door.

Marquez came at me again. I ducked his left hook, which grazed my ear, and returned a jab of my own. It landed on his nose with a satisfying crunch that would probably alter his movie star profile.

I expected, hell, I prayed, for La Nasa and Dougherty to pull us apart, which they did. As well as I'd started, Marquez was younger and bigger and eventually would have beaten me to a pulp.

"You little asshole," he shouted in La Nasa's arms. "My nose is broken."

My ear was red where he'd clipped it, and it was as hot as fire. Dougherty was holding me tightly, but I had no desire to mix it up anymore.

Then La Nasa relaxed his hold and Marquez charged forward to deliver a devastating punch to my stomach.

I bent in two, gasping for breath. Dougherty helped me to a sofa in the living roon.

"Nice clean punch, Sonny," he said sarcastically. "Want me to hold his feet so you can kick him, too?"

"Yeah. Well, fuck all you guys," Marquez said, wordsmith to the end.

Clara McGuinn descended the stairs, frowning. "What in heaven's name is . . . Coley, what happened?"

I was still having too much trouble catching my breath to answer.

"Little mix-up," Dougherty said. "Nothing serious."

Marquez was still glaring at me and dabbing at his nose with a red-spotted handkerchief. He turned to Clara McGuinn and said, "Listen, ma'am, we're tightening security here. I'm sorry, but this is gonna be your last visit."

"That's nonsense—" she began.

"Oh, please, lady," Marquez said. "You're not gonna give me attitude, too? C'mon, I'm heading home. I'll walk you to your car and try to explain my position."

She turned back to me. "You feeling all right, Coley?"

I nodded my head and managed to get out, "Fine."

"He'll be okay," La Nasa said. Easy for him to say.

Marquez had the front door open. "Make sure Killebrew's out of here in ten minutes," he told Dougherty. "You coming, ma'am?"

Clara McGuinn paused to give me one more worried look. I waved to her and she followed him out.

It was more than ten minutes before I was ready to stand and walk. "Got your wind back?" Dougherty asked me.

I nodded.

"Sonny's not a bad guy, really," La Nasa said.

"He's a prince," I said, dragging my battered body to the stairs.

Dougherty winced and said, "Uh, I don't know how to put this, but Sonny's calling the shots. So you gotta leave. 'Course, I don't think it'd hurt if you were to tell the lady good-bye."

"She's asleep," I said.

"Well, then . . ."

I nodded, moved gingerly to the door and took my sore stomach home to bed.

51

AT JUST after five A.M. I was jolted from a dream of flying by the creak of a floorboard near my bed. I opened my eyes.

A man was standing a foot away, pointing a gun at me.

He didn't move. But, I admit, I blinked. And blinked again.

It was DEA agent Dougherty and he was not his usual smiling self. "Get up, Killebrew," he ordered.

Confused, I slipped from the bed, wincing with fresh pain as I bent my abused body.

While dressing I tried to get the agent to tell me what was going on, but Dougherty remained silent except to urge me to hurry.

As he led me to the front door I was surprised to find two strangers, a man and a woman, slowly and quietly searching my living room.

"What the hell *is* this?" I demanded. "What are they looking for?"

"You'll find out," Dougherty said. "If you don't already know."

That was a laugh. I didn't know what day it was.

I was expecting to return to the house in Cheviot Hills. But our destination was a restaurant in downtown L.A. called The Pan Handler.

"I'm not hungry," I said.

"You're not here to eat."

Though its charms held little appeal for me at the moment, The Pan Handler had a colorful history. Originally an open-twenty-four-hour steak and eggs short-order house serving blue-collar workers, it had been discovered in the sixties by Elvis Presley when he was shooting a film nearby. Where Presley went, there went America's youth, and The Pan Handler began an expansion that doubled and then trebled its working space. The counter ran for nearly a quarter of a block. A series of dining rooms opened, manned by waiters in traditional black trousers, white shirts, black bow ties.

In the seventies, as both the city and Elvis grew older and fatter, the steak house lost some of its allure and most of its trend-seekers. In the eighties, when grazing became the lunch option of choice for health-conscious Los Angelinos, The Pan Handler closed off some of its rooms and once again reverted to its original clientele, the downtown blue-collar workers. But in the nineties it began to regain some of its former allure as a place where rebellious film execs and lawyers and others of that ilk might thumb their noses at California cuisine and maintain that aggressive edge by scarfing down as much bloodred beef as possible at one sitting.

Dougherty led me past a breakfast counter that was remarkably busy considering that the sun had just risen. Then it was down a hallway to the rear of the restaurant, where we paused before a closed door. Dougherty knocked.

The portal was opened by an attractive red-haired woman in a no-nonsense pantsuit. Past her I could see a medium-sized room with its walls covered by black-and-white blowups of Elvis Presley snapshots. Elvis with Ed Sullivan. Elvis with Sinatra. Elvis in the Army. Elvis with Stella Stevens.

There was one long table with a white tablecloth. Seated at its far end were five people—four men and another woman. The dress code was pretty eclectic. The guy at the head of the table was wearing a dark blue pinstripe. He looked like a fifty-year-old self-made million-aire who had no respect for anyone who wasn't.

To his right was a robust young black woman with a modified Afro, wearing a tank top and jeans tight enough for her stomach to drape over the belt. The two men to the self-made millionaire's left were in early middle age, wearing sport coats and open-neck polo shirts. The guy sitting next to the black woman was in his twenties, dressed in a rumpled brown jumpsuit with a shoulder patch reading DEPARTMENT OF PARKS AND RECREATION.

None of them seemed to be Elvis fans. All of them were glaring at me.

"Report," the millionaire said.

Dougherty shifted his weight from one foot to the other and said, "Engine of his car wasn't quite cold, but that could have been from the drive from Cheviot Hills. Gun found in living room on first pass. Clean. Wrong caliber. They're going over the place from stem to stern right now."

"Tell me about him," the millionaire said, as if I were a member of the animal kingdom.

"Asleep. I'd say he wasn't faking."

"So, Mr. Killebrew, what've you got to say for yourself?" the millionaire asked.

"I'd say my home has been broken into and I've been kidnapped."

"Sit down, Mr. Killebrew." The millionaire indicated a chair next to the man in the park uniform.

I sat. The redhead in the pantsuit brought me a cup of coffee.

"My name is Quarles," the millionaire said. "How much do you know about our organization?"

"What organization is that, Mr. Quarles? The Grand Poobahs? The Holy Rollers? The Mighty Ducks?"

"As I think you are aware," the man said without an ounce of sarcasm, "we're with the Drug Enforcement Administration."

"Then I do know a few things about your organization. You think you're above the law of the land, and you don't believe in little niceties like civil rights of citizens. Though, of course, it's citizens who pay your salary."

Quarles smiled. "Ah, then you *do* know about us. Well, there are a few more things. Our primary mission is to enforce the drug laws of this fine country. That means we hunt out people involved in the illegal growing or manufacturing or distributing of controlled substances and we also regulate the people who are legally allowed to create and distribute controlled substances. In other words, we're split into two operations—regulatory and enforcement. With me so far?"

I nodded.

"The regulatory branch is staffed by Division Investigators. Nice fellows on the whole, but a bit on the stuffy side. We, the people in this room, are on the enforcement end. We're called Special Agents and we like to think we are pretty special. We can make arrests, perform search-and-seizures, conduct criminal investigations, infiltrate, confiscate. All sorts of good things. Even drag a feisty little guy out of bed at five in the morning and bring him down here to the Elvis Room."

I looked at a photo of the King on the wall. "Speaking of controlled substances," I said.

"Hey, now, Mr. Killebrew," Quarles said with a frown, "let's not put down the King. Please remember, the late great Richard Nixon once made him an honorary agent of the Bureau of Narcotics and Dangerous Drugs."

"Was he on your team?" I asked.

Quarles gave me a bleak smile. "The thing about us Special Agents, Mr. Killebrew, is that we really do think of each other as family. I know it's a cliché, but we're old-fashioned like that. We take care of our own. Maybe we bend the rules a little, but we think of it as loyalty.

"Anyway, that should explain why it would behoove you to answer a few questions as truthfully as you can. Because if you don't, we're just liable to see to it that a lot of bad things happen to you. Am I clear?"

I sipped my coffee and wondered yet again what the hell I'd gotten into. I knew it involved a gun, since my automatic had already been discussed. And I knew it also involved a DEA agent. The answer came to me at just about the same time that Quarles asked, "Where were you tonight from approximately two to four A.M.?"

I noticed that the redhead in the pantsuit was sitting behind me, pencil poised above a notebook. A minirecorder rested on the table about a foot away.

"At two, I was still with that guy," I said, indicating Dougherty. "By about two-twenty, I was at my home. By 2:25 I was asleep."

"When was the last time you saw Special Agent Degarza?"

"I don't know any Agent Degarza."

"His operating name was Marquez."

"Was?"

"Agent Degarza was murdered at approximately three this morning. When did see him last?"

I looked at Dougherty for confirmation. "I don't know. Somewhere around 1:45, I guess."

"This was at the Cheviot Hills safe house?" Quarles asked.

I nodded.

"Where Degarza beat the tar out of you?"

"With Dougherty holding my arms, yes."

Quarles's eyes moved to Dougherty briefly, then back to me. "I take it you didn't like Agent Degarza."

"That's correct."

"Why not?"

I hesitated, then decided to dive in. "He wasn't much of an agent."

"Oh?"

"He was supposed to be keeping someone out of harm's way. Instead, he purposely exposed her to danger."

"Lea Starbuck?" Quarles asked.

"That's right."

Quarles stared at me for a few beats, then said, "Degarza was shot four times at close range just outside his home in Sherman Oaks. The sound of gunfire woke up his wife. She got to the door just in time to see a car pulling away."

"What make?" I asked.

"It was too dark. The street he lives on . . . lived on, is one of those Valley stretches that look like they haven't been completed. No sidewalks. Lots of trees. No lights. Mrs. Degarza doesn't have any idea what kind of car it was. She was too busy looking at her husband, bleeding to death on the sidewalk.

"One of the neighbors must have called the cops, because an emergency wagon got there while Degarza was still breathing. On the way to the hospital he even said something to one of the attendants. Four words, actually."

Quarles paused. For dramatic effect, I assumed. When he didn't appear inclined to continue, I bit and said, "Okay, what are the four words?"

"Degarza's last words were 'Starbuck woman' and 'jealous asshole.' So, can you figure out why we immediately thought of you?"

"Maybe the paramedic misunderstood him," I said.

"He said Degarza repeated them in English and in Spanish. The paramedic is Chicano, too, so it's doubtful any mistake was made."

"There's another possibility," I said. I had the attention of everyone in the room. "Mar— Degarza misidentified his killer. Maybe the guy was short like me."

"Degarza was a pro," Dougherty said. "Considering the range at which he was shot, he wouldn't have made that kind of mistake."

"Marquez, or Degarza, left the safe house fifteen minutes before I did. Assuming he went directly to his place, wherever that is, how did I get there fast enough to kill him? In fact, how did I know where he lived? I didn't even know his real name."

Quarles looked at Dougherty questioningly. Dougherty nodded disgustedly and turned away.

"And even if I could have followed him and shot him, then what? I drive to my place and tuck myself into bed and wait for one of Marquez's buddies to come find me?"

"Your comments are not without merit," Quarles said.

"Aren't you people forgetting something?" I asked.

"What's that?"

"Another of your agents was killed a month ago. Vickie Salazaar."

"Not by gunshot," the black woman pointed out.

"But the same case."

"What're you talking about?" Quarles asked.

"I didn't just fall off the turnip truck, Quarles. You and I both know that Vickie was assisting Raymond Starbuck on a case involving possible misuse by a DEA agent of confiscated thoroughbreds. She died rather mysteriously, and an attempt was made on Starbuck's life. Degarza was in charge of the investigation. Just yesterday afternoon he picked up a copy of the list of people who attended a cocktail party at my restaurant the night Vickie was murdered."

Quarles shot a hostile glare at Dougherty.

"Sonny didn't say anything to us about any cocktail party," Dougherty said.

"Was there any list on the body or in the car?" Quarles asked.

"Degarza told me he was going to feed it into the computers today," I said.

"None of the investigating officers mentioned a list," Dougherty said.

"Anybody back up your claim about Degarza going to your restaurant, Killebrew?"

"Lea Starbuck was with him."

"Anybody else?"

"My maitre d'." I gave them Jack's name and phone number. Dougherty left the room.

"There's something else you might find interesting," I offered. "A jockey named Dewey Lane, who was also at that cocktail party, hasn't been seen or heard of in several weeks."

Dougherty returned in a few minutes to report that Jack Hayward had corroborated my story about Degarza looking at the catering book. Poor Jack must have thought the early morning call was a desperate summons to a soundstage somewhere.

Quarles sighed. "Well, Agent Dougherty, I think you can take Mr. Killebrew back home now. But stop off at his restaurant first and get a copy of that list. He makes an interesting point about there being a connection between the two deaths. And perhaps we should be a little more candid with local law enforcement. Let them do some of the work for us." He turned back to me. "That's it, Mr. Killebrew. Thanks for dropping by for this chat. We'll keep in touch."

52

QUARLES MUST have laid it out very neatly for the police, because by noon, when I had reawakened and was attempting to remove a day's growth of beard, the radio in my bathroom was filled with news of the murder of two DEA agents—James "Sonny" Degarza and Helena Diez. Diez's body, discovered nearly five weeks before, had been misidentified as Victoria Salazaar, the pseudonym she used when in the field.

An unnamed spokesman for the DEA, probably Quarles, had issued a statement that the agency was eager to provide the Los Angeles Police Department with whatever it needed to vigorously pursue its investigation into the murders of Degarza and Diez. Thus far, no arrests had been made, but Lt. Olaf Burns of the LAPD had announced they were "pursuing a very promising lead."

Was I that lead? I wondered. I wasn't about to call Burns—let him find me—but I did get on the phone to Parker Center and asked for my pal, Detective Sean Wiley.

"Coley, before you say anything, this better be a social call."

"Sean—"

"It used to be, I'd hear from you, it'd be a tip on a horse or to talk about the Lakers or the Bruins, or just some kidding around. But lately, Coley, every time you call it's trouble."

"How about those Lakers, huh?" I said. "And how about that DEA agent who got drilled last night?"

"You're not mixed up in that case, for Christ's sake?"

"That would depend on a colleague of yours named Olaf Burns. Would it be possible for you to find out if *he* thinks I'm involved?"

"Burns is a good cop," he said in a way that indicated he wanted to hear more details.

"Even good cops get screwball ideas."

"I'll call around," he said.

An hour later Sean got back to me.

"Want to hear the good news or the bad news first?" he asked.

"The bad, always the bad."

"Burns thinks you shot this Degarza dude."

"Great. What's the good news?"

"I'm sleeping with a twenty-one-year-old movie star."

"I hope that's a joke."

"Just trying to lighten the mood, buddy. The good news is that there's no real evidence linking you to the crime. And Burns is so straight-arrow he's not gonna make any moves on you until he's got some. So you're a free man. For now, at least."

"Thanks for the vote of confidence."

53

O N THE way to The Horse's Neck I dog-legged into Cheviot Hills hoping to see Lea. It was a faint hope; the odds against her still being at the safe house were insurmountable. But I had to make sure.

A For Sale sign had been stuck into the lawn approximately where I'd noticed the divot the night before. Still, I got out of the car and peeked in enough windows to convince me that the place was deserted. I hoped the new safe house lived up to its name.

Getting back into my Cherokee, I spied a dark Ford sedan parked down the street. When I drove away, the Ford followed at what might have been considered a discreet distance.

The tail knew what he was doing. By the time I arrived at the restaurant, I'd lost sight of him. But I had a hunch the reverse was not true.

Working my way quickly past the late luncheon crowd and the mildly harassed staff, I went to my office for a pair of binoculars. The windows of the empty upstairs dining room offered the widest view of the street. The Ford was parked about a half block away. Training the binoculars on the car, I zeroed in on La Nasa and an unfamiliar agent sitting in the front seat.

So they were watching me. Nothing to do about that. I threw myself into the general duties of a restaurant owner, the normal everyday worries about menus and staff conflicts and problem customers and machinery on the fritz. All through the day and evening I expected Lieutenant Burns to drop in, officially. But the time passed uneventfully.

That night, after closing up, I noticed that the Ford was no longer parked near the restaurant. Nor did I catch sight of it as I drove home. Nobody seemed to care anymore. Not the police. Nor the CIA. Nor even my old buddies from the DEA. I couldn't remember ever feeling so lonely.

But there was a message on my machine, the one message I'd been hoping for.

"Coley, darling. We've moved. I wish I could tell you more, but they've tightened the security to a point where I'm not even sure where we are. Agent Dougherty is watching while I talk to you. They've asked me to assure you that Dad and I are well and as nearly happy as we can be cooped up in a . . . Sorry, but I can't even give you a description of this place. I miss you. I want to be with you. I want this to be over. I love you."

54

I SLEPT well that night and awoke with a freshly optimistic out-
look. But in the midst of an especially ordinary day at The Horse's
Neck, I realized that even normality must be taken in moderation. By
evening, without another word from Lea, depression had set in again.

I was in the midst of greeting diners during the second seating
when Jack Hayward notified me I was wanted on the phone.

"Who?" I asked.

He raised one eyebrow in disapproval. "She said to tell you it's the
little girl on the white horse."

My face must have brightened a little too much. Jack exited in a
huff. My restaurant employees were starting to act as if they were all
Lea's older brothers.

Even if I'd wanted to, I doubt I could have made Jack believe that
my excitement over a call from Angela Carmody had less to do with
Angela than with her father.

She sounded animated and very happy. "Well, Coley, I've decided to
take your advice."

For a moment I wasn't sure what advice she meant. "Good," I said.
"Some people have done well taking my advice."

She laughed. "You don't know what I'm talking about, do you? I
mean I'm ready to get back on a horse again."

"That's great. What made you change your mind?"

"I . . . I met someone. At an art show. He said the same thing you
did, that the only way for me to conquer my fear of riding is to ride."

"I don't remember saying that exactly."

"Well, whatever you said, it inspired me."

"Not as much as this guy at the art show, though."

She giggled again. She was positively giddy. "Oh, Coley, would you
help me, please, please, please?"

"How?"

"I want you to come here and spend a few weeks helping me to ride again."

"Angela, I'd love to, but . . ." I paused, pretending to consider her offer, while my mind was racing over the possibilities. Without even knocking, opportunity was being handed to me on a silver platter. This was a way to get back inside the Carmody compound and snoop around for that hard evidence Starbuck was talking about.

"But what?" she asked.

"I'm kinda persona non grata around there, as far as your father is concerned."

"Actually, I already mentioned this to him. He didn't throw his usual fit."

"Maybe he just had something else on his mind. Like planning on the Belmont. Or running for President."

"Seriously, I take that as a sign that he thinks better of you than you imagine. How soon can you come?"

"Well—"

"Tomorrow? I want to get started immediately," she said, with all the impatience of the very young. And very rich.

"Late tomorrow," I said.

"I'll have someone pick you up at the airport."

55

"COLEY," LEW Totter said, greeting me the next morning at the door to his office in the SportsNet Building. "Come on in."

"I couldn't find anybody downstairs, so I just walked up."

"Yeah. Loretta's in New York. Sit down. *Que pasa?*"

"I'm taking a short trip and was hoping I could get a check from you for my stints at the Derby and Pimlico."

Lew winced. "Bad timing, amigo. Barry has to sign it and he's in New York."

"A little early for the Belmont, isn't it?"

"Some sudden big powwow was scheduled. Barry and the lovely Loretta flew out yesterday. Listen, I'm sorry we're dragging our feet on the check."

"I guess I can shift a few accounts around."

"Where you headed?"

"Lexington," I said casually. "Jaydee Farms."

"What?" Lew couldn't have been more astonished if I'd said I was taking the shuttle to Venus. "I thought he had you pegged as the anti-Christ."

"I guess he saw the light. I'll be hanging out at his place."

"Helping with his campaign?"

"No. Helping his daughter with her riding."

"You dog." He gave me a lascivious grin.

"Strictly platonic," I said.

"Sure. Say, is Carmody running For Cupid's Sake in the Belmont?"

"The last I heard."

"Any chance we could put the documentary back on track?"

"Maybe, if I ever get paid for the work I've already done."

Lew held up his hands. "Let me phone Barry. Maybe he can cut the check in Gotham. The filly missing the Preakness takes the edge off things a little bit, but Carmody's still Carmody."

"Gallen's mood improve any?" I asked. "That last day in Baltimore he looked like he was ready to jump off a bridge."

"Barry generally bounces back. One of the benefits of a short attention span. But actually—" Lew leaned forward, lowering his voice though there was no one else within earshot. "—he and Clara McGuinn have split the blanket."

"No kidding?"

"She locked him out, I hear. He's moved his stuff downtown to the Athletic Club. I'm supposed to be looking for a new place for him."

"You TV producers wear many hats," I said.

"Right. All the more reason why I'm anxious to get this documentary closed out. Any chance you could talk Carmody into letting a cameraman—your pal Walrus, maybe—join you in Lex and mosey on to the Belmont?"

"All I can do is ask. Assuming the check comes through."

"I'll get on it pronto."

On my way to the airport I made a stop at Spinoza & Co. to check on Walrus's availability. But Gigi was minding the philosophers and theologians on her own.

"John is in Bakersfield," she said proudly, making the town sound as prestigious a destination as Carnegie Hall or the Vatican. "He's setting up our booth at the New Age Fair. I'll be joining him on Friday."

"I don't suppose you could give me a number where I could reach him?"

"Don't try. Please."

I didn't.

56

THE FLIGHT to Lexington was a white-knuckler, with a thunderstorm bouncing the jet around the heavens like a pin ball. When it touched down, I got the impression the trip might get even rougher. Richard Sandford and Franklin, the large bodyguard, were waiting for me. You'd think the trainer of Jaydee Farms would have better things to do.

Franklin tossed my bag into the trunk of the car, then stationed himself on the rear seat. I rode up front with Sandford.

The trip to the Carmody spread was a silent one, until I asked Sandford, "Is Cupid going to run in the Belmont?"

"If that goddamn medicine gets out of her system," the trainer replied nastily. "Why do you ask?"

"I'm just surprised you'd take the time to chauffeur me around. Franklin looks like he can drive a car."

"I wanted to make something perfectly clear, Killebrew. You fool around with Angela and I'll make the payback permanent."

"You do a lot of that, Sandford?"

"A lot of what?"

"Threaten to kill people."

"Not a lot. Only when I'm willing to back up the threat."

We paused at the gate to the estate just long enough for the guards to show Sandford they had the routine down. Then the trainer drove me to a guest house not far from the main building. My temporary home was a handsome little ranch-style structure with its own goldfish pond in front.

"Door's unlocked," Sandford said. "They're expecting you at seven for dinner in the main house."

Franklin made no move to bellhop my suitcase, so I retrieved it myself from the trunk. "There goes your tip," I told the bodyguard.

Sandford put the car in gear and roared away, spraying me with pebbles and coating me with dust.

Welcome to friendly Jaydee Farms.

57

THE GUEST house was very western, rough-hewn and sturdy. Toss your saddlebags in the bunkhouse, podnuh. But in stark contrast were electronic gadgets that were like a time traveler's anachronisms scattered throughout its four rooms. The state-of-the-art kitchenette included a microwave that could do anything but balance your checkbook and a computerized coffee maker. The living room contained a big-screen TV with digital VCR. All the rooms had phones that looked like plastic slabs.

I picked up the living room phone, and an electronic voice asked me, "To whom do you wish to speak?"

"Angela Carmody."

"Thank you."

After an assortment of buzzes and beeps that sounded a lot friendlier than my human welcoming party, Angela was on the line, happy to hear that I had arrived.

I told her I hoped she hadn't changed her mind about wanting to ride.

"Sandy and I have discussed it and we're both ready and eager."

We agreed to talk about it a bit more at dinner.

I was showered and dressed by six-thirty. I spent the spare half hour strolling around the grounds, checking out the stables, the facilities, and the horses, all of which appeared to be in fine shape. No one seemed to pay me any notice. But while I was admiring a particularly handsome yearling, a figure loomed up behind me.

I turned apprehensively, ready for anything. But this member of the Jaydee Farms staff was one of the friendly ones, a tall weathered chap sucking on a dead meerschaum and extending a hand roughly the size and texture of a skillet.

"Howdy," he said. "I'm Horace Jinks, stable manager."

"Coley Killebrew," I said.

"Yeah, I know. Glad to have you with us, Coley. If there's anything I can tell you about or show you, say the word." He sounded quite sincere.

"You have quite a setup here."

"You don't know the half of it," Jinks said. "Horses and barns may not change much, but our computer system is strictly twenty-first century. You fond of computers, Coley?"

"I'm no hacker, but I like anything that makes my life easier."

"Come on down to my office, then. You got to see this."

As we walked, Jinks pointed out the equine and floral sights along the way by gesturing with his pipe, which was so crusted it seemed to be growing stalagmites. When we got to the office, he booted up the terminal on his desk and started his spiel. Jinks may have looked and sounded like a stable hand, but the heart of a frustrated computer nerd beat behind that denim work shirt.

"Would you believe we can keep track of everything about our horses' progress and health right here in this box? The complete history of every animal Mr. Carmody owns or ever owned or, if you're talkin' about the breeding operation, is *gonna* own, is on the central computer, and I can tap right into it by punchin' a few little buttons. Just watch this."

He demonstrated by hitting the control key and F1, then typing in the letters S-I-D-E. Suddenly, the screen went black and, beginning at the top, started to fill with a color photo of a thoroughbred named Sidecar.

Almost as quickly as the picture appeared, it was replaced by a menu offering a series of headings, among them lineage, foaling, disposition, injuries, illnesses, medication record, training record, race record, breeding schedule, offspring, and death.

"That's amazing," I said.

"Every step old Sidecar ever took's documented right here. I can call up a full family tree, charts of all his races, winner's circle pictures, X rays of his fractured cannon bone, what you might do to make him kick you, who he bit and when and where he bit 'em, what mares he got bred to and how many times and if he got 'em in foal or not, who his kids were and how they did on the track. Even when and how the poor old guy bit the dust. It was a twisted intestine. That gets too many of 'em."

"Could you punch up For Cupid's Sake?" I said.

"Sure 'nough." Jinks hit the control key and F1, followed by C-U-P-I, and the filly's recognizable portrait appeared almost instantly.

I was wondering which of the list of menu choices, shorter than Side-car's, would be most likely to tell me something I could use, when our technology lesson was interrupted.

"What the hell's goin' on here?"

Sandford was standing in the office doorway, glaring at us. His bris-tling hostility caused Jinks's jaw to drop, his pipe hitting the desktop with a clunk.

"J-Just showing Coley the computer," Jinks said.

Sandford looked at the computer screen, where For Cupid's Sake's menu appeared. "You let any bozo who walks in here look at the files?"

"Miss Angela told me Coley has the run of—"

"Miss Angela your new boss?" Sandford asked.

"No, sir," Jinks said, thoroughly deflated. I felt sorry for getting the stable manager in Dutch.

Sandford lost some of his officiousness when he turned to me. "They're expecting you at the main house. You want any more infor-mation about how we do things here at Jaydee, I suggest you ask Mr. Carmody."

Right. And if you have any questions about Hughes Aircraft, just ask Howard.

58

I WASN'T the only guest for dinner. Vida Barker, Carmody's pro-
posed running mate, was among the group gathered for cocktails,
along with a rumpled middle-aged man named Douglas Rider, well-
known as a political manipulator and spin doctor. Having already met
Burt Lincoln, I realized Carmody and Barker, unannounced candidates though they might be, were building a veritable Dream Team of
campaign managers.

When we went into the dining room, I found myself seated between Mrs. Barker and Lula Dorian. Lula seemed unusually quiet and
possibly drunk. That left me to the mercy of the evangelist, whose
charm wore thin fast.

Over the traditional oyster course, the only one our host truly
seemed to enjoy, Ma Barker treated me to her unusual theological
views, to wit: there were certain rules the great mass of temptation-
prone Christians had to follow to keep themselves on the straight and
narrow path, but once a person achieved a certain level of intimacy
with the Holy Trinity, strict interpretation of those rules no longer applied. She didn't put it exactly that way, but you could read between
the lines.

Accompanying the entrée were her views of the afterlife, which she
felt her electronic flock were not quite ready for.

"Some chosen few, Coley, and not many, who have been especially
faithful and effective leaders of God's work on Earth, will be given the
opportunity to become gods themselves."

"Imagine that," I said.

"Oh, I'm not a polytheist; don't get me wrong. But I think that
God, the one true God, runs a sort of laboratory, where His chosen
few can create life on other planets and test alternate delivery systems.
Isn't that an exciting idea, Coley? I might just start with my own Garden of Eden."

"One where Eve never eats the apple?" I offered.

"What fun would *that* be?"

From there she moved to her political views, much like Carmody's and much more familiar, but to my ear no less nutty. I was almost the exclusive object of her attentions throughout the meal until, over dessert, she began chiding Carmody playfully about his association with the sport of kings.

"I'm not sure the simple folks out there in Kansas and Mississippi will give their vote of approval to a man who flaunts his participation in games of chance," she said.

"That's where you come into the picture, Vida," Carmody piped up with a wide grin. "You're the voice of morality and integrity in this campaign."

Vida Barker blinked her long lashes in mock humility. "You give me too much credit, Jim. I'm human, after all, with human faults. I like a good stiff one every now and then." She turned to me. "I mean a drink, of course."

Some of us smiled politely. Some, like Sandford and Angela, seated across from us, just gawked at her.

Carmody asked Rider what he thought about the racing issue.

"Well," the campaign manager said expansively, "considering the rate that legalized gambling is spreading in the U.S., and the amount of loot the poor fish are throwing away trying to beat the state lotteries, I'd say a presidential candidate who loves horse racing might be perceived as being pleasantly quaint."

At that point Vida Barker leaned against me and whispered, "You know what's on my mind right now?"

"Rum baba?" I asked, indicating the dessert.

"A different kind of delicacy," she said, licking her lips. She meant it to seem sexy and inviting. But the image she conveyed was that of a praying mantis who, I read somewhere, devours its mate right after the act of lovemaking.

"I think I'll just settle for the rum baba," I said, removing her hand from my leg.

"It's damn fine stuff," Lula Dorian said, her first words of the evening. "But I'd be just as happy if they'd hold the baba."

Vida Barker wrinkled her nose in distaste, but Lula didn't seem to notice.

"What my lady wants," Carmody said, and sent one of the waiting staff off to whip up whatever rum drink Lula had been potting herself with all night.

"Demon rum," Vida said sharply. "Maybe voters have become more *liberal* where horse racing is concerned. But there are still some things they will not abide." She smiled sweetly at Lula.

"We might as well get something straight right here and now, Vida—" Carmody began.

Douglas Rider headed off the confrontation by interrupting Carmody to suggest that the three of them have a short get-together in the office, "to go over a few pressing matters."

Thus did the dinner come to a close.

"Coley, you've ignored me all evening," Angela said as the would-be politicians deserted us.

"Don't blame me," I said. "Blame whoever made the seating arrangements."

"Well, we'll have to make up for it now."

"We could take a stroll around the east eighty," I suggested.

"I'd rather a drive into town," she said. "There's a new club called Hoofbeat I'm anxious to see."

"Not a good idea," Richard Sandford grumbled, sending hot-eyed daggers my way. "Too many crazies out there. Especially at clubs."

"For God's sake, Dickie. You can't expect me to stay cooped up here forever. If we meet up with any 'crazies,' Coley can handle them."

"I'll go with you," Sandford said.

"No," Angela said adamantly. "If I have to have a bodyguard, I want Franklin."

Sandford looked about to blow his top, but he kept the lid on with an effort. "I'll get him," he said.

If the big bodyguard was annoyed at having been called into service at a moment's notice, he didn't let it show. He stoically chauffeured Angela and me into town.

"Tell me about your friend," I asked Angela.

She stared at the back of Franklin's neck and shook her head. Then the apprehensive look on her face was replaced by a smile. "I had another image two nights ago," she said. "This one was wonderful. I was in it, wearing this long white dress, a beautiful, flowing dress. At first I was in a building with stone walls. But then the walls opened and I stepped into a valley filled with beautiful flowers. And it was as if I was lifted up and began floating just over the flowers, like on a magic carpet. But there was no carpet."

"Just the other night I dreamt about flying, too," I told her.

"But this wasn't a dream exactly. I wasn't asleep. I was sitting in my room, listening to music. This image flashed in my mind for just a second."

"What do you think it means?" I asked.

"Freedom, of course. Freedom on the back of my beautiful horse." She leaned forward suddenly and said, "Turn left there, Franklin."

That led us onto a dark, semideserted street in Lexington's warehouse district. "I don't like this neighborhood," the big man said, making me realize he and I had more in common than I had suspected.

"We'll be fine," Angela said.

Hoofbeat was several blocks past the last streetlamp, a dim, ominous beehive of dubious activity in a three-story brick building. Its front door was guarded by a young, shirtless bouncer with long peroxided hair and the tattoo of Beavis, or maybe Butthead, on his right arm and several earrings dragging down his left earlobe. He welcomed Angela with a lopsided smile, then moved to block the door before Franklin or I could follow. "Sorry, we're full up."

Franklin invaded the guy's space, stood about a foot away from him. "We're with her," he said without emotion. The threat was in his eyes, his stance. Maybe the bulge under his windbreaker helped.

The bouncer stood aside.

"What a treat, huh?" Franklin said as we strolled down a dark corridor flanked by other patrons of the club. "Jee-sus, aren't they something?"

They were, indeed. Tattoos, body piercing, and hair art seemed to be all the rage. Baggy gangsta garb ran a close second to black leather and T-shirts.

Hoofbeat's main salon was aswirl with people I would have preferred never to have encountered in my lifetime. Baby halogen bulbs shined down from the flat black rafters like miniature spotlights hanging in a bogus midnight sky. In the far distance were tables, but most of the area was taken up by a dance floor that surrounded a stage. There, a muscled lad in black leather sat at what appeared to be a console, playing records. He wore earphones, and I wondered if he was listening to a ball game while inflicting his recorded cacophony on the crowd.

Angela was moving across the dance floor. She seemed to be searching the crowd. Then she turned, waited for us to catch up. "There's an empty table," she said.

It was toward the back of the room, against a wall, beneath a Day-Glo version of Picasso's Guernica.

Franklin gave the area a quick eye dust and nodded. We'd barely squatted on our chairs when a transvestite wearing a Hoofbeat T-shirt over his protruding breasts arrived for our order. Angela asked for a glass of white wine. I wanted a bottled beer. Franklin, as designated leg-breaker, opted for a Coke. "Just bring the can," he said. "I'll open it myself."

"I love that in a man," the waiter said, "fanatic caution."

A rock group aptly named Horse's Ass performed a ditty called "Stallion City," complete with snorts and whickers. Angela assured me it was the number one record in Lexington and I took her word for it.

All through the song her eyes had been darting around the room. It didn't take a genius to figure out she was looking for somebody in particular. As Horse's Ass deposited another number, she leaned over to me and said she'd be right back.

She was away from the table and into the crowd before Franklin could get to his feet and follow. I was surprised the big guy's reactions weren't quicker. Maybe he was into the music. He searched the crowd, a worried look on his face.

"She's just gone to the ladies' room," I said.

"Richard says I'm not to let her out of my sight. Anything happens to her, it'll be my ass. Yours, too." Then he moved into the crowd, craning his neck.

At that point I wasn't really worried. This was a grungy part of town, true, but it was just a club, and, for all their pierced navels and bizarre hairdos, these were just Gen-Xers without anything particularly sinister on their minds. But after a few minutes I started to get anxious myself and ventured into the crowd to find out what had become of Angela and Franklin.

Several of the dancers and drinkers seemed stoned, but they were minding their own business. The problem was that there were several rooms off of the main area. A video bar. A poolroom. A small showroom with a comic with porcupine hair screaming about how fucked up the world was.

As I rejoined the crowd in the main room, I spotted a figure that looked somehow familiar—a male body moving away in a graceful lope, ponytail bobbing. I knew I'd seen him before, but I couldn't quite bring the memory to the surface.

When I got back to the table, Angela and Franklin were both there, sitting in silence.

"What's the problem?" I asked.

"She was with some punk," Franklin said.

"They treat me like a baby," Angela said. "I'm an adult, for God's sake. A lot of women are married with children by now."

"They don't have daddies like yours," Franklin pointed out.

"Tell me about it," she said.

"Who was the guy?" I asked.

"My friend from the gallery. I told you about him."

"The one who thinks you should start riding again?"

"Yes. And this oaf scared him away."

"I was just doing what I was told," Franklin said defensively.

"Have you noticed? Nobody is willing to accept blame for their actions anymore," Angela said. "Come on, Coley, I've just about had it with this place."

59

BACK AT Jaydee Farms, I walked Angela to the main house while Franklin put away the car. Before going inside, Angela said, "I'm going to do it tomorrow."

"Good," I said, hoping she meant get on her horse and not run away from home. "We can get an early start."

It was nearly one A.M., but I was too restless to consider trying to sleep. Instead of going to the guest house, I ran to the section of the barn that was used as a garage. Franklin was just locking up.

"I'd like to borrow the car," I told him.

"Why?"

"To drive it, I guess."

Franklin shrugged. "Richard didn't say you couldn't. Ah, Killebrew, do you think we could maybe forget to mention the little incident at the club to Richard? It'd just make him crazy."

"He won't hear it from me."

Franklin nodded and tossed me the car keys.

Pausing at the gate to tell the guard I'd be back in a few minutes, I drove to the nearest establishment I could find that appeared likely to have a pay phone. It was a bar called The Rusty Nail, catering to neighborhood drunks.

I dialed my home number. There were four messages waiting for me on the machine.

Lieutenant Burns asked me to call. Sure. Get right on it.

Lew Totter glumly reported that he was not able to get Barry Gallen to write a check. "Poor Barry's in a daze, doesn't care about anything. Clara McGuinn really gutted the guy, not that he didn't deserve it. But anyway, pally, I don't know what to tell you about the documentary, except that Gallen couldn't care less, about it or anything else. You want to talk about it, gimme a call." He left a New York phone number.

The third message was from Walrus in Bakersfield, wondering what I'd wanted when I stopped off at the store.

The final call was from Lea.

"Hello, darling," her recorded voice said. "Where are you, anyway? What's going on? I want to hear your real voice and not the machine. I miss you. I think even Daddy misses you. He's giving the guys here holy hell. Something is up with them, by the way. Dougherty left the country this morning. I heard La Nasa telling his replacement that he's deep in Dope Country, which could mean anything, but I suspect it's Colombia. Anyway, I don't know whether to be angry or jealous or . . . uh-oh, here they come and here I go. Love you, and want you."

60

ANGELA WASN'T as ready as she thought to get back on a horse.

The next morning, she and I spent an hour or so leading Sandy around the half-mile Jaydee Farms training track. Once, she got a toe in the stirrup. But Sandy, possibly sensing her fear, whinnied and backed away, nearly dragging Angela along. I helped her get her foot free and kept her from falling in the dirt. It wasn't a serious mishap, but to Angela it was magnified beyond its importance.

"Coley, I just can't do it," she said, tears of frustration shining in her eyes. Her chin quivered a little, but she brought herself back under control with an effort. "Today, I mean," she said more quietly. "I can't do it today. Maybe tomorrow."

"Sure," I said.

She whirled around and marched back to the main house, limping slightly, her self-confidence in tatters. Sorry as I felt for her, her withdrawal from the fray allowed me to use my time more profitably.

I spent the rest of the morning poking around the stables, acting the part of a curious but not vitally concerned houseguest. While I was familiarizing myself with the operation, I was also watching for an opportunity to get at the computer in Horace Jinks's office. I was pretty sure a chance would come my way eventually. The security around the perimeter of Jaydee Farms was so elaborate, some of the procedures within its boundaries were surprisingly lax, at least when neither Sandford nor Carmody was at hand.

At noon, when Jinks went to lunch, he left his office unlocked. I didn't waste any time getting to the keyboard, following the procedure I'd observed the night before and pulling up the file on For Cupid's Sake. I absorbed as much of the data about the filly as I could from a quick glance. The sire, I noted, was Tara's Pride, a horse I'd won a couple of races with years ago for Carmody.

Curious, I typed in T-A-R-A. In the offspring section was the information that a filly sired by Tara's Pride had been foaled at Jaydee Farms on the same day For Cupid's Sake was born, but this filly's name was an unfamiliar one, Scarlet Lady. Maybe the original For Cupid's Sake, the one bought from the DEA auction, had been worth only a few bucks, and maybe the three-year-old who was showing so much potential wasn't For Cupid's Sake at all but Carmody's own Scarlet Lady.

But then why would Carmody have gone to such lengths to buy For Cupid's Sake when any similar mare of the proper age would have served the same purpose? It didn't figure.

I was about to call up For Cupid's Sake again, but I heard some of the other workers returning from lunch. I waited until they'd passed and slunk out of the room.

Back at the main house, I found Angela just finishing lunch with her father.

She seemed a little mad at me for some reason. Mad at the world, more likely.

Carmody's mood, on the other hand, was expansive. While I waited for the kitchen staff to whip me up a smoked turkey sandwich topped with sun-dried tomatoes, the master of Jaydee Farms explained his good humor: he had just received word from his man in New Zealand that a business deal had netted him another few million dollars.

Angela rolled her eyes and stood up. "Oh boy," she said. "Now maybe I can get some new curtains for my cell."

"You need new curtains?" Carmody asked, concerned.

"Just a joke, Daddy," she said between clenched teeth. "Just a bitter joke." She looked at both of us like a matched set of road kill and stomped out of the room.

When she was gone Carmody sighed and shook his head. "She calls this place a prison. Well, I guess maybe it is for her, at that."

"She needs to be around people her own age," I said.

"Nobody's stopping her," Carmody said defensively. "She can go wherever she wants, within reason."

"But she has to have Franklin or somebody like him tagging along."

"Of course," he said. "You surely must see why. She's my point of vulnerability."

Not a comment to get him elected Father of the Year.

He stood up to leave. Then he paused and added, "Richard thinks you have designs on Angela."

"Richard should worry about his own designs," I replied.

"Then he's wrong?"

I smiled. "Your daughter is quite a prize, but she's a young man's prize. Anyway, I'm already taken."

"Oh? You don't strike me as a married man," Carmody said guilelessly. I stared at his simian face and wondered if he could possibly have ordered Lea's kidnapping, not to mention Vickie Salazaar's murder.

"Not married. But taken all the same."

"Good," Carmody replied, his interest waning as he made his exit. "Well, think twice before having any children. Most times they're a damned nuisance."

61

IT TOOK me four days to get Angela on a horse. I convinced her that continuing with the spirited Sandy was like trying to run before you could walk. The stables provided an older, more gentle animal named Brewster, who earned his keep as a lead pony for Jaydee Farms runners. By week's end she was actively enjoying the riding experience, and I was sure the next time she approached Sandy she'd get all the way onto the high-strung Arabian's back.

I spent the next few mornings with her and the horse, afternoons poking about the stables, asking the odd question about For Cupid's Sake. Evenings were either quiet or, when guests like Vida Barker or business associates of Carmody's were present, vaguely disquieting. The visitors weren't Carmody's friends, so their conversations were forced and the atmosphere a bit too tense.

There were no more jaunts to Hoofbeat nor any references to Angela's shadowy boyfriend. If she was seeing him, I couldn't begin to imagine how.

Each night, I left the compound to visit the pay phone at The Rusty Nail. Lea's messages were like manna to me, warm, loving, funny. What they usually weren't was newsy. But one night, seven days before the running of the Belmont Stakes, her message contained information about the DEA's progress.

"Dougherty is still among the missing. But Daddy found out the thing that sent him off to Bogotá was the list of people who attended the party the night Vickie died. Evidently, one of the guests turned up in her dossier, but nobody will tell us which one. They won't give us any names, but they say it was a personal affiliation, not a business one. Maybe a guy she dated. Or a woman she became pals with while she was undercover.

"Daddy thinks the DEA is doing some sort of background check to see if this person could possibly be tied to Paolo Rodriguez. Meanwhile, he keeps going over the list and getting frustrated and furious because there are at least a dozen guests he doesn't know. And there's no guarantee that it isn't somebody he knows very well. Anyway, wherever you are—not Colombia, I hope—I send you all my love."

Lea's message sent me back to the same exercise that was driving Starbuck crazy: mentally reprising the list of guests at The Horse's Neck that fateful night. I was still thinking about it as I walked from the barn garage to my guest house. I entered the dark house, closed the door behind me, and was crossing to the bedroom when I first sensed I was not alone.

"Somebody here?" I asked.

"Just me," Angela said.

"Why are you sitting in the dark?" I ran my finger along the wall and found the light switch.

She was on the sofa, dressed in jeans and a tiny tank top.

"Been to Hoofbeat?" I ventured.

"No. The stables. Talking to Sandy. Tomorrow's going to be the day, Coley."

"Good. If you're sure you're ready."

"Don't you think I am?"

"It's what you think that counts."

"Then I'm ready," she said firmly.

Though it wasn't out of character for her to hang around my quarters to make the dramatic announcement, I was a bit uncomfortable about her being there. It was the sort of thing that might provoke Sandford to rush in with guns drawn.

"Fine," I told her evenly. "Now maybe you'd better get some rest, if we're going to be riding tomorrow morning."

"Not in the morning," she said, getting up from the sofa and walking toward me. "I was thinking more like the afternoon."

She stopped a few feet from me. There was a bright light in her eyes that I prayed I hadn't put there.

"Precisely at three tomorrow afternoon," she told me.

"Why then?"

"Because," she said, playfully mussing my hair, the front of our bodies making light contact, "it's the exact time I took my fall."

With that, she walked past me and out the front door.

It was one of those situations where you don't know whether to be disappointed or not. I stood in the doorway and watched her head back to the main house. A large figure emerged from the shadows to join me in staring after Angela.

"Turned out to be a nice uneventful night for all of us, right, Killebrew?" Franklin said.

He strolled off in Angela's wake. I wondered if the big bodyguard wasn't taking his job a bit too seriously.

62

AT PRECISELY three the next afternoon, Angela mounted Sandy for the first time since her accident. A bit tense but not fearful, she began to let the animal know who was in control. Astride a handsome thoroughbred named Sapporo, I watched appreciatively as the two of them began to work as a team.

I couldn't help being proud of her progress. But there was the last hurdle to take.

Angela flashed a quick smile in my direction. "C'mon," she said. "It's time."

She applied her boots and the Arabian bounded forward. Angela's face registered a momentary fright, but she didn't lose her seat and stayed with the horse. I dutifully followed at a quick trot, content to let Angela set the pace.

For a half hour we cantered and trotted around the grounds. Angela was the happiest I'd seen her, virtually a part of the horse. She turned tour guide, pointing out plants and birds and other small wildlife, and I saw more of the seemingly limitless Jaydee grounds than I had since my arrival. As she guided our travels, I had an inkling she had some specific destination in mind, but I had no idea what it was.

Finally we arrived at one of the northernmost sections, only fifty yards or so from the electric fence. It was a heavily wooded area, thick with trees and shrubbery. Angela reined Sandy and began to search the grounds. She was frowning.

"What's up?" I asked.

"He said he'd be here at three-thirty."

"He?"

"My friend. You know, from the art gallery."

I nodded. "And from Hoofbeat."

She grinned. "Exactly. Franklin can chase him off, but he can't stop us from talking on the phone. I told him I'd be riding today, and he said he wanted to see the miracle. That's how he put it. 'See the miracle.' He's so sweet." She looked around some more. "But he's not here."

"You're looking on this side of the fence," I pointed out.

"Well," she said sheepishly, "they're doing some repairs about a mile to the south and I knew that the power was going to be off this afternoon."

"That wasn't smart," I said. "For one thing, what if they changed their plans? Let's get away—"

"What's the hurry?" said a voice from the nearby trees.

The speaker was young, dressed in denim, his face distorted by a stocking mask. He was pointing a Wilson Combat Custom 2011 pistol at us.

"Off the ponies," he said.

"Who are you?" Angela demanded.

A movement to my left drew my attention to another man, slightly shorter and slightly stockier than the first, but wearing the same sort of mask and carrying the same brand of weapon.

"I'll give you to three," the first one said. "Then I shoot the horses out from under you."

I swung my leg over the saddle and, hanging onto the bridle, slid off Sapporo. With some degree of nervousness, Angela dismounted, too.

On the ground, Sandy's reins in her hand, she faced the first man with a foolhardy display of fury. "What have you done with Ro—"

"Shut up," he interrupted. "Come on with me."

Taking a step toward them, I felt the second gunman's sidearm poke into my back. It didn't look hopeful. But then came the almost comforting sound of Franklin's voice. "Drop the guns, scumbags."

The big man was standing just behind the second scumbag. He took a step forward to retrieve the scumbag's weapon and a shot rang out from somewhere just behind me. Franklin leaped sideways as if slapped by an invisible hand.

I heard Angela cry out, "Oh, my God."

As I turned to her, the gunman nearest her held another weapon in his left hand. A taser. He pointed it at Angela, and when it hit, she twitched, made a gagging sound and fell to the ground. I took a step toward her and something very hard crashed against my skull. It turned off my powers of observation for a while.

·   ·   ·

It could have been a minute or an hour later that I was awakened by someone not too gently slapping my face. Richard Sandford, purple with anger.

"What happened to her?" he shouted.

I seemed to be in the same place I'd fallen. The smell of grass and the scenery were identical, but the personnel had changed. Behind Sanford, Carmody was leaning against an open Jeep, a cellular phone in his hand. His grating voice was barking instructions into it, but the only word I could make out was "ambulance."

"I said: What the hell happened?" Sandford repeated.

Shaking my head, trying to clear it, just increased the pain. "How's Franklin?" I asked.

"He'll live," Sandford said, as if it didn't matter much either way. "I want to know about Angela."

"She told some boy she met at an art gallery that the fence would be off today. They set up a meeting here at three-thirty. Instead, two guys showed up with guns. Make that three. The two that I saw and the third one who shot Franklin."

"And you didn't recognize them."

"They wore stockings on their faces. Blue jeans. Sweatshirts. They seemed athletic. Young."

Carmody joined us. "Ambulance'll be here any minute now," he said.

"It was probably the rock geek and his mafioso buddy who took her," Sanford said to his boss. "Maybe Killebrew's in on it, too."

"Don't go simple on us, Sandford," I said. "I sure as hell didn't know the fence would be off."

"I better get back to the house," Carmody said, "and wait for their call. You handle it, Richard. No police. None, until we find out what they want."

I got to my feet and woozily staggered toward Franklin's body. The big man was breathing heavily. The gunshot wound on his right side had soaked through his shirt and coat. His eyes were still closed, but he coughed and licked his lips.

"I'm gonna kill those guys," Sandford said. "Even if they don't touch a hair on her head, I'm gonna cut out their fucking hearts."

I took off my windbreaker, rolled it into a ball, and placed it under Franklin's head. A siren screamed in the distance, got steadily louder and closer, then stopped abruptly. Moments later an ambulance rolled into view.

When the emergency guys jumped out to take Franklin to the hospital, one of them asked me how the man had been shot.

"He's a bodyguard, Doctor," Sandford replied before I could say a word. "Licensed to carry a gun. He fell off his horse. The gun went off and caught him in the side. It's an unfortunate accident."

"I'll be asking you to sign a statement to that effect," the doctor said, not fully convinced.

"Sure," Sandford said. "I'll be glad to."

63

THE CALL we were all expecting came at five that evening. Carmody picked it up on his office phone. Sandford and I were standing by.

"We have your daughter," the muffled voice said.

Following Sandford's instructions, Carmody said, in the most subdued and humble voice I'd ever heard out of him, "Thank you. I intend to cooperate completely. I'll do whatever you want to get Angela back safely."

"Good. Then this should be easy. The first rule is no police."

"Understood. But please let me speak with Angela. I have to make sure she's all right."

A moment later her voice came through, clear and reasonably composed. "I'm okay, Daddy. Just do what they want."

The muffled voice returned. "Satisfied?"

"What is it you want?" Carmody demanded. "Do you want me to pull my horse from the Belmont? It's done."

"We don't give a shit about your horse. We want money. I'll call you later with details."

And that was it.

Sandford and Carmody looked at me. I took a guess at what they expected and said, "This isn't Halcyon and Martin Grosso, if that's what you're wondering."

"I'm afraid you're right," Sandford said with a sigh. "That means we don't know who we're dealing with. And I don't know what the hell we can do about it."

The kidnapper with the muffled voice checked in regularly every hour after that, mainly to reiterate what he'd already said. It wasn't until the nine o'clock call that there were specific instructions.

"Three hundred thousand in small, nonsequential bills," the voice said. "We want it Thursday. We want you to deliver it yourself in a plain brown bag to the lion's cage in Taylor Zoo."

"Taylor Zoo? I never heard of it," Carmody complained.

"On Beauclare Street. In Elmont, New York. You're gonna be there for the Belmont, right?"

"I . . . I'm not sure. . . ."

"Figure it out. I'll call back." Click.

"It's bad," Sandford said wearily. "For one thing, they're not asking for enough money."

"Meaning?" Carmody asked crossly.

"Meaning you're the target. This is all an excuse to get you into the open."

Carmody expelled a long, weary sigh. "Great. Either I willingly go to my death or they kill my daughter."

Sandford slumped in his chair. "They're gonna kill her anyway," he said. "According to what Killebrew tells me, Angela probably knows one of them."

Carmody stared at him. His mind normally worked like a steel trap, but his daughter's abduction had slowed him down.

"In other words," Sandford said, spelling it out, "she knows what he looks like. They won't let her go."

"My baby," Carmody said. The pain in his voice made me reach for an optimistic note.

"They'll keep her alive as long as they need her," I pointed out.

"Meaning what?" Carmody asked.

"Meaning you have to play for time. Tell them you can't get the money before Friday. Or you can't get to New York. Anything. Only push for another day."

"What good is one more day?" Carmody demanded.

Instead of answering the question, I asked one of my own. "Have you ever heard of a woman named Vickie Salazaar? Or maybe Helena Diez?"

Carmody looked perplexed. "No. Neither one."

"It's two names for one person," Sandford said. "I worked with her at the DEA."

"Was she involved in the capture of Paolo Rodriguez?" I asked.

Sandford seemed to be mulling over how much he should say. But he obviously knew he had no future with Carmody if he withheld any information now.

"No," he said finally. "But she knew Rodriguez. She'd spent some time in Colombia. Got pretty close to his inner circle, but she did a dumb thing and we had to pull her out."

"What was the dumb thing?"

"She got involved with some guy down there. She was convinced he wasn't a player, and she may have been right. But it had been a dumb thing for her to do, under the circumstances, and she was yanked back to L.A."

"She was killed there, shortly before the Derby," I said. Sanford looked at me blankly. "Remember the name of the man she got involved with?" I asked.

"I don't think I ever heard it. What's this got to do with Angela?"

I turned to Carmody. "Weren't you aware that Vickie Salazaar and a detective named Raymond Starbuck were investigating your purchase of For Cupid's Sake?"

Carmody looked dumbstruck. Sandford wrinkled his nose. "What the hell is there to investigate?" he demanded.

"Tell me what happened to a filly by Tara's Pride named Scarlet Lady," I said.

"The bastard stole her from me," Carmody exclaimed.

"And what bastard was that?" I demanded.

"This is none of Killebrew's business," Sandford said.

"What the hell difference does it make now?" Carmody said, raising both hands in a who-cares gesture. "I had certain financial interests in Bogotá. Nothing even remotely illegal, but quite delicate. That snake Rodriguez threatened to blow the whole deal out of the water unless I sold him some of my livestock for a ranch he had in Florida. Included was this lovely little filly that showed a great deal of promise. He requested her particularly."

"How did he know about her?" I asked.

"I didn't find out until much later, but he bribed someone who was working here, someone I trusted, to clue him in."

"Your former trainer, Gandy Dawes?" I guessed.

"Damn it, Killebrew," Sandford exclaimed, "you seem to know an awful lot about our business."

"I'll take that as a yes," I said. "And if you expect me to help you, I'll need to find out a lot more." I turned back to Carmody. "So Rodriguez stole the horse from you, and you, with Sandford's help, stole her back."

"Don't answer that," Sandford said.

"What are you, his lawyer?"

"Richard, for Christ's sake," Carmody said. "It's foolish to deny it. Yes, that's precisely what happened. I actually planned the whole damned thing—Rodriguez's capture and trial in this country—for that one reason. The fucker stole my horse."

"And now he's trying to have you killed to get the horse back?" I wondered.

"He's trying to have me killed to get his respect back."

I slumped in my chair and looked at the ceiling. "Salazaar is murdered because she's investigating the sale of the horse. But wouldn't Rodriguez want the sale to be investigated? You'd be embarrassed, and you," I said, looking at Sandford, "might even go to jail for rigging the auction."

"That's your story," Sandford said.

"Unless Rodriguez didn't know she was investigating that deal," I said, thinking out loud. "Unless he was just gaining back his respect, as you put it, by taking care of an agent who'd infiltrated his operation."

"How is this going to help my Angela?" Carmody asked plaintively.

"I don't know," I told him, but it wasn't the complete truth. A gnat of an idea was buzzing in my ear.

The next and final call of the night came an hour later. Carmody told the muffled voice that he wouldn't be able to get the cash and fly to New York before Friday.

There was a pause, then, "Okay. Friday it is. Noon at Taylor Zoo. Any questions?"

"I . . . I'll want to talk with my daughter Friday morning. At eleven o'clock, just before I leave for the airport."

"I'll think about it."

"If I don't hear her voice, I won't be there," Carmody said.

Click.

The three of us looked at one another for a long couple of minutes. Then, feeling we'd done as much as we could, we called it a night.

As I exited the office a board creaked to my right. A shaft of moonlight outlined the unmistakable figure of Lula Dorian moving swiftly and almost silently up the rear stairwell.

64

THE NEXT morning, Sandford dropped by the guest house. He seemed to have grudgingly decided we were on the same team. "I'm going into town to talk to the owners of those two art galleries Angela visited," he said. "It might help give us a line on this boyfriend. Want to tag along?"

"I thought I'd see how Franklin is doing," I said.

"Yeah?" He made it sound as if the idea would never have occurred to him. "Well, debrief him while you're there. Maybe he saw or heard something that'll help."

"I'll tell him you asked about him," I said.

"Whatever."

As soon as he left, I set out for the hospital.

There, I discovered that Franklin's first name was Lawrence and that he was in a private room on the third floor. A nurse on that floor informed me I could see him only if he was awake.

Which he was.

He was lying on his back in bed, needing a shave and pale as death. He seemed to have aged a decade.

"Hi," he said. "Richard with you?"

"He's checking out the art galleries."

"The bastards ask for a ransom?"

I nodded.

"When I fuck up, I fuck up big," he said.

"There wasn't anything more that you could do," I said. "You took a bullet for her. You couldn't have known she was arranging a meet with the boyfriend."

He sighed. "Richard wanted a tap on her phone, but the old man put his foot down. Still, I should have—"

"Don't beat up on yourself," I told him.

"I keep going over it in my mind. What I could have done differently."

"Can you describe the guy who shot you?"

"I didn't get much of a look at him. Average height. Wearing a stocking mask like the others."

"What about the guy who was talking to Angela at Hoofbeat? Could he have been one of them?"

"Maybe." Franklin groaned, either from pain or frustration. "Hell, it could've been my brother and I wouldn't have recognized him."

"Tell me about the Hoofbeat guy."

"Pretty boy. Dressed like the rest of 'em. Leather jacket, like that. Only they're sort of pale and unhealthy, and this guy had a deep tan."

"What about his hair?"

"Slicked back in a ponytail."

It sounded like the description both Lea and Dr. Carl Forrester had given of her kidnapper.

"Tell me exactly what happened. You saw Angela talking with this guy, then what did you do?"

"I headed for 'em. She spotted me, leaned in and said something to him. He turned and saw me. Then the fucker winked at me and gave me a two-finger salute. He was walking away by the time I reached Angela."

"What did she say when you got there?"

"She was just pissed off. Said I was interfering with her life. Then she closed down entirely."

"Thanks, Franklin. Get well, now." I started for the door.

"Uh, Richard say anything about coming by today?" the big man asked.

"He's got a lot going on right now."

"Yeah," Franklin said gloomily. "Well, tell him I'm sorry I let him down."

"You did all that anybody could."

"Try that one on Richard and see what he'll say."

The first thing I did on returning to the Carmody compound was to dial the number in New York Lew Totter had given me. The SportsNet producer was in reasonably good spirits and looking forward to the upcoming race. When he started in on the chances of the various runners, I cut him off as gracefully as possible.

"Do you remember a conversation we had a while ago, about Barry Gallen spending the night with the sister of a policeman in Panama?"

"Yeah," he said with some degree of caution.

"When was that, exactly?" I asked.

"It's stale news. Five, no, maybe six years ago. Why?"

"Was that the trip, L.A. to Panama and back?"

"No. Actually, that was one of our real long runs. We were in Brazil for a week, then we moved on to Bogotá for some jai alai. We stayed there eight or nine days. Then the night in Panama and we vamoosed, sadder but wiser. Why the interest?"

"Anything happen in Bogotá?" I asked.

"Like what?"

"Like Gallen shacking up with anybody?"

"Man, that was a while back. And there have been plenty o' women. But as I recall, one of the SportsNet people down there introduced him to some bimbo and she and Barry were not seen again thereafter. What's this all about?"

"Just curiosity."

"Right. I'll bet that's what Woodward and Bernstein told Deep Throat."

"Are you guys commuting to the Belmont from Manhattan?" I asked.

"Nope. We're leaving soon for the Commodore on Long Island."

"Not the Garden City?" The hotel near Belmont had long been the horseman's hostelry of choice.

"It was Barry's call. Maybe he's got some lady stashed in the joint. Actually, it's a comfortable old place. Food's pretty good, too. You coming in for the race?"

"Flying in this evening. Think it's too late for me to get a room at the Commodore?"

"Have no fear," Lew told me. "I'll take care of it. It's the sort of thing I do best."

Sandford returned from his art gallery trek at noon. I met with him and Carmody in the office, where he relayed the description of Angela's new friend as provided by the art gallery owner.

"Guy called himself Mr. Dover. Tall, good-looking. Well-dressed but a little flashy. Just started showing up recently. No address for him. He wasn't on either gallery's mailing list. Didn't know much about art. He just seemed to appear a few minutes after Angela would arrive. And he'd leave minutes after she did."

"They mention his hairdo?" I asked.

Sandford frowned, initially confused by the question. Then he said, "Oh, yeah. Ponytail. How'd you know?"

"I didn't," I said. "It's just that guys wear their hair all sorts of distinctive ways these days."

Sandford stared at me. "Franklin have anything to say about the kidnapping?"

"The third guy looked just like the others, face covered by a mask," I said. "Franklin's feeling pretty low."

"He should. The son of a bitch let us all down."

"The son of a bitch almost died trying to do his job."

"He's getting the best attention money can buy," Carmody said. He turned to Sandford. "What do I do, Richard?"

"I'm assembling a team for your 'meeting' in the park," Sandford replied. "We'll have that end of it taken care of. But I don't want it to get to that point. We have to reach Angela earlier. I've got a phone guy who swears he can do a trace in less than a minute. As soon as they call you to let you speak to Angela, we'll know where she is."

Unless, I thought to myself, they're calling from a mobile phone or using any of a number of electronic tricks to mask their location. I was sure that Sandford knew as much about that as I did. He was just trying to ease Carmody's burden.

"I'm leaving for New York this evening," I said. "If there's anything I can do . . ."

"Stick around till tomorrow," Sandford said. "That's when I'll be flying out with the horses."

I looked at Carmody. "You're still planning on running For Cupid's Sake?" I asked, somewhat incredulous.

"Richard and I feel it's best if things look normal. Otherwise, the press will be on the phone wondering where the horse is. Naturally, if . . . if it doesn't do go well for us on Friday, the horse race will be the least of our concerns."

I nodded. "I'll see you in New York, then," I said. "I'll be staying at the Commodore if you need me."

Carmody nodded. "Good hotel," he said. "A little far from the track. I haven't stayed there for ages, but I've always liked the place."

65

THE COMMODORE proved to be as pleasant as advertised, but I was much less interested in the amenities than in spending a few minutes with Barry Gallen. The desk clerk informed me that Mr. Totter had taken care of my registration and all that was needed was my signature.

It seemed like a natural follow-up for me to ask casually, as I signed my name, "Are the other members of our party here already?"

"Let's see," the clerk said, letting his fingers wander over his computer's keyboard. "Misters Totter and Gallen have arrived, as has Ms. Simmons."

"Anyone else?"

"No. I don't believe so."

"A Mr. Paragon?"

"I don't see a reservation for Mr. Paragon."

"Is there a free room near Mr. Gallen's?" I asked.

He punched a few more buttons, then frowned. "He's in suite 932. I'm afraid the closest I can get you is 916, but it's right next to the elevator."

"That'd be fine," I said.

Two minutes after the bellhop left my room I was standing in front of suite 932.

No one answered my knock.

I tried the door. Locked. I pressed my ear to it. An image flashed through my mind—Angela Carmody inside the room, bound and gagged.

A foolish and desperate thought. If Gallen were involved in the kidnapping—and there was only circumstantial evidence to support that theory—he certainly wouldn't leave a bound woman in a hotel room where cleaning ladies would be poking their noses into every nook and cranny. There wasn't even a Do Not Disturb sign on the door.

But if she wasn't there, where was she?

The top priority was finding Gallen. It didn't take Sherlock Holmes's deductive skills to locate Lew. He waved to me as soon as I stepped into the hotel bar.

"Coley, join me for an after-dinner drink," the producer said, waving his glass at me.

"Actually, I haven't eaten yet," I said. "I need to find Barry Gallen."

Lew looked pained. "Look, I did the best I could to get that check—"

"It's not about that. Have you seen him?"

"He was in the dining room a half hour ago."

Peering into the fashionably dark dining room, I was confronted by a French-accented maitre d' all primed to do his where-can-I-find-you-the-perfect-table number. He deflated like a fallen soufflé when I told him I was looking for Mr. Gallen.

"Ah, you just missed him and the other gentleman."

"What gentleman was that?"

"I didn't catch the young man's name."

Hoping Gallen and his dinner companion were headed to his room, I raced to the elevators. Crossing the lobby, I saw the two men exiting the front door of the hotel.

By the time I arrived at the door, Gallen had just taken a seat in a maroon Lexus sedan and was pulling the door closed. His dinner companion, the ponytailed legacy at SportsNet, Roddy, was behind the wheel.

The sedan roared away just as I arrived at the curb.

"Need a cab, sir?" the hotel doorman asked.

"You bet," I said.

"I'll have one here in just a few minutes," he said, stepping into a street absolutely void of taxis.

"Thanks," I said, "but I won't need it then."

I walked back inside the Commodore, feeling frustrated and defeated.

Lew was still in the bar, looking for company. "Sit yourself down, amigo. Waiter, can you bring my friend a libation?"

"Sapphire martini," I said to the waiter. "And enough olives to make up for a missed dinner."

"I can bring you something from the grill, sir."

"See what I mean about this place?" Lew said as I ordered a steak, medium-rare. "Whatever you need."

"What I need is some information."

"What I have is yours," the producer said.

"When did Roddy show up here?"

Lew shrugged. "I didn't even know he was in town until I spotted him in the dining room with Barry. I don't think he's staying at the hotel. I didn't book him here."

"Where else could he be staying?"

"I don't know. I don't have much contact with the Rod man."

"Could Roddy's last name be Rodriguez?"

"Something like that," Lew said. "Yeah. I think that sounds right."

"Some legacy," I said.

"What do you mean?" Lew asked, sobering a bit.

"Nothing," I said, and welcomed my martini.

We talked to no apparent purpose for as long as it took my steak to arrive and be consumed. Lew suggested we drive into Manhattan to check out the nightlife. But the nightlife I was interested in was right there in the hotel.

I begged off in the name of exhaustion and went upstairs to my room.

66

IT HAD been a busy day, but I had no intention of falling asleep. I sat in an armchair in my room, in the dark, with the door open several inches so that I could hear the elevator when it arrived. Which it did, innumerable times as the evening wore on. But never with Gallen aboard.

By one A.M., in spite of my anxiety, I found myself nodding off. Under the circumstances, I couldn't fight the tendency with a book or TV. But I knew I had to stay awake . . .

I awoke with a start. The elevator doors had opened. I leaned forward in my chair, straining to hear.

Suddenly, two men were standing in my doorway. They entered the room, closing the door behind them.

"Mr. Killebrew," said a familiar voice. "Whatever are we going to do with you?"

A light went on in the room. The man nearest me was Lawrence B. Singleton of the CIA. Across the room, beside the light switch, was a shorter, swarthy man in a suit slightly too large for him.

"This is Agent Pantera," Singleton said.

The man nodded. He was a sight to behold. There were huge welts going from under his chin to his cheeks, scars that might have been made by the claws of a large animal.

"What in the world do you think you're doing here?" Singleton inquired.

"No business of yours," I replied. "Have you been following me?"

"Absolutely not."

"Then how'd you get here?"

Singleton sighed. "This hotel is under observation."

"Why?" I asked.

"Oh, come on, Mr. Killebrew. Who do you think you're kidding here?"

"I don't think I'm kidding anybody. I asked a question."

"You mean to tell me you don't know that James Carmody has booked the Penthouse Suite upstairs and is flying in tomorrow?"

I looked blank. But my mind was racing. Had my mentioning the hotel influenced Carmody to change whatever other accommodations he had? Or had he been planning on staying there all along? In which case, there might have been a reason why Gallen and Company were there, too.

"Then tell us why you *are* here, Mr. Killebrew," Singleton asked with exaggerated forbearance.

Well, hell. Why not give him just enough of the truth to keep him happy? "I'm here to confront a Los Angeles businessman named Barry Gallen."

Singleton and Pantera exchanged glances. "Confront?" Singleton asked.

"I think Gallen may have killed a DEA officer whose street name was Salazaar."

Singleton smiled. "I'm familiar with the crime. I have not heard Mr. Gallen's name connected with it."

"Salazaar had moved into your former buddy Paolo Rodriguez's inner circle when she made the mistake of getting involved with the wrong guy. Gallen was in Bogotá at roughly that time. And he had an affair with a woman he met through the SportsNet office there."

Singleton looked at Pantera and they both grinned. "Imagine that. Gallen and the Salazaar woman, lovers," Singleton said.

I could feel the anger rising. I wanted to wipe the smirks from their faces. "I don't suppose you know anything about the young Colombian named Rodriguez working for SportsNet. He's been described as a legacy, which makes me think that Paolo Rodriguez might be at least a part owner in the company. Big surprise to you guys?"

Singleton shook his head. "You're very colorful, Mr. Killebrew. And you've got quite an imagination."

"Do you know what Gallen is doing here?" I asked.

"Just a wild guess, but: Going to the Belmont Stakes?"

"I think he and the guy he works for, Geoffrey Paragon, are trying to kill James Carmody. Or, failing that, to discredit him."

Singleton chuckled. "Why would they do that?"

"Maybe they're working with you."

The indulgent smile left Singleton's face. "We don't kill people or set people up."

"Tell it to the *New York Times.*"

"Carmody is setting himself up," Singleton said heatedly. "Do you know the circumstances behind the sale of For Cupid's Sake?"

"The first sale, when he sold the horse to Rodriguez? Or the second one, when he bought it back?" I asked.

"Then you do know that the main reason Carmody sent his mercenaries into Bogotá to unlawfully apprehend Paolo Rodriguez was to get the bloody horses."

I stared at Singleton. "What difference does that make? Rodriguez was a trafficker in drugs, a murderer, a thug. Who cares what Carmody's motive was?"

Singleton turned to his partner. "Perhaps you can explain it to him."

"There will always be drugs in Bogotá, Mr. Killebrew," Pantera said. "That is a fact of life. Paolo Rodriguez was all the things you say, and possibly he is even worse than that. But we had come to a point of agreement with him. It meant that, to a certain extent, we could control the flow of narcotics coming into our country and achieve certain other goals. Now we are being forced to court Rodriguez's replacements. And the courtship does not go well."

"In other words," Singleton said, "to buy back a horse on the cheap, Carmody sold us out in Bogotá."

"That's one way of looking at it," I said.

"What other way is there?" Singleton demanded.

"I'm not about to discuss aspects of morality with a CIA agent," I said. "There's no point."

"Just keep one thing in mind, Killebrew. We do what we do for the good of our country. Carmody only gives a shit about Carmody."

I couldn't deny that. "What is it you want from me, Singleton?" I asked. "Just tell me and, who knows, maybe I can accommodate you."

"I want you to go home," he said. "I want you to get out from underfoot. We don't want some loose cannon knocking down all the work that's been done."

"Work? You mean you know about Gallen and the murders?"

"I'm telling you to forget Gallen. He's not even a part of this mural. And that's the last thing I will tell you. If you're not out of here in the morning, we'll take steps to help you leave."

They departed and I sat slumped in my chair, suddenly realizing that they didn't care if Gallen had killed the DEA agent. I'd almost gone against Carmody's wishes and told them about Angela's kidnapping. I doubt that would have impressed them either. For all I knew, they had arranged it. It was all too dark and too deep.

I went to the door and set all the locks. As added protection, I wedged a chair under the door handle.

And so to bed.

67

A RUDE knock woke me up. Aching and stiff, I staggered to the door to find Lew Totter, bright and energetic.

"Nearly nine," he said. "Man, you look like my liver feels."

"Thank you very much," I said, staggered into the bathroom and turned on the water in the washbasin.

"You said you wanted to check in with Barry. I'm meeting him for breakfast in," looking at his watch, "seven minutes."

The basin was nearly full of cold water. I dunked my face into it, wiggled it from side to side and withdrew with a yell. "I'll be right with you," I told him. "Keep my seat warm."

I shaved and dressed in record time and paused only long enough to take my handgun from my suitcase, snap it together, load it, and slip it into my coat pocket.

I needn't have hurried.

The guy seated at Lew's table in the dining room was not Barry Gallen. The producer introduced him as Mick Karpis, a somewhat grizzled specimen from Manhattan who, he informed me, usually spent his time taping semiporno performance acts for the blue channel. He was Lew's pick to finish off the documentary.

We lingered over breakfast until ten, during which period Lew tried Gallen's room three times without getting a reply. I was about to go upstairs and bribe a maid to let me into suite 932 when Loretta Simmons arrived, lovely as ever but a bit haggard.

"Coley?" She was obviously surprised to see me. "I . . . ah, Lew, Barry just called. He's sorry he couldn't make breakfast, but he's sort of tied up."

Lew rolled his eyes. "What is it this time—blonde, brunette, or redhead?"

"Unless he was fibbing again, he was all by his lonesome."

"It's important that I see Barry as soon as possible," I said to Loretta. She stared at me, frowning.

"Look, if the money is that important—" Lew began, still as confused as I wanted him to be about my insistence on seeing Gallen.

"It's not the money. It's . . . about Clara McGuinn," I improvised.

"Give me a minute," Loretta said.

She took at least ten, but when she returned, she said, "He'll see you right now."

Lew stood up as if to join us, but Loretta said carefully, "I think Barry wants to speak with Coley privately."

Lew shrugged and pulled a piece of plastic from his pocket. "Here," he said, handing it to me, "before I forget. I thought you might be able to use this." It was a press badge for the Belmont.

"Thanks. But I don't think I'll be making the race tomorrow," I said, handing the badge back.

"Hang onto it anyway," Lew said. "You never know."

He was right. I never do.

68

LORETTA LED me to a rented sedan in the hotel's parking lot. "I don't know what's been going on with Barry and Mrs. McGuinn," she said, "but whatever it is, it's driving him crrr-azy. I hope it's not bad news you have to tell him."

"It should make him as merry as Christmas," I lied.

She drove us into Manhattan, showing a cool expertise with New York traffic that impressed the hell out of me. Los Angeles freeways are alleged to be challenging, but to my Southern California sensibility, the free-for-all New York motoring was indistinguishable from London or Rome. Still, on the way I didn't forget to at least try to gather information.

"How well do you know Roddy Rodriguez?"

She wrinkled her forehead. "SportsNet Roddy? I don't know him well at all."

"I heard he was a ladies' man. Don't tell me he's passed you by."

She smiled. "Not my type, chum. I'm not into boy toys. I prefer a mature man."

"Like Paragon?"

"I wish," she said.

"Is he here, by the way?"

"Not that I've heard. But he doesn't always consult me."

Our destination was a beautiful old three-story brownstone in the Nineties. It sported an ornate cut-glass front door behind the barred front alcove. Loretta dug through her purse for the key.

"This is owned by SportsNet," she explained. "Sort of a home-away-from-home for the execs."

Inside, with its polished wooden floors, high ceilings, and antique furnishings, it reminded me of another age entirely. A more civilized, elegant age.

Loretta called Barry's name. There was no reply.

"He must be upstairs," she said.

We passed through a formal dining room. Two meals, only partially consumed and now congealed, rested side by side.

"Must be the maid's day off," I remarked.

Loretta, looking a little concerned now, called Barry again. Again there was no reply.

"He was in bed when he called. I guess he might still be there." She sounded more worried than the words implied. She led me up a wooden staircase to the second floor.

The door to the main bedroom was open a few inches, just enough for us to see Barry Gallen sitting up in the huge king-size bed. He was wearing purple pajamas, with a tufted quilt drawn up around him.

"Barry?" she asked tentatively. Barry Gallen didn't reply. He continued to stare at a spot on the wall opposite the bed.

A chill went through me as I started to get the idea. I moved past Loretta and entered the room. Gallen's purple pajamas had once been white. Now they were crusted with his blood, blood that was too dry for him to have been able to invite me to come see him just that morning.

As I belatedly reached under my coat for my gun, someone, probably Loretta, bounced something off the back of my head. I stayed conscious just long enough to record the irony; it had landed on the precise spot where I'd been hit during Angela's kidnapping.

69

I AWOKE to a blinding whiteness that was like a knife piercing my eyes and going directly to my brain. Everything was white and hot. I closed my eyes, wanting to start over. First you take inventory.

I was lying on my back, hands tied behind me, ankles bound. I opened my eyes again, more cautiously. Above me were the glass panels of a solarium. The afternoon sun was baking the room. And me.

Through the open door, leading, I guessed, to the third floor of the SportsNet brownstone, I could hear two people talking. One of them was Loretta Simmons, dear lady, the other a male whose voice I didn't recognize.

". . . only then will he feel like a man again," the guy was saying.

"I hope they finish it at the park," Loretta said.

"If not, we move to Plan B."

"Plan B sucks, Roddy. In broad daylight? There'll be cameras all over the place, videotape. If the park fails, I say we skip B and go directly to A."

Plan A? Shouldn't Plan C follow Plan B? Didn't these people know I had a headache?

"It's too messy," he replied. "So many others would have to die. Even the animals. Plan B is, how they say, fail-proof."

"That's easy for you to say. All you have to do is watch."

"But it's so simple, *bonita mia*. Just a little prick."

"Yeah, well, I hope they get the big prick in the park."

I turned my head and could see them, seated in what appeared to be a den adjoining the solarium. They made a handsome couple, sipping their tall drinks and discussing murder.

Loretta was on a white couch, elegant legs crossed prettily. Across from her, on a matching stuffed chair, was the man with a ponytail and cheekbones more prominent than Jay Silverheels's. Roddy Rodriguez.

"What about *him*?" Loretta asked, meaning me, I guess. "He'll be waking up soon."

"*Mi patrón* says we keep him here. It is all a matter of drugs. Speaking of which . . ."

Roddy got to his feet and walked out of the room. The last part of their conversation had been even more alarming to me than the murder talk. Its threat was more immediate and up close, you might say.

Loretta stood, too, and started toward the solarium. That was my signal to close my eyes.

I could hear her footsteps approaching, high heels tap-tapping on the tile floor. They paused very close to where I was lying. I could smell her perfume, a subtle citrusy scent I'd always liked up until then.

I heard more footsteps. Heavier. Masculine. The dapper Roddy coming to join her. Adding an excessively applied aftershave to my aroma blacklist.

All I could do was keep my eyes shut, think unconscious, and hope they'd go away.

But Roddy moved closer. What the hell was he doing?

Too late, I felt the sting of a needle entering my neck. By reflex I pulled away from it. Roddy cursed, then said, "He got enough."

I felt warmth spreading through my body. A soothing warmth that mixed with the warmth of the sun and made me think it would be so very nice to drift off to peaceful sleep. But I still had a kernel of awareness that told me to resist sleep as long as I could.

"It'd be simpler just to kill him," Loretta said, her voice coming from a far-off place.

"We can always do that," Roddy replied. "He's not going anywhere."

But I guess I went *somewhere*, because that's the last thing I heard for a while.

70

THIS TIME I awoke in darkness. Choking. Gasping for breath. Something was stinging my nostrils. A pungent odor. Ammonia. I rolled away from it, until I bumped into a post. I sat up, straining my eyes and seeing nothing. I brought my knees to my chest and pulled on the rope around my wrists until I was able to work my bound hands past my butt and feet and up and over my drawn knees. My hands in front of me now, eyes watering, I drew my bound feet under me and pushed upright. Then I hopped back to keep from falling.

My shoes came into contact with something on the floor. It crunched. Glass. I squatted again. The smell was too strong. My eyes filled with water and I couldn't breathe at all. The fingers of my bound hands scrabbled for a section of broken glass on the floor. The one I found was wet with ammonia.

I stood and hopped away from the smell. Carrying the broken glass. Carrying some of the toxic odor.

Panting, I leaned against a wall and placed the piece of broken glass between my knees. It took me forever to saw through the rope around my wrists, and slightly less than forever for me to cut my ankle ties.

I tossed the broken glass aside. The crash as it hit the cement floor was punctuated by a scurrying sound that I didn't like at all.

I felt my way along a wall until my hand contacted a light switch.

Reflexively, I closed my eyes against the sudden painful brightness. Opening them slowly and tentatively, I saw I was in a room filled with boxes and cleaning utensils. An ancient heating system sent its metal tubes through the ceiling. A staircase led up to a closed door. Breathing heavily, I climbed to the top of the steps and grasped the knob.

The door was locked.

According to my watch, it was nine o'clock. Day or night? I had no way of knowing.

My gun was gone, but I still had my wallet. And my press badge. Whoopee. Just the stuff I needed.

I felt my neck. It was almost as sore as my head. My brain was fuzzy. Sore and fuzzy. Fuzzy and sore.

I could see the remaining pieces of the ammonia bottle on the floor. It seemed to have fallen from a shelf. Other items on the shelf were disturbed. As I moved closer, a large rat scooted from behind a paint can and scurried along the shelf, leaping off into a dark corner of the room.

As I jumped back in surprise, I think I yelped. But I didn't hear a thing come out of my throat. The idea I might have lost my voice alarmed me. What if I wanted to scream? What if I had to make a noise? Could I? As a test, I screamed at the top of my lungs. That I heard. But it alarmed me, too. What if I was losing my grip, raving, going crazy?

I kept a wary eye on the rat in the shadows. How many more of his relations were down there, sharing my space? Didn't I have enough trouble without having to deal with rats?

On the other hand, hadn't it been the rodent who woke me up by knocking over the ammonia? If he hadn't, I would probably have stayed drugged until the Rod man returned to administer the next dose of drugs or the coup de grace. The rat was my pal.

But I still didn't like him. Or her.

So it was nine o'clock. What to do? Smash through the door? And alert Roddy? No. The conservative approach was definitely the way to go.

I looked around the room, considering the materials available. Use your brain, Killebrew. It's still working. Do what you can do, then turn the damn light off, before the man with the needle returns.

It was just under an hour later when the door at the top of the stairs finally opened. The light came back on.

Roddy paused at the top of the stairs looking down on the body of the poor over-the-hill jockey, lying right where he'd left it. He wrinkled his nose. What was that odor? Ammonia?

He looked at the body again. He started down the stairs. But as he descended, his foot came in contact with something unexpected. Though he didn't know it at the time, it was twine stretched tight across the stairwell. He reached out his hand, and the case containing the hypodermic needle flew from his fingers as he stumbled forward, screaming.

He tumbled down hard, handsome, tanned face scraping wood, chin banging against plank, body sliding out of control. And as he landed on the cement floor and started to rise up, I stepped from beneath the stairwell and swung a heavy skillet against the bastard's skull.

My head was reasonably unfuzzed by now, but after an extra hour in the dark in my underwear, with the rats, my nerves weren't in the best shape. I used a clothesline to tie Roddy to the ancient metal heater, making sure the knots were nice and tight. As Roddy's jacket slipped to one side, I noticed a lump in one pocket. Sure enough, it was my own gun. It warmed my hand, but the rest of me felt a little breezy, so I removed my coat and trousers from the rag and paper towel dummy I'd fashioned.

Redressed for success, I decided the time had come for a little fun. I sopped up some of the spilled ammonia with a rag and stuck it under Roddy's nose. It didn't take long before he was coughing and glaring angrily at his surroundings.

"*Maricón*," he said nastily.

"Feeling poorly, are you?" I asked.

He didn't answer. Instead he said, "That fucking drug was supposed to last longer."

"I had a wake-up call. Where's Angela?"

Roddy stared at me. "Angela who?" he said.

I picked up my gun and aimed it at his left eye. It seemed to alter his mood. "Hey man, I did you a big favor," he said.

"Oh?"

"They wanted me to kill you," he said. "But I ask, why do this needless murder? In twenty-four hours, what will it matter if you are still alive?"

He sounded convincing. I might have believed him if I hadn't overheard him say the only reason he was keeping me alive was on orders from his *patrón*.

I flicked his nose with my finger. He yelled and tears came to his eyes. "Where's Angela?" I repeated.

"She's upstairs. She's okay. I swear. Just, you know, sleeping it off."

I got the hypodermic needle out of its case. "Where do I jab this?" I asked Roddy.

"Hey, don't screw around with that. You can kill somebody if you don't know what you're doing."

"That's why I asked you."

"C'mon, man—"

"Okay, I'll just have to improvise."

I felt my own neck, locating the bump where Roddy had injected me earlier. Then I started to push the needle into Roddy's neck at the same spot. My patient pulled away.

"Close your eyes," I advised him. "It'll be easier on both of us."

He closed his eyes tight and was still as a statue, but it just wouldn't work for me. So I used my gun to knock him out and shot the dope into his arm. It wouldn't act as quickly, but there was no way I could stick a needle in somebody's neck.

With Roddy taken care of, I left the basement and discovered that a new day had dawned. In slightly less than two hours Carmody would be starting his potential death march in the park.

I made a hasty reconnaissance of the upstairs of the house. Four rooms. One was occupied by Barry Gallen, still dead and smelling rather badly. Another was being used as a sort of den, the furniture paying homage to a large-screen TV that filled a wall.

Angela was in the third, a neatly appointed bedroom. She was lying still, a down blanket covering her. She seemed to be breathing easily.

I drew back the cover.

Someone had removed her outer clothes. She was wearing a frilly bra and panty combo, probably selected with a glorious evening with Roddy in mind. It didn't appear that he or anybody else had done more than keep her drugged.

I left her to look for a phone. A neat little cellular number was in the room next to the solarium.

Much to the day clerk's surprise, Sandford took my call in Carmody's suite at the Commodore.

"Cancel the trip to the park," I told him.

"What?"

"I've got Angela."

"Is she okay?"

"I think so."

"Where are you?"

"Manhattan," I told him, and gave him the brownstone's address. "But we won't be here long."

I gave him Loretta Simmons's name and description and that of Geoffrey Paragon. "I'm not sure that *he's* part of the package, but the lady is definitely on Paolo Rodriguez's payroll."

"Got it. I owe you one, you son of a bitch," Sandford said, hanging up. I hoped he meant it in a nice way.

Returning to the basement, I found a set of Lexus keys in Roddy's pocket that carried a tag from a rental car company. The maroon sedan I'd seen Roddy and Gallen in was parked in a closed garage just off the kitchen.

Back in Angela's bedroom, I filled a glass with water from the bathroom sink and sprinkled it on her face.

Eventually she opened her eyes and peered up at me.

"Hi," I said.

Her reactions were slow. Confused and disoriented. Then, when she began to remember where she was, she tensed.

"It's okay," I said. "It's me. Coley. I've come to take you away from all this."

Our escape was accomplished in various stages. Getting Angela up and dressed. Using a towel to wipe away our fingerprints. Helping her down to the car. Finding the switch that lifted the garage door. Using the cellular phone to notify the Manhattan police of shots and screams of horror coming from the brownstone's address. Figuring out how to get from where we were to the Hotel Commodore.

With all that, we wound up on the Long Island Expressway in less than half an hour.

71

ANOTHER DAY, another daughter-father reunion. But this one was a bit different. Starbuck had lowered his guard, albeit temporarily, to welcome Lea's return with a rare display of emotion. Carmody, however, remained as stiff as a brick.

With his monkey face as rigid as if it had been cast in brass, he solemnly shook my hand and then turned to his still-woozy daughter, who was being administered to by a middle-age man of medicine. "You gave us quite a scare, young lady," he said. Yessir, quite a scare. I couldn't figure him out. That night at the compound, he was behaving like a worried father should. A few hours ago he'd been planning on risking his life for her. But that was then, and now it was back to business as usual.

She stared at him coolly, apparently trying to match his lack of emotion. The doctor interrupted the magic of the moment by announcing, "I think Miss Carmody could use a bit of rest and quiet."

We filed out of the room. Sandford was the last to leave, studying the girl carefully, as if trying to make sure she hadn't been infected with vampire blood.

"Top flight job, Killebrew," Carmody said. "Done with remarkable discretion."

"Discretion wasn't my main concern. And, in fact, when the police grab Roddy Rodriguez and Loretta Simmons, they may just drop our names."

He chewed on that for a bit, then said, "There's truth and there's public perception of truth. Whatever happens, we can live with it. Remember this, son, you're a genuine American hero."

The way he said it made me think the bill for the whole party might wind up on my credit card.

I asked Sandford what he was going to do about Loretta and Paragon. "We'll probably nab 'em in the park," he said. Then he stared at me and said, "You look like hell. You'd better get some sleep."

He turned from me to the security guards who'd been assigned to the suite. He gave them their marching orders, then departed to join with the cadre of armed leg-breakers already stationed in the park, waiting for whoever showed to collect the ransom Carmody was supposed to deliver in less than twenty minutes.

I was exhausted, still slightly drugged. I wandered downstairs to a pay phone and made a call to the car rental company to tell them where they might find one of their Lexi, seemingly abandoned in the wilds of Long Island. Then, yawning mightily, I elevated up to my pristine suite.

Just one more yawn away from sleep, I dialed my home number in Santa Monica. Someone had called two days before from a nearby hospital to inform me of their new health plan. Lieutenant Burns had called yesterday, presumably not about my health. And Lea had called last night with a message short but sweet. "I love you, I miss you, I want to be with you. Sleep well." How could I refuse?

I woke up eleven hours later with Lea still on my mind. I dialed Jack Hayward at The Horse's Neck and told him I'd be returning on the morrow.

"Mission accomplished?" he asked.

"Sort of," I said, wondering if Sandford had been successful in rounding up Loretta and the others.

"If Lea should call," I said, "she can reach me here." I read the number on the base of the telephone.

That accomplished, I cajoled room service into providing me with a cheeseburger and a dish of rice pudding, and munched and watched the middle part of a Late Show movie. From what I could gather, the hero was a hit man whose love for a sexy environmentalist moved him to bump off a bunch of greedy businessmen whose companies were destroying the planet.

I was mildly curious about how the movie would end. Would the guy get away with murder because it was for a good cause? Would he wind up standing trial with a dream team of lawyers riding roughshod over the prosecution? I never found out. There must have been some vestige of the drug still in my system, because I fell asleep in front of the TV. I didn't wake up until late the next morning with an animated

Man-Lizard cavorting on the small screen. He seemed to be trying to save the environment, too, only a bit less lethally, using his tail in lieu of a .45.

I dressed and went down to the hotel dining room for a leisurely and solitary lunch, buying several morning papers to keep me company. The various sheets, from top to tabloid, each offered a vivid description of the discovery of Barry Gallen's body, a mystery complicated by syringes and other drug paraphernalia. According to no less dependable a source than the *New York Times*, the house was empty except for the body. Unless the police were concealing some information, Roddy must have flown the coop. I probably should have scrubbed up that ammonia.

After lunch I went up to the penthouse to see how the Carmodys were faring. One of the security guards stationed in the hall informed me that Miss Carmody was resting comfortably in the suite. But Mr. Carmody had gone to the track.

It had never occurred to me that, after all the events of the last few days, Carmody would still go to the Belmont. On the other hand, why not? His daughter was okay; he had plenty of security; and his filly, which had finally thrown off all traces of the procaine, had a chance to accomplish, as the morning papers noted, what no filly had done since 1905.

I'd have enjoyed seeing the race in person myself, but I decided it was probably too late to drag my tired and sore body out to the track. So I returned to my room, leaned back on the bed and relaxed over the sports pages for a while, figuring I'd catch the classic on TV.

My favorite nag, Sabisa, was now the choice of the chalk players off his strong run in the Preakness. Appetizer would be running again and would no doubt have some support from the New York partisans, but I doubted he could get the mile and a half. Another New Yorker, Glory Regained, had skipped the Preakness and hoped to live up to his name on home ground. Halcyon's Derby champ, Headbanger, would be back in action, too, having recovered from his poisoning siege. The Lundens, though, convinced they were Triple Crown snakebit, had kept their hotshot Hotfoot back in California.

It figured to be quite a contest. I still thought For Cupid's Sake, whatever her original identity, might do it, and if she didn't make it, Carmody could start running her against fillies instead. That had been his alternate plan—

Alternate plan. The words set off a gong in my brain.

I shot to my feet, feeling like ten kinds of idiot. With Angela back and safe, I'd been thinking and acting like the crisis was over. But it wasn't. The conversation between Loretta and Roddy came back to me like icy fingers on the back of my neck. If the assassins missed Carmody in the park, they would move on to alternate Plan B, rather than alternate Plan A. Alternate Plan B. If A and B did not signify alphabetical progression, then it was a good bet that plan B was . . . Plan Belmont.

72

I REMEMBER somebody telling me that time is the longest distance between two places. It was true that day.

I spent priceless minutes trying to get through to the Belmont
switchboard. Failing that, I called the guy at the front desk and told
him I was headed down and needed a cab right away. The bellman
had just flagged one down as I cleared the front door.

The driver, a young African American whose name, according to
his license, was Marcus Aurelius Fly, told me it would take twenty
minutes to get to Belmont, assuming traffic was light. The voice on
his car radio was counting down the minutes before the race.
Seventeen.

"Twenty on top of the meter," I told him, "if I make that race."

"Let's say twenty plus a speeding ticket," Mr. Fly said, "plus another
fifty because I'll probably have to go to court to argue—"

"Let's say a flat hundred," I said, ticket or no.

"What a beautiful day," he said, the cab taking off like a greased
rocket. "We'll just take the Long Island Expressway to the Cross Island
Parkway. Not a red light the whole trip."

We were on the expressway when he asked, "You trying to get a bet
down before the race?"

"Something like that," I said.

He lifted a cellular phone. "I can take care of it for you right here."

"There's a little more to it," I said.

"Uh-huh. I don't suppose you got a tip you'd care to share?"

As a matter of fact, I did. If I was right, only one horse would be
winning the race. "For Cupid's Sake," I said to Mr. Fly.

"He's at three-to-one."

"She," I corrected.

Steering the car one-handed in and out of the expressway traffic,

Mr. Fly bet the hundred I'd promised him. When he put down the phone, he grabbed the wheel with both hands and really put the pedal to the metal.

We arrived at the crossroads of the Belt Parkway and Hempstead Avenue in twelve minutes. I fumbled in my wallet and laid two fifties into Mr. Fly's plastic drawer, then ran across the Belmont Park parking lot.

For all my visits to Belmont as a jockey, I had never been there as a spectator. Still, I had a fair idea where the owners and trainers congregated. The press pass Lew had so thoughtfully provided would get me through all turnstiles and past all checkpoints.

Time was getting short, but there was some advantage in that. I could belt through the crowd like a maniac on wheels without anyone taking notice of me. They were all transfixed, focusing their attention on the eight horses entering the starting gate. At most American tracks, the start for a mile and a half race would be somewhere on the backstretch, but since the race was just one circuit of the big Belmont oval, the gate was in front of the stands.

I found the owners, and trainers, section just as the last horse was loading. Looking down from a railing above the grandstand section, I saw some familiar figures, among them Halcyon and Martin Grosso, there to root for Headbanger, and the plump salsa maker who owned Sabisa. At the instant the horses were breaking from the starting gate, I located Carmody's box.

He and Sandford were avidly watching as For Cupid's Sake settled into a comfortable third place going to the first turn. Their three bodyguards, by contrast, were the only ones in the owners' area looking anywhere (and everywhere) but the track. I had to shift my focus to avoid making eye contact with them and attracting their unwelcome attention.

"Whaddaya t'ink of Appetizah?" said a guy standing next to me above the seat section, binoculars pressed to his eyes. In powder-blue suit, black shirt, and orange tie, he was a living stereotype who might've just walked in from a straw-hat theater production of *Guys and Dolls*.

I grunted something noncommittal.

"They're ratin' him today, huh? People think he needs the racetrack, but he don't."

As great as the race sounded, I wasn't really giving it that close attention. At each of the previous Triple Crown races, Geoffrey Paragon had arranged for seats in the same position relative to the Jaydee Farms party. And, assuming I was right, he'd be in that same general vicinity now.

But I couldn't spot him.

There was a cry from the crowd and I glanced at the horses as they passed the five-eighths pole. The favorite, Sabisa, was running third, a couple of lengths behind Headbanger and For Cupid's Sake, who were neck and neck in the lead. I shifted my gaze back to the crowd, counting heads, counting rows, counting seats. Evidently, Lew had not come through for Paragon. The special seats on the aisle, four rows in front of Carmody, were occupied by an elderly couple.

The woman was directly on the aisle. She was wearing a hat that covered much of her white hair, a dark pleated dress, pearls, white gloves. Her beau was dressed in a dark blue blazer, sporting a tan panama. They had the appearance of old-money horsepeople, and they were watching the race like everybody else. Still, there was something off about them.

The woman gestured with her hand, and I saw the sun glisten off a ring on her finger. A ring on the outside of her glove.

"Headbanga's out of it and here comes Appetizah," exclaimed the Damon Runyon dropout. "Look at 'im go."

As if taking the invitation too literally, I grabbed the binoculars out of his hands.

"What duh hell you t'ink you're doin'?" the fan demanded, justifiably outraged.

"Sorry, but this is a matter of life and death," I said. That kept him quiet for a few seconds. I trained the glasses on the elderly woman's hand. Her ring looked remarkably like the one Paragon wore for the Kentucky Derby. And at the party at The Horse's Neck.

What was it Roddy had said in his conversation with Loretta at the brownstone? "Just a little prick." He hadn't been talking about me. And we didn't have bugs at The Horse's Neck. And it hadn't been Gallen who'd had the affair with Vickie Salazaar.

I returned the binoculars to their owner with a mumbled apology and started down the stairs toward Carmody's box. As I did, the crowd was rising to its feet. Appetizer was making a surprising late move to take third, passing Headbanger. But by then, For Cupid's Sake was breezing across the finish line a length in front of Sabisa for the win.

The crowd was screaming. It looked like everyone in the owners' area was trying to get to Carmody, shake the winning owner's hand.

I was only a few feet away from him now, but the aisle was filling up on me, the crush of spectators pushing me back.

Carmody struggled to get to the aisle. When he got there, he headed down the stairs toward the winner's circle, moving faster than his bodyguards, as usual. Here, I realized, was what Sonny Marquez had called the moment of vulnerability, the one window of opportunity that Paragon had been waiting to open up since the Kentucky Derby. He'd even tried to help it along by getting rid of For Cupid's Sake's main competition.

Pushing past Sabisa's plump, disappointed owner, I fought my way to within an arm's grasp of Carmody. That was when I felt someone's powerful grip on my shoulder. One of Carmody's guards, probably. I twisted away, not looking back. Someone shouted angrily.

The elderly woman with Paragon's ring was turning to greet Carmody. In what seemed like slow motion, she raised her free hand to grab his in what appeared to be a gesture of congratulation. I felt the bodyguard's fingers reaching for me again, and I wanted to shout at him, "I'm on your side, damn it. I'm trying to save your boss." I leaped away from his grasp toward Carmody and the woman. My hand found her wrist and clutched it desperately, my forward thrust pulling her and Carmody with me down the stairs.

By now the whole crowd knew there was something unusual going on—a madman attacking the winning owner and an elderly female patron. Everybody seemed to be screaming and yelling.

We had landed in a painful human sandwich with Carmody on the bottom. The person I was lying on top of, whose wrist I held, was definitely a woman, but she was young and strong, struggling to free herself.

One of Carmody's bodyguards stuck a gun in my ear and was bellowing something at me, but I kept hold of the wriggling woman's wrist. Below us, Carmody was wailing in pain.

The woman turned her face upward to me now, teeth bared in a furious snarl as she tried to bite my hand. I was staring into the vaguely disguised features of Loretta Simmons, her gray wig and dainty hat comically askew. When she couldn't get her teeth on my fingers, she tried to punch me in the head. I dodged, my grasp on her wrist weakening.

"What the hell's going on, Killebrew?" demanded Richard Sandford's voice somewhere up above me. The trainer was flanked by the second bodyguard.

"The ring," I shouted to the trainer. "Poison."

Sandford acted quickly. He grabbed Loretta's hand and pinned it to the cement while she cursed and tried in vain to kick him.

I rolled off her bucking body. The first bodyguard was still pointing his gun at me. I looked past him at Paragon, in his elderly turf patron guise, pushing through the shocked crowd on his way to an exit.

"Stop him," I screamed. "Stop the guy in the hat."

The bodyguard, unable to cast off the idea that I was the lunatic, was confused.

"Do what he says! Stop the bastard!" Sandford yelled at him as he struggled to drag Loretta off Carmody.

The bodyguard lumbered after Paragon, yelling for the track security guards to head the man off.

Television cameras moved in past the startled crowd as Sandford jerked Loretta to her feet, awkwardly twisting her arm behind her and trying to stay clear of the deadly ring. Members of the track's security team moved to assist him.

Carmody sat up with a grunt. I offered him a hand. He slapped it away. "Goddamn you, Killebrew," he bellowed. "Feels like you broke my fucking leg."

73

IT WASN'T Carmody's accusation that made me extricate myself from the nearly slapstick situation as quickly as possible. I wanted to make sure that Paragon didn't escape. He'd made it at least as far as the exit from the grandstand.

The stands were still packed with people, most of whom seemed to be gawking at me. They had no idea why I'd attacked Carmody or why some security guards seemed to be ignoring me while snapping cuffs on one of my victims, while others were racing after some elderly gentleman. The up side of being thought of as loony and dangerous is that crowds open up to let you pass. I was out of the grandstand in jig time.

I could see Paragon cutting across the parking lot, hatless now, with his pursuers closing in. Still, he moved purposefully, presumably heading for the section of the lot where his car was parked. But with the big race over, the exits from the lot were filling with departing patrons. So Paragon reversed his field and tried to make his getaway on foot.

As he reached an exit, police cars, their sirens wailing, braked only a few yards away. Uniformed cops hit the asphalt and Paragon turned to head back inside the lot. But the security guards were waiting there. He was trapped.

Thinking the police might need some information from me, I trotted across the parking lot myself. As I walked through the maze of parked cars, my former companion with the binoculars turned up alongside me.

"Did you have him ta show?" he asked.

"What?"

"Appetizah. I was on'y on him ta win. I figured you musta had some dough on him, too, the way you grabbed my glasses when he started makin' his move. Matter o' life an' death." He laughed. "I like a guy who really gets into da action."

He had me pegged.

By the time I reached the parking exit where the real action was, Paragon had surrendered to the police. As an officer cuffed him, the SportsNet chief turned his head, saw me and threw me a pernicious scowl.

"You are an annoying little man," he said.

"Happy to be of service," I replied brightly.

74

IT WAS considerably later when the police finished with our statements and sent us on our way. By then a doctor had convinced Carmody that his leg was not only not broken, it probably wasn't even sprained. The news cheered him up enough to offer me a lift back to the hotel.

I accompanied him and Sandford up to the penthouse to say goodbye to Angela. She had watched the whole bizarre day at the races on television.

"But I still don't understand why they wanted to kill Daddy so badly," she said.

"I assume that Paolo Rodriguez didn't like your father winding up with For Cupid's Sake. I think it's that simple."

"Amazing," she said. "And they actually had a backup plan in case the park plan didn't work."

"Actually, they had two backup plans. B and A."

Sandford said, "Rodriguez may come at your father again, sometime. But we'll handle that, just like we handled these."

I was wondering if I should remind him that they hadn't exactly handled the day's two attempts, when Carmody beat me to it. "Actually, Richard," he said, "I was thinking maybe we should send all your crew home and just hire Killebrew."

Sandford scowled at me, then relaxed. "Yeah. You did some good work today," he told me. "It wouldn't hurt to have you around."

"I'm flattered, gentlemen, but I've got more work than I can handle in Los Angeles. Which is where I'll be headed on the next plane out of here."

"Well, at least let us give you a lift to JFK," Carmody said. "We're heading out ourselves, soon as the bags are packed."

.   .   .

We made the trip in two limos. The Carmodys and three bodyguards rode in front, with Sandford and me and two more bodyguards bringing up the rear.

The sun was just setting when we arrived at the airport. I checked in, and since I had an hour to kill before my own flight back to L.A., I decided to see the others off. By the time I jitneyed to the private hangars, For Cupid's Sake and the other horses were being led aboard by two handlers in overalls.

I bid the Carmodys and Sandford good-bye and watched them board the plane with two of the bodyguards. The other three waited until they were inside, then departed in the twin limos.

Before returning to my terminal, I stepped inside the hangar to a pay phone I spied just outside the men's room. I dialed my home number. With Loretta and Paragon off the streets, I thought, Lea might even be there to answer. If not, perhaps there was a message.

The sky was a deep red, marked with little purple puffs of clouds. The phone rang once, twice, then clicked. I shifted my feet and felt something scrape under my shoe. It blinked in the light of dusk, a brass button from a uniform.

On the phone I once again heard Lieutenant Burns's somber voice requesting a return call. I made a mental note to contact him once I got back to L.A.

The second message was from my old high school, reminding me of an upcoming reunion. Then Lea's recorded voice called my name.

Inside the rest room someone groaned.

Still holding the phone, I pushed the door open with my foot. A man was lying on the floor in his underwear. Unconscious. He'd been hit in the head hard enough to break the skin of his forehead just above the right eye. His assailant was standing beside him in the gloomy tiled room, pointing a gun at me.

Roddy Rodriguez looked quite dashing in his pilot's uniform— minus one button. "Amigo," he said chidingly, "you're a real pest, you know it?"

He plucked the phone out of my hand, listened for a beat, smiled and replaced the receiver, eyes and gun still focused on me.

"Broad in there says she loves you, man. It's nice, being loved, huh?"

He gestured with the gun toward the waiting plane.

"Actually, I'm ticketed on United," I said.

He shrugged. "I could punch your ticket right here."

So I accompanied him up the ramp and into Carmody's private plane.

On board, the two men in overalls were holding guns on the Carmodys, Sandford, and the bodyguards. Angela gasped when she saw Roddy.

"Plan A for airplane?" I asked him.

"Bingo." Roddy winked and headed for the cockpit.

I sat beside Sandford. The two guys in coveralls watched us in silence. Blond and burly, they resembled each other enough to be brothers, but one of them had a blank and vacant stare, a guy who was better at strong-arm stuff than anything involving thought process. The second one might not actually have been more intelligent, but he looked liked he could put his shoes on without help. I mentally tagged them Thumper and Thinker.

The plane took off into the darkening sky. Considering that the so-called handlers, Thumper and Thinker, were busy with us, the horses in their traveling stalls seemed to be pretty calm.

I remembered that, back at the brownstone, Roddy had been resistant to Plan A. It would be a big mess, he'd said to Loretta, killing people and animals. I decided to share that memory. "How are you guys fixed for parachutes?" I asked Thinker.

His eyes flickered to his partner. "We don't have any," he said.

"That could be a problem," I said, "because as soon as we get to the right location, where there's not much chance he'll get tangled up in trees or electric wires, your pal Roddy will be leaving us. And my guess is he's planning on you guys staying on board for the plane crash."

"Bullshit," Thumper said. "Roddy's a stand-up guy."

"Then I must be wrong and he probably isn't wearing a chute himself."

We were steadily gathering altitude now. The bad thing was that I was upsetting Angela and Carmody had gone sickly pale. The good thing was that a layer of sweat had appeared on Thinker's brow.

"Just what is the plan, huh?" he asked Thumper.

"Look, Roddy knows what he's doing—"

"He surely does," I said. "But do *you* know what he's doing?"

"Shut up!" Thumper said.

"What did he tell you?" I asked. "That you'd fly us over the ocean and dump us out?"

Thumper smiled. "Something like that."

"Then he wouldn't need a parachute," I said.

Thinker moved forward, concentrating on the closed door to the cockpit. As he crossed in front of Thumper, I pushed off from the seat and leaped forward, driving my shoulder into his exposed side.

He sprawled into Thumper, both of them hitting the deck. Thumper's gun went off. I kicked it from his hand. Then Sandford and the bodyguards were all over the two of them.

The cockpit door flew open and Roddy stepped through it, gun in hand and parachute on back. The plane must have been on some sort of automatic pilot.

"What's all this?" he asked sardonically, looking at the men on the floor.

The two gunmen stared at Roddy. His smile. His gun. His parachute.

Roddy shut the cockpit door. Then he tried the handle and seemed satisfied that the door was locked from the other side.

He circled us, heading for the exit door.

"You can't do this," Carmody said, entirely without conviction.

"If we rush him," I said, "he can't shoot us all."

"Just some of you," Roddy pointed out.

He struggled with the door, but he couldn't open it one-handed. That rattled him a little. He ordered Thumper, whose real name was Lou, to open it.

"Screw you, Jack," the gunman said.

And Roddy shot him in the head.

"Now you," Roddy said to Thinker. Thinker licked his lips, looked down at his dead partner and decided to cooperate. He reluctantly grappled with the door until he had it open to the night sky.

The gunfire and the wind screaming through the open door had caused the horses to kick up a fuss. They were panicked and whinnying, thrashing against their restraints. A hoof smashed through a wooden barrier.

Roddy, still standing at the door preparing to make his jump, may have been distracted by the restless horses, or he may have been concentrating on Carmody's bodyguards in the rapidly darkening cabin. But he couldn't be looking everywhere, and he certainly wasn't looking where he should have been.

The bullet knocked him against the cabin wall. Startled, he looked down to see a spot of blood blossom on the middle of his uniform jacket. Then he raised his eyes to the source of the shot. What he saw was a frail young woman holding the gun dropped by Thumper. And she wasn't finished.

Angela pulled the trigger once more, and I moved my head just quick enough to see a still-astonished Roddy do a little backward hop out the exit door into the night.

The horses were going wild now. One five-year-old stallion, an allowance runner named Vituperation, broke free of his wooden confines and kicked out, throwing Thinker against one bulkhead, howling in pain. It looked like his leg was broken.

Sandford raced for the cockpit door.

I ran to the exit door. The handle was just a few inches too far away. Vituperation moved to the other side of the cabin and the shift in weight tilted the plane in that direction. The exit door swung shut.

Up front, Sandford and the bodyguards tried to smash down the cockpit door. Carmody put his arm around his daughter and took the gun from her hand. Vituperation, eyes wild, pranced around the cabin.

I spoke to the animal in as calm a voice as I could muster, getting a hand on his halter.

"Okay, boy, just settle down," I said, my throat dry as dust. "That's a boy."

Maybe he was waiting for someone to tell him what to do. For whatever reason, the words worked. I led him back into his broken stall. Then I slipped the belt from around my waist and used it to secure the broken panel on Vituperation's box. All the while I continued to talk to the horses.

Carmody and Angela were sitting together, holding one another. I was starting to relax when the plane went into a sharp dive.

I was thrown forward into the wooden horse pens. The Carmodys fell to the floor. From the front of the plane came yells and grunts and the sound of the cockpit door giving way.

Downward we plummeted.

The horses' hooves clattered as they tried to regain their balance. My hooves were clattering, too.

When we leveled off, I fell back on my butt. I stayed there, lying on the deck until the sense of panic subsided. Then I started working on the horses again.

Once they'd calmed from frantic to only mildly skittish, I headed for the cockpit, past the Carmodys, who were huddled in their seats. The old man's arm was around his daughter protectively. If nothing else, the adventure seemed to have resulted in at least a temporary family bonding.

In the cockpit, Sandford, seated at the controls, was shaking his head.

"The son of a bitch smashed most of the instruments," he said. "I can't tell how high we are or how fast we're going. And the radio is as dead as that guy in overalls back there."

"Other than that?" I asked.

"Other than that, we're out of gas."

I watched him wrestle with the wheel while the plane bucked like a bronco.

"I've gotta find some place to ditch."

"How far to the water?" I wondered.

"Who knows? It's almost pitch-black down there. My guess is we're over trees, but the fact is, I don't know where the hell we are."

"Oh, sweet Jesus," one of the bodyguards exclaimed. "What do we do?"

"Relax," Sandford told him. "Dying doesn't require any experience. It happens or it doesn't. You might want to get tucked in. In case we don't explode or go up like a torch."

I went back to the rear and found a seat for myself beside the horses. They were getting restless again, and who could blame them? Especially when the plane went into another nosedive.

I heard Sandford shout, "C'mon, you sweet bastard."

I tried to calm the horses with more soothing sounds. The plane seemed to be leveling off now. Maybe Sandford was getting it under control.

Then came a jolt that sounded and felt like the plane's wheels were making contact with terra firma. It seemed too good to be true. A glance out the window showed me we were bouncing along on the ground, but we sure weren't out of the woods. Literally. Sandford had found enough of a clearing in the moonlight to touch down in, but at the rate the trees outside were whizzing by, it was only a matter of time before we made contact with one.

I was telling the horses how wonderful everything was when the plane hit the first tree. That one sheered off the right wing.

The second tree caved in a portion of the left side of the body just aft of the cockpit, and Sandford screamed in pain.

The third tree stopped the plane in its tracks, spinning it 180 degrees.

One of the bodyguards immediately made for the side door, threw it open and leaped out. The other bodyguard, a bit more job oriented, helped the Carmodys to the door. They seemed to be uninjured.

I ran to the cockpit, where Sandford was on the floor, blood coming from his nose and a gash in his forehead. I shouted for someone to help, and the more conscientious bodyguard lifted Sandford and carried him from the plane.

That left the gunman with the broken leg and the horses. I chose the horses, easing them from their shattered stalls, murmuring that same soothing nonsense and hoping they wouldn't take it into their heads to rear up and trample me. By some miracle, none of them seemed to be harmed. But they were skittish about jumping the distance to the ground. The crackling and sparking of the plane's electrical system proved to be the spur they needed. They leaped out one by one without another thought.

A fire had broken out toward the front of the plane. I hurriedly dragged the wounded gunman to the door and rolled him out. Then, exhausted, I jumped myself.

"We better move back," I yelled to the others. Over my shoulder I could see that the whole interior of the plane had taken on a red glow.

As we were scurrying away a small explosion rocked the craft and a plume of black smoke was sent skyward. The plane began to burn merrily.

Less than half an hour later, an Army helicopter, alerted by the fire and smoke, hovered above the clearing where I was seated next to the Carmodys and the bodyguards. A blinding light circled us and an amplified voice told us from on high that help was on the way.

Then the chopper banked and headed away. Angela looked at her father and me as the spotlight illuminated us through the tall trees. She exclaimed gleefully, "It's the image I saw, Coley. You and Daddy, and the fighting and the giant bird and the sounds. It's all come true."

75

LEA AND her father were both waiting for me at LAX when I arrived the next day. The Starbucks were still among the walking wounded, she on crutches, he using a cane. But they were blissfully, happily, free.

My first order of business was to engage Lea in a long, fervent, to-hell-with-the-spectators kiss. The embrace got too long for Starbuck, who felt the need to interrupt with a news report.

"They caught the whole bloody gang," he said, "the ones that hadn't crawled back to Colombia."

"How'd they do it so fast?" I asked.

"Deathbed confession," Starbuck said. Then he chuckled and added, "Only the bugger didn't die."

"Who?"

"Luis Rodriguez, Paolo's nephew."

"You mean Roddy?"

"They told me his name was Luis. Anyway, he was picked up by New Jersey cops hanging from a tree in the northwest corner of the state with two slugs in his torso. They tossed him in the hospital and put his ID on the computer, and a passel of New York cops raced over to ask him a few questions. Seems his prints were all over the brownstone where Gallen died. I'll be getting the complete transcript, but right now let's go out and celebrate." He paused and asked, "Hope you don't mind if I drag Clara McGuinn along."

I didn't mind a bit.

A few days later he called to say that the promised transcript had arrived. When I dropped by the beach house to pick it up, I was pleased to note that routine had been reestablished. Choo-Choo was puttering about at his various duties and his boss was building another birdhouse out on the deck. The cane was still in the picture, but Starbuck was ignoring it a lot of the time. Was I developing a deep, warm family feeling for my future father-in-law? That might be overstating the case. But he was definitely easier to deal with now that romance had entered his life.

"Transcript's too big to copy," he said. "I'll need it back, but I thought you deserved a look at it."

I thanked him and made off with the bundle. That night, in my office at The Horse's Neck, I worked my way through it, interrupted only a couple of times on restaurant business. The transcript managed to answer most of the outstanding inquiries, as well as being entertaining reading in its own right, especially if you conjured up the image of Roddy assuming he was making a deathbed confession.

He agreed to tell all, which included pinning the tail on Geoffrey Paragon and Loretta Simmons, in return for the promise that his body would be transported back to Colombia for burial there. Perhaps the state of New York would eventually carry out its end of the bargain, but first there would be many years of incarceration for the Rod man, whose wounds were definitely not fatal.

What he had to say was that Geoffrey Paragon was an international assassin with a list of victims that rivaled Carlos the Jackal's. Several years ago he had retired from that profession to become the European and eastern United States representative for Paolo Rodriguez and his Medellín associates, overseeing the narcotics traffic in those countries, all the while operating under the more or less respectable umbrella of SportsNet Cable TV.

From his jail cell Paolo had ordered the assassination of Carmody, the man who'd put him there. But the billionaire, who was subject to paranoia even before he got mixed up with Rodriguez, had not been an easy victim. He'd arranged for security so effective that, after numerous failed attempts, Rodriguez finally asked Paragon, the man he considered the world's best assassin, to work out a plan of attack.

"Geoffrey came up with this far-out scheme to take out Carmody," Roddy was quoted as saying. "Elaborate, you know, took him a year of waiting to get the job done. But he liked that kind of shit. In the meantime, Tio Paolo—my uncle, I mean—gets word that this female DEA agent is snooping around Carmody. To make it worse, turns out it was this same agent who'd played my uncle for a chump back home."

"That would be Helena Diez?" the interrogator asked.

"Diez. Salazaar. That's the broad. Geoffrey was supposed to kill her

years ago, but I think women are his weakness. He and the Diez broad
screwed a lot, and when the time came, he let her go. She never even
knew he was part of the cartel.

"But Uncle puts in a demand now that Geoffrey take her out, too.
And Geoffrey's of a mind to do it, anyway, since the bitch is interfering with our current plans for Carmody. So he flies out to the West
Coast and he sticks her with this ring. That's what I mean—the guy
doesn't use a gun or a knife, he's got this goddamn poison ring. Too
fucking tricky. But, hey, it worked for him for a long time. You see,
the poison isn't really poison, but some kind of medicine that speeds
up the heart or something till the person croaks. Looks real natural.
Carlos used it, too. Geoffrey told me Carlos got the idea from him.

"Anyway, he finds out that this guy Starbuck was working with
Salazaar and he tries to take him out, too. When that didn't work,
that's where I came in. I'm just a minor player in this whole thing,
y'know?"

"Go on, please."

"I got assigned to snatch Starbuck's daughter so we can get him to
keep quiet. With the one broad dead—"

"Diez?"

"Diez. Salazaar. Whatever. With her dead, nobody else is supposed
to get hurt. Except Carmody. Once he's dead and Geoffrey's safely
back in Europe, Lea Starbuck would be free as a little bird and she and
her father could live happily ever after. See, I'm not the guy my uncle
uses when there's killing to be done."

The transcript of a second session with Roddy described his wit-
nessing Paragon's anger upon discovering that Gallen had hired Coley
Killebrew, the fiancé of the kidnapped Lea Starbuck and the sometime
business associate of her father.

But according to Roddy, that anger had turned to amusement when
Paragon decided to "play Killebrew's game. Assuming the ex-jock was
snooping around, we'd be in a better position to keep track of him if
we knew where he was and what he was doing. And if he did find
anything that might screw up the plan to get Carmody, well, he could
be taken out quickly."

To make certain how much I knew, Paragon and Roddy broke into
my hotel room in Louisville to see if they could find notes or anything. While they were going through my possessions, they heard
someone at the door. Paragon grabbed one of my ties and slipped beside the door, leaving Roddy in the middle of the suite as a decoy.

They were expecting me to step through the door. Instead, a black man entered, a stranger to them. Andrew Gunderman. Before he could say a word, Paragon used my silk tie as a garrote.

"I didn't know he was gonna kill him, I swear," Roddy told the police. "The guy was dead in a second. Then Geoffrey went through the stiff's pockets, but there wasn't anything to tell us any more than the guy's name. But something was weird, because he'd picked the lock. And he was carrying a gun.

"He mighta been a thief. But Geoffrey figures he's more than that. Maybe he's somebody worked for Carmody. Anyway, he wasn't no friend of Killebrew's, breakin' in like that. So we got out of there."

Poor Gunderman, I thought. The wrong place at definitely the wrong time.

According to Roddy's final deposition, Barry Gallen, during most of the years he worked for Paragon and SportsNet, had not known that the company was funded by drug money. It was not until Gallen got into some trouble with a very young girl in Panama that he discovered the power of the people he was working for. One phone call from Paragon to Paolo Rodriguez, and Gallen walked away from unavoidable imprisonment and disgrace.

"Barry was worried about where his money was comin' from," Roddy said. "He had this bullshit about being a moral man. But he was a real weak man. My uncle built his empire on the bones of weak men."

To stay alive and relatively wealthy, Barry agreed to help Paragon get as close as possible to Carmody. "But toward the end, there, Barry, he sort of went wild. Too much pressure. Especially after the fuck-up at the Preakness, when Carmody's horse wound up not running. Hell, it wasn't Barry's fault no more than Geoffrey's, but Geoffrey made like it was. All that did was drive Barry even more nuts. And then his bitch, his woman, has to tell him she'd found somebody new. That's when Barry lost it completely. He flew back to L.A. and killed the drug agent."

This seemed to confuse the interrogator. "Barry Gallen killed DEA agent Degarza?"

"Hell, yeah. He was gonna kill somebody. Big macho man, gettin' the horns put on him. See, he's got this thing all figured out. When he's in Baltimore, he calls his woman and tells her he's gonna be late getting back, that he's going to some party and won't be in L.A. till the next day. So she don't know he's in town and he can follow her to her lover's place and bang-bang-bang.

"He even rents a car she wouldn't recognize. So the plan goes great.

He follows his old lady, sees her go into this house. Then she comes out with this young stud. She drives off and he follows the stud to another house, and when the stud gets out of his car, it's like shootin' fish in the swimming pool."

Which is what Degarza/Marquez was trying to tell the ambulance driver, that the "jealous asshole" who shot him had thought he was involved with "Starbuck's woman."

When I returned the transcripts to Starbuck the next day, there was one loose end I thought still needed tying. Not sure if I'd missed it, I asked him, "Did Roddy Rodriguez happen to mention who killed Gallen?"

"He didn't have to," Starbuck said. "Loretta Simmons confessed. She claims self-defense, that he was trying to rape her. It's some story. I imagine Paragon realized that Gallen was too far gone to be trusted. But it's up to New York to prove the lady killed the guy in cold blood. In any case, they've got her for the attempted murder of Carmody."

"Don't you just love a happy ending?" I asked.

76

THE NEXT day the other shoe dropped.

I was in the kitchen at The Horse's Neck, observing a mechanic working on one of the freezers at sixty dollars an hour, when who should drop in but CIA agent Singleton, alone.

"Let's take it to your office," he said.

"Sure," I said. "Bring you something to drink or eat?"

"No, thanks."

When we were safely behind the office door, Singleton laid it out for me. "Here's the drill, Killebrew. It's a live-and-let-live scenario."

"Come again?"

"You stay out of the Agency's mural and we'll stay out of yours."

"I'm a simple man, Agent Singleton," I said. "What exactly are you trying to tell me?"

"Later today there will be a news announcement regarding . . . certain parties. When you hear it, you are to express surprise, curiosity, dismay, happiness, you name it. You are not to provide the press with any information you may or may not possess pertaining to the announcement."

"Let me guess," I said. "This is about James Deth Carmody, right?"

Singleton answered with a forced smile.

"Is he going to jail?" I asked.

"It's not that wonderful," Singleton said.

"But it won't be good news for him."

"It most certainly won't."

"You've been plugged in to his operation for a while, haven't you?"

Singleton didn't reply.

"Do you know a lady named Lula Dorian, Agent Singleton?"

The half smile left Singleton's face.

"A while back," I said, "Lula was seen chatting away with a Latino with facial scars. Your associate, Agent Pantera, fits that picture. If she was sneaking around, talking to Pantera, then . . ."

"That's precisely the sort of speculation I'm telling you not to attempt," Singleton said.

"Or you'll do what?"

"Or we'll add a bit of information to the record on Andrew Gunderman's murder. Namely, we'll explain how his body got from your hotel room to the street in front of his motel."

"I imagine his killer, Geoffrey Paragon, took it there," I said.

"That's the prevailing assumption, though the Louisville Police Department certainly didn't go to any lengths to confirm it. I imagine it would take very little urging to get Paragon and Luis Rodriguez to state officially that the body was left in your room. Then I bet an eyewitness or two might be found who saw Gunderman's body being transported from the hotel."

"Big deal," I said. "Paragon murdered the guy."

"I'm no lawyer," Singleton replied, "but I imagine that whoever moved the corpse might just be considered an accessory after the fact. Actually, who's to say Gunderman really was dead when Paragon and Rodriguez left him? Maybe you finished him off yourself. You had a motive."

I sighed. "Just between us girls, Singleton, was it you who sent the Racing Commission that letter about Sandford undervaluing horses for Carmody, the letter that started all this?"

"Me, personally? No. Of course, if I had, I'd deny it."

"Did you know it was Paragon who was trying to kill Carmody?"

"We don't condone murder, nor are we murderers in the CIA." Singleton smiled.

I flashed back to Roddy's insistence that he was no killer. So many people getting killed in this world with so few killers.

"But you're not above blackmail," I said.

"Not if it's for a good cause."

"I suppose your fellow agent Aldrich Ames may have felt the same way about selling secrets to the Soviets."

"You're not a very pleasant man, Killebrew. I'd be real happy if our paths never crossed again."

"Amen to that, brother."

That evening the newscasts all led off with the top story of the day: "Original certificates of birth and other documents, including forged papers, surfaced today indicating that tycoon James Deth Carmody may have acted illegally when purchasing a number of thoroughbred horses, including the recent winner of the Belmont Stakes, from the Drug Enforcement Administration. Carmody has refused to reply to the allegation, and the DEA is remaining silent on all charges. But Congress has ordered a full investigation. And a long and very dark shadow has been cast over Carmody's plans to enter national politics."

I could almost hear Paolo Rodriguez's laughter all the way from his prison cell.

77

O N A bright sunny morning some two weeks later, Lea turned up unexpectedly at The Horse's Neck. I walked into the kitchen to find her talking conspiratorially with Chef Antony. When they saw me, they parted with false smiles on their faces.

I knew they weren't plotting a surprise party, because it was nowhere near my birthday.

"Coley," she said brightly, "I have something to tell you."

"Something since breakfast?" I asked.

"Yep. Come with me."

Not being CIA, she didn't insist on going behind the door of my cluttered office, but we did find a remote booth, far from any of the employees preparing for the lunchtime rush.

Antony found us, though, to personally deliver a bottle of the best vintage champagne from the Neck's well-stocked cellar. He placed two glasses in front of us, opened the bottle with a Gallic flourish, and poured us each a glass. Then he placed the bottle in an ice bucket and said, "Enjoy! Enjoy!"

Much as he adored Lea and would do anything to please her, for my temperamental chef to play waiter was unprecedented behavior. They both smiled and Antony trotted off, a spring in his step.

"Am I about to become a father?" I asked.

Lea shook her head from side to side. "Not yet."

"You've won the Nobel Peace Prize for keeping your father and me from killing each other."

"No, but when you hear this, you'll want to kiss him, not kill him."

"News doesn't come that good."

"Yes it does. Cheers."

We clicked glasses. I didn't know what I was celebrating, but when the bottle's open, you might as well drink it. Especially when you're paying for it.

"Good stuff," I said. "Okay. Give."

"Would you go back to riding if you could?"

The question seemed almost too serious for our mood. "I don't know," I said, quite honestly. "Would you want me to?"

"I want what you want."

"What's this all about?"

"The Jockey Club has reversed its decision to bar you from racing." I stared at her.

"And any mention of their earlier decision will be expunged from the records. You'll also be receiving a letter of apology."

For a moment I was too surprised to talk. Finally I said, "Your father did this?"

She nodded.

"How?"

"It was Dewey Lane," she said.

"Beg pardon?"

"Dewey Lane is the one who caused the accident. He did it deliberately, working with your old girlfriend, Francie. They were the ones who planned the whole thing."

"That was why your father was keeping my file open?"

"Andrew Gunderman investigated every jockey in the race and discovered some heavy debts that Dewey Lane paid off shortly after the accident. Then it was a matter of pushing and shoving until Lane broke. The night of the Derby party, Daddy forced him to come here to sign the confession."

"Is that why he ran away?"

"No. That lowlife Rodriguez didn't want him riding Jake Lunden's horse. And threatened him. So, with the help of somebody in law enforcement—Daddy doesn't know who—he's been hiding out. But he's back now. And since the statute of limitations has run out, he won't be charged with a crime. But he'll never race again. And you can, whenever you want."

"It's . . . amazing."

"Will you race again?" she asked.

I slid closer to her in the booth. "I'll think about that tomorrow," I said.

And her lips tasted like champagne.

ABOUT THE AUTHOR

BILL SHOEMAKER retired as a jockey in 1990, after winning a record 8,833 races. He continues to work as a trainer on the Southern California circuit. His previous novels in the Coley Killebrew series are *Stalking Horse* and *Fire Horse*.